...e for *Trapped in Yosemite*

"Prepare to be captivated by this heart-racing, page-turning reunion story. Dana Mentink weaves together a thrilling tale of danger and intrigue—and a villain I didn't see coming!"
—Lynette Eason, *USA TODAY* bestselling author of the Extreme Measures series

"Fast-paced from start to finish, *Trapped in Yosemite* by the talented Dana Mentink is a story of second chances, faith, forgiveness and the unexpected, all expertly combined with surviving a natural disaster."
—Jenifer Ruff, *USA TODAY* bestselling author

"Mentink opens with a bang and the tension only escalates from there. This is a skillfully crafted story with twists that will keep readers turning pages long into the night."
—Jessica R. Patch, *Publishers Weekly* bestselling author

"*Trapped in Yosemite* is a pulse-pounding suspense and kept me turning the pages to reach the gripping conclusion. The intricate plot and complex characters give the reader an exceptional, satisfying story. Bear will steal your heart!"
—Darlene L. Turner, *Publishers Weekly* bestselling author

"Crisp, original writing along with a riveting plot make *Trapped in Yosemite* a book you won't want to put down even after the satisfying ending."
—Susan Sleeman, bestselling author of the Truth Seekers series

"*Trapped in Yosemite* is an emotionally charged story with an intriguing mystery that kept me turning the pages!"
—Terri Reed, *Publishers Weekly* bestselling author

"Action-packed and fast-paced from the very first line, Dana Mentink's *Trapped in Yosemite* is a powerful suspense that's hard to put down."
—Lenora Worth, author of *Retribution at the Ranch*

DANA MENTINK

TRAPPED IN YOSEMITE

LOVE INSPIRED

Stories to uplift and inspire

LOVE INSPIRED®

Stories to uplift and inspire

Recycling programs
for this product may
not exist in your area.

ISBN-13: 978-1-335-00904-3

Trapped in Yosemite

Love Inspired
22 Adelaide St. West, 41st Floor
Toronto, Ontario M5H 4E3, Canada
www.LoveInspired.com

Printed in U.S.A.

To my soulmate, Mike, who helped me believe in myself.

Chapter One

Stella Rivers scoured the dense shrubbery like she'd been doing for the past hour as if the branches might somehow reach out and snatch her van off the mountain road. Ridiculous, but the isolation raked her nerves.

No sign of anyone around, even the person she was supposed to meet. She opened the notes on her phone, confirming for the fifth time that she'd arrived at the correct mile marker.

Easing to a stop, her gaze went to the rearview mirror to check the back. A silly instinct since she'd already left nine-month-old Hannah with her aunt. The empty car seat stoked her anxiety.

She'd told herself it wouldn't have been optimal to bring the baby to this client consult—the cold, the winding roads, the weather unsettled...or maybe that was her overprotectiveness winning out. Babies were resilient, her mentor Kip often insisted. Larger than their size would indicate.

She knew otherwise. The ache spiraled through her again, a gray, misty sadness that pinched the corners of her vision like incoming clouds. *Not now.*

There was no reason to worry about Hannah. Aunt Zoe was doubtless spoiling her rotten.

The wind rattled the pines that screened the hard Yosemite sunlight. Their pointy tops were not yet snow covered, but they might be in a matter of hours. A bird erupted with a scream from the canopy a millisecond before the ground began to bounce under her tires. The windshield rattled. She clung to the wheel. Another one?

She'd felt the first jolt when she'd stopped to change Hannah's diaper blowout before they'd reached Zoe's.

Abruptly, the shaking died away without a trace. She exhaled. Should she head out? Was it a precursor to a larger seismic event? Weird. Earthquakes were uncommon for this area of the Sierras.

She scanned the trees and jumped.

A man stood on the opposite side of the road, dressed in all black. Her heart hammered against her ribs. Where had he come from? Surely, way too young to be her client. The brim of a baseball cap hid his face, long blond hair touching his shoulders. She fumbled for the gears. His hand snaked into his pocket, long white fingers pulling out a cigarette as he ambled slowly away from her, smoke trailing in his wake.

Her breath came in harsh spurts. Clearly, no threat. A man out for a walk before the storm.

She must be unsettled by the quake, or tense at being separated from Hannah.

Sure, it was an out-of-the-way place to meet a client, but not unusual for her line of work. An arborist had to go where the trees were, and new arborists drove farther afield until they established themselves. Kip, who was now her boss, had forwarded her the number. "Guy saw our website and called asking for you. Job's yours if you want it. Otherwise, I'll farm it out to someone else."

Of course she wanted it. As a newbie, she had to prove to herself, and to him, that she could handle the legwork part of the biz, baby or not. She mentally replayed her phone conversation with the client, Matt Smith.

Want your opinion on a bunch of trees. Maples. They look real sick. If it's bark beetles, they'll have to come out, right?

She'd gently informed him that bark beetles snacked on coniferous trees, not maples. The native beetles had decimated millions of Sierra Nevada pines already stressed from years of drought, bringing Kip dozens of phone calls from anxious locals. "Beetles are my bread and butter," was his mantra. She'd arranged to meet Smith at Old Pine Road, Mile Marker 42.

With a storm system projected to land in the next few days, she'd rather have cuddled up with Hannah in their thimble-size apartment in Fresno, but a single mom with rent due couldn't be too choosy. She'd decided to make a trip of it. A small reward for surviving sleepless nights and long winter days, alone.

Matt had even offered to pay for her gas. What a blessing. She didn't take them for granted anymore. Her pregnancy had revealed how tenuous life could be, and what a divine gift she'd been given. Sweet and bittersweet.

A massive yawn teared her eyes. If she closed them she could almost hear Hannah's happy babbling, picture her strawberry hair, like her father, Von's. Pain pricked her chest.

Von Sharpe was another echo from the past that nudged the tender, dark place inside her. Her mind insisted on traveling to those sad memories, like a tongue prodding at a broken tooth. At least the sensation was mostly resignation now, instead of anger, with a side helping of guilt folded in.

She peered out the windows for any sign of her client, or the solitary hiker. The mile marker was clearly visible a yard from her front fender, near a mailbox colored with equal parts yellow paint and rust. Drifting pine needles drew her attention to the canopy. There was no sign of bark beetle damage on these sturdy pines, but Smith sounded positive his trees were infected.

Matt Smith. Such an innocuous name, she thought idly. The name someone might choose as the perfect alias.

Alias? She sat up straighter. The muscles in her belly quivered. Just anxiety talking, her constant companion. There was nothing to worry about. She smoothed her hair and smoothed it again. But what if the meeting wasn't what it seemed to be? A branch scuttled across the windshield. She jumped.

Intrusive thoughts, Stella. You know how to deal with that. She was doing her job. *But what if…?*

Smith didn't know his trees. So what? Not everybody was a plant person. Still, the Yosemite region was a wild place, where people didn't subdue nature as much as they learned how to thrive alongside it. But who wouldn't be able to tell a maple from a pine?

She stilled her bobbing knee and tried to reason her way through her unease. Locals in the area knew each other, depended on one another. Had Smith mentioned how he'd heard of Kip's business? A neighbor's referral? And why had he chosen her from the trio of arborists pictured on the website? She patted down her hair and twisted a strand until it cinched tight.

The situation is fine. You are fine. She freed her finger from the knot.

Was it illogical to feel suspicious? Or was it prudent?

She sat on her hands and considered.

Her fears were probably groundless, her distrust of his bland name, his weak grasp of botany. She gnawed at her lower lip.

Von would've said she should trust her instincts, but since their engagement imploded his advice was no more than an echo from the past. Besides, she wasn't sure how to separate instinct from fear. Not anymore.

She was reaching for her phone when a man appeared on the steep drive, his plump body filling out a puffy white jacket, a knit cap framing his full-cheeked smile. This had to be her client. She exhaled as he raised a hand in greeting, his breath steaming the air. She rolled down the window a few inches.

"Hello, Ms. Rivers. Matt Smith. Thanks for meeting me. Did you feel an earthquake a few minutes ago?" Friendly. Innocuous.

"I did." Chagrined at her imaginings, she got out and took his offered palm.

He wiped his brow. "That's what we get for living in California. I should never have hiked down from the cabin." He patted his stomach. "With this boiler? I'm gonna need a winch to get back up."

She smiled and considered the trees. It was time to do her job and get to Zoe's. "I don't see much in the way of bark beetle infestation around here."

He lifted a shoulder and jerked a thumb past the mailbox. "That's cuz my place is up the road about two miles. You can't see it from here. Those trees, man. Swiss cheese with all the beetle holes. They look like they're gonna fall over at any moment. I'm worried with the winter storms coming. Drive on up. We can talk there. Maybe you can give me a lift, huh? Save me from a heart attack." His gaze darted to the tree line, brows crimping. After a moment he smiled at her again.

Over his shoulder, she caught the remnants of a painted name on the mailbox, now peeled and almost obliterated. Only the last two letters remained. An I and L? Two Ls?

"You said you own the cabin, Mr. Smith?"

"Call me Matt. Cabin's been in my family for years. Granddad and Dad lived here before me. As a kid, I used to come up here every summer and do some whitewater rafting on the Tuolumne River, but it's just me now."

Why did the answer sound so pat? Almost like it had been rehearsed. The skin on the back of her arms prickled. If the cabin belonged to the Smith family, shouldn't the last two letters of the mailbox name be "th"? Instinct or paranoia? It no longer mattered. She didn't feel safe. Time to go. Casually, she looked at her cell phone, finger poised over the emergency button.

"Mr. Smith, I'm not sure my van will take that slope. Tell you what. How about you text me a video of the pines? I'll work up a quote and send it to you."

His smile dimmed. "I'd really like you to eyeball it yourself. I arranged this consult and all."

She edged a step away from him. "I'll waive the fee."

His geniality faded into something more serious. "Ms. Rivers, I really need to talk to you." He reached into his pocket.

"No," she said, fumbling for the door handle.

He pulled out an envelope. "I'm not…"

Something exploded through the air. A high-pitched whine drilled her eardrums as a projectile streaked past her cheek. She screamed, recoiling from the sound. The phone flew out of her grasp, hurtling into the shrubbery.

Her client stumbled back. He dipped his chin to look at a spot of red blooming on his jacket. For one second Stella could only stare in horror as blood saturated the fabric before he collapsed to the ground. The envelope flew from his limp fingers and landed almost on her feet.

Only the convulsive twitch of her shoulders saved her from the second bullet that shrieked past her ear. She grabbed the envelope and leaped into the van, slammed the door, locked it. Fingers clumsy with terror, she wrenched the key in the ignition. A bullet whammed into her rearview mirror, nearly severing it. Something, no, someone, was moving in the bushes, slashing through the foliage. The man in the baseball cap.

The scream stuck in her throat. *Go, go, go,* her brain demanded.

She floored the gas, and the van wobbled.

In the rearview she saw Smith twisted and still on the ground, the wide splash of crimson spreading from his body indicating he was most likely dead. The van fishtailed onto the road.

The mirror caught the shrubs parting, and the man in the cap sprinted toward her. She punched the accelerator and widened the distance between them, jerking another look back in time to see him bend at the knee, pull a rifle from over his shoulder and aim.

No.

Pedal to the floor, she surged along the mountain road. Rocks pinged against the fender, or was it the sound of bullets striking her van? She was too terrified to tell. The shooter was not there in her rearview anymore, but he probably had a vehicle and he'd be coming for her.

Choices ribboned through her skull. Should she try to get back to the highway? But that would take forty-five minutes along twisty roads where he might ambush her. With her cell phone lost, she couldn't even call for help.

No phone. Twenty miles from the nearest town. Should she press on for Cloud Top or try to return to Hannah at Aunt Zoe's cabin?

Oak trees flashed by as she drove, their limbs bare of leaves. Only the pines held on to their vibrant green. Her attention darted between her front windshield and her rearview mirror. Her pulse slammed in her throat with sledgehammer force.

She'd just seen a murder.

And almost been killed herself.

If she hadn't delivered Hannah to Aunt Zoe, her baby would have been in the van for the whole horrific situation.

The metallic taste of blood on her lip made her realize she'd bitten it. Indecision clawed at her stomach. Taking the side roads to Zoe's remote cabin could lead the shooter there. Pushing forward to Cloud Top might be disastrous if the assassin overtook her. *Which way?*

Cold sweat beaded on her upper lip. Aunt Zoe's, she decided. If she was going to find the closest shelter, it would be there. They'd lock the windows. Barricade the door if necessary and call the police. *You're running out of time.*

With clammy fingers she turned the wheel. If she made the wrong choice, would her family pay the price? She could not lose Hannah or Zoe. It was too much even to consider.

Teeth clenched, she took the trail to Zoe's cabin. She was certain of only two things.

She'd witnessed the murder of Matt Smith, if that was his name.

And the shooter had every intention of murdering her, too.

The hiking trail was quiet, save for the birdcalls and the swish of needles in the frosted pines. Von relished the opportunity to get away from the yammering visitors at the wilderness camp. They were paying clients of Mountain Dog Wilderness Guides, his cohorts reminded him, but all they wanted to do was bend his ear about his military experience. He shut down that line of questioning as politely as he could manage, which wasn't very polite at all. Today they were all jazzed up about the earthquake. It hardly rated a blip on the weird-o-meter in his view.

He pulled an energy drink from his backpack. Bear gave him that look. How did the dog know the doctor had told him to ditch the drinks? Bear had the audacity to whiffle out a judgmental breath.

Von fingered the pull tab. "You're not my mother."

Bear stared.

"I am a grown adult and I've cut back, haven't I? Some law against me having one now and then? I need the caffeine." Precisely what his doctor said he should curtail, but his fatigue, mental fuzz and lack of spunk were incomprehensible, and if a neon concoction of sugar and chemicals would help, so be it. A crutch, pure and simple, but he didn't know what else to do. He'd give it another fifteen minutes, he decided, and if the bracing air didn't wake him up, he was downing the energy drink, dog or no dog.

Bear barked, his attention now caught by a silver-tailed squirrel that appeared on a low branch, chittering its annoyance. Bear looked from Von to the squirrel, as if to say, "Easy jump. I can get him."

"He's living his best life so leave him in peace."

The Malinois cocked his muzzle and stared. Too many confusing words in Von's communique. "Leave it," he said simply. If dogs could give dirty looks, Von would have been drilled.

So many things had been confusing to his furry partner since Von's injury caused their exit from the air force three months before on the cusp of Von's thirty-seventh birthday. Hanging up his Grey Beret would have killed him if he thought it was permanent. Joining up with Tate and Camy at the Mountain Dog Wilderness Guides camp was another odd and painful adjustment, at least for Von. Leading extreme wilderness tours, survival classes and corporate camps was a massive career shift neither of them had gotten used to. He felt like an entertainer, a glorified tour guide.

All those wannabe outdoorsmen, like the Driscoll family and their two employees currently in camp, the camp Von's brother had founded. Memories of Ronnie made Von's stomach churn. The fresh pain of it hacked through him like a cleaver. Daily reminders of his brother made him think he'd made a huge mistake stepping into Ronnie's job. *Temporary assignment*, he reminded himself. With a sigh, he stowed the energy drink in his pack, pushed aside the battered book about rare seeds he'd intended to pore over and hunkered down on the trail next to Bear. "I know you didn't ask for this, either." Bear hadn't physically needed to retire from special forces with Von, since he was a healthy six-year-old protection dog, but there was one problem the dog could not overcome. Bear could swim out to sea far past sight of the horizon, remain calm while parachuting from a helicopter, but he simply could not adjust to losing his "dad" Von. The air force had tried to reassign their valuable canine asset, but some emotions went deeper than training.

"You picked the wrong guy to be your dad," he muttered. If his broken engagement with Stella had taught him anything, it was that Von Sharpe wasn't family material.

The squirrel wisely moved on. Bear's ears pricked and he trotted away, up the boulder-strewn hiking trail they'd tackled for their morning escape. From there, Bear would have an excellent vantage point. Von chuckled. You could take the dog out of the service, but you couldn't take the service out of the dog.

A lone flake of snow drifted onto Von's beard. Soon, the whole Yosemite region would be blanketed with white from the glorious El Capitan in Yosemite National Park to the surrounding valleys and pristine meadows. Snow excursions wouldn't be a problem for Bear. Von might require some support for his stiff knee, which Uncle Sam wanted to label a permanent disability. *Not permanent.*

Bear's ears arrowed up and his back went rigid. Von stared. Bear's hearing was four times better than Von's. Was he sensing another quake? The uptight campers would be all in a twitter about that.

When his own subpar human ears picked up engine noise a moment later, he blinked in disbelief. A car? Driving along what was clearly a hiking trail? Sure, it joined up with the main road in another mile but there was no legit reason a vehicle should be encroaching on a byway meant for hikers.

Anger warmed his belly. He stood next to Bear, glaring down at the turn where the vehicle would soon become visible. Too fast, he thought. The driver was not only taking the wrong road, but he or she was also doing it at a ludicrous rate of speed. He pulled out his binoculars. Cloud Top, the nearest town, twenty miles away from the MDWG campground, had only a tiny police station manned by volunteers when the one assigned sheriff was in another part of the county, but Von would be sure that this license number was provided to the station anyway. Hand delivered if necessary.

A windshield reflected the sun, blinding him. It was attached to an older model white van with a tree logo painted on the side. The vehicle bumped and bounced over the dips in the trail. The driver was pedal to the metal. Likely some reckless kids out for a joyride.

"Hey," he shouted, waving his arms. "You don't belong on this trail!"

If the driver heard him, they gave no indication.

A few yards distant a squat boulder had rolled loose, maybe from the earthquake, and come to rest in the middle of the path. No way to get around it with the bushes crowding the trail on both sides. Maybe the van would smash right into the rock and rip out its undercarriage. That would end the joyride in a hurry, he thought with satisfaction.

Bear was standing, tense and ready. If there was a crash, one simple command and the dog would be the first at the scene ready to pull out a victim, or subdue them, whatever the occasion required.

He hollered again. "Stop!" The last word thundered along the ravine, but it was still not enough to be heard over the engine. He scrambled down the incline, taking a good amount of soil with him, and Bear plunged in at his side, undeterred. He would get the plate number by hook or by crook. He raced on, tracking the van as it joggled over the rough trail, rocks clanging against the sides.

The main road was narrow, steep, bordered on one side by a thick fringe of pine trees. On the other shoulder there was a drop-off that led to a creek, full from the early-November storms.

He was working so hard to keep up the pace he almost missed it when a Jeep surged into view behind the van. The driver goosed the gas pedal, closing in on the van. He gasped.

What was he witnessing? An ambush?

The van was halfway through the turn when the Jeep's bumper thwacked into it. The impact forced it sideways off the road. Von dialed his phone and rapidly outlined the situation for the police.

The van slid faster and faster until the tires caught some resistance from the rocks and flipped over, then righted itself again. With a bone-jarring shudder, it slammed to a stop in the water, the front windshield fracturing. Up above, the Jeep had pulled to the shoulder.

Von finished his call and ran, paralleling the winding slope. Bear legged it at his side, outpacing Von as they trampled down toward the river. The Jeep had stopped, but the driver hadn't gotten out.

Enemy. Clearing the brush, he could see the smashed white metal of the van. His nerves went wire taut as he switched gears from pursuit to rescue.

"Recon," he shouted to Bear, circling his index finger at the sky. The dog immediately headed to high ground where he could get a proper view. If Jeep Guy did exit his vehicle, Bear would be the first to know and to report. If Jeep Guy compounded his error by approaching in a threatening manner or drawing a weapon, he'd meet Bear in a hurry. The dog would handle security. Von's priority was the victim. Charging on, he ignored the pain knifing his knee.

Suck it up, Von. Remember all those deep-water training drills? His brain noted the pertinent details. The ambient temperature was dropping. Water poured in through the broken windshield, water that was likely hovering at thirty degrees. His boots sank into the mud as he plunged ankle deep into the freezing creek. Behind the broken glass a woman blinked at him, eyes huge in her pale face. The shock stopped him cold. *Stella?*

His former fiancée peered at him through the broken glass, her once long brown hair now cut to the jaw, grazed a freckled cheek and honey-colored eyes he knew were flecked with bits of jade.

Stella Rivers gripped the wheel, looking much younger than her twenty-seven years. Wiping water from her lashes she pressed one palm against the door and shoved. The motion tore through his immobility.

He yanked on the handle to assist, but the door was wedged deep against the bank. Without a shovel, that avenue was inaccessible. Options... The passenger window was tipped toward the sky and he could get her out that way, but the move might aggravate any injuries. He searched the fissures in the windshield. Best to extract where the accident had fortuitously provided a sizable crack. He jumped up on the slippery hood of the van.

"Cover your face," he shouted.

Stella curled away and cocooned her head in her arms. He rammed his boot into the broken glass to widen the hole. After three kicks that sent his nerves howling, it gave way. With a circular swipe of his heel he busted away the sharp remnants. He reached in, took her wrist and prepared to assist her from the wreck but she scrambled out under her own steam. Encouraging, unless she was in shock and unable to feel her injuries. That would be textbook Stella. She was the poster child for acting in haste, repenting in leisure. He could hardly believe it was her.

She splashed through the water and waded up the bank. Right behind her, he did the same, shooting a look at Bear. She'd met the dog only once before, and that was from a distance. Bear was alert, not telegraphing concern. The Jeep was now gone.

Stella sank down onto her knees, huddled into a shivering ball, breathing hard. He'd forgotten how petite she was, how young, ten years his junior. All the questions he'd meant to fire at her got scrambled in his mouth and refused to come out. Brain buzzing, he busied himself pulling off his pack and retrieving a nylon jacket from a waterproof pouch.

Wordlessly, he held it out to her.

She reached out a shaking hand. "Thank you," she said through chattering teeth.

"Injured?"

She shook her head, a strand of chestnut hair plastered to her temple, and shifted as if she was going to stand. "Stay still anyway. Possible internal…"

She ignored his comment as she stood. "I need to get to town, to the police. Do you have a phone?"

"I called them. They're dispatching a…"

She stared up at the road. "The Jeep's gone."

To add to his irritation at being interrupted, she appeared not to be listening at all. With a shake of his head, he moved closer. "You can't…"

He hadn't gotten the word out when a sound like a rumble of thunder split the air. Rocks began to cleave from the cliff face and roll with frightening speed toward them.

He grabbed Stella around the waist, lifted her into his arms and ran. Around them the earth writhed and roiled as if the solid ground had suddenly turned liquid. He stopped abruptly, almost sinking to one knee as a massive tree ripped loose from the soil and crashed to the ground. The thunderous impact jarred him. A cascade of branches fell so close he felt the blast of air on his brow. Stella buried her face in his chest as sharp twig arrows flew by. He reversed course and skirted around the fallen tree, calling for Bear. The dog reached them as they slid to a stop on a patch of wet meadow grass, clear of the trees.

The earth beneath his feet continued to lurch as if under the impact of an attack missile. Solid ground acted like waves, heaving and breaking apart.

Not a missile, his unbelieving senses offered up as he gripped her hand.

A quake.

Chapter Two

A groan emanated from deep inside the earth as the shaking knocked them to the grass. Von thrust out an arm and she clung to him, feeling as if the earth itself was trying to buck her off. Her instincts screamed at her to run, escape the tumult, as if she could outpace the disaster, but she was thrown sideways, onto one hip, as the ground dipped and rolled. Von crashed down beside her. His fingers encircled her wrist.

Bear barked, staring at his paws as if he didn't quite believe it, either.

A tsunami of soil broke loose, gathering rocks and branches from the higher elevations, sweeping past them toward the riverbank. She covered her face to keep from inhaling the clouds of choking debris.

"Von," she screamed as she felt herself sliding from his grasp.

Bear leaped into the fray, seizing her by the jacket and holding her in place while Von braced from the other side. The dog tensed with the effort but his hold did not loosen, even when a second wave of dirt rushed past them.

The air went dark, thick. Would she die here? Cut off from Hannah and Zoe? Her stomach clenched. Resolutely, she dug in her heels. She could hear the fabric of the jacket ripping in Bear's teeth, Von's fingers pinching as they fought to hold her.

Gradually, almost imperceptibly, the movement eased, slowed, vanished. She lay there, tethered in place, gasping.

Bear relaxed his jaws and flicked the down feathers from his muzzle that had escaped her jacket. She swiped a sleeve over her dirt-encrusted eyes, blinking at the slice of sky that was somehow still overhead. The patch of ground where Von crouched was ribboned with cracks. He still held tight to her arm.

"Okay?"

She nodded, not sure any words would come out.

Warily, he let go.

She sat up, dirt trickling from her clothes and hair. It wasn't the same landscape that had existed five minutes earlier. She tried to take in the upturned tree and pockets of caved-in soil and the reality that she'd experienced the deepest fear of every Californian. The big one...an earthquake that eclipsed all others.

The display of gargantuan power all around them stunned her. "That was...unbelievable."

"Roger that." Von's breath puffed steam into the air. He, too, looked around, the glacial blue of his eyes reflecting the altered terrain. Both their gazes drifted to the distant profile of Half Dome, the iconic 8,800-foot granite marvel.

"Still standing," she said shakily.

"Wonder if any hikers were caught."

Her heart squeezed. Von had climbed Half Dome, covering the sixteen miles of elevation, sharing pictures with her of Vernal Falls and the steel cables hikers used to hoist themselves up the vertical rock face. The cables for climbers were taken down in winter, but plenty of people still hiked the surrounding trails. Her attention flicked back to Von. Was she really sitting there in a pile of rubble talking to her ex-fiancé?

Dirt streaked his forehead and cheeks, collected on his beard. "Had to have been at least a seven on the Richter."

Below them the water churned around her van, rocks settling slowly. The roots of the dislodged tree thrust like skeletal fingers toward the sky. Bear gave a shake, as if sloughing off the strange experience. It appeared he was still on alert for human enemies, but no longer overly concerned about natural ones.

"There'll be damage," Von said ominously.

Damage, on a large scale. This quake was more massive than any she'd ever felt, even the Loma Prieta quake she'd read articles about. That one resulted in localized catastrophe, collapsed freeways, people trapped in their cars, dozens of fatalities. How many deaths might this one have caused?

Hannah. Her panic was electrifying as she scrabbled for footing. How much damage had Zoe's cabin sustained?

Von touched her arm. "What?"

There was no way she could talk to him, or anyone. Yes, she'd decided after tons of prayer that she needed to tell Von about Hannah, should have told him months ago. But not now, when the world had quite literally turned upside down. It was all Stella could do to manage her current situation. Later.

Debris continued to slide and swirl around them. She tried to orient herself as she stood, swallowing down the tears. In which direction was Zoe's house from their current location? East, she decided. Three miles maybe, four, though she'd never been good at judging distance. With the van inoperable, she'd have to head there on foot. Von was talking, she realized.

"Calling the station again. I told them about the Jeep and the accident, but that was before." In the unearthly quiet, she heard the line ring and ring with no answer. "I'll try again in a minute. What happened? Why was that guy after you?"

She captured her lip between her teeth. "He shot someone I was meeting."

He outright goggled. "What?"

She looked at her mud-coated sneakers with their soggy pink laces. "And then…" She gulped. "He tried to kill me, too. That's why I was running. I saw him do it."

"Where? When?" Von bent to look her in the eye. She remembered the way his voice would go quiet in a crisis, low and calm while hers soared into another octave. "Who tried to kill you?"

"I can't talk now. I have to go."

A vein in his jaw jumped. "You need medical attention and police and rescue are going to be overwhelmed. If you can walk, we can get to help in less than an hour." He paused. "And if you can't walk, I'll carry you."

"Carry me?"

His cheeks went ruddy. "Well, I mean, Bear and I found a baby deer with a broken leg we transported and it probably weighed about the same as you." He rubbed a hand over his dusty face and groaned. "Forget I said that."

In other circumstances she might have enjoyed his discomfiture. Open mouth, insert boot, he'd often said about himself. She turned away and took a few steps. When she wobbled, he reached out but stopped short of touching her.

"You can tell me more details on the way to the camp." He sounded impossibly certain.

"That'll take too long. I need to get back on the road now."

"Be reasonable. Your van is wrecked. When you're dry and away from whoever tried to kill you…"

"I need a ride, that's all." A shrill pitch crept into her voice and she breathed it away. "Don't you have your motorcycle?"

"I was on foot when you drove down the hiking trail, and right now your life is at risk." His clipped tone earned a curious glance from Bear. "You know about hypothermia, Ella."

Ella. She cringed at the use of her nickname.

"The temp is twenty-nine degrees and falling and you're wet. We have to move."

She stood her ground even though she felt like lying down and wailing. "You're issuing orders."

"So sue me. I'm not going to let you develop hypothermia while we continue this debate. We're going to camp." He stood and thrust out his palm to her.

This man who had been her everything and was acting as if he still was… She glared at him. "Please try the police again."

"Then you'll go with me?"

She forced a breath. "Yes."

A busy signal was all he got when he redialed. Without giving her a chance to renege, he turned to the dog and called. "Move out."

When he led the way toward the trees, Bear ran off to flank them. "He'll alert us if the hostile returns."

She was shivering violently now so he removed his coat and thrust it over her other jacket, ignoring her protest.

"How will he know?"

"He'll know."

She hugged the jacket and tried to keep the despair at bay. It wouldn't help Hannah for her to fall apart. "W-where is the camp from here?"

"Two miles as the crow flies…the MDWG campground." He paused. "I work there now."

Her mouth dropped open. "You work *there*?" *The place his brother Ronnie started?*

"Yeah."

His tone was like flint, but she had to ask. "Did…did you retire from the Grey Berets?"

"How 'bout we stick to the more pertinent points? Like the name of the guy trying to kill you?" Clearly, that was a sore subject. Mechanically, he fell in on her right side. A memory intruded.

Stella swinging their joined hands as they strolled. *How come I never get to be on the street side?*

Because if a vehicle jumps the sidewalk, it's gonna meet me, not you.

And you'll subdue an oncoming car for me?

Yes, ma'am.

The memory popped like a bubble, leaving determination in its wake. Von wasn't her protector anymore. He never had been, and she'd been wrong to try to make him one. Von could not be what Stella needed. No one could.

Von stood next to her, eyeing her suspiciously.

"I can't go with you. I'm sorry. Thank you for helping me." She pivoted to head for the main road but he was at her side in one long stride.

"What do you think you're doing?"

"Leaving."

He was incredulous. "You can't go. We've just had a catastrophic earthquake."

She brushed the mess from her pants as best she could. "I'll be okay, and you have other people to help, I'm sure."

"Stella, whatever you're thinking, it isn't going to work." His voice was like stone, his face equally as set.

Her last shred of self-control evaporated and to her mortification, the tears overrode her control. "I have to get to Zoe's."

The granite expression flickered and softened. He'd met her aunt Zoe, knew how much the woman meant to her.

He cleared his throat. "I understand you're worried about her, but the roads and trails will be impassable in some places. Plus, we're likely looking at rockfalls, sinkholes, and a snowstorm's rolling in." He held his phone to her. "Here. Try calling her."

"I can't. Her phone's not working." Her aunt had explained the situation when Stella had dropped the baby off before the whole day had skidded into chaos.

Had Zoe and Hannah been hurt in the quake? Had Zoe's

home collapsed? *Hannah, my baby.* Another flood of tears threatened, but she breathed them down. Calm. She had to be calm.

Tentatively, as if she was an unexploded ordnance, he touched her wrist. "We'll go to the camp," he repeated calmly. "Get some wheels. I'll take you to her."

"I..." But what was she going to say? *I don't need you to help me?* The fact of the matter was she'd been the victim of a murder attempt, experienced a massive earthquake and had no way to get to Zoe and the baby. Their baby, the one he didn't yet know about. Her words died away in the face of the facts. Like it or not, she very much needed Von Sharpe.

He didn't wait for a reply. "Recon," he told Bear again before he pulled a bright yellow knit cap from his pack. "Here."

She was shivering too much to take it so he crammed in onto her head. Great. Now he was dressing her as if she was a helpless child. *Get it together, Stella. You have to be strong.* Resolutely, she made herself straighten the cap and swallowed the tears. Hannah was fine. Zoe was fine.

He was staring at her. "You sure you can walk?"

"Yes." Her quivering limbs suggested otherwise.

He gave one final look around, and she followed his gaze up to the road from which point she'd been forced into the creek. A huge section of it was crumbled away, exposing a black asphalt scar. There was no sign of the Jeep. Maybe the earthquake had knocked him off the road like he'd done to her.

She remembered the shot, saw Matt Smith on the ground, face slack with shock, blood bubbling up through his white coat. "Wait." She ran toward the creek.

"Stella..." She heard Von's muttered complaints as he ran after her.

He didn't catch her. Bear could have, but instead, the dog kept pace with Von. She splashed into the water, reaching through the broken windshield and pulling out the envelope, soggy and splashed with Matt's blood, along with her wallet, which she shoved in her pocket.

Von was furious as he eyed the envelope. "What? You wanted to save your car registration or something? Whatever you've got in there is not worth it."

She jabbed the envelope in his direction. "The man I was meeting tried to give me this before he was killed."

That shut down his retort, and he had the decency to look chagrined. "Oh. Right. We'll take a look later."

No, we won't, she thought, as she stowed the envelope carefully in a zippered pocket of Von's jacket. There wasn't a *we* except for her and Hannah. And then she was scurrying to keep up with him as he picked a path through the ravaged landscape, hoping her prayers would be answered once they got to camp.

Questions pounded her nerves with every step. What had happened to nearby Cloud Top? Her aunt's cabin? Would anyone reach Smith in time to help or was he already dead? Her instincts had told her the stricken man was her enemy, but now she wasn't sure. Maybe the envelope would reveal the truth.

But she was just an arborist. How could she possibly have gotten mixed up in a murderer's business?

Didn't matter. Her mission was to get to Hannah and Zoe even if she had to crawl every inch of the way. She had no idea how she'd accomplish the thing, but there had to be some method of transportation at the camp she could borrow without asking Von for help.

She trailed Von and Bear, her wet jeans and bloated shoes weighing her down. The arduous hike forced her to concentrate. Each mile was mined with patches of unstable ground and shifting detritus. The terrain did not appear to bother Von. He kept them moving steadily up the hilly trail crowded with juniper and black oak. Every ten minutes or so he'd stop and check their surroundings, probably more to give her time to rest than for reconnaissance since Bear was loping along, alert as ever.

He offered her a bottle of water, from which she drank greedily, washing the dust from her raw throat.

"The camp... Are there guests there now?"

"A group of five. Paul Driscoll, his wife and son, two of his employees. More were expected today. And the three of us that run it. Camy and Tate and me."

"Tate Miller?"

"Yeah. You met him when we visited my..." He shrugged. "You remember."

She knew Tate better than he realized. She'd met Von's buddy at a picnic when they'd started dating. Visited him and Camy at the camp when they'd gone to see Ronnie's new venture, a wilderness camp in its infancy. Family friend Kip Owens, who would later become her boss, had been there, too. Von didn't know that Tate and Kip had been her lifesavers when she was pregnant, though she'd lost touch with Tate since Hannah's birth. "Yes. I remember. I didn't know he was still working there. So you three manage the camp together?"

"Yes."

She wanted to ask how Von had possibly come to work at the place that had been his younger brother Ronnie's dream. How could it not tear at his heart to immerse himself in daily memories of his lost sibling? When they'd ended their engagement, he could hardly utter Ronnie's name aloud.

He turned away before she'd capped the bottle.

"Are we almost there?"

"Another half mile." He didn't meet her eye.

They hiked on without further conversation until they reached the apex of a rocky slope that brought them to a winding dirt road. A metal gate with MDWG and a dog emblazoned on a plaque stood open to welcome visitors. The main road that led to the gate had collapsed in several places. There would be no vehicles entering or exiting that way.

Von was practically jogging as they entered the sweeping

graveled drive. The sprawling property was hilly and rugged, the slice she could see of it, backed by a majestic wedge of the Sierras. The alpine lake was as she remembered, peeping through the canopy of pines that had stood sentinel there for hundreds of years. As they moved in closer, she spotted a cabin in the distance and white canvas structures raised on wooden platforms. All new since she'd visited.

She heard Von's breath hitch. The rectangular building now in view on their left was damaged. Badly. One wall was partially crumpled under the weight of the twisted metal roof. She pressed a hand to the stitch in her ribs. "What's inside?"

"Vehicles. It's a garage. Nobody likely hurt in there." He continued on, hurrying toward two log-sided structures. They stopped once as the ground shook underneath them with an aftershock that revved her pulse. Several trees lay near the road and she ached to see the beautiful old trunks splintered and ruined. How many years had they survived the punishing mountain storms and seasons of drought before the earthquake had felled them?

The larger of the cabins was two stories, set apart with a wooden Mountain Dog Wilderness Guides Office sign above the door. It faced the road, toward the garage and front entrance. The second was across a pasture, closer to the lake. Spaced along the grassy carpet stood the tents with plastic-covered windows and wooden doors dark against the white canvas walls.

Von's expression was grave. "Stay here. I need to do a sweep of the admin cabin. If there's trouble, Bear will alert me and I'll come back."

Trouble? Like the man in the Jeep returning? They'd been playing cat and mouse since he'd scared her onto the hiking trail. But the killer couldn't possibly know she'd come here after he'd driven her into the river. She tried not to let fear ice her body. Von hesitated, perhaps waiting for a reply. She gave him none. A plan was forming in her mind, one that required some distance to come to fruition.

"Close watch, Bear," he commanded the dog, before taking off at a sprint toward the closer building. She chewed her lip. A car, a motorcycle, even a mountain bike, would be sufficient to carry her to Zoe and Hannah. Von wouldn't take her anywhere until he'd finished securing the camp and that might gobble up hours, so she was left to help herself to what she needed. She was comfortable on a motorcycle, having ridden with Von in their dating days. He'd taught her, and she'd come to love riding because he did.

Again, she checked to be sure he was hustling toward the office and away from her before she examined the garage. Three of the walls were intact and that meant some of the vehicles might be also.

When she took a step toward the crooked side door, Bear stood and poked her thigh with his muzzle. She stopped. "Did you just push me?"

An ear flick and a hard brown stare was all she got in response.

He was a handsome Malinois, with a narrow tapering head and a muscular body. His intensity reminded her of Von. She'd known Von had been assigned a dog on his last tour, and she'd met Bear, but only briefly and with a comforting space between them. The dog was kept on base when Von was stateside. Would he prevent her from going? Maybe bark to let Von know she was on the move? What exactly did the command "close watch" entail?

She looked him straight in his mud-colored eyes. "Listen, dog. Von told you to watch me and I know you're going to do your job, but I'm a mommy and I'm going to do mine. Watch all you want but don't get in my way. Are we clear?"

The dog was still as the deep waters of Yosemite's Mirror Lake. After a fortifying breath, she slowly sidestepped. Bear slid so close to her shin his whiskers brushed her damp jeans. Heart pounding, she kept going, careful to look for any broken glass or other pitfalls. Bear kept silent vigil at her side.

For the moment he would not interfere or summon Von.

And all she needed was a couple more to enact her plan.

As he jogged, Von's thoughts scattered in all directions. Someone tried to kill his fiancée. *Former* fiancée. The last two words hardly penetrated the cloud in his head. After the earthquake when he'd reached for her wrist she'd recoiled. Was he some kind of poison in her mind? Their split had been frostily cordial, hadn't it? Businesslike as detaching two lives could be.

A million additional questions rolled through him, but snowflakes were trickling down and triage was in order. As Von reached the office door, he almost collided with Tate coming from around the back, face ashen, his search-and-rescue Labrador Opie by his side. Tate's startlingly blond hair was streaked with dirt, and blood oozed from a cut near his brow.

"You hurt?"

Tate shook him off. "I was on a ladder getting down some cables in the supply shed. I fell but not far. Bridget Driscoll and Paul's doctor are sheltering in the amphitheater."

"Some MIA?"

"Paul was out for a trail ride with his son. Archie saddled up and went to find him."

Archie, Paul's stable manager for the Driscoll resorts, would be able to handle spooked horses if necessary.

"But Camy..." Tate panted, pointing to the cabin that served as an office building and an apartment for his twin sister. "I can't call her, my cell's offline and she's not answering her texts. Opie's alerted that she's in there, but the door's jammed. The rear slider's busted, glass everywhere and debris. I gotta secure Opie if we're going in that way." He touched his dog's yellow fur.

Tate's sister, a former cop, and her tracking bloodhound Flash spent hours in the office cabin, keeping the paperwork in order for MDWG. Unlikely she'd be anywhere else this time of day.

Von threw a shoulder at the door. Wedged tight, like Tate said. He could see where the lintel of the old structure had sunk down at an odd angle.

No point in pitting their strength against a stout beam.

Von jerked his chin. "Side door."

They raced to what had been the former garage before the house was remodeled. It, too, was jammed, but it moved, just enough.

Von nodded at Tate. "On three."

Von and Tate attacked at the same moment. It gave on the second attempt, budging enough that they could enter.

"Camy," Tate shouted. "Flash?"

There was a muffled shout.

"Find," Tate said to Opie. Von heard the fear in Tate's voice.

Tate would keep it together because he was formerly an army medic, but right now they could use Von's special ops brothers. As a combat weatherman, a commando soldier in charge of gathering environmental data, Von had deployed with practically every outfit from Navy SEALS to Delta Force Rangers. Military operations at the highest levels depended on crucial ground data that had to be garnered at great risk in hostile territories. His guys were at their finest when the world fell apart around them, and they relished chaos.

They're not your team anymore.

He brushed away the sting of loss, along with a layer of Sheetrock dust that caught in his beard.

Opie sniffed at the buckled hardwood floor and moved a few steps farther in. Von and Tate followed. The pictures in the hallway of the old house, which had become their headquarters, lay in broken piles on the floor. Ironically, the one of Tate and Opie graduating from search-and-rescue school still hung crookedly, the lone survivor. The other of Ronnie and Von in waders, standing knee-deep in the Dana Fork of the Tuolumne River, lay shattered under the entry table. The photo revealed Ronnie's scratched chin and Von's chipped tooth, courtesy of a heated argument they'd gotten into some days beforehand.

You're getting into trouble. Hanging around the wrong people. Not taking care of yourself.

His brother's contemptuous glare… *What do you care? You're never around since you joined up so don't tell me how to live my life.*

Truth. Ronnie's rebellion was made worse by the fact that chronic complications from his Type 1 diabetes denied him his lifelong dream of enlisting. Von got what Ronnie desperately wanted.

Just look at me now, bro. A glorified camp director.

He swallowed the bile. Tate grabbed the intact frame from the wall and used it to shovel debris to the side, away from Opie's paws. Farther down the hall they came to the double doors Camy had insisted they install to partition the office area from the back bedrooms.

Opie stopped, sitting stock-still, his signal. Tate tried to wrench open the wooden panels but they, too, had been knocked off their tracks and jammed tight. "Camy?" he thundered, pounding a fist on the wood.

"It's about time you got here," Camy called back.

Tate sagged against the wall in relief.

Von blew out a breath.

"Are you and Flash okay?" Tate yelled.

Instead of a reply, there was a sound of scuffling and a vicious kick to the other side of the door. "Why won't this thing open?" Camy continued her assault, which made Von smile. She hadn't risen to the level of police lieutenant by allowing her will to be thwarted.

Tate breathed hard. "I gotta get in there." He started to yank at the door.

"Hold up." Von grabbed a nail protruding from the baseboard and used it to jimmy the pin from the hinge.

Tate quirked a smile. "Work smarter not harder?"

"That's why I'm air force and you're army. We're always smarter."

Tate laughed. "Whatever helps you sleep at night."

Von wrestled the door aside. It gave with a dismal groan.

Camy stood with her bloodhound Flash, a bruise darkening her cheek, neat braid covered with dust. Only a slight quiver on her lips indicated any level of trauma. She wasn't a hugger, but Tate was. He wrapped her up and squeezed until she wriggled free.

He looked her over. "Man, I was scared for a minute, sis. Sure you're not hurt?"

"I'm fine, and so is Flash." She pointed at Tate's brow. "You're bleeding."

He shrugged and she scanned Von. "Where have you been?"

"Long story."

"Why didn't you answer my texts?" Tate asked his sister.

"I was in the attic looking for a box of carabiners, and I left my phone in the bedroom. Quake hit just as I got to the bottom rung of the ladder and I couldn't get the stupid door open."

Opie licked Flash on his droopy muzzle. The hound was completely relaxed. Flash's ability to slip into chill mode was beyond belief. They followed her and the dogs into the adjoining space.

Von looked over the office, collapsed shelves, overturned potted plant, some of the laminate floorboards protruding at odd angles like bones from a compound fracture. Camy's attention was focused on her computer, which returned her stare with a blank screen, cracked down the middle from a chunk of ceiling plaster. She pecked at the keys.

"It's working on battery power, but there must have been a

dislocation of the fiber optic telecommunication lines. I can't get online. Try your cell."

Tate pulled it from his pocket. "Already did. Can't call out."

She huffed out a breath. "The cell tower's damaged. Texts are all we have for now."

"My satellite phone should work." Von tried to dial 911 again, but the call didn't go through. "Emergency lines are jammed, likely. We're on our own for a bit. Garage took some damage."

Tate frowned. "Soon as we get squared away with supplies, and account for all our guests, I'll hike into town with Opie or take the ATV. Might be a while before YOSAR can send help."

"More like *if.*" The Yosemite Search and Rescue Team, nicknamed YOSAR, would be delayed, Von was certain. "With widespread damage, they'll have to prioritize the park visitors and staff before they get to Cloud Top."

Camy shook her head at the ruined office. "My guess is the locals will establish an emergency shelter in town. There's a supply stockpiled at the police station intended for blizzard relief, but they'll work just as well now. Von, can you help Tate clear the rest of the buildings while I check in with the guests?"

"Yes."

She raised a brow. "Why do I sense hesitation?"

"There's...another complication." Von tried to figure out the best way to explain.

Camy put a hand on her hip. "What could be more complicated than a massive earthquake, Sharpe?"

"Thing is..." Words failed him as he stared through the broken window over her shoulder. Stella, flanked by Bear, was sneaking out of the flattened garage, pushing his motorcycle. His mouth dropped open.

Camy and Tate followed his gaze, gaping in twin astonishment. "Is that...?"

"Yes," Von snapped. "I brought her here."

Tate and Camy exchanged a look.

"She witnessed a murder," Von grated through clenched teeth. "Someone wants her dead."

Camy whistled. "Might have dropped that on us sooner in the convo."

The silence was so profound he could hear the soft panting of the two dogs as they all three watched Stella's stealthy progress.

"If you brought her here to protect her from a killer," Tate said slowly, glancing from Von out the window to Stella and Bear, "why exactly is she stealing your motorcycle?"

For that question, he had no answer.

Chapter Three

Stella's heart dropped as Von hustled out of the cabin, moving in ground-swallowing strides. His brows were knitted into an angry line. Busted.

"Care to explain what you're doing?" he demanded, fists on hips.

Tate and his sister Camy joined them, two dogs in tow. She swallowed and decided on a casual remark. "You have duties here. I need a ride."

"So you figured you'd steal my motorcycle?"

"Borrowing, not stealing. There's a difference."

"You taking the dog, too, or just my bike?"

She huffed out a breath that steamed in the cold air. "The dog seems to be attached to my side, thanks to you."

"Good thing. Someone has to…"

Tate stepped between her and Von. "Stella. Good to see you again, even if the circumstances are the worst. Von filled us in on your accident. You hurt?"

"I already asked her that," Von snapped.

Camy's expression was half puzzled, half amused. "Hi, Stella. Heard you had trouble. Fortunate that you and Von met up." She flicked a look at Von. "I think."

Stella nodded a greeting at Camy, as if she wasn't holding on to a motorcycle she'd recently appropriated. With two more uninterrupted minutes, she'd have succeeded.

Tate's radio crackled and he stepped away to listen. "Getting emergency alert notices. NPS and cops are taking inventory, but it sounds like widespread structure and ground failures. We need to survey our roads in and out."

"Main road's compromised. Bear and I will hike up and check the south exit." Von shot a look at her. "If you're done with your road trip idea."

Stella wanted to retort, but she wasn't sure how to get out if the other entrance was impassable. She stayed quiet.

Camy called her bloodhound to her side. "As interesting as this little chitchat is, Flash and I need to check the guest quarters for damage and get our clients situated while you, er, straighten this out."

Tate nodded and turned to Von. "You should help Camy. See what we're dealing with. I'll put up the drone after I find Stella some dry clothes."

Von's brows furrowed, forming that "V" that Stella remembered so well. "I need to hear Stella explain what she's up to."

"Later," Tate said. "Stella and I will mosey on over to the medical tent." Von opened his mouth in what had to be a scathing retort, but Tate cut him off. "You undoubtedly noticed her shivering in those wet clothes, the laceration on her temple and chin." Tate's tone was mild, but Von's cheeks went dusky.

"She needs treatment," Tate continued before Von could speak. "Bring me anyone else in camp who does as well, or radio me and I'll come to you with my gear. It's triage time."

Von was still staring at Stella as if he needed to talk but his throat wouldn't cooperate.

Tate's volume dropped. "Storm's comin', Von. We're going to need an assessment of conditions, and we're data sparse, as you Grey Berets put it." He added softly, "Move out, weatherman."

Von finally shook his head, mumbling, and signaled for Bear. The dog unglued himself from her side and pranced after Von as he strode away.

Stella heaved out a breath. Tate took the motorcycle and rolled it back into the garage. The knot in her stomach tightened until he returned and cut through her fog with a question.

"We've been out of touch for too long. I haven't seen you since your mom's funeral. Kip told me you were having twins. How are the babies?"

Babies. The word unleashed agony like a fractured bone tearing through the skin. For a moment she could not breathe through the pain.

"Baby," she replied, struggling for composure. "Just one. I... I asked Kip not to say anything about...what happened."

His eyes clouded as he comprehended. "I'm so sorry, Stella. I haven't talked to Kip in a while. I didn't know. I should have checked in."

Kip and her aunt Zoe were the only ones who knew the full story. There wasn't any way to explain what she'd endured at the birth anyway. Tate looked as though he might hug her, and she stiffened. She couldn't crumble. Not now. He read the body language and stayed put. "I appreciated you not telling Von I was expecting."

"When you asked me not to say anything, I assumed that you'd be telling him pretty quick." He shrugged. "Now that we're actually working together, it's been difficult to keep secrets from him."

"I never should have put you in that position. I had no idea you'd both wind up here. I was determined to let him know in person and..." She rubbed her forehead. "I don't know, Tate. I should have told him ages ago and now everything is a mess."

He gave her a quick squeeze to the forearm. "Hey. We'll sort it all out. Tell me about your baby."

She breathed the anguish away, or at least, forced it to retreat. "She's with Aunt Zoe. I can't reach them. The phone's out of service."

"We'll get you to her. What's her name?"

"Hannah."

He smiled. "I'm sure she's a sunbeam like her mama."

Stella had to chuckle at that one. She'd only recently begun to feel the sunshine again and only in fleeting bursts. Her spirit had cooled the day she pressed her ring into Von's palm, the engagement broken. Then a baby lost. Her life in tatters.

But she'd begun to right the ship, with tiny steps toward normalcy, a job, self-sufficiency, her own apartment, a church family. The earthquake wasn't going to take away that hard-won progress, nor was the bizarre act of violence she'd experienced. "I need to get to her. Aunt Zoe's in Grass Meadow. I dropped Hannah there before the quake."

"Grass Meadow. South of Cloud Top, right? About an hour from here?"

"Yes." Again, panic swarmed over her, a million biting ants. *Deep breath. Then one more.* "Zoe's cell is broken. That's why I was borrowing the motorcycle. She's miles from her nearest neighbor. There's no one to help." Her fingers clenched, nails biting into her palms. "What if…?"

Tate touched her shoulder and guided her away from the garage. "No what-ifs. Baby is fine. So is Zoe. We'll figure out how to reunite you three, okay?"

Choking down the tears, she followed him. Opie ambled along with them. In spite of his easygoing demeanor, Tate was tense, his gaze roving over the terrain as they walked the flat trail to a nearby tent. The ground was mostly intact, criss-crossed with fissures and sloughed away near the river that rushed nearby. Opie's nose quivered as he took in the new smells unleashed by the massive quake.

Tate cleared his throat. "So now that you and Von are in the same proximity..."

She shook her head. "I'm waiting for the opportune moment." In reality, it was way past time. Her lie of omission had to be made right. And soon.

Tate didn't say anything more until she was seated on a card chair in a cramped tent, filled with well-organized supply drawers. The light switch hadn't turned on the overhead lamp so the room was dim and cold. The earthquake damage appeared to be limited to some tumbled boxes, which Opie set about sniffing.

He foraged through the cartons until he pulled out a pair of navy sweats with MDWG and a stylized dog printed on the front.

"Ronnie had this idea that we should sell merch, but we never got past the prototype batch. These will be big on you." He straightened a standing screen that had been tipped over. "You can change behind there. Here's a plastic bag for your clothes. Need a light?" He reached for a flashlight.

"No. Believe me, Hannah's a touchy sleeper, and I've learned to work in the dark. I could probably make a ham sandwich blindfolded with one hand tied behind my back."

He laughed. "Mom skills."

She squeezed behind the screen and peeled off the jacket Von had loaned her. Goose bumps prickled her skin as she stripped away the wet clothes and pulled on the fleece. Cloud soft, the material nearly made her giggle with joy, until it reminded her of the tiny pink jumper she'd put on Hannah that morning.

She had to reach Grass Meadow. Mentally, she calculated the number of servings of the formula powder in Hannah's diaper bag. Almost a full can and several sterile bottles packed, too. A small pouch of cereal and a cooler container with bits of watermelon, Hannah's favorite, a few bananas, cheese sticks. Would

Zoe know to sliver the cheese to prevent choking? How often to feed and change her? They'd only had a brief exchange before Stella had hightailed it to meet Matt Smith. She realized she was twisting her hair again.

Breathe, Stella. Breathe. Aunt Zoe had helped care for Stella as a newborn. She would know what to do. Her delight at being in dry clothes trickled away as she folded and bagged the wet garments, zipping Von's lightweight jacket on again for extra warmth. Red-hot urgency surged through her veins, yet she could do nothing. It was maddening. She forced herself to take a seat on the stool next to Tate.

Tate flipped on a headlamp, listened to her heart, checked her blood pressure and pupils. Her cuts stung when he cleaned them and applied the bandages.

"Must have rocked your world to run into Von."

"You better believe it. I didn't have an inkling he was back. And working here, no less. That floored me."

"It surprised Camy and me, too, but honestly, MDWG would probably have folded if he hadn't arrived three months ago. We hired a bunch of part-timers but no one worked out. Von's an absolute master of survival skills. He's made for the job, except he's not fabulous at schmoozing the guests."

She laughed. "Von's not a schmoozer."

"Fortunately, the clients seem to feel it's part of his rugged mystique and he's gotten away with it, at least so far."

"What happened? Why's he working at the camp?"

He stripped off his gloves. "Short story is he's injured."

She stared. Von would never confess to any physical injury, no matter how minor. Sickness was another matter. It had always amused her that when he was home on leave a simple cold would render him in need of everything from humidifiers to homemade chicken soup. But injuries…he'd never even admit the possibility. She'd actually witnessed him suture his own wound in their tiny apartment bathroom instead of going to a clinic.

If she had an injury, though…he'd treat her like she was a bone-china teacup. Had he been shot? Hurt himself jumping out of an airplane? "Is it serious?"

"Knee."

She relaxed an iota, reeling in her imagination. Likely a minor injury. His work at MDWG was keeping him busy while he rehabbed was all. "When is he going back to his unit?"

He hesitated, not quite meeting her eye. "I'll let him fill you in."

Tate had been embedded on various missions with Von. There was a loyalty bond she couldn't fathom, part of the military brotherhood that had made her feel like an outsider at times. And she'd inserted a wedge between them asking Tate to keep her secret.

She was plunged into a memory. Tate had stumbled on her crying on Kip's shoulder after her mom's funeral reception, just as she blurted about her pregnancy to the man who felt more like a father than her own. Tate knew him, too, since Kip had tended to the trees at the camp. Tate had stepped in with both feet, cobbled a plan together and talked through a scenario with Kip. He'd even helped her pack up and move into a spare room in Kip's rental property in Fresno.

That day she'd asked Tate not to tell Von and he hadn't, but Von's being a part of MDWG left Tate in an unbearably awkward position of having to continue the secrecy, his promise to her at war with his loyalty to Von.

And now here we are, all together in the same cozy campground. She pressed a hand to her throbbing temple. "I'll tell him. As soon as I can."

Tate cleaned the grit from a scrape on her arm. She hardly felt the sting. The idea of having an extended chat with Von smarted worse. It was inevitable and necessary and right, but it

was going to cause them both indescribable pain. Tate continued to clean her abrasions until she could not endure it a moment longer. She heaved herself to her feet.

"I've got to get to my daughter and Aunt Zoe."

"I know but we need to make that happen safely. There are
only two easy exits from camp, and the north entrance where
you came in leads away from Cloud Top. It's wrecked. The
south exit is steep. I'll send up the drone to check the condition. If it's clear, we'll take you out that way the first moment
we can, but..."

She slumped. "But for now I stay here?"

"Give me a few hours to help Camy and Von get things
under control."

"By then it will be dark." Her aunt and the baby would likely
be without power, enduring a cold, frightening night. She tried
again. "I can go by myself. I don't need..."

He shook his head. "Yosemite is a maze of sheer granite
walls, primed for rockfall."

He was right. Rockfalls were a deadly hazard in the region at
all times. Recently, several large ones had occurred at El Capitan, the granite monolith looming 3,000 feet on the north side
of Yosemite National Park. It was only by the grace of God that
no one had been killed. Now that everything was unsettled,
the risk would be severe.

Tate was still staring at her. "You're no good to your daughter if you become a victim."

That had almost happened twice already and not from the
quake. With a jolt, she remembered the envelope she'd taken
from Matt Smith. She was patting her pocket to find it when
Tate's radio squawked with Von's voice, clipped and certain.
"Archie checked in. Two still out of pocket right now, Paul
Driscoll and his son Walker. Minor injuries only for Bridget.
Doc's unscathed."

Tate covered the radio and mouthed to her. "Our resident campers. Paul Driscoll is the patriarch, his wife, Bridget, their son Walker, their stable hand Archie and a doctor in the Driscoll's employ." He uncovered the radio. "Location?"

"They're holding at the amphitheater. Better if you come here."

"On my way."

"Roger that." There was a pause. "Accompanied?"

Tate smiled. "Stella's okay, thanks for asking. We'll both come." He clicked off. "Weatherman's worried."

She grimaced. "Me, too."

"I get that, after the day you've had." He slung a massive back-pack over his shoulder. Opie stood and wagged his tail. "This is going to work out, Stella. We're in problem-solving mode right now. And we'll get you to your baby ASAP."

She zipped the pocket tight. Whatever Smith had passed on would wait. She wasn't going to get out of camp until all the guests were secured, so she'd do her best to help in whatever way was necessary to speed the process along. Her moment to sneak off had passed, but Tate would make good on his word to get her to Hannah.

She just had to hold on and pray Zoe and Hannah were safe.

They took a curved path from the medical tent toward the clearing. The temperature had dropped significantly and she was grateful to be dry. She still wore the hat Von had crammed on her head after her van rolled into the creek.

Not rolled.

Not on its own.

The whole scenario was surreal... Matt Smith, bloody and dying. Tears blurred her vision, but she blinked them back. She'd have to deal with the immediate problems. Triage, as Tate would say.

Von stood in the shallow bowl of land that formed the out-door amphitheater. Tall, so tall, his burnished beard catching a glimmer from the sinking sun. His crewcut was neat and precise. Beard aside, he could never tolerate his hair touching his ears. She'd learned during their engagement how to clip it for him. "Thanks for visiting Stella's Salon," she'd say with a flourish of her comb.

"Best joint anywhere," he'd reply.

And her payment? He'd snag her in a bear hug, twirl her around and kiss her breathless. The memory ached. How quickly love had turned to anger, warmth to bitterness.

As if he could somehow sense her thoughts, he shot a look her way as she, Tate and Opie approached.

A bald man with a flushed face and dark brows knelt next to a tall woman in expensive jeans and a down jacket. She clutched his forearm, her French-tipped nails digging into his wrist. Her other arm was cradled in her lap.

"Doc and Bridget Driscoll," Tate explained. "Doc's the supervising medical man for Driscoll Resorts." He picked up his pace and Stella did, too.

Von thrust his chin toward the two guests. "In spite of the mess, Bear found them in less than five minutes." There was a touch of pride in his statement.

Behind them, the wooden stage used for presentations appeared intact except for a couple of broken boards, but the ground around it was marbled with cracks and loosened rocks. The doctor and Bridget were seated on one of several massive logs intended for viewing presentations. The memory rushed at her before she could stop it.

She recalled a dog-training exhibition, the course marked off in a grassy meadow near Cloud Top. During a visit to her aunt, Zoe had suggested they go to watch the dog tracking and trailing demonstrations. Ronnie Sharpe had given a short educational talk.

Stella had settled next to a big man with blue eyes who smelled of soap and laughed robustly at Ronnie's jokes. When their gazes locked, he'd smiled; she'd done the same.

"That's my little brother, but I taught him everything he knows," he'd joked, engulfing her fingers in his catcher's mitt of a hand. His touch lingered long enough for her to know he'd felt the spark of attraction she had.

"I'm Von."

"Stella." And in a snap they'd been drawn together with the force of opposite magnetic poles.

Infatuation.

Obsession.

Love.

Until it wasn't, for reasons she still did not completely understand. Von changed, closed up, when his brother died from the heart attack caused by his chronic illness. His retreat triggered her disintegration. She'd unraveled, compromising everything trying to reach him, becoming needy, showcasing her immaturity. Their infatuation was not enough. Her "all you need is love" mantra was flimsy as a tissue-paper heart. Feelings weren't faith. And lies, even justified ones, were wrong. As she looked at Von, her heart lurched for her baby. Their baby.

So odd that they'd be together now in the wreckage. Stella and Von. He'd always said they sounded like some sort of vaudeville act.

Tate examined Bridget.

Von sidled close while Stella was trying to come up with a reasonable way to explain the business with his motorcycle. *I needed it to get to your secret baby* didn't seem like the way to go. What were the exact words to use when exploding that kind of land mine?

"You...okay?"

"Uh, yes." She'd been certain he was going to start in on why she'd tried to sneak off. "Scraped, is all. A little sore from the crash." To be sure he didn't follow up with another question, she filled the gap. "What did you find? I mean, about the damage, when you checked the campground."

"One tent unusable because the floorboards are fractured. Water's running but best not to drink it until we're sure the source wasn't compromised. Water heater's knocked loose so it's cold only. No power camp-wide. Gas generators will suffice."

Doc caught Von's comment. "Will we run out of gas? It's cold. Forecast to drop below freezing tonight. How long will we be able to stay warm?"

"I'll get the generators humming in a few," Von said. "They'll supply heat. Hot water can wait."

Doc's expression indicated he might not agree. Tate introduced Stella to the campers.

"We have to find Walker," Bridget said.

Tate started to speak but the woman's lips tightened. "He's out on horseback, and he won't return my texts. He left with Paul. He might have been thrown."

Tate nodded. "We're on it, but Mrs. Driscoll, let's take care of you and Doc first, okay?"

The doctor waved a hand. "I'm uninjured. Bridget fell and twisted her wrist. It doesn't appear broken to me. We were out walking when the quake hit and the jolt of it..." He shook his head. "Inconceivable. I'm sure Walker is fine, though. He's twenty-three. Not a child." Doc's smile was likely intended to soften the remark. Or was there a barb buried in it?

Bridget glared at him. The ground lurched. Von grabbed Stella's arm, but the movement abruptly died away.

"Aftershocks. Bound to happen," Von said.

"More reason to find my son. Walker is out there somewhere. I texted him before the quake, and he said he was on his way back. Don't any of you understand? My son is unaccounted for."

"And your husband, too, right?" Von put in. Stella knew that sardonic tone.

Tate shot Von a "you're not helping" look. He tried to palpate Bridget's wrist until she snatched it away.

"Paul's a good horseman, but Walker isn't. He doesn't even

like riding but his father insists he should know how since we own two resorts with full stables."

"Archie's gone after them," Doc soothed. "No one more skilled, which is why Paul trusts him with the resort horses, right? He'll find them."

She pulled in a breath through her nose and tipped her chin up. "It's a big property with many trails. He'll need help."

"Here." Camy jogged up, waving a sweatshirt. "This is Walker's right?"

Bridget nodded.

"That's all we'll need." Camy offered the garment to Flash, who applied his golf ball of a nose to the fabric before he spun around, ears flapping, and loped away. "We'll find him." She looked at Von. "Archie went up Vista trail. Von, you take the Eagle trail. Tate, when you're done with first aid, see if you can unearth the drone. If it's operational, that'll save search time. Plus, we can get a look at the south access and see if it's clear."

Stella's breath hitched. Clear enough for her to make it to Zoe's? She flicked a glance at Von, but he was shouldering his pack.

Bear stood next to him. Waiting. "I'll drive the Bronco as far as we can. From the peak we can see the whole of Vista and Eagle trails. If Paul and Walker went either way, we'll find them."

"I'll go with you." Stella felt every bit as shocked at her own statement as Von appeared. Why had she said it? To ensure they had time alone so she could come clean? Tell him what he deserved to know? She'd been wrong to keep it from him, but was *now* the opportune moment?

His eyebrow arched, head tilted. "You want to come with me?"

"Because of the horses," she blurted. "There may be two that need to be brought back, right? I can handle those and you can transport the guests, if needed."

Horses were not Von's thing. He knew it, she knew it, and

unless he'd hidden his discomfort with the animals, Camy and Tate had to know it, too. Stella's mom, Francine, on the other hand, had relished the saddle and taught Stella to ride before she'd hit kindergarten. Two photos were next to each other on Stella's battered coffee table, both of them captured at roughly the same age, when Stella and her mother were barely able to straddle their horses. It was hard to tell mother from daughter.

Von's lips pursed as he thought it over. She suddenly wished he'd decline her offer. It was nowhere near the right moment to have their overdue conversation. Or maybe her cowardly streak was surfacing.

"Okay," he said. "Bronco's near the stables. You good here, Tate?"

Tate gave him a thumbs-up as he activated a chemical ice pack for Bridget's wrist. She felt Tate's searching gaze as she turned. Leg muscles quivering, she followed helplessly after Von, fearing what the next hour would bring.

The funk of the stables permeated the air. Von wrinkled his nose. He knew the basics about horses, but even he could see that the three in the corral were agitated, shifting uncertainly from hoof to hoof, a tight trio of manes and tails. He was experiencing an unfamiliar cinching of the gut as well that had nothing to do with the animals.

Stella. Not merely her presence, but her strange actions, unsettled him. In no other area or relationship would he allow such uncertainty to continue. Need answers, get answers was his motto, so why didn't he push her to explain right then? But why should he understand her now when she'd been an enigma since the last months of their engagement? He simply didn't get why her love had changed to suspicion, her mischievous nature to attention-seeking.

Because you left after Ronnie died. Mentally, emotionally.

He'd changed. She'd changed. It happened. At the moment

she looked small and scared. No, more scarred than scared. What was she hiding? And why didn't he come right out and ask?

Mute, he walked on, faster and faster until Bear startled him by poking at the sleeve of the sweatshirt he'd swiped and pulled on at the admin cabin.

"What's wrong?" The dog sat, shook his ears. Von turned to find Stella had lagged several yards behind. Two patches of pink tinged her cheeks, and her lips were parted.

"You're going too fast," she said.

"Oh. Sorry." Von slowed and frowned at Bear. *Since when do we slacken our pace?*

Bear shook his ears again. Maybe he was still tending to Stella and his "watch" duties Von had assigned him earlier. Confusion was understandable, now that there was an unexpected second he was responsible for. A special-ops dog with a nurturing side. Swell.

When he went back as a trainer, he intended to take Bear along. He'd have to reinforce the discipline in order for that to happen. Nonetheless, Von shortened his stride and kept them both in his peripheral vision. He was relieved when they reached the Bronco. Mechanically, he stepped ahead to open the passenger door for Stella. Awkward. He flashed back to the woman he'd dated on his last leave, a rendezvous his buddies had insisted on.

"You need to lighten up. You're about as much fun as a canker sore," they'd informed him.

In spite of his enthusiasm for the blind date being at root canal level, he'd tried his best, shaved off his beard, brushed up on current events, even read an article on dating he'd never admit to, but the moment he'd rushed to open the car door for the woman, she'd laughed. Not a gracious, amused laugh, either.

What are you, my grandfather?

First, he was a canker sore. Then a grandfather. The door

slammed shut on his dating career after that. Had Stella seen anyone since they'd been apart? Acid churned in his gut. Bear huffed a breath through his lips, so quiet, almost imperceptible. He realized he was standing there with his hand on the door. *Like an aged, immobile canker sore?*

Should he have let her open it? Did women want that? Did she? *Sort yourself out, Sharpe.* But Stella simply edged by him, murmured a thank-you and used his extended forearm to lift herself up into the vehicle. That touch…it made his bones ache with loss and hurt.

She cut you loose, Von, remember? Even accused you of cheating.

She'd probably moved on to another relationship. Someone better suited to be a husband. It rubbed against his pride. There was no better Grey Beret than Von Sharpe. It was the way he had to think, to push himself to do what he did, to achieve what he had. Be the best or don't show up. But not in civilian life. They brought out the worst in each other. And then he was plunged into a painful memory.

You don't trust me.

Of course I do. We're engaged, right? Think I'd jump into that if I didn't trust you? But he had jumped, hurtled, in fact, until he began to worry he was losing himself.

You trust your unit. You tell them everything. About Ronnie…

I don't, he'd snapped. *Because they don't badger me to talk all the time. They let me be.*

She tipped her chin up, eyes blazing at him. *No,* she had said evenly. *They help shield you from me.* Shield him? They'd grounded him, been the rope that he tethered to after Ronnie was gone.

While he was on active duty, he was typically able to avoid the dark cloud that descended on him when he thought of her, or his brother. Now he had way too much time to wade in the ruins. One cold snowflake touched down on the nape of his neck, bringing him back to terra firma. He let Bear in the backseat and drove them away from the amphitheater.

Stella clicked on her seat belt. She didn't need reminders anymore, he noted. He used to refuse even to start the car until she buckled up, a practice she would often forget.

Tate gave them a thumbs-up. Doc and Bridget watched the progress of the Bronco from their seat on the log.

"You don't like the guests much?" Stella asked.

He shrugged. "I'm neutral on the doc, but he seems to fawn on Paul Driscoll and Bridget. Paul's got a load of money, and he makes sure everyone knows that. Strikes me as the kind who manipulates people into getting what he wants. That rubs me the wrong way. The kid, Walker, he's early twenties. He's got no discipline, no drive."

She surprised him by chuckling. "Neither did you, until you enlisted, or so you said."

He tried to remember the last time he'd heard her laugh. It was so unexpected it took him a moment to process her comment. "I always had a work ethic, but I was directionless. Didn't want to follow in my dad's military shoes until all of a sudden I did, unlike Ronnie..." He clamped his teeth together, goggling at his loose lips. He wasn't going to talk about Ronnie to a woman who wasn't part of his world anymore. Not like she was sharing with him, either. Behaving like some sort of spy without so much as an apology for trying to make off with his bike.

The Bronco transitioned from the flat ground to a graveled slope. "While we've got time, tell me what happened leading up to the shooting." The debrief would fill up the space so he didn't have to.

She wriggled on the seat. "I was on a job. I work for an arborist."

"Yeah? Like you were considering in college?"

She nodded. "Finally decided and got my license."

The life goal she'd toyed with since he'd met her. He'd encouraged her to pursue it. And now that they were splitsville, she had. Pride and guilt bubbled together. "I'm glad you made that happen. You should be real proud."

She paused. "I work for Kip."

He jerked a look. "Kip Owens? I thought he moved out of the area before we got together."

"He came back to stay in Fresno after my mom's funeral. They were close as siblings in their younger years and, well, I…needed some help."

Help? After Von and Stella had split up, Von had made sure she was taken care of financially as best he could, though she rejected his interference for the most part. He figured she'd go back to school, like she'd talked about, maybe move in with her aunt Zoe. So how did Kip factor in? "Why'd you need help?"

The tone, the comment, the question, were all wrong. He forced himself not to add a bunch more words, which would only mess things up further.

"I was struggling after my mom died."

He swallowed. "I'm sorry, Stella. I would have come when you messaged me, if I could have." He wasn't entirely sure he believed his own statement.

"It was so fast. Even the doctors thought she'd have more time but…" She rubbed her hands over her arms.

He fumbled to bump up the heat.

"And…uh, there was a lot to deal with so Kip and Tate…"

"Tate?" That floored him. Tate was a shirt off his back kind of guy, sure, but why hadn't he mentioned he'd assisted Stella?

He was about to interrogate her when he stopped. He'd find out about Tate's involvement post haste. But what difference did it really make anyway? Stella wouldn't have wanted Von's help. The text when her mother died had been too late.

He'd sent a card with a short note, nothing that would further shred each of their tattered hearts. What else had Tate been withholding? An issue to be dealt with later.

"Anyway, Kip offered me an apprenticeship with him while I finished my schooling and I accepted."

That little tidbit grated. The fact was Von didn't care for Kip. He wasn't exactly sure why. Maybe it was the way the guy seemed to be…what was the word? Complacent? Content? Von couldn't relate. Contentedness seemed to him an excuse for mediocrity. Plus, Kip wasn't afraid to cut corners and skirt the rules when it suited him. Ronnie let drop a few remarks when Kip had managed some tree removal in the early days of MDWG.

He corralled his emotions and assembled the facts. "Before the shooting, the victim called Kip's company and requested you personally. You didn't think that was odd, since you're new to the field?"

She sniffed. "No, Von. My brain was saying, 'Wow. An actual paying job.'"

He ignored the sarcasm. "Kip should have wondered."

"He's a busy guy, and he knew I'd be happy to get some work. I've been paying the bills as a medical transcriptionist until the arborist job got some traction. How could either of us have known what was going to happen?"

"The envelope. You said Smith gave you one before he was shot," he said suddenly. "What's in it?"

"I haven't looked yet." She drew it from her pocket and fingered the paper, which was still damp. Her mouth crimped tight. "I keep picturing him there, bleeding." Her hazel eyes brimmed. "Do you think there's any way that he's still alive?"

"Uncertain. Police are aware. I did leave a message even though I couldn't talk to anyone. There's nothing we can do about it right now until we get communications back online." He wouldn't tell her he'd also texted a buddy in Cloud Top about the situation. No sense getting her hopes up with some fantasy that her client had survived. Generally, a person didn't take a bullet to the chest at close range and lie there with uncontrolled bleeding for hours and live to tell the tale.

It wasn't what she wanted to hear, not what she needed. But he'd never quite figured out what she needed from him. A partner, someone to listen, and support, which was what he thought he'd delivered, but he'd been wrong. At least now he could tell she longed for reassurance so he reached out and touched her knee, a quick pat. "You never know. I've seen people come back from all kinds of injuries that should have killed them."

She nodded, a little stronger, and he felt pleased.

He cleared his throat. "Why don't you open that?"

She stared at it without moving as if he hadn't spoken.

He gestured to the envelope. "We need to know."

We? Her gaze said.

We? His brain demanded. "MDWG is sheltering you and we should be apprised of what we're dealing with. The guy was following you, obviously, when he gunned Smith down." So much for reassuring. "Normally, it'd be best not to handle it since it's evidence, but it's already been waterlogged…" *And we've got a shooter on the loose and we're cut off from the cops for the moment…* At least he'd refrained from adding that last bit aloud. Minimal points for sensitivity. Very minimal.

She peeled back the flap and removed a sodden sheet folded in thirds. He could tell it was some sort of printout, blurred to the point of indecipherable.

"I can't read it. The ink's all smeared."

"Spread it out so it can dry. We might get something from it later."

She smoothed it flat on her lap and flipped it over. "Hold on." Gingerly, she peeled a 2" by 3" rectangle off the back of the letter. A photo? She tucked her hair behind her ear and leaned close. "It's a school picture, I think."

"Who's in the shot?"

"I'm not sure. It's damaged and fuzzy but…"

He heard her sharp intake of breath. "But what?"

"Von," she whispered.

He hit the brakes and leaned close. It was a portrait, badly warped and bubbled from the moisture. The only undamaged part was an edge that showed a pale cheek, with the barest hint of freckles and a dimple, low down on the right cheek.

"Stella…is that you?"

"I think it might be." Her fingers went to her hair, twisting tight. "But I'm a kid in this picture, no more than seven maybe. Why would Smith have a photo of me?"

And how had he gotten it? He drove farther on, guiding the Bronco around a pile of rubble loosened from the mountain slope above them. "Smith calls your company and asks for you personally. You drive to meet him and you sense something is off. What felt wrong to you?"

"He didn't know his trees. Had trouble hiking down the drive from his family cabin, yet he said he'd lived there for years. And the mailbox. I couldn't read the last name painted on it, but the last two letters weren't 'th.'"

"Then you decide to leave. He tries to stop you…"

"Yes. He told me he really needed to talk to me and he pulled out this envelope and then…" Stella stared at the image and shivered. "I don't understand what's happening."

"Got enemies?"

She blinked. "Me? No. Why would I have?"

"Everybody does. You're no different." He couldn't even swallow his own lie. She was different, completely, and he didn't know how to communicate with her, how to behave with her so close. She'd landed unexpectedly in his world again and he'd morphed into a bumbling clod.

"No, Von." Her tone was sharp. "Not everybody has enemies. Plenty of people have friends and people they don't like as much, but not outright enemies. The civilian world isn't all secrets and us against them."

She was naive if she believed that. "Says the woman who barely escaped being shot."

She shook her head and looked away, out the window, jaw set. It made him feel easier for them to be adversaries. That was a playing field he could understand.

"I'm not trying to make this difficult," she muttered.

"Then how come you're not telling me everything?"

Her head jerked toward him. "What?"

"You're holding something back." He jutted his chin in her direction. "Hair twisting. That's new. You used to bite your lip when you didn't want to tell me the truth."

Her complexion blushed a fiery red, and she shoved both palms under her thighs. Her throat convulsed as she swallowed hard. Whatever it was, it was big. He pressed on, ignoring his own discomfort at pushing her.

"Now's not the time to withhold. We're going to be on our own for a while in the face of this quake. I need to know the truth. All of it. Now."

"The truth?" The look she gave him was so raw it stopped his heart and dried up his interrogation. A bottomless well of simmering emotion wiped away the distance between them. Anger? Betrayal? Her eyes were not the playful, flirty ones he remembered, nor were they filled with fire. They were ragged with pain almost…battle hardened. For a moment he wasn't sure how to proceed.

Camy's voice on the radio jarred them both.

"Flash has got a scent. Following Walker's location. Looks like he left the trail heading in your direction."

"We're moving to intercept."

"Any sign of Archie and Paul?"

"Negative."

She clicked off. He goosed the gas, but the loose debris kept him to a crawl. The rough jostling gave him something to focus on besides the woman sitting next to him, simultaneously familiar and strange.

Her body was rigid, her thoughts hidden from him as she

clutched the door handle. Above them, drifting on the current, three vultures glided in lazy circles.

Not a good sign.

Not good at all.

He noted the ridgeline, the earth pockmarked and broken in some places. Unsettled and ripe for a landslide.

A horse emerged from the bushes, turning its long neck to take them both in. No rider.

Stella already had her hand on the door. "A mare. Is it one from camp? She doesn't look injured."

"Don't…"

But she was out and approaching before he could finish.

"Stella…" A mighty crack from the rocks above them drowned out his words.

Chapter Four

Her eyes were wide, arms flung apart as she balanced against the vibrating earth. A cluster of granite boulders, dislodged from the ridgetop, teetered and toppled, thundering down upon them. Bear raced to Stella's side, pulling up as Von did. The mare bolted for the trees.

Von snagged her wrist.

Together they stumbled away from the largest incoming boulder, but it bounced and changed course.

He barely had time to do the same. Together they flung themselves to the side. He tugged Stella and Bear into his arms, praying he'd gotten them far enough. The rock passed so close it showered them with dirt. He felt the percussions as the jagged granite smashed through trees and shrubs, plowing a path down the slope like the ancient glaciers had done to form the sprawling Yosemite Valley.

He thought of Half Dome, mirror smooth, cleaved as neatly as if it had been done with a blade. Were they about to be similarly savaged right there on that mud-covered slope?

He pressed them closer, teeth rattling from the vibrations.

And then he felt Bear pull from his grip, moving to track the boulder as it hurtled past them over the slope. Von risked a look in time to see the boulder vanish.

Ears swiveling, Bear pointed his snout toward the ridge to pinpoint where the rock had broken loose.

With one eye on his dog, he tentatively released Stella. She sat up.

Her eyes were wide as saucers. "Did another quake cause that?"

"I didn't feel anything, but maybe. Ground's unstable from the big one. You okay?"

She nodded and got to her feet, wiping the dirt away from her chin with her sleeve. Bear started to trot up slope.

"Close watch," he commanded. The dog appeared torn, but he obeyed, moving to Stella's side.

Von got to his feet, hands on hips, observing the wide path ploughed by the rock that might have killed them. Earthquake? Unstable ground? Or had someone helped the rocks along? Was Bear's interest purely ongoing threat assessment or had he scented someone's presence? Most likely the cause was a rockfall set in motion by small tremors still radiating from the giant quake.

When Stella headed for the trees to find the mare, Bear followed. Von pulled out his crackling radio.

"Heard a crash," Camy said.

"Rockfall. Be careful."

"Copy that."

A quick jog caught him up to Stella, who'd found the mare. Horses. A thousand pounds of unpredictable energy on top of four spindly hooves. He'd never felt comfortable around them and he never would. Another difference since Stella adored the beasts. Nonetheless, he moved close. If the thing went wild, he would drag Stella away, whatever it took.

Bear kept pace. The dog wasn't fazed in the slightest. Squirrels brought out the play in Bear, but the horse might as well have been a bag of sand. Determined to subdue his cowardly instincts, Von caught up as Stella was reaching out to stroke the trembling mare's muzzle with one hand, catching the reins with the other.

"There's a good girl. Are you lost, baby? Did the rockfall scare you?" Stella crooned. "She doesn't look injured. Does she belong to MDWG?"

"I guess so." The horse nestled closer to her palm while eyeing him with what had to be suspicion. While she carried on talking to the creature, he summoned Camy on the radio again and gave her their location. "What horse was Walker riding?"

"Buttercup."

Von rolled his eyes. "Well, this thing isn't wearing a name tag. What's Buttercup look like?"

Camy snickered. "You've been here three months, and you can't identify our horses?"

"Sorry. Been busy. Coat's dark, like the way I like my coffee. With no milk." Yep, he was cementing his ignorance.

"That's called a bay, Buckaroo Sharpe, and yes, that's Buttercup. I'm almost to you. Flash is on scent so Walker must be between us." The radio caught Camy's panting.

Ten minutes later Camy and Flash appeared through the tall grass. Flash did not give the two people, dog, or horse a single second of attention. He simply barreled across the path, following his quivering nose, strands of saliva dribbling from his mouth. Camy jogged after him.

"Walker's close," Camy said before she disappeared into the bushes across the trail.

Von wanted to follow her, but he was loath to leave Stella. He scanned the shrubbery where Camy had vanished. All kinds of problems might have befallen Walker, who didn't appear to be rich in survival skills.

"I've got something for you," Stella said to the mare. She pulled a bag of cut-up apples from her pocket and poured them into her cupped hand. Buttercup nosed at the treat. The slices were almost paper thin, the peels removed, and the horse gulped them up with one lick of a jumbo-size tongue.

She spoke soothingly to the animal, but her gaze flicked to the place Camy'd disappeared. "Does she need help? It'll be dark soon."

Yes, and they'd have another level of difficulty added. Especially if it snowed. He pulled his radio free. "I'll give her another few minutes. Flash is closing in." Ronnie used to call Flash "robo hound." Von almost smiled at the memory. His brother would have been thrilled to see the bloodhound he'd trained completing a mission.

Again, the strain pinched Stella's face. Was she worrying about her aunt?

The branches crackled and Camy and Walker Driscoll emerged. Walker was moving well, no outward sign of injury to the skinny twenty-something. He was good-looking, Von supposed. His weatherproof jacket was smudged with dirt, but there didn't seem to be anything else pointing to an injury. The long dark hair showing under the kid's Yankees cap was the same shade as his mother's.

Kid? He was twenty-three if memory served, only four years younger than Stella. Von wondered why he hadn't been more reluctant to date a woman a decade younger, but there was something about her that dazzled him like a crystalline sunrise over Glacier Point. From the moment he'd sat next to her at the dog-training exhibition, he'd not hesitated in his pursuit of Stella Rivers.

But you should have. Look how it all turned out.

She couldn't take the military lifestyle, he'd told himself. Plenty of relationships dissolved from that strain. Except that he knew it wasn't the truth, not all of it anyway. He cleared his throat. Walker eyed Bear hesitantly, as he'd done since the Driscolls arrived in camp three days prior. Bear wasn't the tail-wagging pet to which people gravitated. Neither was Flash, who'd sprawled out on the grass, the small treat and chew toy Camy supplied to reward his successful find disappearing in his fleshy maw.

Camy radioed Tate to tell him Walker had been found.

"What happened?" Von said.

Walker shook his head, exasperated. "I didn't even want to go on a stupid trail ride in the first place. Horses aren't my thing."

A point in Walker's favor. "Why'd you go, then?"

Camy shot him a warning look. Nosy question, she was telling him. "His father asked him to."

Walker glared. "He didn't ask. He threw down that whole drama that it was the least I could do. Expensive trip he'd planned, riding lessons he'd paid for since I was two, blah, blah, blah. Anyway, about ten minutes into the ride, I got a text from Mom that she felt a quake and wanted me to come back. I didn't feel anything, but I was amped to have an excuse to turn around. Dad didn't want to. Big surprise, right? Dad isn't going to be deterred by anything Mom says. I got about halfway down that steep section of trail and the whole ground went mushy. Shaking, rocks sliding everywhere." He took off his cap and shoveled a handful of hair away from his forehead. "The horse spooked and threw me."

Camy raised a brow, her police officer's instinct indicating she was listening to a lie. "Hard to picture Buttercup unseating anyone. I was riding her when we encountered a mother black bear who charged us, and she didn't throw me."

Walker blushed as he caught her expression. "Okay. I guess it was more like I kinda freaked out and slid off. I ran toward the nearest tree to hide under."

Not the smartest idea, but Von refrained from saying so. See? He could show social restraint.

"When the shaking stopped, I couldn't find the horse and my phone wasn't working, either, so I've been walking along trying to find the trail down. I got disoriented. I figured I'd hike to a higher spot where maybe I could get a signal."

"Texts might work, but calls are iffy and there's no internet without a satellite phone. You aren't going to get a signal until the cell tower's repaired," Von said.

Walker gaped as if Von had just told him the sun was shorting out. "When will that be?"

Von countered the peevish question with an expressionless answer. "No way of knowing. People survived before cell phones. We will, too."

Walker shook his head, unconvinced.

Camy listened to her radio. "Tate's got the drone up. He has a location for Paul one mile northeast but the trees are obscuring his view." She pointed to the Bronco. "Von, can you take Walker back to camp? And Flash, too? He needs a rest." Indeed, the massive bloodhound had fallen asleep snoring with his rubbery head atop his chew toy. "Tate's going to ride the ATV up if Paul needs transport."

"I'll drive them down, Camy," Stella volunteered. "You might need Von's help."

It was true Von's medical training exceeded Camy's. He didn't like the idea of Stella driving alone. It wasn't merely the secrets she was keeping. They had a shooter at large. "Not a good plan."

"Yes, it is." The stubborn tilt of Stella's chin stirred something inside him. He'd always loved her fire.

"Your trustworthiness is nil. You tried to steal my bike not an hour ago."

"I solemnly promise not to make off with any more of your vehicles."

"No." He flatly refused to be charmed.

Stella stared at him.

He couldn't read her. Perhaps mad about his rejection of her plan? He was uncertain. Before she'd let her emotions stream out like petals in the wind, but now he found she was inscrutable. Ironic, since his stoicism had been a point of frustration for her. What had happened in the eighteen months they'd been apart? And why did the need to know burn his insides? He folded his arms, ready for a fight. "You're not driving back to camp by yourself."

Camy made a "T" with her hands. "All right, time out. To speed this along, we'll change it up. Walker can drive back to camp, I'll follow on Buttercup and you two can hike up and assist until Tate gets there. How's that?"

He gave a curt nod. "We'd better move. Losing daylight."

It was the best option that suited all their needs. Stella would be close and that was where he intended to keep her until he got answers to his questions. Every last one of them.

Stella jammed her hands into her pockets as Walker slid behind the wheel. The dirt that had infiltrated her jacket during the rockfall was uncomfortable, but she was determined not to think about it. Camy coaxed her sleepy bloodhound into the backseat and mounted Buttercup. Von signaled the path to Bear and they set off. Stella pushed herself to keep up. The sooner they got Paul to safety, the sooner she'd be able to set out for Zoe's. She'd promised Von she wouldn't take one of his vehicles, but she hadn't said a peep about not borrowing a horse. *Hannah…* Her insides twisted up again but she refused to let all the terrifying possibilities loose in her mind. Hannah was fine. Zoe was fine. She put the thought on repeat.

She could tell Von the truth. Right here. Right now. But he was so grim faced and marching with such vigor it took all her energy to keep up with him. No. Better to get to Hannah and worry about the revelation later. With her mental health so tentative, she could not handle his emotions until she had her baby back in her arms.

As she hiked uphill, she kept her attention primed for any ground movement, wondering how she'd shake Von long enough to make her escape. He was determined to find out everything. He'd be surprised when he did. The straight line of his shoulders reminded her of their last big fight and the humiliation she'd felt when he'd walked away. It was the culmination of a series of her adolescent attempts to pull him back to her.

She'd not known what else to do. The more he'd closed himself away from her after Ronnie was laid to rest, the more desperate she'd become. Her efforts were silly, in retrospect. She'd dyed her brown hair platinum. Bought trendy new clothes she thought would catch his attention, had her nails and makeup done, even tried to arrange outings with his military buddies and their wives, but nothing seemed to turn his attention back to her.

Another woman, she'd decided. Von had to be cheating on her. That day, that terrible day when he'd gone to a party with his buddies, she'd actually followed him. Spying from the bar, she'd inhaled a drink, though she was unused to hard liquor. When the leggy blonde arrived and headed for the room where Von and his cohorts were assembled, she'd lurched off the bar stool, plowing into the banquet area just as Von hugged the woman on the threshold.

Is she the reason? she'd sputtered, stomach heaving as she stalked over to him. *Why weren't you man enough to tell me?*

Von's expression, incredulous, at a loss for words, was the first indication that she'd made a grave mistake.

The dozen men, his unit buddies, mostly bearded and nursing drinks, quickly looked away, as if to spare her for a brief moment from what she was about to discover. Her gaze drifted over to the cake with the photo next to it of the blonde woman Von had hugged. In the photo her arms were around a man in an air force uniform, her fiancé. The cake confirmed it.

Congrats Deena and Stu.

The woman, Deena, gave Stella a pitying glance before she turned her back to the gathering.

Stella, stunned and mortified at her own behavior, reeled outside where Von joined her. His fury drove into her like bolts of lightning.

What just happened? he said.

She was wondering the same thing.

You were drinking?

She ignored the question. *I thought you were having an affair. You didn't invite me to this party.*

I didn't invite you because you don't like my guys.

Yes, I do, she'd flung back at him. But she didn't. Not really. She was jealous, pure and simple. He loved his unit, wanted to spend more and more time with them and less and less with her.

You thought I was having an affair?

Why wouldn't I? We barely talk. You find every excuse in the book to be away from home. What was I supposed to think?

That we're engaged, and I wouldn't cheat on you.

You don't love me, not anymore.

That's not true.

But she'd seen then, through her misty eyes and whirling head, that it was true. Whatever had started when Ronnie died, had pulled Von away so far that her love wasn't enough to bring him back. She wasn't enough. He confirmed it by turning and walking away from the restaurant, calling derisively over his shoulder.

I'll get you a cab.

She blinked away the horrible memory.

Von appeared to be favoring one knee as they crested the rocky meadow, but perhaps she was imagining it. He certainly didn't slow. She and Bear arrived a moment later at the top, giving them a view of the canyon spread out below. The late sun required them both to shield their eyes.

A thin man with weather-beaten skin and bushy brows

whirled to face them. He stood next to two horses tied to a low-hanging branch.

"Glad you got here," the man said.

"Stella, this is Archie Thorndike."

Archie nodded, thumbing a battered brimmed hat. Von was already at the edge, peering over.

"Found Paul's horse wandering," Archie said. "Took me a while but I finally spotted him down in the ravine. Called to tell you but no cell and my texts are nothing but swirling dots. Been trying to figure a way down to him."

Von removed his pack and extracted a coil of nylon rope, which he secured to a tree.

"Has he moved at all?" Stella asked.

Archie shook his head grimly. "Not that I've seen. A ton of rocks between here and him. Coulda' conked himself a dozen times on the way down. Did you find Walker?"

"Safe and sound. On his way back to camp," Von said.

Archie exhaled. "We're two for two then. I'll go down the rope with you and help get him up."

Von shook his head. "I'll do it solo. I'll need you to lower down a second rope when I'm in position. Tate will be here shortly and he'll have a backboard."

Archie frowned. "I should go. He's my boss."

Von quirked a smile, trademark cocky as he said, "I outrank you." And then after a signal to Bear, he was working his way over the edge.

Archie blew out a breath. "Seems like a real Captain America type."

She hid her smile.

Archie bent to empty a rock from his boot. The movement brought him closer to Stella. Bear reacted by crowding close to Stella's hip and issuing a throaty growl that urged Archie away a few steps.

He raised an eyebrow. "Is that dog your bodyguard?"

"He seems to think so." Bear pressed right up to her, alternating focus between Archie and his master shimmying down the rope. She wanted to comfort the dog with a gentle pat but she knew it wouldn't be right. Bear was doing his job and so was Von. She and Archie watched as Von scrambled down until he was alongside the fallen man.

"Paul should have listened. He's not the world's best horseman despite his delusions."

Archie was the second person she'd talked to who wasn't overly fond of Paul Driscoll. Or maybe the third if she counted Bridget, his wife. "That's what his son said, too."

Archie rolled his eyes. "Father-son angst. I told Walker when he was feeling low that his father didn't even ride a horse until he was almost a grown man. Moved near my family's ranch in Yosemite when he was a regular Joe who didn't know one end of the horse from the other. I taught him about riding." He sighed. "Guess I didn't teach him enough about staying in the saddle, though."

"Not many people could control a horse if it panicked during a quake like we just had."

"True enough. How bad's the camp?"

"No power or communication except for texts right now."

Archie quirked a brow at her. "How'd you get here anyway? This place is miles from the nearest town."

There was simply no way to explain her presence so she condensed it to the bare bones. "I was driving and I had an accident. Von found me. Coincidentally. We're...old friends."

Friends? It definitely did not feel that way. Von was more like a big, glowering shadow. "I know Tate and Camy, too." As she and Archie stood there, a frigid wind swept over the canyon top, slicing through her clothes. The sun slipped below the horizon, bathing them in bronze light. In the distance a granite peak jutted against the sky, beautiful and severe. She shivered, grateful that Bear was lending her some warmth. Every small noise from the wind or crackle of branches made her worry that more rocks might come loose and tumble down on Von and Paul Driscoll.

Her worries spun faster. Had her aunt and the baby experienced any ground failure? They were likely without power, too. Did Zoe have some way to keep them warm? Were she and Hannah suffering? *Stop, Stella.* They were tucked away inside Zoe's cozy cabin with plenty of blankets. She realized her hands were clawed and she forced them to relax.

Archie pulled his denim jacket tighter around his bony frame. Von shouted, and Archie immediately slung the rope over the ridge.

"Is he alive?" Archie called down.

Von's answer was lost in the rumble of an engine. Tate jerked the all-terrain vehicle to a stop and got out, freeing a rigid plastic stretcher from the back. After a nod to both of them, he grabbed the second rope and vanished over the side. Stella kept a wary eye for any movement, the slightest sign of more rocks raining down. She would be able to do nothing but yell a warning to the rescuers, but it might buy them a few seconds to get out of the way.

She and Archie both strained to see in the growing darkness as the two men worked on the victim. Between them and with Archie hauling from the top, the rescue party made its arduous way back up. Paul, eyes closed, was strapped on the stretcher. She could barely make out his features, strong chin, graying hair cut stylish and short, every inch the successful patriarch, even though he was unconscious. Would his arrogance about his riding skills be the cause of his death? But accidents happened to every rider at some point, no matter how experienced. If he'd only come back when his son did.

"Is he…?" Archie started.

"Alive, but not in great shape," Tate finished. He and Von

fastened the stretcher to the back of the all-terrain vehicle and added an extra blanket tucked around the victim.

Archie moved close. "Paul, can you hear me?"

"We need to get him out of the elements pronto." Tate pointed to the horses. "Archie, can you get them back? I'd like Stella to ride with me."

Archie nodded.

"And Von, since you and horses get along like pancakes and ketchup, you and Bear can shove in behind my seat. It'll be tight for a delicate flower such as yourself, but darkness and hiking don't mix."

Without argument, Von squeezed his big frame into the rear space while Bear decided on Stella's lap instead of the cramped backseat. She couldn't even see out the windshield around his blocky body, but his presence was consolation, which she desperately needed. By now her limbs were chilled and her tension was ratcheting up into uncontrollable levels. There was only so much she could do to keep her worry in check. Once they got back to camp, how would she ride to Zoe's in the dark? With everything unsettled by the quake? Tears threatened, and she busied herself stroking Bear's fur. She'd figure it out.

Tate started the engine. From his set expression, she knew Paul's injuries must be grave. She prayed for him as they sped back to camp, the dog somehow staying steady on her lap. She'd seen a man shot down in front of her that morning. She had no desire to see another die on this terrible day.

An image of her chubby-cheeked baby rose in her mind's eye like a flickering flame. All she could think about was how to get to her daughter as fast as possible. Then she could face whatever life tossed at her.

Von helped Tate carry the stretcher to the medical tent before he cleared out the fallen boxes and stacked supplies to make room for a bed for Paul and a chair for his wife.

Camy had gotten both generators up and running in their absence, which was enough to power small heaters and lights to four of the tents. Bridget had her own tent with Walker, Archie and Doc in another. Von and Bear would sleep in the same one they'd been occupying for the three months of their employment and the remaining went to Stella. Camy bunked in the office building though she would be working through the night, doubtless.

He didn't like the idea of Stella holing up a mere fifty feet from his location. His brain was still humming, trying to figure out what was really going on with her and how in the world they'd suddenly landed in each other's lives again. The year and a half they'd been apart wasn't enough for him to have put all his feelings to rest. Hurt, guilt, disappointment had led to resignation, or so he'd thought until he'd pulled her from that van. Now, here she was again, knocking the wind out of his lungs.

Fatigue weighed down his eyelids, but he slammed down a cup of strong coffee Doc had produced instead of an energy drink. At least the Driscolls' personal physician had contributed in a practical way. Doc had already relinquished medical responsibility to Tate, claiming that he'd only treated minor complaints for so long he was rusty.

Camy, Stella and Walker were preparing a meal while Archie tended the horses. Coffee distributed, the doc hovered nervously over Tate's shoulder as he treated Paul, which no doubt aggravated Tate, but as always his friend was gracious.

Gracious was not a word anyone had ever applied to Von. Stella had been the one who paved the way for social interaction for their couplehood. She could be at ease with people she'd just met. He couldn't. God hadn't wired him that way. Hospitality wasn't what was called for post-quake anyway. Crisis management, organization, problem solving, he could bring all that to the party. The others could pick up whatever slack was left over.

Natural disasters brought out the best and worst in people, and for the moment it seemed everyone was pitching in. Hauling the nicked wood table into a better position so he could maintain his watch out the plastic square that served as a window sent his pain receptors howling. Worth it, since he could see Stella's platform tent and the squat cabin at the top of the rise that functioned as a dining hall and assembly room. His stomach rumbled. How long before they would run low on food supplies?

He wished he could ask Tate for a chemical ice pack to numb the needling pain under his patella, but he wouldn't add to Tate's load at the moment. Plus, he had more to say to his comrade that required privacy.

With Stella in the dining hall he'd left Bear on duty keeping watch from their own canvas and wood frame shelter while he pored over the drone controller, which displayed the aerial images Tate had collected.

Not good.

The heavy wall of clouds obscured the view of the south road to the extent that he could not be sure it was passable. While on duty, he'd have a dozen high-tech instruments to construct a forecast that might determine whether or not soldiers were inserted in any given area, but with computers down and his phone not accessing the internet, he'd unpacked the old-school tools, a barometer and an atmospheric thermometer. He was dismayed by the information his gadgets were providing. The temperature was hovering at zero degrees Celsius, and the air pressure was dropping. In other words, snow was on the way.

He scrubbed a hand over his beard. If he'd been alone with Bear in camp, he wouldn't have a concern. He'd stayed alive in harsher conditions in his career. But with guests, a gravely injured man and someone hunting Stella, it wasn't the time to test anybody's limits.

He was still frowning over his data jottings by the light of an emergency lantern, when something landed in his lap. An ice pack, tossed through the tent door by Tate before he stepped in.

"Figured you could use it after our rappelling expedition."

"Thanks." He activated the pouch and rested it on his knee, willing it to numb faster. He'd been in such a rush to scan the weather info he'd forgotten to swallow the ibuprofen he'd laid out. Subtly, he covered the pills with a notepad. No need to advertise the degree of his discomfort.

"Weather report?" Tate inquired.

"Snow."

"Swell. Perfect timing." He rolled his shoulders. "Yosemite in winter. Whatcha' gonna do?"

"How's Driscoll?"

"Unresponsive, head injury to front occipital region. Vitals are okay and that's the best we can hope for at the moment."

"Is he going to make it?"

"I'm just a humble medic, Von. Don't give me too much credit."

Von shot him a look. "You're also a pretty good secret keeper."

A ripple of something passed over Tate's face. "If this is about Stella…"

"That's exactly what it's about. You didn't tell me she needed help after her mom's funeral."

"Von." Tate's tone was sharper than Von had ever heard. "Stella wanted to keep her business private. I honored that."

"Is there anything else I don't know?"

"You'll have to ask her."

His slight hesitation activated Von's radar. "She almost got killed today. If you're keeping things from me…"

"What do you take me for? What Stella's dealt with has nothing to do with some guy taking a shot at her. If it did, I would have insisted she tell you."

"It wasn't random." He told Tate about the photo. "You don't know what information might be relevant."

Tate's stoic expression wavered. "Fair point, but it's her business, not mine. I'm sure you've already pressed her in that sensitive way of yours. She told you the major parts."

"She's keeping something back, something big."

"Her decision to share or not, like I said." He hooked his hands on his waist and looked at his feet. "For what it's worth, I've been uncomfortable, knowing things about Stella that you didn't, but at the time I found out, you were deployed and she was here and she needed help."

"I could have made arrangements," he stubbornly insisted. "But you took it upon yourself to shut me out and never said a word since we've been working here together." The rest didn't need saying. *We served together.* Disloyalty wasn't a part of the soldier bond.

He huffed out an exasperated breath. "And if the roles were reversed?"

"I sure wouldn't have been happy to hear Kip enter the equation."

"You've made it clear you don't like him."

"He takes shortcuts. I don't trust his ethics."

"Stella didn't need him to teach her ethics. She already has those. He's known her since she was a little girl, longer than you."

"A regular Mary Poppins." Von knew he was coming off as a jerk, but how was he supposed to respect Kip, a guy who fudged on his taxes and mooched free Wi-Fi? "Her aunt Zoe lived close. Why not her?"

"As I understand it, after Stella's mom died, Zoe became the full-time caregiver for Stella's grandpa when she wasn't working full-time. They have a minuscule cabin in the boondocks. She didn't have the space, time or funds to help. It was only recently Joe was moved to a facility."

More facts he hadn't known. His knee throbbed and his biceps ached from hauling Paul up the cliff. *You've been slack-*

ing on your workouts. Slacking on a lot of things. He'd had three months stateside to check on Stella, and he hadn't so much as sent her a text.

Tate wasn't through. "Besides, Von. I don't see where all this irritation is coming from. You weren't engaged to Stella anymore when all this occurred. You broke up and to be brutally honest, she didn't *want* any help from you."

That stung. Bad. Made sense, though. Every time they were together, pain was the result. "She's stubborn."

He laughed. "Pot and kettle thing."

He sighed as the fatigue overtook his ire. "Right. Sorry for mouthing off. I, uh, feel uncomfortable hearing that she was having a hard time and I didn't know it."

"What would you have done if you had?"

What had he done the last time someone really needed him? He already knew the shameful answer but he refused to speak it.

Tate clapped him on the shoulder. "Listen. If you do find out…certain things down the road, remember that she made it through by being so strong it would take your breath away. It had nothing to do with me or Kip or anyone. You should be proud of her."

Certain things? Proud of her, why? For handling her mother's death and finishing her arborist certification? What was Tate hiding on Stella's behalf?

"Tate…" He broke off as Bear's rumbling bark cut through the night.

A dark silhouette crossed the ground, sliding toward the mess hall.

His notebook fell to the floor as he sprinted for the exit.

Chapter Five

At Bear's intense barking, Stella almost dropped the tray of food she was carrying. Through the screen door of the dining hall, she saw the dog standing on the porch, a sharp silhouette caught by the weak light of the battery-powered lanterns left there.

Camy rushed in from the kitchen area, hands trailing foamy soap onto the floor. Bear barked nonstop, body angled forward, ready to spring.

A man's voice was almost drowned out by the din. "Down, you mangy mutt." It wasn't Von, and Bear only barked louder.

"Is it a guest? Should we...?" Stella started a step toward the door but Camy stopped her.

"Bear doesn't take commands from anyone but Von. Besides, we don't know who's out there."

Her stomach flipped over. Maybe whoever'd gunned Matt Smith down and continued his rampage at the creek had found her.

"Go to the kitchen." Camy wiped her palms on her jeans and

reached for her phone, dashing off a text. Before an answer arrived, more male voices mingled together.

One stood out.

"Easy," Von said to Bear.

Von and Tate entered with a now relaxed Bear.

A familiar grey-haired man stepped inside after them, breathing hard.

Stella put down the sandwiches. "Kip." She flung her arms around him with a squeal. "I didn't recognize your voice."

His plump belly added padding to their embrace. Sweat dampened his brow. "Hey, kiddo. Fancy meeting you here."

Stella let him go as Camy closed in. "You scared us, Kip."

"Thought you might need some trees trimmed." Kip's eyes twinkled. "Just kidding. Drove in from Fresno to pick up a part when the quake struck."

Von glowered. "How did you get here?"

Kip's thick brows were at odds with his thinning hair, his forehead speckled from sun damage. "It's a wonder I made it at all. And then I almost got eaten by a dog at the finish line." Kip continued to eye Bear.

"Bear doesn't eat people. He stops them, when necessary." Von still scowled.

Tate gestured to the log table. "How about we sit down and talk it all out right after I check on Mr. Driscoll in the medical tent? Doc's with him now. I'll message everyone there's food to be had also."

"Driscoll? Not Paul Driscoll?" Kip said.

Camy nodded. "Yes. Do you know him?"

"Only by reputation." Kip flashed a smile. "That name's connected to Yosemite, since he started buying up parcels a couple decades back. He's the resort guy, right?"

Tate nodded. "We've got the family camping here until the roads are open again. Paul was thrown from a horse, and he's unconscious."

"You're kidding." Kip frowned. "Can you get him to a hospital? Or the clinic at Cloud Top?"

"Not at the present. Battlefield medicine will have to suffice." Tate headed to the door.

"So what are you doing here in camp?" Von repeated.

Kip's mouth twisted. "Not one to beat around the bush, are you, Von?"

Von folded his arms and leaned against a wood beam.

Stella waved Kip into a chair.

"Had to get a part for the chipper. They had a used one in Cloud Top cheaper than what my supplier was going to give me. Figured I'd pay a visit to camp while I was in the area, see if they needed any work done. Could use the extra cash. I was about five miles from here when I felt the earthquake. About knocked my truck off the road. It was a monster and the radio said the epicenter was near Cloud Top, which made me worry since you had the consult, Stella. I got scared for you, especially when you didn't answer my calls. Figured getting to town would be impossible so I drove here, close as I could get, anyway, without blowing a tire, but the road is blocked a quarter mile up by a slide so I came the rest of the way on foot. Figured somebody could help me find Stella." He made a show of wiping sweat from his brow. "What a workout. Thankfully it was all downhill." His gaze turned back to Stella, and her heart stopped.

She knew the question forming in his mouth. Where was the baby? Where was Hannah? He'd forget that Von didn't know and blurt it out. She heard the campers approaching. Von was watching Kip intently.

This wasn't how Von should find out, from someone else. Especially since he didn't like Kip one little bit.

"Kip," she started, but Bridget, the doctor and Walker arrived. She breathed a sigh of relief at the well-timed distraction. She introduced Kip to the newcomers.

"How come that bruiser of a dog doesn't bark at them?" Kip said.

Von shrugged. "He knows them."

"Hmm. Maybe I should have stuffed my pockets with Milk Bones."

Von gave him a look that indicated he didn't think Kip's joke was funny. Fortunately, the guests took seats at the table and helped themselves to the ham sandwiches Stella and Camy had made.

Bridget only sipped coffee.

"Please eat something," Doc said.

She shook her head, face pale and lined, but her makeup still intact. "When will we be able to get Paul to the hospital?"

"Soon as possible," Camy soothed. "Tate's doing all he can in the meantime…with your doc's help."

Bridget smirked. "Doc's a family physician who hasn't treated anything more serious than a papercut in decades."

Doc's face went scarlet.

"Tate can handle it," Von said.

Walker quirked a brow. "You've seen him in action? Like on deployments and stuff?"

Von considered. "Yes. Nothing he can't manage."

Doc offered a wry smile. "That's a relief. Bridget is correct. I'm only a general practitioner. Haven't done emergency medicine since my residency. Not good for much." He glanced at Bridget, but she merely stared at the coffee in her cup.

Archie entered, pocketing a flashlight. "Horses are squared away. No harm done to them. The mare had a shoe loose, but I took care of it."

"Thank you for pitching in," Camy said.

He waved a calloused hand. "This herd is a fraction of what I manage at the resort, so no sweat." He looked at Bridget. "Any…improvement?"

She shook her head.

"He seemed to rouse at first, but now he's unresponsive," Doc said.

"Do people drop in and out of consciousness like that?" Archie rubbed a palm over his tired face.

"Sometimes." Doc selected half a sandwich.

Walker took a large bite of his. "Is he gonna die?"

Stella winced and looked at Bridget, but she did not appear upset by the bold question. He could be in shock, trying to process his father's accident, the quake.

"Impossible to say, but Tate is doing everything he can," Doc said.

Walker swallowed and took another bite. "So how long are we stuck here?"

Camy stood next to Von. "Main entrance is accessible, but the bridge has failed and that's our most direct route into town. With the ground failure on the road, it's unlikely we can get our vehicles out that way, either, not in the dark for sure. We'll know more tomorrow morning."

"What about horseback?" Archie said. "I could ride out on the river trail, skirt the bridge and get help."

"Again, not in the dark, not after a mega quake. It's twenty miles to Cloud Top. We can't predict the hazards in between here and there."

"Can we call for help? Maybe a helicopter or something?" Kip suggested.

Von took a sandwich, one with an extra slather of mustard and no produce. Stella hadn't even realized she'd tailored one for him. Strange.

"I've been calling PD with my SAT phone," Von said. "It rings and rings. They're swamped, no doubt. I'll continue to call but the likelihood of them having a helicopter to spare to transport one person this far out of town is slim."

"Horses are the best option," Archie said.

Camy held up a palm. Her tone firmed into a command.

"Our only move for tonight is to shelter in place and provide care as best we can. As for the weather…"

Von shifted as if he was uncomfortable. His knee? "That's another complication. Snow coming. A storm, hard to know how severe."

Archie toyed with his sandwich. "So Paul's just going to stay there in the tent? And we all sit around hoping he'll come to?"

"What other choice is there?" Bridget sloshed coffee. Doc grabbed the teetering cup and Archie mopped up the liquid underneath with his napkin.

"We'll be fine here together." Doc patted Bridget's arm but she moved out of reach. Stella caught the disdain that tightened her mouth. Doc's attention appeared to be more aggravating than soothing.

"I'm going back to Paul," Bridget said.

Walker bobbed his chin, continuing to devour the remaining sandwiches.

"I'll…" Doc started.

"By myself," she announced and strode out.

Archie looked puzzled as he watched her go.

Camy fetched a clipboard and flipped through the pages. "We're well supplied here. Not to toot my own horn, but Ronnie and I drew up awesome emergency plans." Her words were cocky but the tone was soft, as Stella had noticed it always was when she spoke of Ronnie, the man she'd loved. Stella didn't know Camy well, but every time Ronnie had called Von, he'd refer to Camy as his "one and only" or "Double O" as he'd nicknamed her. Stella had been terribly impressed with the romantic nickname at the time, her heart still wrapped up in such things. She'd wished for something more sentimental than "Ella" but when she'd heard Von say it after her van crashed, it had surprised her how much emotion it birthed.

Camy pulled a pencil from behind her ear.

"We'll be fine with the generators. They've got three thousand hours before we run out of propane. They'll fuel the heaters and emergency lights and the stove. Food and water supplies will hold for several weeks if needed. We'll work on getting the hot water heater repaired as soon as we can, but in the meantime, taps are flowing for washing. Stick to bottled water for drinking."

"Several weeks?" Walker said, midchew.

"If needed," Camy repeated. "But I'm sure it won't take that long to clear the roads. The national guard is probably deploying along with the YOSAR teams after they secure the park."

Stella could relate to Walker's obvious discontent. Even a few days was too long. But Kip had made it in, hiking part way to get around the slide. Thanks to him, she saw her chance to get to Hannah.

She nibbled at a sandwich without tasting it, willing them all to disperse so she could present her case to Kip.

"I'll add you to the guest list, Kip," Camy said. "You can bunk with me in the office. There's a love seat that didn't take too much of a beating in the quake. Structure seems sound enough, except for the mess everywhere."

"Five-star accommodations. I'll take it," Kip said. "Sure would like to text some of my guys who live in this area, but I dropped my phone and I think it's busted."

Camy pulled a spare from a drawer. "You can borrow this one."

Von threw his napkin into the recycle container. "Going to reach out to my contacts."

Camy ticked off an item on her clipboard. "And I need you to check the river while I break out more blankets. I expect some ground failure and we'd better be prepared if the water's going to flood the amphitheater area. If so, we'll all be on sandbag duty."

"Roger that." Von and Bear rose simultaneously. Von hesitated next to Stella. "Thanks for the sandwich. Appreciate you customizing."

Her cheeks went hot. He'd noticed that she'd fixed it to his taste, even if she hadn't realized it herself. Her unease grew. It had been a Herculean effort to pluck Von from her thoughts after they'd split, but she'd done it. How was she supposed to handle his abrupt reentry into her life?

And how would he react when he learned about Hannah? One thing she knew for sure was that Von deserved to be told in private. He would detest processing his emotions in front of strangers.

Von and Bear departed, and moments later so did the others. Stella and Kip tackled kitchen cleanup while Camy climbed a ladder into the storage loft to hunt for blankets. Stella told Kip about what had happened on the isolated mountain road.

Kip dropped the plastic platter with a crash. "You could have been killed. The baby…"

She picked it up. "I'm okay. Hannah's with Zoe but I can't reach them on the phone. I have to get to them. Tonight."

He twitched an eyebrow. "Why do I get the feeling there's a plan afoot that involves me as an accomplice?"

"I can't ask you to come with me, but I need to get to your truck. Can you tell me where it is?"

"No."

Her breath caught. "No?" Was he going to refuse to help her?

"No, ma'am, not unless I'm going, too."

She shook her head. "It's dangerous. You heard what Camy said. And Von…" She heaved out a sigh.

"It's finally dawned on me that you haven't told him yet."

She shook her head. "I was going to write, try to call him, but… I needed time to get myself together, and the longer I waited…" She shrugged.

"You don't have to explain it to me, but somethin' tells me your ex isn't going to like you haring off like this. Can't say I would blame him, in this circumstance."

She pressed the damp towel flat to dry. "I have to get to her.

Then I'll straighten it all out with Von. I need to go now, while he's checking the creek."

"All right. If you're sure, we'll tackle this together. What Von doesn't know won't hurt him."

If only that were true. What Von didn't know, she feared, was going to hurt him beyond measure.

"Ready?" He zipped his jacket.

Not even close, but to get to her baby she'd do what needed to be done. "Ready." Throat dry, she hurried out of the tent after him.

Von photographed the ground failure at the creek. A large shelf of soil had sheared off and unloaded itself into the frigid waves. The water was fast and high but thus far the banks were holding. Farther downriver, the flow channeled into a deep, tumbling racetrack with the hanging bridge overhead that presented another difficulty. The structure had been damaged.

Another thing he should check more thoroughly at sunup and erect a barricade if necessary. Last thing they needed was for someone to try and cross a compromised bridge and fall to their death. He was texting Camy with his findings when he saw the lights of a vehicle twisting along the road a quarter mile away. Bear saw them, too. His ears swiveled.

He pulled the night-vision binocs from his pack. A truck, moving away from camp. His nerves went instantly from zero to sixty. Had to be Kip's truck. But why would he immediately hike back to his vehicle and depart when he'd just arrived?

Stella.

He tried to talk himself out of it. She couldn't have concocted a plan to sneak away with Kip.

And why not? his good sense demanded. She'd tried to take his motorcycle that morning and she was keeping secrets right and left. With Bear at his heels, they ran back, past the amphitheater, directly to Stella's tent. Empty. Confirmation he'd been right. Unbelievable.

Camy was coming out of the dining hall with her arms full of blankets when he sprinted over. Flash meandered along after her, sniffing at a damp patch of grass.

"Is Kip here?"

Camy tossed the bangs from her face. "No, only me and Flash. Maybe he went back to the office."

"No, he didn't," Von snapped. "I saw headlights of a truck leaving and Stella's gone, too. They left together."

"Left? Where would they go?"

"Her aunt Zoe's at Grass Meadow."

"No way. They heard me say how dangerous it was."

Von huffed. "They heard but they didn't listen. I'm taking the ATV and going after them."

Her tone went steely. "So you're not listening, either? I don't have anyone to spare to back you up on this, Von."

"Got Bear." He also had a sidearm in his backpack.

"Von..."

He stopped. "What?"

"I know you're mad, but Stella has good reasons for risking herself like this and she's not alone. Don't go after her and make it worse."

Good reasons. That again? Von could hardly believe the subtext. Camy knew along with Tate the big secret. Figured, since she and her brother were tight. Fury and hurt left him shaken. "Since I'm not privy to any good reasons, all I've got is facts. She took off unprepared with a guy whom I don't trust. Neither one of them is armed, and Stella's got someone gunning for her. Any of her *good reasons* override those particulars?"

Camy stayed quiet.

Emotion aside, it was "go time" and every moment he delayed they'd get farther ahead. He knew her destination anyway, even if he wasn't quite sure where it was on the map. They'd headed for her aunt Zoe's. For some reason good old Kip had accompanied her on this wild mission, probably even encouraged her instead of talked her out of it. He couldn't wait to hear Kip's explanation.

"Von," Camy called as he jogged off, but he didn't turn. He didn't want to entertain any more justifications for why Stella had good reason for risking her life. If she did, he'd hear it directly from her.

He beelined for the ATV and Bear leaped in next to him. The sheer recklessness of her actions floored him. This wasn't a sleepy safe mountain vacation. It was a no-man's-zone. Hadn't she realized that when they'd almost been obliterated by the rockfall?

The ATV's headlights carved out sections of the road as he worked his way upslope to the point now covered by a ragged pile of stone ranging from pea-size to bigger than he was. It was a substantial slide, covering the road with debris that would take hours of work and a backhoe to clear. To get around it, Stella and Kip would have gone down the grassy hillside and looped around the wreckage to make it to Kip's truck. To clear the obstacle with the ATV, he had to thread the vehicle between a huge fallen trunk and a half-buried boulder.

Back on the road, he dared not push the speed too much and he hoped they hadn't, either. The darkness was thick as ink, the trail strewn with obstacles that might bust out an axle or puncture a tire if he didn't move with extra caution. Maybe Kip wouldn't be as careful and he'd flatten a tire, allowing Von to catch up. *Just don't get in a wreck. Please.*

His level of worry for Stella surprised him. They'd gone their own ways, cut the lines that tethered them, like detaching a parachute rig after hitting the ground. Why should his stomach be cascading with concern for a woman whom he no longer loved? Her choices were hers and she made them with her eyes wide open.

When her escapade resulted in disaster, it would fall on Tate and Camy and the MDWG, the only oasis of safety at the moment, to pick up the pieces. It was unfair of her to put them all in that situation with her stubborn refusal to listen to reason. Selfish, even, to risk adding to the victim list.

"She was always a pie-in-the-sky, it'll-work-out kind of person," he grumbled.

Bear glanced at him. Talking to himself now?

He flashed on a memory of her rushing to his study one spring afternoon in a panic, her fingers cupping a flimsy twig construction.

"Von, we have to put this nest back. It's got eggs. The wind knocked it down, but only one broke. Can you help me? Please?"

He'd been in the middle of reading a report, which he put down to examine the nest with three speckled eggs.

"Honey, I think maybe these are goners. Some of them have cracks." He pointed out the barely perceptible fractures.

She shook her head, sending her hair flying. "No. That's just dirt, not cracks. They'll make it if we put them back right now. I know Mama Bird is waiting out there somewhere. Will you? Please, Von?"

Please, Von. As if it was in his power to say no to that exquisite, passionate, vibrant woman. He'd climbed the ladder, returned the nest to a sturdy crook of branch and received a lingering kiss from her for his trouble. How blessed he'd felt to be her hero in that moment, as if God had gifted him well beyond what he deserved. But he hadn't stayed a hero, not for long.

He'd never told her he'd climbed up again when she wasn't home to check the nest.

The three eggs were cold and lifeless. He'd stood there on that ladder step and actually teared up, though why, he didn't know. It was sad, seeing those eggs for which Stella had such hope. In her mind they'd hatched into beautiful birds and he'd let her believe it. Why hadn't he told her the truth? Truth and facts were what kept people alive.

Facts, not feelings. Feelings were wild, unpredictable things that made him behave like a fool. He never should have jumped into an engagement with Stella no matter how in love he'd felt. She was young and so was he, emotionally. He'd thought since then many times about what Tate had said about marriage.

If you aren't tied together by God, the world will tear you apart in short order.

Their tumultuous engagement wasn't based on faith, nor maturity, not on his end anyway. They'd changed, the two of them, like lots of people. And why was he feeling pained about that right now, on a busted-up road after a busted-up engagement eighteen months stale? She was simply one more thing that God had stripped away from him. So much for a loving Father...

He gripped the wheel. *Pay attention, why don't you?*

After an hour passed, he lost hope of overtaking them. Best he could do would be to catch up when they stopped at Zoe's. He'd not actually been to her cabin before. Stella had pleaded with him to go, for them to stay with Zoe for a weekend away a couple of months after Ronnie died, but he couldn't abide the thought of making small talk, watching Stella chatter about plans to decorate their living room. He'd convinced her to go without him.

The headlights were all he had in the dense forested area and twice he'd nearly lost the road altogether where it had been concealed by a deluge of broken branches and loosened earth. Picking up the path again took him another half mile.

When the road branched off he was forced to get out and search for signs of which route they'd taken. Both were narrow and wooded. The earth on the shoulder was damp enough that he was able to detect the imprint of a tread.

As he drove on, the clouds slowly smothered the moon and flakes began to patter his windshield. The storm would not wait any longer. Great. Another layer of complexity on top of a badly planned expedition. How were Stella and Kip expecting to get to Zoe's if the snowfall reduced visibility to zero?

He jerked the ATV to a stop and considered. No sign of their headlights. Where were they? He'd been driving for an hour and a half and he should have caught up. In spite of the fact that he didn't want to involve Camy, he could see no other way.

After yanking out his phone he texted a request he should have made hours before.

Camy, text Kip and get a location.

He pressed Send. When had he become so abrasive? He added Please.

She texted back in less than three minutes.

Text sent. No reply from K.

"Naturally," Von grumbled. Can you track his phone? he texted. He knew Tate and Camy could access each other's location info. She'd loaned Kip a phone. Maybe it was linked.

Camy answered quickly.

I shouldn't be doing this. He would have told us if he wanted us to know where he'd gone and why.

He was trying to get his fat thumbs to reply with all the reasons why necessity should outweigh privacy when her next text appeared with a latitude and longitude.

"You're the best, Camy," he said aloud as he texted a thank-you. Her information told him he'd missed a turn. Reversing in a manner that almost left his tires dangling over a wooded precipice, he doubled back until he found it. A weathered pole lay in the bushes attached to a rusted sign that read Grass Meadow.

"This has to be it." A trail more than a road…easily missed. He felt the tingle, the strange combination of excitement and clear-headedness that he hadn't experienced since he was pushed out of the air force. It made him ache with longing to recapture it, all of it, to return to the world where his life made sense and he made a difference. Maybe he couldn't be a deployed Grey Beret anymore with his age and knee, but he could be a trainer. It hurt, but if training was the way to rejoin, then so be it.

He had a wealth of knowledge to pass on to new recruits along with the irreplaceable gift of experience. He'd "been there" everywhere from Afghanistan to Alaska. And he'd "done that" including embedding with countless units on bases all over the world. He was well enough, too, his knee pain down to a hushed murmur instead of a roar, when he wasn't rappelling anyway. A trainer, not an operator. Better than nothing. His only chance and he wouldn't miss it.

Braced, he drove the narrow, curved path until he emerged in a wooded glen with the world's tiniest cabin nestled on it. Kip's truck was parked nearby. A massive branch had fallen so close to the structure it had busted out the back window. A curtain fluttered in the breeze through the broken glass. No attempt had been made to board up the window. Not a good sign. The flickering lantern light inside indicated the electricity was out. Also not optimal. Had Zoe been hurt? Or worse?

Best to get in there and assess, but as soon as he turned off the motor he was doused in uncertainty. What exactly was his role here?

A self-assigned rescue worker?

A soldier on a mission?

A civilian sticking his nose in where it didn't belong?

And why? Stella clearly didn't want him involved. She wasn't his fiancée or even his friend anymore. So what gave him the authority to barrel in like some angry bear and take over?

His jaw clenched. Because it was an emergency situation

whether Stella saw it that way or not. They needed someone to talk some sense into them and if it had to be him, he wouldn't back down. He shoved open the door and hustled toward the porch when he remembered the way Stella had looked in that crumpled van. The memory slowed his steps. There was something he wasn't understanding, his instincts told him, like a sudden undetected sandstorm that would flip a plane on its nose.

Bear twitched an ear in his direction, his way of saying, "Why the wait?"

Move it. Snow sifted down as he again marched to the front door. Once more, he hesitated. Where was his righteous anger that she'd done something reckless? *She could have made herself a victim by not heeding your advice, remember?* Pride pricked its way up his spine. He raised his hand to knock.

Again, he hesitated. Instinct told him that Stella hadn't made the choice to run to Zoe's to spite him. Zoe was important to Stella, like her mother had been. Maybe even more precious now that her mother had passed and her grandfather was ailing. Was it his place to insert himself into her decision to help her family?

Well, he'd followed her all this way and he wasn't about to leave until he made sure everything was secure at Zoe's house at least. If his help wasn't needed, he'd take off. His knuckle had almost made contact with the door when it opened.

Stella faced him, gasping in shock.

His jaw dropped a second later. Stella wasn't alone. Behind her was Kip and Zoe, but drawing his attention like a flare on a stormy night was the baby cradled in Stella's arms.

An infant? His gut screamed. Not a newborn. Reality buried him like an avalanche. Stella had moved on all right, and she'd found a new man who'd fathered her child. No wonder Tate and Camy hadn't wanted to tell him. *She told you she didn't need your help, but you wouldn't listen.* His mind floundered in circles. Sweat dampened his neck.

Stella stumbled back a step, clutching the baby tight. "Von."

Von felt like she spoke from a hundred miles away. She stood there, hair gleaming in the light from Zoe's lanterns with a child that wasn't his, a life that he wasn't part of. Her baby flung up a tiny hand from the blanket cocoon.

As the silence lingered, Bear looked from Von to Stella. Von could not make himself speak. Stella hadn't come merely for Zoe. She came for a child...her child. "A baby," he finally said around a boulder in his throat. "That's why you were so desperate to get here, huh?"

"Yes." Her voice was unsteady.

She tucked the blanket around the baby and put the bundle to her shoulder. What would she say next? How could he have not seen this coming? Stella wasn't his anymore, but seeing her there with another man's child in her arms cut him.

"Didn't take you long to move on from us, did it?" he mumbled, horrified at what had emerged from his pie hole.

Her eyes flew wide.

The retort shamed him, but he could not take it back. *Just keep your trap shut, Von.*

She breathed out, long and slow. "Come inside. Please."

"Nah." He turned on his heel, intent on salvaging some shred of dignity. "I shouldn't have come. You're welcome to return to camp where it's safer...all of you. You made your own decisions and I butted in." Clearly. And her choices didn't involve him in the slightest. Hadn't for some time.

"Von." Her voice was high and tight. He didn't dare slow. He had to get to the ATV and depart before his confusing emotions spilled over into any more humiliation.

Kip stepped out past her. "Zoe's cabin's been damaged and there's no power or heat."

That stopped Von. He half turned as Kip continued.

"We decided to return to camp but I can't fit everyone and

the car seat in my truck so I was going to make two trips, but now that you're here..."

His mortification turned into fury. Kip was standing in as the guardian now for Stella and her baby? Calling the shots? The guy who cheated on his taxes and paid his people under the table and cut corners when it suited him? This was the person Stella had chosen for support? He wondered where Stella's husband was in all this. Could be in the service. Deployed. For some reason it hurt more to imagine that Stella might have chosen another military guy to fill his spot.

Von was still trying to sort out what to say when Bear barked a millisecond before the shot sizzled through the night and exploded the front window.

Chapter Six

Stella's scream stayed bottled inside, replaced by the frantic need to get Hannah away. Body curled around her daughter, she lunged over the glass-strewn step. With a sickening rush of horror, she realized Kip wasn't behind her. He must have fallen from the porch. Shot? She turned to look, but Von shouted at her.

"Keep going!" He'd dropped to a knee with Bear right next to him and returned fire, once, twice, deafening punches of sound.

She tumbled onto the entry floor. Zoe appeared in the hallway, holding a lantern, mouth slack with fear.

"Get down," Stella screamed.

Zoe dropped the lantern with a crash and crouched as another explosion of bullets ripped into the wall, peppering them both with flakes of paint. It was as if the world was fracturing around them again, torn apart by bullets instead of seismic waves.

Zoe crawled to Stella. "What's happening?"

"He found me," she squeaked out.

Zoe reached out a trembling hand. "The baby..."

"She's not hurt. Take her. Crawl behind the sofa in case any bullets penetrate the walls."

Zoe accepted Hannah with trembling hands and scurried behind the overstuffed sofa. Stella shook the glass from her hair and tried to think how she could help Von or Kip. The phone Camy had loaned Kip... Had he left it in the cabin? Was it a satellite phone? Would it do any good to call anyway?

At least if she could get through to the police it would be something, a record of what was happening. Maybe they'd have an officer in the area working on disaster relief who could respond. Her reasons were flimsy but she could think of no other way to help. She grabbed a pillow to clear a path through the glass shards as she eased her way across the floor. The door crashed open.

Von ran in, dragging a grimacing Kip. Streaks of blood smeared the floor. Bear was beside them, hunched low.

"Kip," she cried.

Von deposited him next to Stella before he crawled back to the door, shut it with a kick of his boot and turned the bolt. More shots peppered the porch.

Von pulled a blanket off the sofa, wadded it up and jammed it against Kip's shoulder. She hurried close and immediately began to apply pressure to the wound. The flow was steady but not spurting. She tried to breathe through her panic.

Von turned off the lantern, leaving them in darkness except for the moonlight filtering through the window. Stella felt caged, a trapped rabbit helpless as the wolf approached.

Zoe peeked around the edge of the sofa.

Von whispered to her. "Back door?"

Zoe pointed a trembling finger. "The patio slider is that way. Opens into the yard."

"Fenced?"

She shook her head.

Von gave Bear a hand signal and the two crept past. Hannah began to cry and Zoe joggled her up and down.

Von disappeared through the patio door.

Stella tried to refocus on Kip. His lips were pressed tight in pain. "Is the baby hurt? Zoe?" he rasped.

"We're fit as fiddles," Zoe stage-whispered, patting Hannah on the rump as she soothed her.

Stella lifted a corner of the blood-stained blanket under her fingers. "How bad is it?"

He offered an arrogant wave. "Winged me is all. Same guy who shot your Matt Smith?"

"Has to be. What are the chances there are two people trying to kill me?" she said with a shaky smile. "Do you have the phone?"

"Was going to get that out of the truck when he shot me."

"He? Did you see the person?"

"Nah. Funny. I've had plenty of women who wanted to take my head off in my lifetime but they'd never resort to a gun."

Stella had to smile again at that one. "Let me see what we're dealing with here." She unbuttoned his shirt and peeled the sleeve away, exposing a long, narrow gouge skimming his deltoid. She scooted to the diaper bag, avoiding a shattered lamp, and extracted her first-aid kit. At first, her fingers shook so badly she was unable to open the bandage, but finally it came free. Quickly, she applied the dressing and wrapped several loops of gauze around to hold it in place. It would do until Tate could dress the wound properly...if they lived long enough to return to camp.

"Ouch," Kip said. She realized she'd bound the wound too tightly.

"Sorry." She loosened it. Her mind was somewhere else, on Von and Bear. The look on Von's face when he'd seen the baby... Her chest tightened. And what would happen when Von and Bear encountered the shooter? What if she never had the chance to tell him what she should have disclosed months before? Not fair that he should be out there facing a killer for her. Tears brimmed and she forced several deep breaths. *It's going to be okay.*

But how could it? Von might be gunned down like Matt Smith had been. And for what? How was it all related to a school picture from decades ago? Fear crept up her throat. She tried to read her watch. How long had Von been gone?

Bear barked viciously from outside. Another burst of gunfire had her close to screaming again.

Kip gripped her hand. "They'll be okay. They know what to do."

She prayed and squeezed his fingers in response.

The minutes stretched by until they heard the sound of the porch slider opening. Stella leaped to her feet, though Kip tried to pull her down.

If the shooter had gotten past Von...

Her throat went dry. Whoever it was, he wanted her. Kip, Zoe and Hannah could still get away. She grabbed Kip's keys from the end table and tossed them to him. "Get to the truck. Hurry."

"No way," Kip said. "We aren't leaving you here."

"You have to protect yourselves and my baby." Tears blurred her vision as a dark form drew closer. She grabbed up the only thing within reach, a yellow pot with a lush fern in it.

Von stepped into view, Bear next to him.

She sagged in relief.

Von looked at her and the corner of his mouth quirked. "Gonna take me out with a flowerpot?"

She couldn't reply.

He slid the door closed and locked it. "He escaped."

"Did you see him?" Kip asked.

"Not up close. Young, by the way he moved." Von stroked a palm over the dog's back. "Bear got a piece, though." He held up a scrap of fabric before shoving it in his pocket and moving to the window. From behind the shredded curtain, he trained his night binoculars into the gloom. After a moment he turned back to them. "We need to move. He could return. I'll be in front in the ATV with Kip. Draw fire if necessary. Can you three...?" Stella noticed he was studiously avoiding looking at her and the baby. "Fit in the truck? This is an emergency so we'll have to do it in one trip."

Stella forced a nod. "I'll drive. Zoe can hunker down in the jump seat with Hannah for extra protection."

Zoe got to her feet with Hannah, whose cries had subsided to whimpers. "Good thing I've been keeping up with my Pilates. Let's go, Pookie Pie."

Still, Von didn't look at Stella or the baby. He simply gripped his gun and headed for the front door. "Give me five minutes. Bear will alert if the guy comes back. Then move quickly to the truck. Follow me back to camp. We'll figure out how to switch it up when we get to the landslide point. Okay?"

They all nodded in agreement.

Before she could get out a word, Von was gone.

Zoe checked the family room clock, which had somehow escaped damage, ticking off the prescribed minutes, but Kip's gaze was on Stella. She knew what he was thinking.

Von had seen the baby.

The bomb had detonated.

How would she go about explaining?

The question she'd been grappling with for months. She grabbed the diaper bag and Hannah's blanket and crammed them in before she scurried to the kitchen to retrieve the bottles from the dish drainer. She thanked God again that she packed enough formula and bottles to last for a week, if she could find a way to sterilize them. The diaper supply would run out sooner but that was a problem for another day.

The sheer incredulousness of the situation swept over her. Here she was, stranded by an earthquake, pursued by a killer and confronted by her ex. And all of it with a baby in tow. A list of harms that could befall Hannah began to scroll through her until she snatched up the supplies, shoved them into a plastic bag and returned to the living room.

"That's five minutes." Zoe repositioned the baby. "Are we ready?"

No, Stella wanted to scream. She was prepared for precisely none of this. The thought, the very notion, of carrying her baby outside with a shooter possibly waiting to try again, left her hardly able to draw breath. Nonetheless, she nodded and helped Kip to his feet. When she reached for the door, he blocked her. "I'll go first. He's already gotten a chunk of me."

And it could have been so much worse.

Kip stepped out, as the cold air flooded in.

"All clear." Von spoke in that no-nonsense way that erased all his warmth and humor. Move, she commanded herself. She took the baby from Zoe. "Help Kip. Hannah and I will be right beside you."

"Wait." Zoe grabbed several heavy coats out of the hall closet and a bag she slung over her shoulder. "All right. Prepared as I'm going to get." She stepped out and Stella followed with the baby, hauling the detachable car seat over one forearm. Every snowflake that flickered down jolted her. He was out there in the storm, waiting for another chance. She could not imagine how he'd found her at Zoe's. How long would it take him to find her again?

As fast as she could, she went to Kip's vehicle, accessed the small jump seat while Zoe helped Kip into the ATV with Von. There was no proper place for Hannah's carrier, so they wedged it as best they could in the small space with Zoe crouched next to it to soothe the baby. Hannah fussed until she found her thumb, sucking contentedly.

"Stay low as you can in case there's more shooting," Stella said.

Zoe nodded and hunched down.

Stella turned the key and started the wipers to clear the collecting snow. Wind splattered more against the glass.

There would be a storm coming in more ways than one, back at camp.

She exhaled slowly and thanked God that for the moment, they were all alive.

Von beat back his stupefaction as they approached the landslide area close to camp. He'd not exchanged one word with Kip for fear that his anger would funnel out in a mortifying rush. No further attacks. At least that had gone right. He'd informed Camy via a brief text what had occurred. When they got close, Tate would hike up to the landslide with a stretcher in case Kip needed immediate treatment or couldn't walk under his own power. Would Stella be able to carry her baby down?

Her baby... They'd discussed waiting until they'd been married a while before trying for children if they decided they wanted some. She'd obviously abandoned that plan with her new guy. He felt as if he was dreaming, until he brought himself to heel. *Get them all to safety. Don't think about anything else.* Bear panted next to him on the seat, tired.

"Good work, boy."

No chew toy or dog biscuit required. Bear had never been one for external rewards. He'd chased the shooter and gotten a mouthful of his clothing, which was the second best outcome to bringing the guy down altogether.

Von was not nearly as satisfied. When they reached the landslide, he maneuvered carefully around it. Stella parked the truck.

Tate was waiting as promised but Kip insisted he didn't need a stretcher. Kip climbed into the ATV and Tate took the wheel. Opie crammed in behind, taking the opportunity to lick Kip's cheek.

Tate glanced at Von. "I can offload and come back. Take more passengers."

"Might as well walk down," Von said. "ATV isn't safe for

a baby if it flips." Pretty ridiculous since they'd just escaped a shooter.

Tate didn't say anything, but his brow quirked.

Yeah, I know about Stella's baby, no thanks to you, Von itched to say to his buddy. But he said nothing at all, daring Tate to continue.

Tate simply saluted. "Radio if you need me."

He trekked up to the truck. Zoe held the baby while Stella fished out supplies from the jump seat. She struggled with a diaper bag and then the baby seat.

"Here," he said, taking the carrier from her without meeting her eye. He snagged the diaper bag, too, though she resisted.

"You don't have to…"

He ignored the comment. After a moment she strapped on some kind of sling gizmo and nestled the baby inside and wrapped another blanket around the outside. Her arms went around the bundle as if it was an extension of her belly. Shoulder to shoulder with Zoe, she started through the falling snow.

Von figured there was no way the shooter could have followed them without him knowing, but he still carried the car seat in his nondominant hand, free to draw his gun if needed. And there was Bear. For extra insurance Von took out the scrap and let Bear have a refresher sniff. Bear wasn't Flash, but he'd sure remember the quarry that had eluded him.

Bear's eyes said it all. *He won't get away a second time.*

Von stowed the scrap and patted his dog. "You're the best, Bear, but stay safe, okay? Don't want my good boy getting hurt." Probably the same way Stella felt about her baby. *Right, Von. Equate the baby with a dog, why don't you? Totally clear why you aren't the parenting type.* He briefly wondered about Stella's new man. Had they gotten married? Become the solid family unit she and Von hadn't managed? He'd not seen a ring on her hand, but then again, he'd not been looking.

He and Bear brought up the rear in grim silence.

Camy met them at the bottom, bundled in a hat and coat with extra blankets under her arm. Flash greeted the new arrivals with a lethargic tail wag. Tate had already installed Kip in the medical tent. Camy walked with the women to Stella's tent. Von made sure the generator was supplying heat and delivered extra water bottles and another battery lantern. What else would she need for herself and an infant? Food? What kind? Did the baby even have teeth?

He stood several yards from their tent, unable to return to his own. He felt rooted to the spot, trying to think of another task that begged to be done. Anything but return to his bunk alone with his thoughts rampaging like flood water about to overtake a dam.

Archie approached as if he'd just been to the stables, his collar turned up against the cold. Never too far away from his horses. "More guests?"

"Kip and Stella are back along with Aunt Zoe and Stella's baby."

Archie raised an eyebrow. "A baby?" He nodded. "Oh, I see. Tate said you two busted up but she went on to greener pastures, huh?"

Von tried to squelch his scowl. Last thing he wanted was to hash out the baby situation with a nosy guest. Archie was more his type of guy than the Driscolls, but he was still a stranger. "Something like that."

"Happens."

A change of topic was required. "What's going on with Paul?"

He shrugged. "No change. I overheard Camy on the radio. Shots fired? Catch the guy?"

"No."

"We kept calling the police station while you were gone. Rings and rings and no answer."

"Overloaded with callers. Probably not much they can do for us right now anyway."

Archie nodded. "Weird that some guy's taking potshots. Any idea why?"

"Negative."

Archie exhaled long and slow. "Not my business, you're saying, but it kind of is, right?"

"How do you figure?"

Archie jammed his hands into his pockets. "Shooter's after your ex and she's here, so that makes us all targets, correct?"

Von didn't know how to refute the point. Guy was right.

Archie shrugged and yawned. "I'm running out of juice. Going to get some shut eye if you think all the excitement is done for the day. Wake me up if you need help. I'm no sharpshooter and my vision's not 20/20 anymore, but I know one end of the rifle from the other."

"I'm going to secure the bridge from our side tomorrow. Thought maybe you could circle around on horseback to the other side and do the same."

Archie grinned. "Sure. You prefer boots on the ground than in the stirrups, I take it."

Von didn't answer. He and Bear returned to their tent. The interior was cold so he turned on the space heater along with the lantern. Bear made himself at home on the second cot, soaking in the warmth.

He tried the police one more time with no better result than Archie had gotten. Fatigue swamped his muscles, dulled his senses. He had to get some sleep, shut off his thoughts, recharge for the morning. He rustled in his backpack, fished out his book and inhaled the soothing smell of aged paper. He'd allow himself a chapter maybe. The book of rare plants fell open to a photo of the suicide palm in Madagascar, which lived for fifty years, bloomed once and promptly died.

One bloom, one shot at reaching potential. If you missed it…

Bear cocked an ear, catching Stella's presence at the partially open tent flap before he did. She was holding the baby. Von got up so fast that the book catapulted from his lap and skidded under Bear's bunk. Alarm bells pinged in his mind. "What's wrong?"

She shook her head, snowflakes speckling her hair. "Nothing. May I come in?"

Odd that his mouth wanted to say both no and yes at the same time. "Oh. Sure."

Von saw a tiny fist thrust free from the fleecy wrap. Wasn't it too cold for babies to be out of their pens or cribs or whatever? He tried to figure out what to do with himself. Shove his hands in his pockets? He'd look like a kid. Fold his arms behind him? Pretentious. He settled on picking up the book he'd dropped and straightening the papers on his makeshift desk. "Something you needed?" As if she was any other visitor to the camp. That worked.

"Yes. I...wanted to talk to you and thank you for saving us. I know you put yourself and Bear at risk. We could all be dead if it wasn't for you."

He shrugged. "Doing my job." Or what *used* to be his job. Serving others, not babysitting campers. He heard her gulp.

"And I wanted to explain about the baby."

Aww man, she was going there. He caught himself from recoiling. No way did he want to discuss that. With her. Now. Or ever.

She gently pulled back the blankets. He saw the soft crown of head, fuzzed with hair, the porcelain curve of an impossibly small cheek. Stella stared at him as if she was waiting for some sort of reaction. What was he supposed to do? Admire the kid? Offer to babysit? Why would she want to rub it in like this? He cleared his throat. "Stella, let's not talk about this. We broke up. You moved on to someone else. You don't have to explain anything to me." He was prowling now, grabbing his jacket. "I have to check the water level in the river."

"Please listen to me for one minute."

I don't have to. I don't want to hear this. "Like I said, you don't owe me any explanations. We are both living our own lives. Marriage, kids, whatever, right?"

She reached out and snagged his sleeve. "Von, look at me."

He dragged his gaze to hers. What was that emotion shining there? Tender and tentative, and strong and scared all at the same time. It caught him, immobilized him.

"She has red hair," Stella whispered.

He barely heard. She said it a second time.

"She gets it from her dad." He heard her swallow again. "From you, Von."

He stared at her, uncomprehending, as if she was speaking a language he didn't know. Her dad. Red hair.

He opened his mouth to ask a question, but nothing came out. Nothing at all.

"You're her father," Stella said.

Chapter Seven

Stella put the baby to her shoulder. Hannah was fully awake now, reaching for Stella's hair to tug, her favorite pastime. Could she feel the anxiety spiraling through her mother at that moment? The way Stella's legs trembled and her arms tensed as she squared off with Von? Bear swiveled his giant ears, taking in the wiggling baby. He trotted over, sat at Stella's feet, transfixed, but she hardly noticed. Her gaze was locked on Von as he stared from her to Hannah and back again.

"She's...mine? *I'm* the father?"

"Yes." Stella swallowed the boulder in her throat. "I should have spoken up. It was wrong. I decided to tell you during your next leave. I didn't know you were already home. I've been so busy with work and the baby and I hadn't talked to Tate in a while..."

Von stopped her with a shake of his head. "Hold it right there. Tate knew. And Camy. And Kip. And your aunt Zoe. They all knew."

The words were switchblade sharp and she deserved the pain.

"Yes," she said, after another hard swallow. "I asked them not to say anything until I had a chance to tell you face-to-face."

"Why face-to-face? You could have called. Texted. Sent a letter even. You did *none* of those things."

She couldn't argue. It was probably true that her insistence on telling him directly was a way to put off this very moment. She exhaled long and slow. No more stalling. She'd take his wrath on the chin, atone for her choices. "You're right. No excuses. I'm sorry."

His face was stony in the lamplight, his mouth unreadable behind the beard. She didn't need to decipher his facial expressions anyway. It was clear. "How old is she?"

"Nine months and three days."

He shook his head slowly. "Nine months of pregnancy and then nine more. Eighteen months and you didn't say a word, Stella. A year and a half of keeping this from me."

She felt the slow burn of grief, long-suppressed emotion and the tiniest kiss of anger. "We were over…"

"Justifications," he spat. "You should have told me."

She breathed out, long and slow. "Yes. I should have." God had convicted her of that. She'd known she'd have to take the anger that would come with cleaning up her mess and she wouldn't shy away from it, but it wasn't as clear-cut as he thought. Bear swiveled his tail back and forth in time to Hannah's gurgling; his long tongue flopped out through his teeth.

Von's countenance was thunderous but his volume was low, intonation almost flat. It was worse than a shout. "And if you hadn't run into me before the quake? How much longer would you have waited before you tracked me down and told me?"

"I don't know. I've had a lot on my plate to sort through." An excuse, but an honest one.

Von's eyes glittered, shoulders braced in a wide, unforgiving wall. "So that's it? You gave birth to my child, kept it from me and you think an *I'm sorry* is going to smooth it all over?"

My child… The spark of anger kindled to a small, hot flame. "No. It doesn't negate my actions. I did what I thought I had to do for me and the baby."

"Concealing your pregnancy? Shutting me out of the chance to be at the birth? That's what you two needed?"

Her jaw clenched tight. Even if he'd known, how could he possibly understand? About going into the hospital to give birth to two children and leaving with one? About what it was like to experience joy and desperate grief at the same time until you thought you'd go mad from it? Of concealing your true feelings lest you be thought of as a bad mother? Guilt, anguish, fear, mourning, love. As the rage rose in a red tide, she moved to leave.

"Wait a minute. You're leaving?" His jaw was slack with surprise.

Better to go than to let her feelings rip them both apart.

He followed her. "Stella…"

She whirled on him. "Think about it, Von. We broke up because you didn't want me around and I wasn't mature enough to give you the space you needed after Ronnie." He flinched at his brother's name but she barreled on. "I learned how to do things on my own. Independent, right? Mature and self-sufficient. All those things you wanted me to be when we were together. Well, now I am and I'm admitting what I did was wrong. I'm sorry that I didn't grow up sooner, but at least I did. I wonder when you will."

He gaped. "Are you joking? You're blaming me for being mad? I have a right to be, Stella. You robbed me of nine months with my kid."

Anger flamed into outright rage. "Get real, Von. This isn't about lost time with your daughter. It's about your pride."

"How do you figure that?"

She could almost taste the bitterness flowing from a deep well. "You aren't angry that you missed any precious moments.

You're irate because other people knew and you didn't. Your dignity is hurt, not your heart."

His lips thinned. "You get to tell me how I feel now?"

"It's clear in every word you've said."

"Don't make this about me. You made choices."

She clutched the baby tighter. "I did. Choices that seemed right at the time. I was scared and weak and fragile and imma-ture, but God grew me up. Now here I am, apologizing. I've come and introduced you to your daughter, and all you've done is rage at me for lying. Guilty, I totally deserve that, but Von, just one thing." She turned Hannah around to the delight of Bear. Hannah kicked chubby legs under the blanket and shoved a fist in her mouth. "Did you even look at her? Really look at this baby of yours?"

Von blinked in confusion. "I…"

"No, you didn't want to see her. Too busy expressing your outrage at what I did to you. Fine. Maybe at some point you can get off your high horse and at least ask what her name is." She was shaking now, full-on tremors. "Or maybe someone else can tell you, if you're ever curious enough to ask. When you feel up to it, I'll tell you the rest." Dagger thrown, she practi-cally sprinted out.

She heard him take a step toward her, the clatter of Bear's nails on the wood platform floor, but she didn't pause until she returned to her tent and tried to yank the door closed. It took her two tries thanks to her shudders.

Zoe's face tightened with uncertainty as she stared at them. Silently, she reached for Hannah, taking her before Stella's knees gave out and she collapsed onto the cot. Great violent gasps thundered through her.

"Oh, Stella, I'm sorry. At least it's over. Nothing to hide now."

"I need a minute," she whispered to her aunt. "Would you…?"

"Of course."

Zoe gave Stella space to sob. She cried into her pillow lest the sound carry into the night. It was important to cry, she'd learned, to let out the grief instead of binding it to her soul by keeping it in, but she desperately didn't want anyone in camp, especially Von, to hear her sobbing. She'd handled the conversation totally wrong, wrong, wrong.

Finally, when the tears had gone, she dragged herself upright. The day had been endless, terrifying, heart wrenching and everything in between. She was depleted, mind and body, but there was still a baby to be tended.

And that was a fact with which she grappled on a daily basis. What if she didn't have enough resources, physical and mental, to meet Hannah's needs? What if she wasn't strong enough, smart enough, brave enough?

You aren't, but God will give you enough, one day at a time, like He's been doing. She realized she was squeezing her fists in that rhythmical way she'd come to learn was a self-soothing technique. She matched some measured breathing to it until the emotions began to subside enough that she could think.

Zoe had already changed Hannah's diaper while Stella had her breakdown. She pointed to the bedside table. "I gave Kip the nighttime bottle I had in my pocket when we left the cabin. He managed to warm it in the dining hall with a little help from Camy." She was walking in circles, crooning to the fussy baby. Stella pulled herself to her feet and wiped a sleeve over her eyes.

"I'll feed her," Zoe offered. "You don't need to..."

But Stella waved her off as she sat in a folding camp chair and nestled the baby close. No cereal or apple snack that afternoon. The seed pearl teeth unbrushed. No lotion for Hannah's rash-prone skin. The list of missed baby care steps whirled through Stella's thoughts, but there was no way to rectify any of it. She fell back on the strategy that had saved her. Focus on the next thing and only the next thing. Kip would say, "Build a wall around today and don't climb over it."

Get through the night.

The morning would bring its own challenges.

Hannah's lids grew heavy as she drained the formula and slipped into sleep. Stella settled her on the cot. They'd butted chairs against one side in case Hannah might roll off in the night.

Before joining the baby, Stella forced herself to drink half a bottle of water and wash her face and hands in the sink. The frigid liquid felt like a slap. Zoe wrapped her arms around Stella and squeezed.

"I'm sorry it didn't go well with Von."

Stella groaned. That was an understatement. "I handled it badly, but he doesn't care about the fact that he has a daughter. He's only concerned with his pride, that I kept it from him."

"Men," she said, with a massive eye roll. "Might take him a while to come to terms with it."

Her brain knew she was being unfair. She'd kept something precious and monumental from him and asked his friends not to tell him. Wrong, hurtful, a betrayal, but her emotions were out of control. "It can take an eternity for all I care. As soon as the roads are clear and you're back in your cabin, I'm going home to Fresno. I'll talk to the police there and they'll help me. If Von wants to see Hannah he can show up whenever it's convenient for him. And if not…"

"If not, you'll raise her like you've been doing." Zoe's face was grave. "Your mother brought you up practically by herself. You've always been her spitting image in more ways than your looks. No father necessary."

Stella felt stung at her tone. "But Dad wanted to be there. His letters said as much." Those letters had gone ragged from continuous reading. He'd worked on an offshore oil rig, but Stella had grown to suspect there was friction between her parents. She couldn't remember ever seeing him before he died when she was four and her mother was uncomfortable discussing him, nor would she read the letters Stella kept in a fancy wooden box.

"Your mom was all you needed." Zoe's expression was so strange, it brought Stella out of her own misery.

"Did you know my father, Zoe?"

She shook her head. "Never met him." But there was something in her aunt's tone.

"Did my mom tell you about him?"

"No. Didn't matter who he was to me. Francine was the best parent, even though she wasn't even twenty when she had you." Zoe pressed a hand to her stomach as if she was in pain.

"What's wrong, Aunt Zoe?"

Zoe shrugged. "Nothing. Everything. The whole situation, I guess. The violence. Being here. It's…unsettling." No doubt, but she had the sense that she was missing something where her aunt was concerned.

"Aunt Zoe, is there…?"

"Stella." Zoe cut her off. "Honey," she said more softly. "I'm exhausted and so are you. Let's take advantage of the quiet while Pookie Pie is snoozing and get some sleep. All the problems will still be there in the morning, right?"

They would, unless tomorrow brought the reopening of the roads and she could get away, escape to her quiet, safe life. Whatever had happened in the forest would remain a mystery. The killer would not have reason to pursue her any longer. A fantasy she needed to believe in order to make it to dawn.

Time to build that wall around today.

Crawling onto the cot, she rested a palm on Hannah's tummy, calmed by the movement of her breathing, which meant her precious baby was alive and well.

As long as Hannah was safe, she'd be able to bear all the rest.

Zoe switched off the light.

Even the gusting winds did not prevent Stella from dropping immediately to sleep.

★ ★ ★

She awoke with her heart slamming against her ribs. Dark. Cold. The terror slithered through her. Hannah... Her frantic fingers found the little bundle lying next to her, breathing softly. Stella felt her cheeks and nose. Warm enough in her pajamas and the sleeper sack zipped over it. She longed to drape on a blanket but the risks of suffocation were too great. She'd pored over pamphlets, books, web articles about the topic. None of the available equipment in camp was certified baby safe, starting with the cot. What if Hannah got caught on something during the night, even though she and Zoe had tried to imagine every possible danger? When her chest began to ache, Stella realized she was tensed like a sprinter poised for the starting gun. She forced herself to perform a series of calming breaths as she watched her daughter sleep. The tiny rise and fall created the rhythm for both their lives.

She's okay. Thank You, God. Slowly, her senses calmed.

The luminous dial on her watch told her it was barely four-thirty. Hannah would require a bottle soon, followed up by dry cereal and a banana. With a groan, she remembered there were no more sterile bottles, nor any bananas handy unless there were some stocked in the dining hall. The cooler she'd packed for Hannah was still in Zoe's refrigerator in the shot-up cabin. She'd have to go to the camp kitchen and boil water to prepare the day's bottles and forage.

Zoe opened a bleary eye as Stella eased off the cot. "It cannot possibly be morning."

"Soon. I have to go make the bottle," she whispered.

Zoe nodded and laid her head back down. "I'll stay with Pookie." Stella noticed Aunt Zoe's feet covered in leopard-print socks poking out where her blanket had become untucked. With a smile she tossed an extra blanket across her aunt's exposed toes.

After pulling on the sweat suit Tate had loaned her along with the jacket and her shoes, which had mostly dried from her plunge into the river, she gathered up the bottles and the formula canister and eased into the freezing predawn. Instantly, Bear poked his nose from Von's tent door, nostrils quivering. Von must have assigned him guard duty again. At least she knew no one would get close without Bear's approval. There was no sign of Von. Emotions scudded through her like storm clouds.

I'm sorry that I didn't grow up sooner, but at least I did. I wonder when you will. She cringed. Had she really said that? So much for humbly accepting responsibility for her behavior. But she was right about him acting out of pride; of that much she was certain. He might possibly come to love and appreciate Hannah, but at the moment his focus was on how Stella had wronged him. Probably a natural reaction. It was for him anyway.

You mistreated Von. You don't get to decide how he should feel about it. She blew out a breath that puffed misty white against the gloom. Pockets of snow had collected on the ground and the iron sky promised more. The amphitheater was empty. Down the road at the distant stables she could make out someone tossing feed to the horses. Archie, no doubt, since Walker didn't care much for them.

Weak light shone from the medical tent where Tate was on duty caring for Paul Driscoll, the proud man who manipulated his son and possibly even his wife. Perhaps the injury made the pettier disagreements fall away. Stella had never understood why her own mother rarely left home, refusing to travel to SoCal to visit Stella and Von, or Cloud Top to stay with Zoe. It was part of the reason Stella had been eager to move away with Von from the claustrophobia of her mom's life. When her mother fell sick, those earlier irritations faded until she realized she didn't have to understand her mother to love her. Maybe Bridget felt the same way about Paul.

Though she knew she was safe at the campground, since no one could get close enough to shoot at her without being seen, she still moved at a near jog until she reached the dining hall.

Camy had told her the night before to use whatever she needed, even pointing her to a storage closet where they kept the accumulated lost and found items. The camp did provide family friendly courses in the summer so there might be some extra baby clothes left behind that she could scavenge.

The first order was pouring water into a pot and setting it to boil.

While the flame did its work, she tidied up the kitchen, folding a batch of clean towels, wiping down the counter, and starting a pot of coffee to brew. Her attention was caught by a series of photos pinned to the bulletin board under the cabinets. It was a sort of dossier, she realized, to prepare the MDWG staff for their guests, Paul, Bridget, Walker, Archie and Doc.

She read over the material. Paul Driscoll appeared to be a self-made man, having purchased various properties in the area over the years until he'd acquired enough to build a luxury resort outside Yosemite National Park. Driscoll's "camping focus" at MDWG was to "build deeper corporate camaraderie." Strange, she thought. He'd brought only his wife, son, his private doctor and his stable manager. Not really a corporate-size event. It was puzzling, until she remembered Von had said the rest of the team was scheduled to arrive Thursday, today, the day after the quake leveled the region.

Plans had been ripped apart by that thirty seconds of shaking. Plans, lives, futures. Hers along with everybody else's in camp and the whole Yosemite region.

Bridget's interests were listed as botany, birding and various conservation efforts. She was a classic beauty in her picture, no lines of exhaustion or worry carved into her face as they had been when Stella met her before Paul was found.

The candid photo of Walker appeared to have been taken at some sort of beach party. He grinned, saluting the camera with a bottle, alongside a half dozen young men playing volleyball in the sand. A compatriot photobombed, giving Walker the rabbit ears. Something struck her about the photo. Walker? The setting? The background? She couldn't say exactly what. Walker's interests were left blank, his age the only fact listed besides his food preferences—no eggplant or liver, heavy on the meat options and spicy food.

Doc Yanis Johnson was also pictured with a much younger Paul Driscoll. They stood together with fishing poles near a swiftly moving stream. Doc had apparently been involved in the family business for decades, then. No food preferences listed. Archie got a section, too, expert horseman who would eat anything but sushi, limited climbing experience.

The bubbling of the pot spurred her to turn off the heat and submerge the cleaned bottles into the steam along with the nipples and plastic fasteners. When she'd used tongs to lay them out on a clean towel to cool, she grabbed a smaller pot to prepare a batch of formula. Grateful that the generators were powering the refrigerator, she loaded the fresh bottles inside, keeping one out for Hannah's morning feeding. The camp kitchen had no microwave, so warming the bottles would have to be done the old-fashioned way. Inconvenient, but nothing to moan about.

Poking through the cupboards she was thrilled to find an unopened box of puffed rice cereal and a tin of canned peaches. Snack and bottles, done. Now for the lost and found. The storage closet was in the back of the empty dining room. Only a few of the lights powered on when she flicked the switch, leaving the space in shadow. The closet smelled of old wood and musty linens, which were piled high on the middle shelves. The rest was filled with a hodgepodge of items from shoes to charging cords to a half dozen books and magazines.

In one cardboard box she found miscellaneous adult clothing. A couple of pairs of sweatpants that might work for her and Zoe and several men's sweatshirts that could be rolled up and worn. And glorious bulky socks more suitable for camping than her slightly damp ones and Zoe's thin leopard-print pair. She piled the items together and rolled them into a tidy bundle.

A second box contained a collection of children's clothes, the majority much too big for Hannah. Likely, there were not many babies toted along to wilderness survival camp, but perhaps the tot-size articles had been left by the various summer events. At the bottom she discovered small socks that could be made to work, and several toddler shirts. No diapers, she thought ruefully. That was going to be a problem sooner rather than later. As she was about to close the door, she noticed something on the top shelf. It was a bouncy infant seat complete with straps.

"Score." After pulling a chair over, she climbed up and tried to wrestle it free. Wedged as it was on the narrow shelf, she had to grab it tightly with both hands and yank. It came loose, the movement causing her to overbalance and teeter. Braced for a fall, she felt strong arms steadying her, helping her down from the chair.

Von.

Her grip on the baby seat tightened as he set her on her feet. "I... Thanks," she mumbled.

He let go of her abruptly, as if touching her burned. "Found some supplies?"

"Yes. Um, this seat and some clothes. Rice cereal and fruit."

"She eats real food?"

Honest confusion played across his face. "Yes. Formula and finger foods."

"Right." He stroked his beard. "Uh, you sleep okay?"

"No. Not really, to be honest. You?"

He shrugged, and she knew he hadn't. He'd been the type to be able to sleep through a brass band playing before Ronnie passed and then he'd turned into a complete insomniac, slugging caffeine to function. Long nights she'd lain awake, too, trying to figure out how to get him to express the darkness that had taken hold of him.

"Not drinking those energy drinks, though, right?" She cringed. What was she doing bringing back a topic they'd argued about when they were still engaged?

He frowned and his expression said it all. *You don't have the right to tell me what to do.* "Checked on Kip. He's uncomfortable, but okay."

"Good news." She blew out a breath. "Von, I'm sorry about what I said last night. I was out of line."

He looked away. "Me, too. Let's forget about it."

As if that was possible.

He fidgeted. "It'll be a busy day ahead. I'll cordon off the bridge access from this end. Archie's helping secure the other side. Then I'm going to try and get to town."

"To the police?"

"If I can. My buddy's a volunteer. He said he'll try to meet me there and take a report about this clown that's taking shots at you."

"I have to go, too, then."

"No."

"I need to tell them what happened, give an eyewitness account."

"I can relay the info."

"Von, I have to tell them what I saw. That man was gunned down right in front of me." She swallowed a lump.

"You've got a baby."

A baby…their baby. Exasperation and irritation tumbled through her, pumping her volume. "I'm aware, Von. And that's why I need this to be over quickly. As soon as the roads are clear I'm getting us both out of here and I'm not coming back so the cops need to know what happened."

"What if the trouble follows you? We don't even know how the shooter found you at Zoe's."

"I go to the cops again. I'll deal with it."

"It's too much."

She gripped the baby seat as if it was a gladiator's shield. "Who are you to tell me what I can and can't deal with?"

"I'm the guy you sent to the basement because you thought the garden hose was a snake."

"All grown up now," she snapped.

He folded his arms and leaned back. "Write out your statement. I'll deliver it."

Tate walked in with Opie. His jaw was shadowed with blond stubble and he looked cold. Stella carried the baby seat to the dining table to calm herself. "Hi, Tate."

"Morning. I would trade my molars for a cup of coffee."

"The coffee is ready. You can keep your molars," Stella said. They returned to the kitchen and poured themselves mugs while Bear and Opie waited patiently. Von filled bowls of kibble and water for both dogs.

"I heard you arguing as I came up the walk," Tate said, after a yawn.

Stella felt her face warm. She hoped none of the guests were up and about to hear their bickering.

"If I may offer a compromise, I'll go with you both to town. Help with the security watch on the road. Can't be much of a threat once we get there and it's critical I go."

Von drank coffee and watched Tate over the rim, waiting for an explanation.

Stella couldn't wait. "Why? Don't you need to stay with Paul?"

"He requires an IV to stay hydrated. I've set him up with one, but I need more supplies. This is only a stopgap until we get him to a hospital. They've got a clinic in Cloud Top and maybe if I present the case they can come up with a way to get him out. Or it might be possible to move him in the Bronco if the roads are clear after the initial slide area. I'm not going to risk it unless I can scope out road conditions in the ATV."

"Good reasons," Von said, in that way that might have been a dig at Stella. "But that leaves Camy alone."

"Fortunately," Camy said as she strolled in and headed for the coffeepot, "Camy can run this campground blindfolded." After two deep slugs of the bitter brew she fed Flash, who buried his face in his food bowl. "Archie's volunteered to manage horse care. He tends to sizable stables for the Driscolls from what I gather so he'll be in his element. Zoe and Kip are on KP duty, and I'm going to strong-arm Walker into keeping a fire going in the amphitheater and help me fiddle with the water heater."

"Think he's going to comply?" Tate said.

Camy rolled her mug between her palms. "I am persuasive."

"Understatement," Tate said.

"I'm supporting this wild field trip only because rescue resources are diverted elsewhere." She paused. "The damage is worse than we could have imagined. There's a full-on rescue going on to get to a group of hikers near Half Dome and…" She sighed. "Partial collapse at the Ahwahnee."

Stella gasped. The gorgeous historic hotel inside Yosemite National Park had been standing since 1927 and housed illustrious guests from Queen Elizabeth to Walt Disney during its decades. Picturing the regal stone walls crumbled and collapsed was too much. She didn't want to ask how many guests might have been injured or trapped. Every available National Park ranger and rescue group would be called up to aid hikers, visitors in the various Yosemite campgrounds and now the hotel guests.

Tate blew out a breath. "Catastrophic."

"Right, so go do your excursion." She flicked a glance at Opie. "He might be able to assist if no SAR people have reached Cloud Top."

"You sure, sis?"

Camy huffed. "Is that a serious question?"

"No. Merely being polite." Tate raised his mug at Von. "Okay, then. Three adults and two dogs crammed in an ATV for a rough ride. Sounds like a good time to me."

Von dumped out his coffee and rinsed the mug. "This is a bad idea." He strode to the dining area, snatched the baby seat and clomped to the door. "I'll bring this to your tent," he muttered.

"Thank you."

Tate grinned at Stella as the door banged shut. "Mr. Sunshine's at your service."

She smothered her smile, grabbed the bottle and clothing and followed Bear to catch up with Von. He was silent until they got to her tent where he held the door for them to enter first. On the step he suddenly stopped, shifting, tense.

As they passed, Hannah gurgled. Bear's ears swiveled and his tail ricocheted back and forth.

Von cleared his throat and looked at some vague spot over her shoulder. "What's her name?"

The question took her breath away for a moment. "Hannah Catherine," she managed.

He didn't reply. After a curt nod, he simply plowed inside, deposited the baby seat and immediately departed.

He was clearly unhappy with her for insisting on going to Cloud Top, but she knew it was the right thing to do. Hannah would be safe at camp, and the police could not possibly discount the seriousness of her situation if she was there to spell it out. The only thing she could do for Matt Smith was to tell the story of his death, word for word in a legal statement, and try to get some justice for him.

Bear lingered, sniffing.

Von knew their baby's name. Strange, and oddly sweet to think that Hannah now officially had two parents, dysfunctional as their relationship was. "We've got a long day ahead of us, Bear." She watched Von stalk to his tent without looking back.

Very long.

Chapter Eight

The whole matter was illogical. Stella should be staying with her baby. He mentally corrected. Their baby. Hannah Catherine.

The name chimed around in his head on permanent repeat. Hannah Catherine. Not simply any baby, but a named human who made gurgly noises and had his hair color. He tried to shake away the fog of exhaustion. Their. Baby. He was an actual *father*.

Father was a title he'd only considered sporadically over his lifetime. The new identity struck him with alternating waves of terror and awe. Awe? That surprised him. He'd never actually pictured himself as a father. Their conversations about having children felt more theoretical than concrete. His own dad did his best but it was clear that once their mother passed, he'd been in holding-it-together mode, scrambling from one day to the next until both boys were legal adults. Von and Ronnie's father viewed his job as mission management, a mission made harder by Ronnie's tumultuous experience with diabetes. Ronnie had been diagnosed at six, and their mother passed away five months later. It had been a constant struggle to keep Ronnie's disease in check and during his rebellious young adult years, Ronnie hadn't wanted anyone badgering him about his health, including Von and their dad.

Von figured he barely understood himself, so why would he want to attempt to navigate the parental waters?

But when Stella dropped it on him that they'd actually produced a *person*, that God had combined their DNA and made a human being…

Fear rose to the top now, ice on a frozen lake. Von hadn't even shown up for Ronnie and now here he was…a commissioned parent. And maybe she'd not seen fit to tell him because she knew he wasn't going to be any good at the dad thing. A sickening thought. He readied his backpack on the table in such a way that he couldn't help glimpsing Stella through the plastic-covered window of her tent. She sat in a hard-backed chair, rocking slowly as the baby squirmed in her lap. It looked uncomfortable, but she kept at it until Hannah stopped her fussing and latched on to the bottle. The puff of red hair, that carroty hue that he'd been teased about since he was walking age…

He traveled back in his memories to the day when he was a pimple-faced middle schooler, facing down his three tormentors. He'd had enough of their muttered asides, comments about his father being a "jarhead" marine, Von's beanpole stature, his ginger hair.

Von was ready for a fight, but the kids had brought reinforcements and quickly Von's lip was split and his eye almost puffed shut at their showdown in the field behind the school.

And then, bursting onto the scene, was his seven-year-old brother, fists flying, leaping into the fray to defend Von. Von was furious. Humiliated. Outraged at his brother, until one of the boys knocked Ronnie over. Inside, a switch flipped at that moment. Von's anger was swallowed up by a ferocious, primal need to defend Ronnie. He'd gone at the other kids with such vehemence that his attackers scattered and ran, leaving Von and Ronnie alone. Bloodied and bruised, he'd been ready to shout at Ronnie, berate him for what he'd done.

But Ronnie got to his feet and fired off a gap-toothed grin. "You were like a superhero, Von."

A superhero to his brother. Far from it.

He hoped Ronnie knew how much he'd meant, how much Von loved him. Why hadn't he come out and said it when he had the chance? Remorse was a wasted emotion, he thought bitterly. God didn't dole out second chances, at least not to him. His chest ached as he zipped his pack and exited the tent.

Through the window Stella smoothed Hannah's strawberry hair.

His gut tightened. No one was ever going to get away with teasing his kid.

His kid?

Stella cupped Hannah's cheek in her palm and kissed her forehead.

Bear poked him in the thigh. He'd been standing immobile as a stalled car, the snow falling around him and collecting on his collar. What was he doing there? He spun away, marched to the tool shed to collect the materials to secure the bridge. On the way he remembered Stella's comment, dripping with disdain.

When you feel up to it, I'll tell you the rest. What else could possibly be coming? Something more she should have told him months ago? He wasn't sure he wanted to know. With Bear in tow he hurried to the bridge.

The silvered wooden structure spanned a creek now glutted from recent rains. Snow collected on the beams, falling through the gap where a half dozen slats had broken off and now dangled. The entire contraption was no doubt compromised. It'd be expensive to fix and labor intensive. How would Camy and Tate manage when he returned to the military? They'd recruit someone else to take his place.

And how would Stella fare?

Just fine, he told himself. Like she'd been doing perfectly without him. He'd provide support, of course, take care of his responsibility, but it didn't appear she'd need more from him in the way of parenting.

That was a relief.

Stella arrived as he was nailing the last beam across the bridge entrance. She carried a roll of yellow caution tape.

"Camy said you'd need this."

"Thanks." He took it, her cold fingertips brushing his wrist. Didn't she have gloves? He'd ask Camy for a spare set. No good her getting frostbite. Without asking, she took an edge of the tape and held it to the wood where he stapled it in place. The unspooling allowed him space from her and he welcomed it. Stella confused him. She was the same Stella, spunky, warm, funny, but completely different, too, in her reserve, the stillness both inside and out and the undercurrent of fear. Where was the impish impulsivity? The constant laughter and joie de vivre? There was something quieter about her, deeper, that he could not fully define. Was it the *growing up* she'd referred to? Her insult pricked him.

He finished the job and they returned to her tent so she could check on Hannah once more before they left for town.

"It's wrong." The voice coming from inside Stella's tent stopped them. Zoe's. "It's a lie."

Stella shot Von a startled look.

"Not a lie, a promise," said a voice in reply. Was that Kip? Had to be.

"An old one. Things have changed," Zoe said.

"Not for me," Kip answered.

Von would have stayed quiet, eavesdropping as the conversation played out, but Stella was already stepping into the tent. He followed.

Zoe faced Kip and both jerked toward Stella and Von. Hannah lay on a blanket on the floor, holding on to one of her feet in an impossible display of flexibility. Bear sat at Von's side, watching her.

"What's a lie?" Stella said.

"Oh, hey, Stella." Kip's arm rested in a sling. "I came to check on you and the bambino."

Stella frowned. "What did you mean about promises and lies?"

"Ah, nothing. We were just shooting the breeze."

Stella eyed Zoe. "Aunt Zoe?"

Zoe grimaced, arms wrapped around herself. "I know that sounded strange, but it's nothing, like Kip said." She smiled. "Kip is going to help me with baby duty today. We're going to hang out in the dining hall first to find some breakfast. Easier for Pookie to eat at the table if I hold her in my lap, right? I figure some dog or other will clean up whatever she drops." She eyed Bear uneasily.

"And I volunteered to help," Kip said. "Even though I've only got one good wing."

Stella frowned until Zoe stroked her arm. "Really, honey. Everything is okay."

Von didn't buy it. He wondered if Stella did. His gaze crept to Hannah, who was working her legs as if she was prepping for the long jump. She had a toy in her hand, colorful plastic keys on a ring. He caught a tiny gleam of white in her gummy mouth. She really did have teeth, smooth edged like melon seeds.

"Are you sure Hannah is safe around the dog?" Zoe asked.

"Bear won't hurt her." As a matter of fact, he'd die protecting her if Von gave the word. Von watched as Bear sprawled on the floor a foot from the baby, tracking every tiny movement and sound, ears twitching. When Hannah let loose with a gurgle, Bear's tail swished in a happy arc. Hannah launched the baby keys into the air with a squeal.

"Catch," Von said.

Bear leaped up and snagged them midair. He laid the toy gently on Hannah's blanket and settled down to watch some more.

Von found himself smiling at the dog's enchantment. He'd never seen Bear play with a child before.

Not just any child, he reminded himself. *His* child.

That thought felt unnatural and strange. Proof that he wasn't cut out for the job. Any paternally minded man would have been overjoyed at the news, not experiencing sweaty palms and acid reflux.

Stella laughed. "Dog slobber aside, that is the sweetest playmate Hannah's had."

Zoe waited until Von called Bear before she snagged the toy. "I'll just give it a wash in the kitchen."

Stella gathered up the baby and bundled her in a blanket, sliding on a fuzzy hat and socks. She gave the diaper bag to Kip and turned to Von. For one terrifying moment Von thought she was going to hand him the baby. Instead, she passed Hannah to Zoe.

He hoped the terror hadn't shown on his face.

Before they left, Stella buzzed a soft raspberry onto Hannah's cheek that made her chortle.

It floored him, that teensy warbling laugh, the way she grabbed her mother's hair, the complete ease Stella displayed in the role of mom, a job she hadn't landed until a scant nine months before.

Nine months he'd been denied, he reminded himself, stoking his irritation to incinerate the strange confusion that had settled over him. Not to mention the whole pregnancy period. She'd kept the truth from him for a year and a half. No wonder the whole idea felt weird to him. It was like being dropped into a mission without a briefing. He stopped in his own tent to give himself some space, grabbing his pack, SAT phone and solar charger. His weapon had already been cleaned and reloaded.

He still knew it was the absolute wrong idea to take Stella

into town, but he had to admit that it would give the cops an eyewitness account if they had the time and staff to sit down with her.

Tate and Opie met them at the ATV. "We'll take the rear," Tate said, though Von would have preferred not to be sitting next to Stella. They wrestled their way into the back with Bear. Stella buckled up and sat, fingers roped together as they drove.

He cleared his throat. Might as well not bother with small talk. "Kip and Zoe are hiding something."

She jumped as if she'd gotten a shock.

"What are you talking about?" Tate said from the backseat.

Von relayed the conversation. "They said it was nothing." He glanced at Stella. "But you don't believe that, do you?"

Stella chewed her lower lip. "I'm not sure what it was all about, but I know neither one would ever hurt me."

"Lies hurt." He sounded petulant and he regretted the comment.

Her hazel eyes zeroed in on him. "Yes, they do, but I trust their motives."

"But..."

"Big picture. I know Kip and Zoe. You don't." She settled back into the seat, conversation over.

That pie-in-the-sky attitude had attracted him like a bear to a blackberry patch back when they'd been young and in love. Though now she was more world weary and harder somehow, she still believed in people more than she should.

He decided he'd be keeping a close eye on Kip and Zoe no matter what Stella said. It made him uncomfortable that those two were back in camp responsible for his baby.

His? Theirs? Why could he not seem to fix on the right label?

The southern exit from the camp was the most direct route to Cloud Top, but it was also a series of tight turns and rising and falling terrain. As expected, they soon encountered a stretch where the entire slope had collapsed onto the road, rendering it impassable.

"Now we find out how well this ATV can perform." Tate pointed out a horse trail that enabled them to skirt the obstruction, but it was so precarious Stella was clutching the door handle in a death grip. When he stopped to give them a breather, she asked for his phone to text her aunt.

"I forgot to tell her how small to cut up the peaches," she said, fingers flying.

That seemed like a ridiculous concern, but maybe the size of peaches was crucial data. The intensity with which she waited for the return text was astonishing until she read the reply and heaved out a big breath. "Hannah's fine. She's okay."

It sounded like she was trying to convince herself. And then she was back at it, firing off more instructions about rice cereal and formula. Was it that stressful to care for an infant? His mom had passed before he hit his teens but she'd seemed more resigned than fearful.

"Boys will be boys," was her motto and certainly his father wasn't concerned unless they came home after curfew. But what did he know about mysterious things like mothers and babies?

The first of a series of detours took them off the main road and back on it again in quick succession. Fortunately, the snow had not yet covered the granite boulders and the maze of pine and oak. With Tate and Stella warning him of obstacles from their vantage points, he avoided wrecking the axle or tires. After three hours of backtracking, segues and bone-jarring terrain, they reached the final span into town at eleven o'clock.

"Oh no." Stella's hand flew to her mouth.

The approach to the historic downtown left Von reeling, too. In his deployments he'd seen and prepped for every type of weather-related natural disaster, hurricanes, typhoons, blizzards, sandstorms and flash floods, but geological wreckage was a different beast altogether. He tried to force his senses to take it all in. The asphalt road was neatly split into two levels, one side of the fracture a foot and a half higher than the other. A compact car was tipped, front end down into the fissure, the sides crumpled. No victims inside.

Tate heaved out a breath as Von kept the speed to a crawl. On either side, chaos. At the corner, set apart from the other buildings, was a historic theater; the old windows on the second story were broken and the flat roof partially caved in. As they passed, another half dozen bricks cascaded from the upper floor and splashed into the river that backed the building.

"My mom told me about that place," Stella said sadly. "She acted in some of the plays there when she was in high school."

There was no way that building could be restored. It would have to be razed and rebuilt from the ground up.

Tate grabbed the front seat. "Hazard, at your ten."

"Got it." Von squeezed the ATV around a sinkhole the size of a bathtub only to find another five yards farther, filled with water that had not yet frozen. They weren't going to get emergency rigs in here without some repair work. He dared not increase his speed, in case there was concealed damage.

Finally, they got a glimpse of the main drag.

Tate sighed. "The place is a wreck."

The post office building had partially collapsed, sections of roof and walls tumbled in piles of white snow. Next to it was a gift shop, mostly intact except for the shattered windows. Beyond was the charred remains of a restaurant. Likely the gas or electrical lines had blown. Even with the windows up Bear and Opie's noses quivered with the acrid scent of smoke hovering in the air.

"Look." Stella pointed.

In the distance he spotted the massive water tank, suspended on steel-reinforced legs. It was crooked, tipped to one side like a hobbled spider, water spilling from a rupture in its metal body.

"Clinic's only a block from there." Tate's voice was grim.

Von knew where it was. He'd visited a doctor a few weeks back, trying to sniff out some help for his knee. Not wanting to dull his reflexes with pain meds, he'd stuck to aspirin. Cruising around the next corner revealed another set of ruined buildings. He maneuvered the ATV, skirting the rubble piled onto the sidewalks and lampposts bent like hangers.

Scattered in bunches were groups of citizens working together to haul broken beams, sweep up glass, and some handing out coffee and bottled water. Several small canopies had been erected to keep off the snow. A generator connected to a small heater provided warmth for the workers who gathered under the coffee tent.

A food truck was parked at the crooked curb. A man handed paper plates of steaming tacos and wads of napkins out the window to a guy in dirty jeans with a ripped back pocket. He pulled a hat from under his arm, jammed it on and trudged away to eat his meal.

Von rolled down the windows and called to the owner. "Is there a shelter set up?"

The man gave the ATV a serious once-over before he pointed a rubber-gloved finger. "One in the clinic parking lot for injuries and overnight accommodations at the middle school. You hurt?"

"No."

"Hungry? We're dishing up free food for everyone until our propane runs out."

Von declined after checking with Stella and Tate, who shook their heads. "Police?"

"One only, and he's working the apartment building collapse on Fourth. More on the way, we're told, but it's hard to get here. We got it handled." The man's gaze darkened. "Any looters decide to take advantage, we'll take care of it."

Von nodded, noting the military baseball cap. His gut relaxed a notch. Good people taking care of their own. That was better than any police presence. He resisted the urge to glance at the leaning water tower. "Thanks."

The clinic parking lot housed two large tents where several people were gathered. He noted one doctor and two nurses in protective gear, triaging the wounded. They, too, had portable generators powering heaters, he was pleased to note. There was some activity from inside; the *whop* of hammers on nails echoed as the broken windows were covered over with plywood. Hopefully, they'd be able to treat patients inside soon, but they were woefully understaffed.

Tate gestured at a completely collapsed feed-and-grain building across the street where a cluster of people in safety vests and hardhats stood together, pointing and talking. The volunteer Cloud Top Fire Department truck was there also.

"I see a YOSAR guy, but no dog," Tate said. "Looks like he's the only one. They'll need me and Opie to zero in on any survivors. Let me out. Meet you at the clinic later."

Stella got out and Tate crawled from the backseat with Opie.

Stella squeezed him in a hug. "Be careful, Tate."

"Ditto." Tate jogged away, Opie at his side.

Von felt an irrational flame of jealousy, which he promptly batted down. Stella and Tate weren't an item any more than he and Stella were. But they could be someday, couldn't they? No, they couldn't, he told himself severely. That'd just be… weird. And besides, anyone who partnered with Stella would be a father figure to Hannah. His stomach bunched into a fist.

Another group was assembled at the water tower. Stella eyed the extended ladder on the utility truck and the people working to reinforce the bent support leg with scrap steel. On the ground, a team of no fewer than fifty men and women filled sandbags to channel the spilling water away from crossing the road where it would otherwise inundate the clinic. Von itched to help shovel sand but he dared not leave Stella alone in this wrecked town. She'd grown paler and quieter the farther they'd driven, the more devastation they'd witnessed.

"You okay?"

She looked small in the seat next to him, startled that he'd asked.

Chin tipped up, she answered. "No choice not to be."

He understood. She had to be okay to take care of Hannah. *And I'll take care of you both.*

He gripped the wheel. Take care of this baby he'd known for one day and the woman who'd lied and broken his heart? That was a hard yes from his heart, though his brain offered a second opinion.

Totally normal response. He'd extend help to any woman and child.

Had nothing to do with the fact that she was the only woman he'd ever wanted. But that was the past. She wasn't even the same Stella. The problem was he was exactly the same Von.

He would do his duty. That was all he was comfortable with.

That was all he needed to remember.

When Stella thought she couldn't stand the sight of one more crumbled building or broken window, they finally reached the police station, a squat, brick-fronted building. Though it did not seem damaged, it looked ominously empty and quiet in the falling snow. Only one car occupied the parking lot, a brown sedan with no official markings. What if no one could take her statement? Von sent a quick text and received a reply.

"My buddy's inside waiting for us."

Relieved, she followed Von as he pushed the door open with Bear accompanying them. They found their way inside the darkened office that smelled of stale coffee. The interior was a wash of dirty beige carpets and cracked vinyl chairs that formed a waiting area.

A short man with a lush mustache greeted them. His eyes

were shadowed with fatigue, and lines bracketed his mouth. He wore a navy jacket with "volunteer police department" emblazoned on the front. He offered a tight smile, displaying a chipped front tooth. "Sight for sore eyes, Sharpe."

Von clasped him in a tight hug. "Legs, I'm glad to see you, man."

The volunteer whacked him on the back and turned to Stella. "Name's Roger. Legs is my nickname, and trust me you don't want to know why. Conference room is being used to store relief supplies at the moment, so we'll park ourselves here." He gestured them to a card table, which had been set up in the lobby. It was neatly piled with papers. A bulletin board on the wall was covered by a map of Cloud Top, stuck all over with pins and labels penciled on sticky notes.

"How we doing?" Von said, taking in the map.

His expression dimmed. "With two volunteer cops including myself, it's a stretch, but the town's rallying and the fire department's been stellar. All their volunteers and full-timers are working around the clock." He grimaced. "Current totals are fifty injured, eight deceased that we know of, which could have been way worse considering, but it's hard to take in a small town like this. Fortunately, the quake didn't hit on a weekend when we'd have a bunch of tourists around. We have a few residents still unaccounted for and you probably saw the water tower situation. There's a shelter set up at the middle school and it's going as smoothly as possible. No outside help yet since weather is locking down flights and our road in is treacherous. How'd you get here, by the way?"

"ATV but it was rough in stretches."

"Don't doubt it." He sank into a folding chair and gestured Stella to sit, too. Von stood with Bear.

Legs quirked a look at the dog. "Still got that fleabag?"

"Yes, sir. You're fortunate he doesn't understand your juvenile attempt at humor."

"Probably a better soldier than you ever were."

"Yes, sir," Von repeated with a laugh. He cleared his throat. "Sorry to pile on, but we have a situation, Legs. Stella needs to give you a sit rep."

Legs nodded and held up his phone. "Okay to record? I'm a little over-circuited. I've lost track of my coffee mug twice this morning. Found it in the custodial closet that last time. I won't interrupt until you're done. Full disclosure, I don't know how much we can help right now, but at least it will be officially documented."

Stella pulled in a breath, then stopped. Thinking about reliving it all tightened her chest. She'd been so anxious to report what she'd experienced but now she felt nothing but dread. "I… I'm not sure where to start."

Von rested a hand gently on her back, surprising and encouraging. "The phone call from Kip telling you about the job. How about you start there? Legs can chime in when he needs clarification."

It was comforting, his touch. She had to resist the urge to reach up and clasp his fingers. She heaved in a deep breath and then related the story. While the details unfolded, icicles formed in her gut. As if he could sense her emotion, Von tightened his grip on her shoulder. How close she'd come to being murdered alongside Matt Smith. One more second, one inch closer, and Hannah would have lost her mother. Nausea gripped her. Bear came nearer, sitting close enough that she could rest her hand on his warm fur. Legs offered her a tissue. She hadn't realized the tears had started to fall.

"Thank you," she mumbled, wiping her face.

Legs frowned at her. "So this Matt Smith had an old photo of you?"

"Yes. The letter's indecipherable, but the photo's all right. He said he really needed to talk to me." She slid over the mangled photo and the ruined letter. Legs photographed both with his cell phone before he stuck his nose close to the picture and peered at it.

"A school photo, you think?"

She nodded. "First grade, maybe kindergarten."

"Did you attend here in Cloud Top?"

"No. I was born in Fresno, and I went to school there."

He leaned close, tilting the photo to catch the light. "Hmmm." His phone pinged with a text. He straightened and quickly tapped a reply. "Sorry. Can you give me a description of the shooter?"

"I only saw a glimpse. Male, young, maybe early- to mid-twenties. He had long hair, unnaturally blond, like it was dyed."

"Could it have been a wig?"

"I suppose."

"Facial hair?"

"Maybe. I'm not sure. I was scared. All I could think of was getting to my baby at my aunt's house." Her voice cracked.

Legs's eyes widened. She saw him flick a look to Von.

"Her...my...our daughter," Von finally managed. He'd cycled through and landed on *our*. Gut reaction probably, but the word made her feel like crying harder. A baby should be *ours*, she thought. But Hannah was his and hers, but not exactly theirs. How had it all gone so terribly awry?

Legs was beaming at Stella. "Congratulations on the baby." He turned to Von. "And you finally graduated to a two-legged child."

Von cleared his throat. "Thanks. Anyway, what can you do to help her?"

Legs was about to answer when his radio crackled. A high-pitched voice filled the room.

"Legs, we've got a downed utility pole on Second and Main. Need assistance securing the area."

"Ten-four. Rolling now." Legs picked up his phone. "I'll

share this with the sheriff's office and the local officer in Cloud Top. I wish I could tell you they'll investigate soon, but…"

Stella held up a hand. "I understand. I'm relieved it's officially reported."

"I'll try to get someone to head to the mile marker and see if there's anything to be done for Matt Smith, or evidence to be collected, or I'll go myself if I can. My advice in the meantime would be to stay close to this guy." Legs hooked a thumb at Von. "He and Bear are your best security until we get the earthquake damage squared away."

Von. Why did her life always circle back to him?

Because you share a child, you ninny. Didn't you realize that would change things?

Legs said goodbye and led them back out to the ATV before he took off.

On their drive out of the parking lot, she noticed water sheeting down the street. Her breath caught. "The water tower?"

"They're diverting the flow away from the clinic, but they can't contain it all."

The water burbled away from the main drag. She followed its progress down the block where it flowed in front of a grocery store into an ever-widening pool. An older man stood outside watching the progress of the water, a burlap bag clutched in his fist.

Her eyes widened. "Wait. I know him."

"Stella…"

But she was out of the car, hopping over the water, rushing toward the man who held a piece of her heart.

Chapter Nine

"Mr. Swenson," Stella cried.

He blinked and squinted. "Stella? Stella Rivers?"

She hugged him and introduced Von. "Mr. Swenson's known me since I was little. He knew my mother well."

He nodded. "Frannie worked for me for years, until she was eighteen. When she left town it broke my heart. So sorry to hear she passed. I sure used to twist her arm to get her to come up and stay with us here in Cloud Top, but she would only ever pop in for a quick visit. Always in such a hurry to leave." He sighed. "Better than nothing."

"Much better. I adored visiting you."

"You always had the toy shelves organized tip-top."

"And you always let me pick out whatever toy I wanted."

He laughed. "True enough." His mournful gaze went to the pooling water. "Now look at it. My shop's about to be swamped."

"Here." Von took the sack from his hand. "We can mitigate."

"Oh, I couldn't ask you to…"

Von ignored Mr. Swenson's comment, seized the shovel and began filling the bags. Stella hurried to hold them open for him. Bear kept an eye on the swirling water from the cement step.

They fell into a comforting rhythm, shovel, stack, shovel, stack. The effort seemed easy and maybe even pleasurable for Von. He'd always loved projects that made him break a sweat. She remembered the garden bed he'd built and filled using a fussily precise ratio of logs to compost to soil. *Gonna be a bumper crop, Ella. Wait until the heirloom seeds get moving. Tomatoes the size of your head, baby,* he'd said as he'd hugged her close. She'd never known anyone who loved seeds more than Von Sharpe.

Von heaved a shovelful of sand. "What are you smiling at?"

"Nothing." She blushed, and she realized it had been a long time since she'd recalled a joyful moment from their past. Her brain must be completely scrambled to dredge up silly memories in the face of such devastation. She snatched up another bag and unfurled it.

Soon, they had twenty sacks full and piled into place, forming a sandbag wall that defied the incoming flow. She watched in satisfaction as the water bubbled away from their makeshift dam and the store's front entrance.

"You saved me." Mr. Swenson clasped his palms over his head in a victory prayer. "I never could have done that by myself."

Von leaned the shovel against a wood bench and wiped his brow. "How much damage inside your shop?"

"Aside from tumbled merchandise and a broken back window, not too much. No power, of course. I've been making care packages for the locals. Say, do you need anything?"

Von didn't get out the "no" before Stella answered.

"Diapers."

"My…" She ducked her chin without looking at Von. "Our daughter Hannah is going to run out of diapers soon."

Our daughter. Maybe if she said it enough, it would feel normal. Strange to think they could share a daughter but not a marriage. There were so many permutations that would have to be squared away in her mind and heart now that Von finally knew the truth. It wasn't going to be clean and easy, not by a long shot.

Mr. Swenson was grinning with delight. "A daughter. Your mother must have been over the moon. Did she…meet her before she passed?"

A pang rippled Stella's heart. "No, but she was excited to find out I was having…a girl." She'd almost said twins. It hurt to remember that Stella's mother had been in pain, tired, worn out from the fight, but hearing about her twin pregnancy had brought tears of joy. It was a blessing, in a way, that her mom had been spared the pain of the lost child. And Stella hadn't been forced to explain what had happened. That would have ripped apart the fragile thread holding her mind and heart together.

You've got to protect your babies, her mom had whispered. *No matter what it costs you.* The odd remark now brought double the pain. How could she protect her little girl when her other child had never even opened his eyes?

Tears threatened as Mr. Swenson clutched her hand. "I'd do anything for Frannie's daughter and granddaughter. But what else do you need? Food? Clothing?"

"Just the diapers and maybe a can of formula if you have one."

He beamed. "Absolutely. This sure is a bright spot in my day, seeing you." He led them into the shop. The aisles had been somewhat tidied, but Von and Stella set about restoring boxes of cereal and canned goods to the shelves while Mr. Swenson fetched the diapers and formula. He returned with the items, along with extra baby things he'd collected, but he'd lost his smile.

"What's wrong?" Stella said.

"Nothing, probably. The earthquake has jumbled up my brain. I just remembered there was a man here asking about your family. Said he was a friend of Frannie's from way back when she used to live in Cloud Top."

Stella's fingernails bit into her palms. "A man? Asking about us? When?"

"A week ago, Wednesday."

Von's mouth was a hard line. "What exactly did he want to know?"

Mr. Swenson's eyes wandered over the shelves as he considered. "He said he'd heard Frannie had passed away, but he didn't get the message until after the funeral. He wanted to find you, Stella, to express his condolences."

"Can you describe him?" Von asked. "Was he young?"

"Not really. Fifties maybe. Short, chubby."

Stella and Von exchanged glances. Not the shooter. Mr. Swenson was describing Matt Smith, the dead man. Her body felt numb with shock. "What did you tell him, Mr. Swenson?"

"Not much. He was jovial and all, and it sounded plausible, but somehow it didn't feel right. He asked if I had your address but I said no. I didn't know where you lived anyway, so it wasn't a lie. I hope I didn't cause any trouble for you."

"No." Stella clasped his hands. "You've been nothing but helpful. My mom would be so happy that we chatted."

He sighed and handed her the bundle. "There are some jars of baby food and a bib in there, too. Soon as you need more, you know where to find me."

Von reached into his pocket. "What do we owe you?"

Von was paying? She felt flustered, confused, to have him stepping in.

"Nothing. I'm giving away supplies to whoever needs them."

"No, sir. That's not right."

Mr. Swenson thrust out his chin. "Yes, it is. I'm an old man. There's not much I can do to help right now, but I've got supplies and it's not right to profit when the town's been knocked to its knees. You're not going to tell me otherwise."

After a moment Von stowed his wallet and offered Mr. Swenson a handshake. "Thank you, sir."

"My pleasure." Stella thanked and hugged him one more time before they returned to the ATV.

Von's phone buzzed and he read a text from Tate. "He's finishing up. We'll go get him in a few minutes. Are you...hungry or anything?"

She laughed. "You know, I think Mr. Swenson tucked some candy bars and water bottles in this pack. He always made sure I had some sweets even though Mom would tell him no."

She lifted out the diapers to move them aside. There was a picture of two babies on the front, with wide smiles and dimpled arms, one wearing pink and the other in blue. Like a massive quake, the grief shook through her in an unexpected wave. The ferocious pain made her gasp.

Von immediately grabbed her wrist. Bear tensed and shoved his muzzle over the passenger seat.

"What? What's wrong?"

At first, she could not force an answer through the wall of despair.

"Ella, take it slow and easy. All you have to do right now is breathe in and out."

She tried. Each breath was arduous, her body fighting against her. "There's something I didn't tell you. It...hurts to talk about."

He considered, his pressure steady and warm on her wrist. "Is it important for me to know now?"

The question surprised her. She expected more of an indignant demand that she come clean. Was it? Important? For him to be privy to an extremely private grief? But it was his flesh and blood, too, his loss, although he did not know it yet. She gulped. "Von, there were two." The truth ripped its way up her throat, carving jagged wounds into her mouth as they exited.

He stared, uncomprehending. "I don't understand. Two what?"

Tears pooled as she clutched the diaper package decorated with two healthy babies. She could not see, but she felt his hand travel from her wrist to gently prize her fingers from the packet and into his. "You mean two babies?" he said softly.

She nodded, unable to do anything more but clutch at him and try and keep her lungs working.

The silence ticked between them as he waited for her to continue. His breathing was slow and easy and they sat almost like a normal couple, except nothing was normal, not one single thing, the wrecked earth around them and the ruined past behind. She wished she could stop time, preserve that moment, the second before he understood the grief that awaited him.

A terrifying thought cut through. Maybe he wouldn't grieve. Maybe it would be to him as if the child had never existed. Or he'd agree with the well-meaning hospital volunteer who'd told her, "At least you have one healthy baby." As if the birth of one child could cancel out the death of another. *Please, Von. Don't say that. Please.* She wouldn't be able to endure it, not from him. But he was still quiet, waiting. Her palms went ice-cold.

"Hannah had a twin, a brother." She shivered. "He died at birth from an undetected umbilical cord defect. We—the doctors and I—had no idea there was a problem. He lived less than an hour. He looked so perfect."

Von tugged her hand and pressed it to his face. "Oh, Stella."

"I'm sorry. I did everything to keep them healthy. I took my prenatal vitamins and drank lots of water and tried to get eight hours of sleep."

He gripped her fingers so tight it hurt. "Stop."

"I read all the books and I always wore my seat belt. Every time. I went to every appointment like they told me and ate healthy foods, no lunch meat or bleu cheese." She was babbling, the stream of syllables bearing all her anxiety and guilt. "But he…" Her throat closed, breathing ratcheting up faster and faster.

"Honey…"

"I had two of everything picked out, outfits, blankets, car seats. Zoe and Kip, we all thought I'd come home with two babies but instead I took home my daughter, our daughter, but I lost our son. Everyone…" She gulped in great mouthfuls of air. "People would congratulate me on my perfect baby, but no one, not even the nurses or doctors, could tell me how to celebrate and grieve at the same time. I didn't know how to do it. I still don't, Von." She ducked her chin, unable to stop the storm of sobs that exploded from the abyss that she fought every day to keep sealed.

Von let go of her hand.

She sobbed harder.

He unbuckled his belt and got out. His departure tore right through her. He blamed her, like she'd blamed herself for a while. Why did it hurt so excruciatingly from a man she knew didn't love her anymore? Von wasn't there at the birth because she'd shut him out and now he was doing the same. Her throat swelled and her legs trembled. Bear shoved his cold nose against her cheek. She hardly felt it through her choking cries.

Von appeared at the passenger door, yanking it open, unbuckling her seat belt and pulling her out. He wrapped her in a fierce embrace, rocking her back and forth, his chin resting on the top of her head.

She clung to him, unable to do anything else.

"Stella." His voice was ragged and broken, choked with tears. "I'm sorry. I'm sorry. I should have been there." She pressed her cheek to his wide chest, feeling the gentle thud of his heart in her ear. "What you've been through…"

Her anguish streamed out and mingled with his, cold flakes falling around them. Somehow, the grief they processed together felt different than what she'd endured alone. Kip told her God meant for grief to be shared, but she couldn't until that moment because she was sure speaking the pain aloud would rip her apart forever.

He held her, supported her, wiped her face with his sleeve and squeezed her close again. When she could not cry any-more, he led her to a sidewalk bench where they sat, her body tucked into the shelter of his.

He cleared his throat. "How did you manage? I mean, how did you care for Hannah while you were grieving like that?" His voice was hoarse with emotion.

"I had help. Kip insisted I go to therapy. I didn't want to, but he drove me himself and watched Hannah for hours while I had my appointments. He didn't know anything about ba-bies, but he read all these books about how to do it. Zoe came up when she could, too."

His eyebrows crimped, but he did not stop her.

"I... I've had trouble with panic, intrusive thoughts, para-lyzing fear, which led to some compulsive behaviors, but the doctor helped, and Kip stayed up nights so I could sleep. He sings her hymns for hours on end."

"Hymns?"

"I think losing the baby kind of changed him, too."

"Are you still seeing the doctor? A therapist?"

"Yes. It's going to be a long journey. It's only been nine months of treatment so far but I'm able to function most of the time, care for Hannah and myself. Support us both."

He shook his head. "I'm going to be helping you now." He looked away. "Money won't be so hard. She'll have what she needs. And you, too."

All the money in the world isn't going to fix what's broken. What did they need? Hannah needed a father, one that was involved in her life, unlike the one Stella knew only through old letters. But Von wasn't offering that, and she didn't blame him. He hadn't even known he was a father until the day before. And now he was a grieving one.

She fished a tissue out of her pocket and wiped her eyes.

The snow had stopped temporarily but it was dark, though it was only afternoon.

Von was silent. She wondered what he was thinking.

She used to ask, but he'd shrug and tell her his mind was blissfully blank. She could not remember a moment when hers wasn't filled with worry, wonderings, wishes. Von would share when he was ready. Oh, how she wished she'd learned that lesson years before. The quiet was broken only by the clang of the workers shoring up the water tank.

"What was his name?" he whispered so suddenly she jumped.

After a swallow, she looked at him directly. "Daniel."

Von stiffened, pulling away to look at her. "Daniel? Ronnie's middle name?"

She nodded. "It felt right. I know how much you loved Ronnie and he never got the chance to live out his life. I thought it would honor his memory." She felt her throat close up again. "I never imagined that our son would be gone so soon. He didn't get to live out his life, either."

Von gasped, stood abruptly and walked away a few steps, staring at the ruins of the town. The tableau was striking; Von broad shouldered, strong, filled with life, backed by a blighted landscape. He'd always defied the world around him, refusing to accept the one thing he could not change, his brother's death. How was he feeling now?

As she watched, the unthinkable happened. Von, the man who never admitted defeat, walled up his emotions as if they were shameful and dishonorable, dissolved. Tears streaked his face, leaking onto his beard, and he bent from the waist. His sobs were wrenched from his body, raw, agonizing.

Bear leaped out the open car door and raced to Von, circling around him in agitation, pawing his leg.

She shot to her feet, unsure. So many times during their engagement she'd tried to offer comfort, connection, and been rejected. She'd responded by acting out in ways she wasn't proud of, the distance between them becoming fathoms they couldn't cross.

In all that time, she'd never seen him cry. He would not welcome anyone being privy to his pain, yet she could not stop herself. Three hesitant steps and she was next to him. She glanced at Bear. Would the dog interpret her as a threat to his distraught handler? Bear was not active duty anymore, but he wasn't exactly a pet, either.

She stared at Bear and reached toward Von with one hand. Bear made no move other than a flick of one ear, so she touched Von tentatively on the shoulder. The violence of his emotion charged his muscles. He did not flinch from her. She was not certain he even felt her fingers on his arm. Bear eased back a step as if to say, "Fix him."

"Von." Slowly, she turned him and he allowed it, head dropping to her shoulder as she clutched him close. His sobs mingled with the scuttle of snowflakes driven across the broken ground. She gathered his big body to hers, absorbing the pain as best she could.

Von could not remember crying since he was an awkward twelve-year-old when his mother passed. Even at Ronnie's funeral he'd felt empty as a dry husk, eyes burning with tears that he wouldn't allow to fall. But with Stella's arms around him, he could not push the twin images of his son and his brother from his soul. She was the only person in the world who'd seen him in such dissolution.

She's the one you were supposed to share your life with. The one who had your children. If he'd been honest with her when Ronnie died, maybe things would have worked out differently. Maybe she wouldn't have gone through unimaginable horror alone. Maybe, maybe, maybe.

One thing was certain; this wasn't the way things were supposed to be. The worst kind of agony shuddered through him in seismic waves as she clung to him. How long it was before he gathered himself, he wasn't sure. When he finally wrangled control and stepped from her embrace, Bear stayed close, nosing the damp spot on his arm where his tears had collected. He forced his lungs into a steady rhythm by sheer will. Mortification didn't cover it.

Tate walked up with Opie. His hair was disheveled; dust coated his jacket. Opie's tongue ribboned from his mouth. Tate offered a smile, but Von knew he'd noticed both their tear-stained faces. Tate didn't miss much. Never had.

Von cleared his throat and sent the nonverbal message. *Not talking about it.* "How'd it go?"

Tate wiped a hand over his filthy brow. "Opie located a survivor. They got her out and she's at the clinic. Looks good for her." The way Tate's mouth tightened, Von realized they'd probably also found a victim or several that hadn't been as fortunate.

Von fished a water bottle from his backpack for Tate. He drank half and poured the remainder into a bowl for Opie, who slopped it up.

"You need to stay in Cloud Top?" Von said.

"No. Another YOSAR guy hiked in with his dog, second to follow. He said they're working on getting a medevac helicopter. Their priority will be Cloud Top, obviously, but Paul's on the list to evacuate when they can, along with the casualties from the Ahwahnee and Camp Curry. I need to get back to him before the snow piles up." He held up a bag. "I got additional IV supplies so we'll be okay for a while."

Stella stood hugging herself against the cold. Von forced himself to make eye contact as if he hadn't just bawled on her shoulder. Emotions still rumbled through him. Grief, most of all; disbelief of what she'd endured. Anger that he'd never even laid eyes on his son. But he'd not reached out to Stella, either, not shown one iota of interest since he'd been back, though he'd wondered about her on the daily.

Something happened deep inside his chest and circulated through his bloodstream when he allowed himself to consider what he shared with the woman standing there in the falling snow. It was so confusing he determined to keep his attention elsewhere. "You...okay to head back?"

"Yes." She was probably more eager than both of them to return. He'd realized on their drive that it was torturous for her to be away from Hannah. Now he understood more clearly her intensity.

It was past time to leave Cloud Top. He'd need all his driving prowess to get them back to camp before the snowstorm hit and they lost the daylight. The return trip would take at least three hours if conditions hadn't worsened. Loaded up again, they set off.

Before they'd gone five minutes Stella immediately texted Zoe.

"Baby's okay?" he asked.

Stella hesitated for a moment and then blinked. "I've got to get used to sharing information, I guess. Yes, she's napping after a good bottle feeding and some diced peaches."

Napping. He pictured her curled up in those footed pajamas he'd glimpsed with pink bunnies on them and the matching knit cap. Adorable. Or did he just think that because it was his child? How did parents discern the truth about their progeny?

They approached the ruined theater and the sinkholes. He couldn't help his thoughts drifting as he edged past them.

Hannah had a twin, a brother.

He'd come to Cloud Top thinking he was the father of one child and now he was leaving knowing he'd had two...a son who'd been taken from him. Anger licked his gut but not for Stella.

They say God's a good guy. What a joke. Ronnie died, like

his namesake. What kind of justice was that? Especially for an innocent baby who hadn't even had a chance to taste life. He snuck a glance at Stella. And why wasn't she enraged? Maybe over the past nine months her anger had morphed into strength she used to corral her rage. No wonder she seemed so much more mature than he remembered. The horror she'd endured had stripped away some of her youth and she was the wiser for it. It was as if she'd gone to battle while he'd stayed tucked in a barrack somewhere. The new Stella attracted him more than the one he'd known. Attraction?

Knock it off, Von.

He shoved down the anger and the confusion. The shadow of the demolished theater crept over the car. The roar of the swollen river behind the derelict structure covered the rumble of the engine. A glint from above caught his attention. Tate's, too.

"Shooter on the roof," Tate shouted.

He had only a moment to swerve the vehicle off the road and behind a tree, as a spray of bullets found them.

Chapter Ten

The bullets ripped into the rear bumper before he drove behind a fortress of sturdy oaks. Bear barked, unscathed. Nerves screaming, he reached for Stella, who was crumpled on her seat. Was she hit? His heart stopped until she peered at him, breathing hard. Relief left him shaky. "Tate?" he said.

"Uninjured. Opie, too," Tate reported.

The trees would provide cover. No way for the shooter to kill Stella unless he came down from his perch.

Von wasn't going to allow him that opportunity. Shooter's dumb choice to isolate on a rooftop was going to be his downfall. "Move out, Bear." He shoved the door open, yanked his gun from his pack.

Tate was out, too, crouched low.

"Stay with her," Von said. "You armed?"

"Bear spray."

Von rolled his eyes. "That'll help against a rifle."

"I'm a camp doctor now. I don't travel armed. We'll stay low. He can't hit us through the trees. Watch your back."

"That's Bear's job."

He thought he heard Stella say something but nothing penetrated over the roar in his ears. He and Bear ran toward the theater. In the scant two minutes since the shooting, he'd scoped out his plan of attack. They headed to the side of the building, opposite the corner where the enemy was holed up. The fire escape he'd noted on their way into town, courtesy of the training burned into his every cell, would be his entrance ticket. Now he just had to hope the aged and quake-damaged ladder wasn't going to pull away from the building under his weight.

He knelt and tapped his shoulder. Bear hurtled aboard, curling around his neck. The added seventy pounds twinged his knee as he climbed. The shooter might be waiting for them at the top so he kept his gun close, stopping twice to listen. Cement crunched and groaned as he ascended, and he prayed the rushing water would swallow the noise.

Six steps up, a rung gave way under his boot, and he barely kept his hold. Bear adjusted with Von's swaying, coiling tighter around his neck until he regained his balance. Rusted metal bit into his palms as he clambered up as stealthily as he could. Before the last rung he stopped. One quick look over the top. The glimpse revealed that the roof was strewn with rubble. On the far end was the rectangular box of an old air-conditioning unit. That was where the shooter was hiding.

He signaled Bear, the silent gesture that meant "here we go" to his canine partner.

In one motion, he heaved himself up over the last rung and onto the roof. As soon as his boots hit the surface, Bear leaped free and glued himself to Von's side. They sped to the nearest pile, crouching behind the busted concrete pieces.

Another burst of gunfire drilled his eardrums. Rifle guy was shooting again at the ATV in the woods.

Buckle up. Von and Bear waited for a pause in the shooting and then ran to the next place of cover, a bigger heap of tumbled bricks closer to their target. Bear shoved him in the arm. He looked right, discovering a hole broken through the roof into which he would have tumbled if not for Bear's warning.

Good dog. None better.

He was close enough to hear the shooter's movements now as he edged to his right to try for a better vantage point through the trees, his shoes scuffling on rubble. Good moment for a diversion.

Von scooped up a handful of debris and gave Bear the signal to crawl in the opposite direction on his command. He counted down with his fingers. The dog was wired and battle ready. At the "one" Von launched the handful of rocks in a lazy, looping arc that pattered down near the air-conditioning box.

He was on his feet, weapon ready, running away from the falling rocks with Bear at his side. As he'd hoped, the shooter's attention was in the other direction as they surged around the air-conditioner and closed in for the capture. The ruse had worked completely. Their quarry was a young guy, thin, silver rings on each of the fingers of his right hand, flannel shirt and jeans with a ripped back pocket. His hair was unevenly cut, as if he'd taken scissors to it, the color of straw.

Von had him cold. "Drop it."

He stiffened, yanking a look over his shoulder. "I said drop it," Von roared as he sighted down his weapon.

The shooter raised his hands but didn't relinquish the rifle.

"You're gonna put that weapon down. That's your only choice here."

Bear quivered with adrenaline.

Von looked closer at the ripped pocket. It was the same guy he'd seen eating at the taco truck, keeping tabs on them, planning out his ambush. *You're rusty, Von. Should have sensed something was off about him.* Still, the rifle remained in the shooter's grip. He needed more persuasion.

"Talk," Von said to Bear.

Bear let loose with the savage spate of barking he'd been suppressing. The shooter jumped, dropped the rifle and spun around, palms raised.

Pale skin, dark eyes, a smirk spreading over his mouth. His back pressed the half wall behind him. Von hoped it would hold.

"Guess you need your dog to do your dirty work." The man's voice was high-pitched and reedy.

Von quieted Bear and thrust out his chin. "Guess you got yourself a new jacket after Bear got a piece of it."

The guy didn't answer.

"Name?"

No answer.

Von allowed Bear to move forward a step and he did the same. "I asked for your name."

The smirk widened. "Abraham Lincoln."

Von forced down his anger at this wiseacre who cracked jokes as if he hadn't almost killed Stella. Twice. "All right, Abe. Why are you trying to shoot Stella Rivers?"

His blond brows arced in the picture of innocence. "Who?"

Von exhaled. "I got no time for games. If you don't want to talk to me and Bear, we're going to tie you up and carry you down the fire escape ladder, trying real hard not to drop you, and take you back to Cloud Top. Not many cops around, but they've got a holding cell. They'll get to you eventually. Should be fun, right? Two days, three, maybe four, tops. Don't worry, though. We'll stay there and make sure you're fed and Bear will be the most attentive buddy you've ever known. What do you think, Abe? Sound good?"

The man suddenly leaped up on the wall. Bear barked like a wild thing.

"Stand down," Von shouted. "The wall's compromised. It's not gonna hold." All he got was that stinking smile.

He could order Bear to grab the guy, but if he fell, he'd take

Bear down with him. Two-story fall right into the liquid deep freeze.

The man fired off a sardonic salute.

"Stop." Von surged forward. His quarry leaped away from the building and plunged out of sight.

Stella screamed as the body plummeted from the rooftop into the river. From far away she heard Bear's staccato barking. Blind panic hurtled her from the car past Tate. He reached out for her but she didn't slow. Her blood rampaged through her veins, propelling her as she ran toward the riverbank.

Von. He'd fallen. If she could get there in time, she could snatch him before he was sucked away. Her feet slipped and slid, grinding the snow into muddy slicks that spoiled her traction. The bank was piled high with branches broken loose in the quake.

If she could extend one out to him, she could tow him to shore.

She strained to pick him out in the roiling water. He was an excellent swimmer, but if he'd been shot, hit his head... A branch snagged her pant leg and she bent to haul it free. It was about six feet long, not enough. She'd have to get closer. As she staggered through the heaps, she tried desperately to spot him.

There? No, only a dark boulder.

How many minutes had passed? Three? More? Her heart thundered. "Von," she screamed, her plea swallowed by the noise.

The crown of a head broke the water and then disappeared. An arm next almost at the opposite bank. She had to get closer before he was too far out of reach. She snagged her foot on a rock and tumbled toward the water.

Tate caught up and grabbed her sleeve, yanking her back.

"I have to help him, Tate."

He was pulling at her, preventing her from grabbing the stick.

She turned to try and free herself and saw Von and Bear hurrying up. For an instant she was frozen in shock. Then she dove into Von's arms and fisted her hands in his jacket. Sobs racked her body.

He held her, letting go only for a moment to stow his gun. "It's okay, Ella."

She couldn't make herself let go. "I thought... I saw..."

He shushed her. "Guy jumped in before I could grab him." She couldn't absorb the information. It was all she could do to breathe and force her tide of fear back into its well-worn channel. With her head pressed to his chest, she could delay the inevitable embarrassment. Von was safe but there was no covering up her reaction. She'd thought it was he who had fallen into the river and she'd been undone. Completely.

Don't think about it, Stella. She commanded herself to let go of him. So as not to have to look at his face, she knelt near Bear.

"Are you okay, too, boy?"

The dog wagged his tail. She held out a hand and Bear allowed her to scratch behind each of his ears.

She realized Tate had been scouring the river after Von arrived.

"Water's moving fast. I texted the fire department, but there's not a whole lot they can do. Hopefully, the guy can catch a tree root and pull himself out."

Von helped Stella to her feet. "Got a description for them, in any case."

"Who was it?" Stella asked to give herself something to do. Von was still looking at her as if she was a pane of glass ready to break into pieces. Not far removed from how she felt at that moment.

"Said his name's Abe Lincoln."

"No doubt his stage name," Tate quipped. "I'm thinking we better get out of here before anything else happens."

She nodded, fighting the urge to text Aunt Zoe yet again. Hannah was fine.

And Von.

Von was, too. She allowed him to open the door for her this time, figuring she would stay silent as a mouse on the way home and try to quell the flood of feelings that had come over her when she thought he'd been swept away.

Von wasn't her husband.

And she didn't even consider him a friend.

He was Hannah's father; that was all.

Surely, that explained the profound terror and relief she'd experienced when she'd thought for a moment that he was gone from her life.

Simple compassion.

Same way she'd feel for anyone.

She prayed Abe Lincoln would be saved, too.

The return trip was rougher and more time-consuming than that original passage to town. They had to stop so Tate and Von could change a tire, the dogs keeping watch while the wind howled around them. A half hour before sunset, they arrived back at camp.

Stella almost ran to her tent, heart aching when she found it empty. Of course. It was the dinner hour. Moments later she stumbled into Von on her way out and her cheeks went hot. She had the oddest sense that his had done the same.

"Dinner's ready in the dining hall. Camy texted."

She nodded.

He kept space between them as they walked, which gave her some relief. They would have to adjust to whatever it meant to parent Hannah, but that was more than plenty. Her emotions had been shoveled up and dumped out and now was not the time to be conjuring up any old love connections with Von.

See that space between you? Keep it that way.

The fire in the amphitheater was blazing, a pocket of gold in the coming dusk. The soft glow cheered her. She was back in camp. Safe, with her baby. The murder had been reported to the police. It almost seemed like a dream what had happened in Cloud Top before the shooting, her confession to Von about their son. But the memories of Von's outpouring would not stop surfacing.

"Do you...?" She wished she'd not started.

"What?"

She'd wanted to say *Do you want to talk more about anything? Our son. Your brother. Whatever broke inside you that allowed you to cry?* She burrowed deeper into her coat. "Do you think Abe Lincoln got out of the water?"

"Possible. We're going to operate under the assumption that he did until I'm shown proof to the contrary."

She sighed. "So he's still a threat."

They reached the dining room and he pulled open the door. "Affirmative."

Everyone was inside with the exception of Tate, Doc and Paul. Stella beelined for Hannah, who was sitting on Bridget's knees at the end seat across from Walker. Archie drained a bottle of water. "Found two horses loose down near the bridge. One has a minor scrape and they're both cold and hungry but I got 'em cleaned up and in the paddock. Musta been spooked from the quake, bolted from a nearby property."

Camy piled an armful of small logs to the hearth. "We can double them up in the stable if they'll tolerate it until after the blizzard passes. If they won't, at least they'll have the lean-to and we can blanket them."

Stella hoped the horses' owners hadn't been injured. The thought of all the wounded and shell-shocked townspeople they'd seen made her hurry even faster to her daughter.

Von joined Camy at the fireplace, ostensibly helping her stack the logs, but more likely, Stella thought, to fill her in on the missing details on what had happened in Cloud Top. Here, in front of a crackling fire and her baby close by, the attack at the theater seemed surreal.

As did her reaction when she thought it had been Von falling into the water. Her hands went clammy. She needed to forget all that and focus on Hannah.

"She's beautiful," Bridget said.

"Thank you."

Bridget sighed as she hoisted Hannah into Stella's arms. "I forgot how sweet it is to hold a baby. I always wanted a bunch but Paul was an only child and that's his perfect family model." Her eyes were wistful.

"Better than having no kids," Archie said.

Bridget shot daggers at him. Stella's teeth ground together. As if children were possessions. *At least you have one…*echoed painfully from the past.

"Who'd want kids anyway?" Walker said. "I never would."

"Maybe not one like you," Archie said with a laugh. After a second, Walker laughed, too. "Yeah. I'm a handful. Just ask my teachers. Right, Mrs. Rivers?"

Zoe smiled and shrugged. "I wasn't sure you would remember me. You were only in my class for eight weeks before you moved back to Mammoth. That wasn't enough time for you to get under my skin."

Walker smirked. "Dad was worried about bad influences."

"On you or from you?" Zoe said.

There was a startled silence and then everyone laughed.

Bridget chuckled right along.

"Good one," Walker said.

Archie grinned. "Don't mess with a teacher. My mom taught private school French, and she always knew when I was up to no good."

Zoe sighed. "I'm glad I retired and work the occasional shift at a coffee shop now. I don't have to do anything but give people their beverage of choice."

Kip waved a slotted spoon as he delivered a pot of vegetable soup and sliced bread and butter to the table. "Soup's on. Literally."

Tate and Doc arrived in a blast of cold air. Tate headed directly to the fire with Opie. "The med tent is warm but as soon as I stepped out it's like the Arctic." He rubbed his hands together. "I'll take my dinner to go so Doc can stay here and have a break. I'm seeing some encouraging signs in your husband, Mrs. Driscoll."

She cocked her head. "Really?"

"Pulse is steady, and we've got some eyelid flickers."

Bridget smiled. "That's wonderful. Thank you for taking such good care of him." She reached for a bowl. "Let me get you two some soup. You must be starved."

Amidst the clank of crockery and quiet conversation, Stella bundled Hannah close and kissed her cheeks. Most of the pieces of her heart slid back into place as they always did the moment she cradled the baby. There was that missing one that never would. She was learning to accept the incomplete peace as best she could. Hannah grabbed her hair. "Were you good for Auntie Zoe?"

"Pookie's been an angel." Zoe slid a plate of cut-up bread cubes and minced cheese on the table. "Two naps and a good bottle. Kip even helped with the diaper changes."

Kip shrugged. "By helped she means I handed her the wipes."

Stella laughed. "You two are a great team." Von was wrong to doubt their intentions. Whatever they'd been concealing wasn't anything to worry about.

Zoe counted out bowls. "Down to our last two diapers, by the way."

"We're resupplied, thanks to Mr. Swenson." She told them about filling the sandbags and diverting the water from his storefront.

"What a dear man," Zoe said. "Your mother said he was the best boss she ever had."

"Why didn't Mom want to return to Cloud Top? She talked about it so often and Mr. Swenson said he'd have been happy to hire her to work full-time but she'd only visit. We could have lived near you."

Zoe wiped a crumb off the table. "It was easier for your mom to live near Grandpa."

Odd, since Grandpa was a fiercely independent man until his later years and Stella had often noted tension between Grandpa and his sometimes obstinate daughter. "The letters Dad sent me…he always said Yosemite was the most beautiful place in the world. Giant sequoias, waterfalls, valleys, monoliths. He wrote about them all." Stella thought she caught a flicker of uncertainty on Zoe's face.

"It's not for everyone," Zoe said.

Stella freed her hair from Hannah's grasp. "Mr. Swenson told us there was a man asking about me. We think it was Matt Smith. He knew things about Mom."

Zoe stared. "How is your mom connected to all this?"

"I don't know." *But it's gotten a man killed*, Stella reminded herself. If Von hadn't sheltered them in the safety of the trees, there might have been another death.

Zoe chewed her lip. "Do you think that photo from Matt Smith is linked to whoever's been shooting at you?"

Von finished stacking the wood into a precise pyramid. "It has to be somehow."

"What's the condition in Cloud Top?" Bridget ladled out additional bowls of soup as Kip carved slices of bread from a loaf.

Von described the damage. "We took some fire from our friend. Calls himself Abe Lincoln."

Bridget clanked the ladle against the side of the bowl. She, Doc and Archie were all riveted to Von's report. Walker kept his attention on his soup.

"Sorry." Bridget used a napkin to retrieve the ladle, which had fallen into the pot. Had she been staring at Walker? Walker was shoveling soup into his mouth as if he hadn't eaten in weeks.

"Did you catch him?" Archie asked. "This Abe Lincoln guy?"

Von accepted a steaming bowl and buttered a slice of bread. "He may or may not have drowned in the river."

"Aww, man," Walker said. His expression was pained.

"You know him?" Von said.

Walker shook his head. "Nah. Burned my mouth on the soup, is all."

Von, Camy and Tate didn't look satisfied with Walker's answer.

"He's about your age, I'm thinking," Camy said, tapping her spoon thoughtfully. "Why don't you describe him, Von? Maybe Walker went to school with him. If so, Zoe could have met him, too."

Von did, but Walker shrugged. "Nope."

"Doesn't ring bells for me, either," Zoe said.

Doc stirred his bowl without tasting it. "Like Zoe said, Walker was only here for eight weeks while Paul was developing the resort."

"On the land he bought from my folks." Archie tore off a chunk of his bread. He dipped it and popped it into his mouth. "Took his sweet time."

Bridget waved him off. "Paul's a perfectionist. You've never seen someone fuss so much over every minute detail."

"That's why he can charge five hundred dollars per night," Doc said.

"Before then we were at our other property in Mammoth Lakes where we have a home." Bridget tasted a sip. "We built a cabin here in Yosemite, too, and Walker loved it so we decided he should go to school here while the Yosemite resort was under construction."

"You call that thing Paul built you a cabin?" Archie laughed. "It's got six bedrooms, a library and a home theater."

"Not to mention the state-of-the-art stables, which you call a second home," Bridget retorted. "I never hear you say he overspent on that."

"Guy who shot at us was about your age. High-pitched voice, nasally," Von said. All eyes were on Walker.

He shook his head. "Don't know him."

"You sure?" Von didn't bother to hide his doubt.

"I don't like your implication, Mr. Sharpe," Bridget said. "Walker said he didn't know anyone like that. He shouldn't need to reiterate."

Camy turned to her brother. "Tate, you said Paul's on the list for a medevac flight as soon as possible?"

"Yes. Have to wait out the storm now, but the amphitheater space is just big enough to land a chopper."

Bridget balled up her napkin and tossed it on the table. "I'll take my dinner to go, too, so I can check on him. Come with me, Walker. You haven't seen your dad since yesterday." She carried her bowl and spoon out, her displeasure at Von clear.

"I'm not done eating," Walker said.

Her mouth tightened.

"I'll go with you," Tate said. "Shouldn't walk there alone. Walker can head over when he's done."

"Yeah," Walker said. "Not like Dad's going anywhere."

Archie spoke low to Walker in a disapproving tone.

Von slid a bowl and a plate with a slice of buttered bread in front of Stella. She realized with a start he'd prepared the meal for her. Thoughtful of him. Her stomach growled. She shifted Hannah to one side, but the baby grabbed at her spoon when she picked it up.

Zoe put her hands out for Hannah, but Von cleared his throat. "I could…uh, hold her so you and your aunt can eat."

Stella's pulse kicked up. *Von wanted to hold Hannah.* Zoe instantly nodded. "Fabulous. I've been on baby duty all day."

Dazed, Stella lifted Hannah to Von. Bear scurried close and sat, watching.

Von clasped her around her middle. She waved her arms and kicked her legs. Frozen, he held her as if she was a hand grenade ready to explode, a look of panic creeping over his features.

"Why don't you sit here next to me?" Stella suggested, patting the bench. "She can balance on your lap and eat her snacks."

He climbed next to her and set Hannah on his knee facing the table. He pulled the plate near. "Does she grab the stuff or do I need to feed it to her?"

Stella tasted the savory soup. "She's an accomplished grabber."

But Hannah wasn't interested. Instead, she twisted her head to the side and gazed at the huge, bearded man holding her, as if he was one of the seven wonders. Von tried a half smile. "Uh, hi. Dinner's in the other direction. Here." He moved her snacks closer.

Hannah reached up and seized a handful of Von's beard. With a squeal she tugged it this way and that.

Everyone laughed, but Von appeared too surprised to make a sound.

"Sorry." Stella went to disentangle Hannah's fingers. "Do you want me to take her?"

"No, it's okay." His gaze was riveted on the baby.

Stella felt a sudden prick of tears as she watched Hannah play with Von's beard. Von finally turned her around so they were eye to eye. "Do you like that?" Von said softly. "Do I look like a big old grizzly bear?"

Hannah gurgled and squealed and tugged for all she was worth. When she tired of the game, he swiveled her toward the table so she could pick up the bits of food from the plate.

"That's it," he said as she stuffed the snacks into her mouth. "Gum it up real good so it all goes down smooth."

Archie finished his meal. "All right, Walker. If you don't

want to visit your dad, you're on deck to help me with the horses."

"Do I have to? I was already told I'm going to help work on the water heater."

"Yep," Archie said. "Hey, when my dad was alive he'd walk around our ranch from sunup to sundown doing chores without a complaint, come in for dinner, content as if he'd found the meaning of life on that land. He did, too. Come on, sonny boy. You could use some life lessons."

"Yeah, your dad probably walked five miles to school in the snow, too, right?"

Archie socked him playfully on the shoulder. "This is why some species eat their young."

Walker didn't answer, nor did he look at any of the others as they left.

"Do you think Walker knows something about the shooter?" Stella said.

Camy swallowed a mouthful. "His mom sure didn't want us to ask him any more questions. If I had the internet up and running, I'd do some research. I'll try again tonight."

When Hannah dropped some bread cubes, Von allowed Bear to snap them up. Bear wagged his tail in delight.

"Bear's going to think she's some sort of vending machine that throws rattles and bread cubes for his enjoyment," Stella said.

"If he gets tired of the job I have two more replacements ready to step in," Camy said.

Stella noted that Opie and Flash were sprawled by the fire, snoring. "As soon as their naptime is over."

Von was studiously guiding the bits of food closer to Hannah's reach with a clean fork.

"She doesn't need to eat it all."

He arched his brow. "That isn't enough to keep a humming-bird alive."

"She gets bottles, too."

"Oh. Right."

Hannah squirmed on his lap, digging a fist into her eyes. When she whimpered, he looked at Stella with alarm. "What's that sound mean?"

"She's tired. I need to give her a bottle and get her to bed."

He carefully transitioned Hannah into her arms and flicked the bread cube crumbs from his beard. "I should try again to call Legs and tell him what happened. Don't walk to your tent until Bear and I come back."

"I can escort her." Camy caught Von's glower and raised her palms. "Or you could do it."

Stella didn't see why Von wouldn't trust Camy, a retired cop, with the escort job. Was it possible he actually wanted to be close to her and the baby? No, she thought. Maybe Hannah, but certainly not her. A wisp of depression poked at her, remnants of what they'd had and lost.

Von left, returning fifteen minutes later as Hannah was finishing her bottle. Kip and Zoe were talking quietly by the fire.

"Ready?" Von said.

"One more thing to do first." She strapped Hannah into the baby bouncer on the table. Hannah fussed as she unfolded a square of gauze.

Von frowned. "What's that for?"

"Because we don't have a toothbrush. Camy gave me some."

He brushed a hand over his beard. "How many teeth does she have anyway?"

"Eight." She had a sudden idea. "Would you like to do the honors?"

"Me? Uh, I've never trained in that kind of thing."

He was so serious she almost laughed aloud. "You can track storm progressions and parachute into the desert. I think the baby tooth care should be a snap, even without training."

He took the square of gauze and bent in front of the bouncer.

"Act quick. Bob and weave," Stella joked. "She's got plenty of jaw strength."

Von probed her gums but he was too slow. Hannah clamped down all eight teeth on his finger.

He winced. "Oww. She's biting me."

Kip chuckled. "Nothing personal. You have a nice, solid teething finger there."

Von didn't remove his finger. Instead, he watched with a look of wonder on his face as Hannah munched away. "She's strong."

Stella laughed. "Yes, she is."

"You keep at it," Von said to the baby, finally freeing his finger from her mouth and quickly swiping the gauze around. "Soon, you'll be ready for steak. I'm the best at grilling up a T-bone. When you're old enough, I'll teach you how to eat one. Medium rare. That's the only proper way for a Sharpe."

Stella smiled. "Or a Rivers. Someday you can teach her how to grill one."

He looked startled. "You think she'd want to learn?"

Her breath caught. "From her daddy? Yes, I do."

Von's azure eyes widened and locked on hers. *Daddy.* How quickly he was accepting the role. She'd hoped introducing Von to his baby would form a bridge between the two, but she hadn't realized how much it would draw Von back to her own heart. Having him there, close, connected, was all she'd ever wanted, and it was so comforting to pretend he could be hers again.

But that's all it was, a pretense. She wouldn't and couldn't make him her everything, the source of her happiness and fulfillment. In eighteen months she'd learned that profound lesson. Von wasn't enough for her, nor she for him. Elevating someone to that level could only lead to disappointment. When and if she ever married, it would be God first, marriage second. Though that wasn't her present reality, there was a family born from their union. She and Von were Daddy and Mommy to their child, whom she hoped would embody the best of them both.

Von threw away the gauze, and she bundled Hannah.

The weight of the day and the uncertainty of the future crashed down on her. This wasn't real; it was a strange bubble in which they briefly found themselves before they went their separate ways again.

Unless...

Perhaps Von wasn't going back to the military.

What if he stayed at the camp? How would she feel about that?

Too tired to feel.

Too tired for anything but sleep.

He seemed to sense her sagging.

"Let me." He took Hannah and the diaper bag before he crooked his arm. "It's slippery outside."

She should not let herself grow attached to this man again, and she wouldn't, but there was no harm in threading her arm through his so she did, secure in the knowledge that he was holding on to them both.

When they got inside, Von joggled Hannah and pulled out his phone. "It's Legs." He activated the speaker. "You're on with me and Stella."

"Evening." Exhaustion colored his words. "I'm clocking off. Got another volunteer in and I need a few hours of shut eye or I'm going to forget my own name. Hoping to look into the identity of your Matt Smith tomorrow if I can. Told Tate the medevac will happen as soon as the storm lifts."

"All good news. Thank you," Von said.

"And there's one more thing. Got a call about a body five minutes ago."

Stella shivered.

"Young white male pulled from the river. Age is similar to your shooter."

"Jewelry?"

"No, but there have been looters. Might have removed them.

Clothing is similar but his shirt was gone. I didn't get word about the back pocket being ripped but it's nuts here."

Von was silent for a moment. What a terrible contrast, she thought, Von holding his own child while someone else might soon be grieving the loss of theirs. Her throat clogged as Von disconnected.

She took the baby to hide her face from him.

"I…" he started then stopped. "Are you crying?"

"No." She moved a blanket from the chair to the bed. "I just feel like tidying up. I like to keep things clean."

"That's new. You used to say 'cleaning is a problem for tomorrow's Stella.'"

"Things change."

"Do you want to talk about what Legs told us?"

"No."

"It should be a relief."

She whirled on him. "It should be, but it's not because someone lost their son and I can't celebrate that."

He locked eyes with her. "I apologize. You're right."

"I shouldn't have snapped. I'm tired, Von."

"Lie down. I'll watch and make sure she doesn't roll off or something."

"Thank you." She lay on the bed next to Hannah, but she felt too self-conscious to drift off. Hannah's wriggles slowed until she slept. Stella got up and sat in the camping chair. "I'll wait until I'm sure she's asleep before I turn in for the night."

He sat down on the cot opposite Hannah, studying the soft rise and fall of the baby's chest. "She's unusually good-looking, isn't she?"

"I've always thought so, but I'm pretty sure that's what every parent believes."

He shook his head. "No, it's objective. Her eyes are bright, and her smile is, like, especially dazzling. And she's perfectly proportioned. I measured her head-to-body ratio."

She gaped. "You did what?"

He didn't seem to hear. "When she was asleep, I took some measurements."

Through the fatigue and the worry, a giggle crept up her throat.

He was dead serious. "And she's intelligent, too. You can tell by the way she observes everything and tries to respond. If she was old enough to take the Stanford–Binet test, I know she'd knock it out of the stratosphere."

Her chuckles turned into full-blown guffaws. He finally tore his attention from the baby, his expression pure confusion.

"What? I'm being objective."

"No, you're not. That's not the slightest bit objective."

"Then what am I?"

Her laughter stilled. "You're a proud papa."

His mouth opened, then closed. He looked from Hannah to her. "How did that happen?"

She simply shrugged.

They settled into silence, lost in their own thoughts. She was sinking into a doze when his question startled her.

"Were they...?" He stopped. "Never mind."

"Ask. It's okay."

"Wrong time. Just something I wondered about... Daniel."

"It's never the wrong time to discuss our children."

"I don't want to cause you pain."

"Talking about them is a good kind of pain. What hurts worse is never speaking about him. Then it's like he was only alive in my memory. I want him to be alive in yours, too."

He nodded and she heard him swallow. "I wondered if they had the same amniotic sac. Is that okay to talk about?"

"Yes. They didn't, though. They had separate umbilical cords and placentas." She sucked in a breath. "Daniel's cord had that defect, which none of us knew about." She blinked hard. "But he was beautiful, Von. Do you...want to see a photo?" She was suddenly stricken with terror that he would recoil, from her, from their son.

His chest moved in a deep exhale. "Yes, I do."

She took the photo book she never went anywhere without from the diaper bag, opened it and offered it to him. "Here. Take a look." *At our son…*

Von's voice shook. "Beautiful. I see the Sharpe genes there in his chin." She heard him swallow. "Like my brother."

"You miss him." She took his hand.

He nodded. "At first it felt like my heart stopped working when Ronnie died. Everything was fuzzy and far away except these massive uppercuts of grief." The pain throbbed in his tone. "Is that… I mean, did you have feelings like that after Daniel?"

"I still do. There have been so many days when I didn't think I could get through it."

"How do you?"

"God gives me just enough." She held up a thumb and finger, a sliver apart. "Barely, sometimes, but enough."

"I hate that you went through all of this alone."

"I didn't. I don't think I would have survived without Kip. He invited me to live on his property after Mom's funeral. He took me to the hospital and when everything fell apart, he stayed. He had no idea what to say or do, but he stuck around and called Aunt Zoe."

"I wish I'd known."

It wasn't blame in his voice, but deep sorrow.

He got up and paced. During their couplehood she would have pressed him, tried to ease his discomfort with a hug or the suggestion of an outing. Now she simply waited.

"And I wasn't there."

Was he talking about the birth or his brother?

"Von…"

"I should go," he said. "Let you get some sleep."

She'd thought he might actually express his deepest feelings about Ronnie, but nothing had changed there. The words remained sealed up in a tomb behind a massive stone she could not roll away.

"All right," she said softly. "But here, take this."

She removed one of the photos of Daniel. Von looked like he didn't want to accept it at first, but she pressed it into his palm. "The nurses took the photo. It's the only image I have, but I had copies made. This one is for you."

His mouth trembled, or perhaps it was the shadows, before he and Bear departed.

Chapter Eleven

Von woke at the sound of a baby crying in between bursts of gusting wind. He pulled himself from the cot, his muscles feeling every inch of the climb up the fire-escape ladder the day before. His gut tightened at the memory, Stella wrapped in his arms, sobbing. No way could she pretend she hadn't been distraught at thinking him drowned. No way he could shake it from his mind. Her, him, an embrace that left him tingling all over.

Tingling? Just adrenaline overload, nothing more.

Focus, Sharpe. Bear was already at the tent door, eager to be allowed to investigate. Where was the man calling himself Abe Lincoln? Drowned in the river? Hiding out in Cloud Top again? Waiting for another chance at Stella? His gut told him Walker had an inkling about Abe's real identity and he intended to press the kid further when his mother wasn't around.

The tip of his finger throbbed and it took him a second to remember why. Hannah's tiny teeth had left a mark on his skin. "She bit me," he told Bear. He found he was smiling at the force with which she'd clamped down. He thought babies were fragile, but this one seemed to have a great supply of strength.

Like her mother.

Sorrow and regret swarmed down on him like a stream of angry hornets. He grabbed up the photo Stella had given him the night before, studying the perfect child with the barest hint of Von's strong chin. Would Daniel, too, have shown the curiosity and excitement Von saw in Hannah? And how had Stella survived it all alone? *She should have told me.* His anger was justified.

But would he have had the strength to help her? Without a clue how to do it?

And she wasn't alone anyway, he reminded himself. She had Kip and Tate and Zoe standing in where he should have been. It was going to be a while before he could let go of that resentment. He breathed away the hurt and the pain. The next wave of storm had arrived and there were bigger issues than his frazzled emotions. He tucked the photo carefully back inside the cover of his plant book, hauled himself from the bunk and into the small bathroom.

The memory popped up. *What kind of a tent has a bathroom? Isn't that called glamping?* he'd teased Ronnie.

His brother had replied, *Camy insists that people aren't gonna want to hike to a communal latrine when the snow's up to their elbows.*

He hadn't said so, but he'd thought it a waste of money.

Now he knew Camy had been right, and Ronnie was wise to take her advice. They'd been a good partnership, multiplying their strengths, dividing their weaknesses.

I miss you, Ronnie.

The freezing water was too uncomfortable to withstand for long. Quickly, he washed his hands and face and brushed his teeth, slicking down his hair and beard so Hannah wouldn't mistake him for a bison. The small heater kept the worst of the chill from the tent. Stella and the baby might not be warm enough. He'd check, maybe move them to the dining hall where the temperature was more easily regulated.

His phone was charged thanks to the solar battery pack. There was a message from Legs.

No positive ID on body. Will update you when I know something.

In other words, *stop bothering me, Von, I've got bigger problems than your shooter.*

His stomach growled as they stepped into the wind, which the anemometer he'd installed told him was hovering at forty mph. Bear wasn't deterred, surging ahead until he reached Stella's tent. Von called out a greeting and waited for a reply before he opened the door.

Stella was attempting to wrestle Hannah into an overlarge snowsuit, but the little girl was bucking like a bronco. Bear galloped over, skidded to a stop on his haunches, risking a quick lick of Hannah's foot when it came close enough.

"Good morning." Von stood awkwardly. "She's not cooperating?"

"No." Stella's eyes were shadowed with fatigue. "And she was up every couple of hours last night. Zoe's gone to start the coffeepot so we can begin the caffeine infusion."

He approached the cot and took a knee to bring him closer to the wriggling baby. "You're trouble, huh?"

Hannah stopped moving to stare at him. Everything about her was like a normal grown-up, eyes where they were supposed to be, nose, mouth, but somehow the miniaturized features were concentrated into a type of perfection from which he couldn't look away. Each quirk of those rosebud lips magnetized him to the spot.

Hannah flung out a fist and caught his beard, tugging him closer. He complied until they were only a few inches apart. "Did I forget to brief you, kiddo? At night you're supposed to sleep and let your mama get some shuteye, too. Those are direct orders from headquarters."

Hannah stared in deep concentration at Von's face captured by her chubby grip. Von had to remind himself to breathe. Stella used the momentary pause to slide on the snowsuit and button it closed.

"Whew. I might have to grow a beard after you leave." She looked away and scooped up the baby while he stood. "I didn't have a chance to ask before. When are you returning to your unit?"

"I'm not, exactly." He didn't want to discuss it, but there was no getting around her question. She had a right to know. Ironic, since she hadn't felt he'd had the right to be told about the babies, but he found his resentment had shrunk since she'd told him about Daniel. Now it was more like a low-grade throb. "They made me retire because of my knee."

Her expression was ripe with sympathy, which made him recoil.

"I'm so sorry, Von."

"No big deal. I've been rehabbing. Gonna go into a training role and hopefully take Bear with me."

"Really?"

"Surprised?"

"Not that you want to return to the military, but I mean, you seem to be doing well here at MDWG. It's grown so much since Ronnie started it. He'd...well, he would probably have been pleased that you took a job here."

Not the moment to discuss Ronnie. Von shrugged. "Short-term. It's Tate and Camy's thing. Not mine."

"Plenty of room to plant the seeds you're always reading about," she joked.

His brows furrowed until he recognized it for the tease it was. "So how about you? What are your plans? Going to stay in Fresno with Hannah long-term?"

"I thought so, but after being here a while, I might change my mind, once the shooter situation is resolved, of course." She took a deep breath. "I like it here. Brings back memories of visiting Mr. Swenson and it'd be good to be near Aunt Zoe. My dad used to say in his letters Yosemite was the perfect spot to raise a family."

"You told me he died young." He helped her pull a knit cap on the wriggling baby.

"Yes, and my mom never wanted to talk about him. I think maybe they had some issues. All I have really are his letters. He was killed working on a TexAm oil rig in the Gulf of Mexico when I was four." She snagged the diaper bag.

Too much for her to carry. Should he snag the bag or the baby? While he tried to decide, she headed to the door with both. He scurried in front of her and held out his hands. "Let me take something. Storming hard out there."

She hesitated, just for a moment, before she handed him the diaper bag. He was both relieved and disappointed. She didn't trust him with Hannah and why would she? He didn't even know enough about babies to keep from getting bitten. He was learning, even if it was the hard way. The wind battered them with falling snow. Stella drew the baby close and bowed her head against the onslaught. Von looped his free arm around her middle.

Odd how natural the move came, how comfortable their connection felt. Her waist was not as narrow as it had been, widened from growing two babies inside. It made her even more attractive. Incredible that her body had been a vessel for their children. Awe-inspiring and enticing. Without realizing it, he'd pulled her closer to his side. Wouldn't be good if she slipped and fell.

Bear shook off the snow and trotted along, ears swiveling as he picked up every sound, the hum of the generators, the *thunk* of logs Archie and Walker were adding to the fire in the amphitheater. The cacophony of the river reminded him to check the level again. The last thing they needed was a breach of the banks and a flooded campsite.

His pulse quickened when Stella leaned close, her lips brushing his ear. Warmth spread down his neck.

"Why are they keeping the fire lit on a day like this?" she called above the tumult.

He turned his head and put his mouth to her cheek, flooded with an overwhelming urge to kiss the tender spot beneath her earlobe. *Kiss? Check that thought on the double. You had your chance with Stella, and God's not gonna dole out another.* He cleared his throat. "They're melting some snow to water the horses." There were plenty of gallons of water left for the humans, but since they had no idea how many more days they'd be trapped in camp it was wise to conserve resources.

He hoped she didn't have another question. His desire to kiss her was way out of left field, and he'd obviously sustained too many shocks recently, which had unsettled his mind. When she was tucked in the cabin with Zoe and Kip, Von left Bear to monitor things and excused himself to check the river.

What he found was alarming. The water level fed by additional snowfall was only two feet below the bank. Sandbags were in order and fortunately, Tate and Camy had already had a pile of sand delivered before the quake hit. He was fetching sacks and a shovel from the utility room when his phone vibrated with a message from Lieutenant Colonel Mackey.

Heart hammering, he listened.

Sharpe, I'm keeping tabs on your earthquake situation. You're there now? How bad's the damage? Nothing you can't handle, right? When the shaking stops, call me. There's a trainer slot opening up, and we should talk. End of message.

Von listened to it twice more before he redialed and got a busy signal. He tried a third time when a voice interrupted him.

"News?"

He spun to find Tate eating a banana and offering him the other.

"What are you doing here?"

"Looking for another shovel. Snow's piling up around the med tent. So what's the word?"

Sparks winged inside him. "There's a trainer slot open. Looks good."

Tate chewed and swallowed, flakes of snow glistening on his jacket. "That's great."

"It is." Von tried not to crow aloud. "It's everything I want."

Tate took in the interior of the shed before his gaze swiveled back to Von. "Everything?"

Tate's searching look infuriated Von. "I'm leaving. Not like I haven't been forthcoming."

"Right. You've been up front from the get-go."

Another telling silence. "What do you need to say, Tate?"

He shrugged. "Thought maybe there'd be more reason to consider sticking around now."

Von huffed out a breath. "Come on. Give me some credit. I'm not going to leave Stella and Hannah without support. Certainly going to make sure they're both safe and financially squared away before I ship out."

"I figured."

Von snatched up a pile of bags. If there was more coming, he wasn't going to stand around waiting for it like a kid sent to the principal's office.

Tate shrugged. "It's not a bad place here, you know. The MDWG does a lot of good for a lot of people, like your brother intended."

Von breathed out against a tightening of his lungs. "No argument, but this is Ronnie's place, not mine."

"Doesn't have to be if you'd let go of your guilt."

He almost dropped the bag he was holding. "My guilt?"

His expression was unreadable. "You weren't there for your brother and it grieves you, whether or not you can admit it."

He stopped himself from recoiling outright. "Yeah, it grieves me. Of course it does, but I didn't realize how serious Ronnie's condition was."

"Yes, you did."

He felt the blood drain out of him as Tate continued.

"I told you it was serious in two different messages and you didn't come. His heart was damaged. You knew that."

You didn't come. "I…"

Tate waved him off. "Point is Ronnie didn't blame you for that, Von. He knew who you were and what made you tick and he understood your decision. Probably supported it, even. You don't have to run away now because you didn't show up then."

Fury cut Von down the middle. "My brother isn't the reason I need to go."

Tate peeled the rest of the banana in silence, which only made Von angrier.

"You got no right to judge me. You kept the truth from me, you helped hide my kid from me, so what kind of man does that make you?"

"I wish I knew."

"You love to be the hero, don't you, Tate? Made you feel good to step in and rescue Stella without telling me so you could put on that shining armor. What is that, some hero complex? You feed on being the good guy so it works for you to make others look bad. Look in the mirror. You're a liar, and your ego is bigger than mine."

Tate sighed. "It's possible, or maybe you're lashing out because I've probed a sore spot."

"Don't make me feel guilty for what I want."

"That's not my intent."

"Then what's your point? That my priorities are messed up? Maybe I should ask God to sort them out for me?"

"Not a bad thought."

"I'm not asking God for a nickel." He threw out a palm. "Take a good look around, why don't you? God has wrecked us with an earthquake. God let Ronnie get sick when he'd finally gotten his dream off the ground. God let my son die before he even got to sit up. Stella's grief will probably never end." He swallowed the wobble in his throat. *Or mine.* "You may believe God doles out happiness and rainbows, but I don't. I know He's in charge and I have to accept that, but I don't have to be happy about it."

Tate shook his head. "News flash. You weren't put on this planet to be happy."

Tate's equanimity only infuriated Von further. "Yeah? Then why am I here, oh, wise sage?"

"To learn how to love."

The comment confused him enough that he stopped talking. Finally, he rallied a response. "Stay out of my life, Tate."

The tension simmered between them for an endless moment until Tate turned, grabbed a shovel and walked away, leaving Von staring after him.

With his insides shaking, Von stalked toward the raging river that mirrored his inner tumult. He struggled to process what had just occurred.

You don't have to run away now because you didn't show up then.

He felt a deep hatred for Tate at that moment. Von hadn't come when Ronnie was sick the last time because he'd heard enough about the medical situation to know his little brother wasn't going to make it. He'd been rendered comatose by the heart attack, the culmination of years of damage and hospitalizations. The doctor's messages about "brain activity" and "kidney damage" were grim. Von's rational side knew the inevitable result, but his soul couldn't face it. The bald, ugly truth was Tate was right. Von hadn't been able to stand watching his brother die. *Coward.*

All the things he'd endured in his life, the training accident that almost paralyzed him, the missions where he was feet away from enemies that would have killed him on the spot if they'd known he was there, Ronnie's rebellion and health struggles, the emptiness in their house when his mother passed…he'd withstood it all.

Until the moment when his brother needed him to show up. And he hadn't.

The shame and guilt filled him until he thought he'd drop. *Ronnie didn't blame you for that, Von.*

The single sentence was all that kept him on his feet.

Tate believed Ronnie understood. Von hoped with everything in him that was true. He'd desperately not wanted to witness the light dying from his brother's eyes as God pulled Ronnie's soul from earth and Von's along with it. Well, he'd been given what he wanted, right? He hadn't arrived home until the funeral, unable to feel, a robot walking through somebody else's life. At that moment the shutters slammed tight inside him, sealing everyone out including Stella. If Von had been put on earth to learn how to love, he'd flunked the lesson big time.

Von picked up a stone and pitched it as hard as he could, sending it sailing over the burgeoning bank. The foaming water gulped it greedily.

His heart was raw and stripped, as if Tate's accusation had flayed away the outer walls and left him bloody. He forced himself to stand up straight. Tate had gotten some of it wrong, though. Von didn't need to leave the camp now because of what had happened two years before. What Von needed was what he'd always needed, a purpose, a way of mattering that was indisputable, public. A way to make sure his life meant something.

The night before in one of his many wakeful hours, he'd caught Stella's shadow gliding back and forth behind her tent walls as she soothed the baby. A confusion of feelings had spiraled through him, and it seemed that he paced along with Stella as she moved.

He pictured Hannah chortling in her arms. A lightning bolt fused him to the floor and he'd realized he loved that baby. Loved? He hadn't loved any living creature except Bear since his engagement ended. What's more, he was becoming dangerously fond of her mother. But that couldn't be, not the way it had been. He and Stella had broken up because they were opposites, she young and rash, he older and closed off, both set in patterns of selfishness. She was a different person now and the notion tantalized him, but the conversation with Tate reminded him that he was not.

Same Von. Same desires. Same shortcomings. And now a father with no better notion how to love someone than he'd had before. Glued to the floor, he'd watched her soothe their baby. He wanted them in his life. It would be incredible to picture the three of them becoming a family in the Yosemite wilderness, like some sort of sentimental Christmas movie.

But he required his duty as much as he needed his lungs to work, his arteries to pump. Stella and Hannah had not displaced the burning desire to regain his lost profession. Because it was more than a profession; it was who he was. He'd failed at being a brother, a fiancé, but he still had one identity intact. God had to know he needed all of it in his life.

So why was he suddenly a heaving mess of emotions? And how was a person supposed to learn to love by having their heart ripped to pieces?

River spray tossed up by the storm dampened his face. He glanced at his phone again, to reassure himself the message was still there, a tangible reminder he could have what he wanted and needed. His brain spat out the plans. Plenty of guys cared for families while serving. It didn't have to be an either-or situation. He'd take on the training role and make sure Stella and Hannah were supported any way they required, with a house, schooling, whatever. He'd be involved as much as he possibly could. The relief was delicious.

Spinning on his heel he marched toward the sand pile, ready to dig his mind clear of Tate's echoing words.

Stella knew Von would object to her joining him, but she sought him out at the sand pile anyway when there was a small break in the storm. She and Bear found him shoveling sand into a sack and adding it to the pile stacked on a utility wagon.

"You shouldn't…" he began.

"Hannah's sleeping and you need help." She pointed to Bear. "And he's missing you."

"How can you tell?" Von leaned on his shovel and wiped his brow.

"His eyes are sad."

Von's furrowed brows told her he didn't believe that for one red second. His mouth was set in a line, and she didn't think it was entirely due to her arrival.

When he took the water bottle from his pocket to drink, something fluttered to the snow. She picked it up, the papery propeller wings that held a seed from the maple tree.

He shrugged. "Found it in my backpack."

She thought of the one lone elm in Cook's Meadow, a regal, solitary tree with Half Dome in the background that had been photographed by millions. She smiled at him.

"What?"

"I'm remembering your seed collection."

"You know I got a thing for seeds."

At their apartment, he'd sprouted an army of plants in pots everywhere from the bathroom to the kitchen sink, but his favorites were the heritage seeds. After every deployment she'd find a couple he'd squirreled away in an empty medicine bottle, treasures from an ancient tree somewhere in the world. Potential, in a bottle.

"Do you still have the one you took from Cook's Meadow?"

"Yeah. Haven't found the right place for it yet. Don't worry, Arborist Stella. I won't plant it here, for sure."

Elms didn't belong in the area, as she'd told him. Cook's Elm would be the last in Yosemite Park, since it was a nonnative species. But the grand specimen had flourished anyway, even though it wasn't home.

She gave him a saucy look. "I like that about you, Von."

"Like what about me?"

"That you still have the urge to plant. It speaks to your optimistic side."

"I'm not an optimist, Stella. Maybe I was, but..." He trailed off, then took a breath and started again. "I dunno."

"You still save seeds."

"Habit."

"No. You're a born helper. With your unit, your service." She waved a hand. "What you do here at the camp. It's you. It's how you're made. To plant. To make things better." The snow fell in a swirling backdrop, shrouding them.

"But I didn't help you." It sounded as if the words were being pulled from him like roots giving up their hold on the earth. She froze, waiting to see if he would continue this time.

"I retreated. Completely. Like I did with Ronnie."

She prayed her response would not push him back into the darkness. "It hurt that you shut me out...but I kind of did the same. I should have been a grown-up and told you about the pregnancy." She sighed. "I learned a thing or two since we split."

"Like what?"

"That people give what they have, when they can."

"I didn't."

"You couldn't, not then, but you are now. God gave you seeds to plant, Von. Somewhere down deep, you know that."

"Tate just told me God put me here so I can learn to love. Now you're telling me I'm supposed to be planting."

She laughed and it felt good. "Maybe it's the same thing."

"I'm confused, about God."

"Me, too, sometimes. I think it's okay to feel that way."

He made no move to retrieve the seed from her, so she slipped it back into his pocket. Without asking, she scooped up an empty bag and held it open for him to fill. He stood motionless.

"Something wrong?"

"No. Right, as a matter of fact." He cleared his throat. "Got a message about the training job."

She made sure to smile and keep her tone light. "That's great."

"Yeah." He began to shovel in some sand. "We'll work it out to get whatever you need for you both."

"Child support?"

Why did that sound so cold?

He nodded. "Absolutely."

"We'll be okay. We don't…"

"It's my responsibility." His tone was hard, and it bugged her.

"Do you think maybe Hannah might need something other than your money?"

He stared at her, the shovel suspended in his hands. "I'm not going to vanish. I'll visit whenever I possibly can."

"And write letters?" She didn't understand until that moment exactly what she'd wanted him to say, that he'd get to know his daughter and allow her to know him. That he'd be a father…the kind she had known only in letters. He had seeds to plant in his daughter if he wanted to.

"I'm going to do my best. It's a new situation for me, right?"

The slight edge of accusation… Their earlier intimacy whirled away into the storm. "Because I didn't tell you. I know and I've apologized, but somehow, I don't think the scenario would be different if you'd known her for nine months, would it?"

"This isn't new. You were ready to sign on to that kind of life, Stella."

"That's when I thought your heart belonged to me and then the service but I was wrong about that." And she was wrong to imagine things would be different with a child in the picture. It wasn't fair to him. People gave what they could, when they could.

His shoulders slumped, and he rested the shovel on the ground. "Stella…"

She wrapped her arms around herself, uncertain of her own disappointment. She'd not expected him to want to be with her again, baby or not. "It's okay. You never painted a rosy picture. I did that myself."

"I'm sorry," they both said at exactly the same time.

She laughed.

"I'm sorry I'm not the man you thought I was," he said.

"I'm sorry I pressured you to give me something you couldn't."

His smile was so terribly sad that she took his hand in her gloved one. "We'll do what we can. Both of us. And we'll try to figure out what's best for Hannah together. How's that?"

He gripped her fingers, eyes poring over her face as if he was trying to memorize it.

"All right."

He turned away and filled another sandbag.

She glanced at the cart. "Isn't this enough?"

"No." His tone was flat, hollow. "But you should go back. Wind's picking up."

It wasn't the way she wanted to end the conversation, but she couldn't think how to do it better. "Meet you at the dining hall later."

Von told Bear to follow her but she shook her head. "He should stay with you. In case you fall in or something, he can let us know."

"I'm not gonna fall in."

"And I'm not going to get snatched by a bear in the fifty

yards between here and the cabin. You can practically watch me all the way."

"I…"

"Von," she snapped. "The shooter's likely been found, and I'm not going to get used to having a guard shadowing me. I can't allow myself to feel like I'm not capable of handling things on my own." Why, oh, why did her voice wobble on the last few syllables? She swallowed hard. "See you in a while."

She wasn't sure if he would insist or not so she marched with purpose. Von was leaving. It was a matter of time. There was no marriage bond to keep them tethered. She and her daughter would be alone to face the world together as they'd done from the start. Why had she allowed herself to entertain, even for a blip in time, any romantic connection with Von Sharpe? All that had vanished long ago.

Her heart was bound together by fragile roots like a newly sprouted seedling. For Hannah's sake, she could not let those roots be broken.

She'd only made it a few steps when Bear barked, hard and urgent.

She knew him well enough to know what it meant.

Threat.

Chapter Twelve

Von charged into the shadows, wielding the shovel like a club. He didn't have to tell Bear to stay with Stella. The dog had already shoved against her legs, urging her backward until her shoulders touched the walls of the shed where no one could attack from behind. Staring into the shadowed riverbanks, the tangled shrubbery, Bear growled low in his throat.

Von skirted the muddied bank. Branches slapped at him, snagged his hair, scratched his cheek. A big cluster of debris had piled up in one section, the perfect spot to conceal someone spying on them as they talked. If he hadn't been so caught up in the emotion of the conversation, he might have reacted more quickly.

The soft snap of a twig under his foot foiled his stealth. Nerves along his arms prickled as he surged forward. The ground gave way underneath his left boot and he tumbled toward the swollen river, the shovel landing in the mud. Only a reflex reaction allowed him to crook an elbow and snag an exposed root. Arduously, he hauled himself up, retrieved the shovel and crept on to the debris pile.

There was no one there.

The ground was snowy, so littered with twigs and leaves cast down by the wind he was not able to detect so much as a heel print. Frustrated, he hastened back to Stella.

Bear was quiet now, but every bit as alert.

"No one," he said.

Her face telegraphed the same worry he felt. "No one there or someone gone?"

"I don't know."

"Would Bear have alerted if it wasn't a human?"

"Possibly. He's trained to tell me when someone or something is near, human, animal, vehicle." He knew she wanted more, but he couldn't conjecture. "Bear and I are walking you back to the lodge now."

She simply pressed her lips together and nodded.

He gave Bear a silent hand signal. The dog loped ahead, ears swiveling.

Stay alert, buddy.

I've got a bad feeling.

Stella moved at a brisk pace, propelled by the storm at her back. The weak glow spilling from the dining hall was a welcome sight since it was still not even 10 a.m. and dark. Von made sure she was settled, before he and Bear ventured out again.

Rechecking the riverbank for an intruder.

She tried to shake away her foreboding.

The wood in the fire crackled an invitation, and the enticing smell of baking bread made her salivate.

Zoe snoozed in the rocking chair next to the mat and blanket they'd laid out for Hannah that morning after their breakfast. Hannah slept in the blissful ignorance of infancy, warm in her footed jammies with her arms flung out like a snow angel. Sometimes Stella couldn't stop herself from imagining them both together, Daniel and Hannah, like one photo superimposed over another. Her son had been whisked away after the delivery, only returned to nestle next to his sister in her arms after it was clear there was nothing more that could be done for him. They'd shared that moment, at least, together as a family, except for Von. She blinked and allowed herself a moment to marvel at her lovely girl. So much had happened since she'd driven to meet Matt Smith. The events that had taken place on that lonely drive caused massive upheaval enough. The quake was a whole other layer, trapping her here, forcing her to deal with Von and everything else.

If God was looking to grow her through the experiences, He was making the lesson unavoidable.

Kip stood in the kitchen, staring at the pictures of the guests and their bios. He looked more rested, less haggard, than he had the day before. He was still wearing the sling on his injured arm, but Tate had said a day or two more should do the trick. He kept his voice low to avoid waking the baby. "Hey there. What's wrong? You look worried."

She told him about Bear's behavior.

Kip sipped gravely. She noticed Opie under the tiny kitchen table and gave him a pat. "Where is everybody?"

"Some on the porch, or maybe with the horses. I'm not sure. I was on my way outside to fetch more logs from the woodpile."

"But your shoulder…" she protested.

"I only need one arm to snag a log, Stella. I gotta help out in some way since Zoe has commandeered the baby unless there's a diaper to be changed. I certainly don't want you out there in light of what's happened. Back in a minute."

She closed the door after him, shutting out the storm, and set about preparing more bottles.

Tate climbed down the attic from the loft, surprising her. He tipped an imaginary cap at her. "Morning."

"I thought you were in the medical tent."

"I'm everywhere, like the wind," he said, wiggling his fingers and adopting an eerie tone.

"Well, your sister always said you were full of hot air."

He pressed a hand to his chest. "You wound me, dear lady. Did you get any sleep last night?"

"No, but they tell me I'll sleep when Hannah leaves for college."

"I doubt it." He grinned, rifling through a box he'd brought down with him. "Where's Von?"

She told him about Bear's alert. "Those two will sniff out any trouble." His smile didn't reach his eyes, she noted.

"What are you looking for?"

"A whiteboard."

Camy appeared, holding an insulated carafe. "Good news. I got on the internet for less than five minutes before it failed again, but that's a good indication we're getting close to reestablishing communication."

"What did your five minutes tell you?" Stella shook up the bottles and put them in the refrigerator.

"NPS has rescued several of the hikers. They're still working on the Ahwahnee. National Guard is tasked with clearing the roads in and out of Cloud Top. They'll make it here soon, but this storm is going to knock them out for at least one or two days."

"Which? One or two?"

"How do I know? Ask the weatherman. Where is he?"

Stella repeated her story.

"That's a concern. Plus, the water level's way too high for my liking." Camy looked at her brother. "Why do you need a whiteboard?"

The porch door, visible via the kitchen pass-through, blew open with a clack. Opie looked up in alarm.

"My bad. Didn't shut it all the way when I came in," Tate said. As he moved to close it, he explained over his shoulder,

"Paul's restless, and he's opened his eyes a few times but he can't speak, as far as I can tell. I thought he might be able to communicate in writing the next time he rouses. Sorry," he called to the porch sitters as he wrestled the door shut. "I'll go snag the whiteboard from your office. Doc's keeping an eye on Paul."

Camy filled the carafe with coffee from the pot and screwed down the lid. "I'll go with. I was fueling up before I try to get on the internet again. I need to pick your brain."

Tate smiled. "Not much of it left, but have at it."

Out the side window, Stella could see vague outlines of people on the screened-in porch, bundled against the cold, probably sipping coffee. She could hear them chatting. The generator didn't power the porch lights so she couldn't make out quite who was there, but there was a fire pit to keep them relatively comfortable while they watched the storm. She hoped the horses were as sheltered and cozy.

"Stella, can you take the raisin bread out of the oven when it's done?" Camy asked. "We're out of regular so I had to improvise. Hope everybody likes raisins."

"I'll eat the picky people's shares," Tate said. Opie merely raised his head when Tate called softly to him. "Some highly trained dog," Tate teased. "You're a couch potato. Don't you want to go find a whiteboard with me?"

Opie wagged his tail, but did not get to his feet.

Camy laughed. "At least you got him over here. Flash is still sprawled on the sofa cushion under my desk. He pretended not to hear me when I told him it was time to get up."

"With those ears he could hear a fly on the moon."

"Only if he wants to," Camy said.

"He'll hear clear enough when it's snack time."

"True story. Let's go. I have work to do."

They let themselves out, and Opie went to curl up next to Hannah's makeshift cot.

Stella followed her nose to the oven and the luscious smell

of bread studded with raisins and doused with cinnamon. The timer indicated fifteen minutes remained so she cut up more peaches and bread cubes for Hannah's breakfast. The menu, written in Camy's meticulous printing, was tacked to a bulletin board. "Sandwiches" was scratched out and "Chili" scribbled in. With ten people and no new influx of supplies, their rations were going fast. Only a day or two more until help arrived. The row of cans on the counter was obviously intended for the chili. With everything on Camy's plate, Stella figured she would appreciate help.

Armed with a can opener, she opened and rinsed the contents and dumped the various beans into the Crock-Pot, added a handful of spices, canned tomatoes and paste, and set it to low. The smell of cumin and chili powder gave her a pang. Her mother had adored chili of all types until she'd become too sick to eat it.

Chili and a buttered cornbread muffin were staples in their tiny Fresno house. When Stella had started local community college, her mother would be sure to have a simmering pot ready whenever she made it home. She missed her quiet, serious mother, who was always stirring dinner with one hand and thumbing through a book with the other.

When the oven timer dinged, she removed the bread, enjoying the warmth radiating through the oven mitts. Ten minutes to cool and she'd tip it out of the pan.

She frowned with a sudden thought. Ten minutes. It had been fifteen to finish baking the bread. Kip hadn't returned with the firewood. She peeked at Aunt Zoe, who had roused and was rolling her neck to unkink it.

"I'm going to step onto the porch for a minute," she whispered.

Zoe gave her a double thumbs-up.

The porch was empty. There was no sign of the people gathered there before she'd gone to supervise the baking.

No surprise they'd not wanted to hang out for long. She tried to think of the experience from the clients' perspectives. It seemed Bridget and Walker hadn't much enthusiasm for the team-building camp in the first place and Doc was neutral at best. Being trapped here by an earthquake with Paul's health precarious and the rest of the team not arrived must be maddening. With the landing of the storm, it would be at least another day until the helicopter would arrive, hopefully followed by the clearing of roads to allow them out of MDWG. In the meantime, they were all marooned with diminishing supplies and no hot water.

Anxiety pricked her skin. Where was Kip? No new logs had been added to the porch where they'd been staging small batches of dry wood to feed the fire, so he hadn't yet returned. The woodpile occupied a space on the other side of a graveled path. She didn't see him as she peered from the porch, so she pulled her coat tighter, stepped into the gloom and crunched her way to the stacked logs, frosted with a layer of white. He wasn't there.

Had he continued on, enjoying some fresh air? The close quarters might be getting to him. But it certainly wasn't optimal weather for strolling.

"Kip?" she said, walking along the path. Overhead, the pine needles clattered and branches creaked. The path curved around past the medical tent, but she would go no farther. Not without Bear or Von. Something rustled in the bushes that lined the path. Stella jumped as a creature crawled into sight—a cat, bony and shaking. Snowflakes stuck to its orange fur. Instantly, she dropped to her knees.

"Oh, sweetie. Have you gotten lost in this storm?" Probably bolted during the quake. The animal had to be close to death. Slowly, she unwound her scarf and laid it gently over the little cat's back. It did not so much as flinch. Gingerly, she scooped it up and brought it to her chest. "You'll be safe now. We'll get you some milk and warm you up. You can stay with us until we find your family, okay?"

As she straightened, she noticed a shadow moving along the path. Her breath caught, nerves surging, but the dark shape lost itself again in the forest. Probably another animal. The region was home to all manner of wildlife from rabbits to bears so it might be anything at all. She wished Bear and Von were with her.

The forest made her feel small and alone, like the cat cradled to her chest. There was no sign of Kip or any indication that he'd passed this way. And no good reason for her to be out in the dark, even if she was only yards from the lodge. She would probably return to the dining hall and find that Kip had merely gone to retrieve something he'd left in the office he was sharing with Camy.

Still, her chilly walk had been worth it. The cat wouldn't have survived much longer in such conditions. The animal meowed weakly, making her wonder if it was injured or frostbitten. Tate would know. He took care of his dog and Camy's, in addition to his human patients. She'd pop over to the med tent and wait with Doc and Bridget if she was there, until Tate returned with the whiteboard and ask him to check the cat. Plus, she could ask him if he'd seen Kip.

She resettled the creature, snuggling it deeper into the warmth of her jacket.

With the wind buffeting them both, she hurried toward the tent. Lights glowed from inside, poking into the darkness of the trees overhead and the storm-clad sky. It might as well be midnight as morning.

"Let's go, kitty."

She just stepped over a frozen puddle when the lights on the med tent went out. Darkness swamped her senses.

"What happened?" She clutched the cat.

The tent was drowned in oily blackness, the interior lights

and porch lamps extinguished. Had the generator failed that supplied the building? Should she backtrack to the dining hall or continue on to the medical tent? Surely, Doc or Bridget would activate one of many flashlights Tate had in the tent. She patted her pocket for the one Von had given her.

Finally locating it, she switched it on. The beam was paltry in the deep mountain gloom. Branches and falling snow cast strange shadows until it seemed the forest was coming alive. Fear twisted her stomach.

Calm down and make a decision.

Best to continue to the medical tent rather than turning around. It was closer and they might need help. She could already hear distant shouts. Probably Camy or Von tackling the generator failure. The machine that powered the med tent was also providing electricity to the dining hall so both would be out.

She resisted the urge to sprint back to her baby. This was a power glitch only. Hannah was fine. Zoe was with her, maybe Kip if he'd returned, and they had a fire for light and warmth. Not to mention a selection of lanterns and flashlights. She should definitely get to the med tent and wait there, assist if she could in case Tate needed to help restore the generators.

Something thudded at her feet and she screamed. The cat squirmed against her. Only a pinecone blown loose. The flakes were driving hard now, surrounding her in a dizzying cone as she patted the cat.

Hurry up. Breathing hard she hustled along with the aid of her flashlight to avoid debris and any more plummeting pinecones until she arrived on the porch. There was no sound but the forest crackling and whirling above. "Tate?" she called. Why did her voice quaver? Silly. "Doc?"

She raised her palm to knock on the med tent door. There was a disturbance in the air as something rushed toward her. Instinct shrilled and she ducked as a thick tree branch slammed into the door where her head had been a moment before. The wood exploded into pine-scented splinters. She tumbled sideways off the step as fragments settled around her.

Abe Lincoln, her mind shrilled. He'd escaped drowning and come for her. Hannah. She had to get to Hannah. On her knees she scrambled for footing, one arm raised to deflect another blow.

Finally able to stand, she jerked left and right, trying to spot her attacker. But there was no one there, nothing but the howling wind and the broken branch lying at her feet. She scoured the night, aiming her meager beam in all directions.

Her light caught nothing but the storm.

Get inside. Get help.

Heart slamming into her ribs, she clutched the cat and pushed into the med center.

"Hello," she called again, stopping when her foot encountered something soft and pliable.

Feet crunched on the threshold behind her and she heard someone say, "What are you doing?"

Looking down, a scream tore from her throat.

Von and Bear sprinted to the darkened dining room. Some weather-related malfunction had caused the generators to fail. No enormous cause for alarm likely, but he was on edge. Even without an intruder in camp, there were plenty of other ways they might be hurt stumbling around in the dark.

The thought, the merest whisper of an idea that they could be injured, had him pounding over the slick ground.

Zoe stood in the doorway of the hall. "What happened to the lights?"

"Uncertain. Are you all okay?" He looked around her to catch a glimpse of Stella or the baby.

"Hannah and I are fine, but we're alone here."

Alone?

She explained that Stella and Kip had gone.

He tried not to bark out the question. "Where?"

"I don't know for sure about Kip. Stella left about twenty minutes ago. I think she took the path toward the woodpile."

He was turning to track Stella when Tate and Camy trotted up with their dogs.

"I'll check the generator. Let's go, Flash." Camy and the dog disappeared at a run.

No further conversation necessary. He and Tate both jogged out. Von tracked the route Zoe thought Stella had taken. Tate was beelining with Opie for the medical tent.

Bear glided next to him. He tried to think of what reason Stella had for going out in the storm, but it must have been a good one. Her tendency toward recklessness had mellowed since she'd become a mother. He trusted her judgment. Where was she? Not at the woodpile or along the path.

She should have had Bear by her side. And that was the way it would be going forward no matter what she had to say about it. They rounded the bend, and Tate stopped so fast Von almost flattened him.

The med tent door was open, banging in the wind. Inside, a flashlight beam zipped around and he heard Stella call out for help.

His blood went icy as he slid past Tate and exploded through the door.

Tate and Opie followed on his heels.

Stella was on her knees next to a fallen Paul Driscoll, Doc on his other side, shining his phone light down onto the floor.

They both jerked at the new arrivals. Bear stood on alert, eyeing the tableau, waiting to see if he was called upon to act.

"Stella," Von panted. "What happened?"

"I was trying to find Kip. He went for wood and didn't come back. I got here and found Paul like this."

Tate eased her out of the way and knelt next to Paul.

"Lanterns," Tate commanded.

Von snagged two, activated them and set them on the bed to help Tate in his examination. Von was busy looking at Stella. She didn't appear hurt, which eased his breathing a fraction. With Bear watching Doc closely, Von pulled Stella to the far corner and bent to look her directly in the eye.

"Hurt?"

She shook her head, breathing hard through her nose. "While I was looking for Kip I found this cat." She unzipped her jacket to reveal a pathetic specimen. "I was bringing it to Tate to examine when the lights went out. A branch almost crashed into my head."

"A branch? How?"

"I don't know. It might have been torn off in the wind."

Or not.

The rest of the explanation trailed out. "I let myself in and Paul was on the floor. I screamed when Doc came in because he surprised me. I figured Tate had to be close so I yelled for help while Doc tried to text Tate."

Von caught the doctor's eye. "Where were you during all this?"

The doctor's gaze flicked back to Paul. "I was sitting with Paul like I've been doing every day. Tate gives me a progress report and such, but today he went to the dining hall to look for something so I offered to stay. Paul was sleeping peacefully, not agitated at all, so I went outside for a cigarette. I saw the lights go out and I lost my way getting back. I arrived to find her on the floor with him."

Stella bit her lip. "Is he…alive?"

Tate sat back on his heels. "Yes. Appears as though he fell. Tried to walk maybe. There's a bruise on his chin. He's unconscious again. Help me get him on the bed."

Von took Paul's heels with Tate and Doc on either side. Together they laid him back on the cot.

The lights flickered twice and turned on.

"Camy to the rescue," Tate said, but there was worry in the pinch of his mouth.

Von checked Stella again to be sure she didn't have a laceration or bruise she was unaware of.

"Hannah…" Stella said.

"She's okay." He brushed a pine needle from her hair; the strands clung to his finger, impossibly soft. "I stopped there before I came here. She was sacked out with Zoe on duty. I promise."

She breathed out and nodded. "Okay."

He went to the porch and used his light to look closely at the branch. Stout as a man's arm and easily capable of crushing Stella's skull. Jaw clenched, he examined the end, which had been attached to the tree. The wood was twisted and sodden.

Had it been sent flying by the wind?

Or used as a weapon by someone hiding in the forest?

Abe Lincoln?

Von's gaze fastened on Doc through the open door.

First on scene.

Lost in the dark? Maybe. Maybe not. Would have been easy for him to pretend he'd just arrived, rather than struck out at Stella with the branch.

His phone buzzed. "Camy's on her way here. Let's get you inside while we wait." She followed him and she seemed steady but he kept his palm cradling her arm anyway until he settled her into a chair.

Von decided on a fishing expedition to extract some information. "Sorry about this, Doc. Not what you hoped for in a vacation."

Doc shook his head. "I didn't figure it would be. Team building exercises for a bunch of people who don't function as a team are a waste."

"You all don't get along?"

"About as well as the rest of the people in the big, wide world. Everyone's out for themselves." Doc removed a cigarette from his pocket and stuck it in his mouth. Von noticed his hand trembled.

"No smoking in the med tent."

"Of course. Filthy habit, right?" He shoved it back. "I don't know why we had to come here anyway. Paul's Mammoth property has plenty of space for corporate bonding or whatever it is we're supposed to be doing. The family home is luxurious. Two swimming pools and a bocce ball court. There was absolutely no need to come play around in the wilderness. No offense to what you all do here."

"None taken. I don't see why you all came, either."

Tate flicked Von a look as he applied an ice pack to the bump under Paul's chin. "We got a message from another person on the team, Lawrence Galleon, asking for a status report. He was supposed to arrive Thursday with the rest of the group."

Doc sniffed. "A lawyer. Doesn't even work on the site. Haven't even met him and I've been with Paul for thirty years."

"You must like working for Paul, though, huh?" Von turned off the lanterns and returned them to the shelf. "You've stuck with him."

"For decades. Watched his son grow up, if you can call it that. Paul's taken care of me over the years."

"Didn't want to maintain a private practice?"

Doc waved his unlit cigarette. "And miss out on all this?"

Camy hustled in with Flash. "Everybody okay?"

Her face tightened as Tate explained things. "Can I talk to you two on the porch for a second?" Whatever she needed to tell them wasn't good.

Stella shivered in the chair. He grabbed a folded blanket and draped it around her shoulders. Her eyes were wide, intense. "Von, I have to get back to the baby. I feel... I know she's fine, like you said, but I need to go soon. Please." Was that rising panic he heard in her voice?

Without thinking, he put his hand to her face and stroked it with his thumb, her cheek soft as down. "I understand, Ella. Couple more minutes, I promise. Can you wait that long?"

She inhaled and gave one quick nod.

His fingertips trailed down the back of her neck and before he realized it he'd pressed a kiss to her temple, his mouth lingering there as if his skin craved hers. His pulse scudded like a tempest-driven cloud. He was submerged with intense longing. To recapture their past? No, the longing was for the woman she'd become, this new person with strength and maturity and faith that fountained from her in an undiminishing supply. Absolutely not acceptable. Full stop right there.

What is wrong with you, Sharpe? He cleared his throat.

Tate and Camy had already stepped outside. He joined them. Camy's face said it all. Bad news loading.

He braced for it. "The generator?"

"An easy fix," she said. "Because it was functioning perfectly."

Tate scowled. "What?"

Her mouth tightened. "The cords were unplugged. That was all."

The quiver of instinct Von had experienced earlier turned into a roar. "Unplugged, as in on purpose."

"Uh-huh. I might buy that one had somehow wiggled its way loose from the socket, but not both. I plugged them in again and the fit is as tight as Auntie Flo's girdle. The generator was intentionally taken out of service."

Their twin gazes swiveled to Von.

"Abe Lincoln?" Camy said.

Von immediately sought Stella, catching her profile as she stood by the window.

Vulnerable.

Unprotected.

Plans whirred in his brain as a silent alarm blared. "We need to make arrangements. Then I'll do a thorough recon with Bear of the entire camp. If it is Abe Lincoln and he's managed to conceal himself, Bear will find him." His words landed like mini explosions.

Camy nodded. "First priority is Paul needs to be moved. Too exposed out here. If this was sabotage, someone may have been after him for some reason and Stella showed up at the wrong time."

Tate grimaced. "Or someone was following her, and his fall was unrelated."

"I'll provide increased security for Stella, Zoe and the baby," Von said.

"All right." Camy pursed her lips. "The med tent is too far from the dining hall. We should move him there. Set him and Tate up with whatever they need in the eating area and shove the tables into the rec room. Move any extras outside to free up space."

"Good plan. It's in view of the office building and I can see it from my tent. Tate will have Opie, and Bear can make it from my tent to the dining hall in sixty seconds."

Camy looked at her brother.

He shook his head. "Not ideal. All my equipment is…"

"No choice," Von said.

Tate stopped him. "I wasn't arguing. I'm saying it's going to require some effort."

"Then let's get moving. Oh, and can you do a quick once-over on a cat?"

Tate's eyes rounded. "I missed something. How'd we get a cat in the mix?"

"Stella found it and she's not one to see something suffer and I want to get her back to the dining hall immediately so I'm going to tell her you'll look at the cat real quick right now. Okay?"

"Okay. One cursory cat exam coming up, but disclaimer…we didn't spend a lot of time on feline anatomy in med training."

"Wing it." Von rattled off the second part. "I'll escort Stella to the hall and pick up the ATV. I'll come back for you and Paul. Supplies after that. Whatever you need, we'll transport it. Get you both situated in the hall."

Camy nodded. "Good. I'll head back with Flash on foot. We'll move furniture around to accommodate before I go explain to Bridget everything that's happened."

"Take a head count when you talk to her." Von's remark earned a sharp look from Tate.

Camy's quirked brow showed she understood his meaning. Bridget, Walker and Archie all had access to the med tent. As did Doc. Von shifted. And there was one more person unaccounted for.

Where exactly was Kip?

Chapter Thirteen

Von kept his arm around Stella as they walked, though she didn't seem to need the support. She was moving at a fast clip with the cat clutched to her chest. Tate had indicated gently that he wasn't sure the animal would survive. Stella ignored that part completely, like she'd ignored Von about the bird eggs long ago.

Doc hadn't appeared nonplussed about the plans to relocate. He'd grabbed a pile of blankets and set off on foot to the dining hall.

Von took advantage of the private moment with Stella. "Is there any way Doc could have tried to hit you with the branch?"

"Doc? Why would he do that?" She shook her head. "I'm sure that was an accident. Broke off from the trees and the wind carried it." Her lashes collected the falling flakes. "That's the most likely explanation, right?"

"Sure." He wasn't convinced but he could not bring himself to heap fear upon what she already carried. He'd handle the suspicion and gnaw on it until the bone was picked clean and any and all perpetrators were bagged. The magnitude of the problem was yet to be determined. The branch and Paul's fall could be purely random accidents. If they weren't, Abe Lincoln might be involved in some way—if he was alive—and if he hadn't gotten close enough for Bear to detect him.

The other alternative was much more dire. Barring an accident or Abe Lincoln, then there was another enemy at play.

One inside the camp.

Bear sensed his agitation and scanned the tree-lined path as they hurried along. The dining hall couldn't come into view fast enough. They hustled inside. Hannah was awake, Zoe bouncing her on her knee and singing something about a bus and wheels. Stella headed immediately to scoop the baby into her embrace. It was astonishing to see the bliss infuse her at the first moment of physical connection. It made sense to him now. Something happened to him, too, when he held Hannah. A thought that could wait to be examined at a later date.

Bear watched the reunion with his tail wagging and sure enough the dog looked happy to see the baby.

"Where's Kip?" he asked.

"Present," Kip said, entering from the porch. "What's going on?"

"Where have you been?"

Kip rubbed a hand along his head, bristled with gray tufts. "What do you mean? Here in camp, same as you."

"You went to the woodpile, and Stella couldn't find you."

"I didn't know she'd gone looking." Kip's brows furrowed. "Why does this sound like you're accusing me of something?"

"He's not..." Stella started, rocking the baby.

"How about an answer to the question?" Kip could call it an accusation if he wanted.

Kip returned Von's stare. The storm-filtered light accentuated the lines bracketing his mouth and the pouched cheeks. Was it sweat on his forehead? Von couldn't tell.

"Well, if you must know, I used the restroom in the shower

building. Needed a minute away instead of using the facilities here. The door jammed when I tried to leave and I spent a good fifteen minutes stuck inside until it finally gave and I was freed from my latrine prison."

"You didn't text anyone for help?"

"Would you? If you'd gotten stuck in the bathroom? And anyway, I forgot to charge the phone Camy gave me."

Von didn't reply.

"Your turn to talk," Kip said evenly. "What crime do you figure I'm guilty of?"

Von explained in under a minute what had transpired. He tried to read Kip's face but all he detected was confusion and fear. Concern for Stella? Von wasn't overly skilled at picking up nuances of truthfulness or lack thereof. The weather was exponentially easier to read than humans. He should have left the question to Camy, the former cop, but she was up to her ears in tending the camp. It was up to him to discern if Kip was involved. "Where's the log?"

"What log?"

"The one you went to fetch, before you got stuck in the latrine."

Kip glared. "I added it to the fire."

"He did," Zoe said, returning from the storage closet with a cardboard box. "I saw him."

Could have snagged it on the way back from the med tent. No good alibi there.

"But how did Paul fall out of bed?" Kip demanded.

Von started to move the largest table out onto the porch as Stella explained it all again to Kip with added details while Zoe took charge of the cat accommodations. When Camy arrived to take over the arrangements, he hustled to the ATV and returned to load up Tate, Paul and the first batch of supplies. He was hauling in the load from his second trip when Bridget, Archie and Walker arrived.

Bridget rushed to Tate, who was prepping Paul for a new IV.

Her hair was pulled back in a casual ponytail and he caught a glimpse of silver threading through the darker strands at her temples. One of her long nails was missing. "He fell out of bed?" she accused. "How could that have happened exactly?"

Walker didn't come close to the cot, Von noted. Instead, he slouched in the corner, hands in his pockets.

Tate was about to explain but Doc interrupted.

"It happened on my watch. He was sleeping soundly so I stepped out for a smoke."

Her lips went white. "A smoke? This is the kind of care you give him?"

"He'd been resting comfortably. I didn't think he required 24/7 observation."

Bridget's lips pinched into a tight knot. "He's been in a coma, not taking a refreshing afternoon nap. And you're supposed to be a doctor."

"I am a doctor, but I'm not here to run an ICU," Doc muttered.

Her eyes narrowed. "What are you here for, then? Oh, right. You're the lapdog."

Doc's mouth fell open, and he shut it with such force Von could hear the teeth snap together.

Interesting. Von hadn't realized there was that level of tension between Bridget and the doctor. Stella, Zoe and Kip were trying not to stare, but it was impossible to ignore the altercation. Tate had returned his attention to Paul. Interpersonal drama was not his cup of tea. Camy, on the other hand, was unabashedly taking in every syllable, like Von.

Archie eased a step closer. "Easy, Bridget. We're all on edge here. Not gettin' us anywhere gunning for each other. Like he said, Doc isn't an ER doctor."

"Correct. I'm paid as a personal physician," Doc finally said stiffly.

"You're paid to do a lot of things."

Bridget's last comment was low and laced with disdain, but Von caught it anyway. He had no doubt Tate and Camy had also. And all three had heard the doctor's reply. Paid to do what?

"You should know," Doc muttered.

Tate pulled off his rubber gloves and gestured to Bridget and Doc. "How about you folks go find something to eat or get a drink of water and let me do what's best for Paul right now?"

Bridget appeared to be about to fire off a retort to Tate, but Archie took her wrist and guided her away. "Normally, I don't insert myself in the Driscoll drama, but let the man do his work, huh?"

Bridget allowed Archie to lead her to a chair in the corner. Doc zipped his jacket. "I'll be in my tent if anyone needs me." The door banged behind him.

Stella walked to Von as he unloaded the last box for Tate.

"Everyone's unraveling," she whispered.

He nodded. "Longer we're stuck here the more that's likely to happen." He paused. "Gonna assign Bear to your cabin tonight."

"He should stay with you."

He was prepared for an argument. "You get me or the dog or both of us camped out on the porch of your tent. What's it gonna be?"

She opened her mouth, then closed it. "I, uh, all right. Bear it is."

Pleased with the victory, he pressed on. "Bear and I are going to check the campground, all of it. I'll be gone a while, probably until after dark."

"To be sure there's...no one hiding?" Her honey eyes were troubled, and he fought the urge to pull her close and fold their baby between them. The powerful need unsettled him. *You don't get to have that, Von. No second chances, remember?*

"Just to make sure it's all clear." Hannah blew a raspberry

and he laughed. She repeated it and he laughed again and poked her gently in the belly. "What are you doing? Trying to crack me up?"

Bear had drawn close, fixated as usual on the baby's shenanigans. When one of her socks went flying, he instantly pounced and brought it back.

Von reached for Hannah's foot. Those toes were the tiniest toes he'd ever seen. And why in the world did he want to kiss that miniature foot? After the sock was in place, he forced himself back a step, away from the intense connection that seemed inconceivable after only three days of knowing his daughter.

Stella jiggled her back and forth. "Please be careful, Von." It sounded so tender when she said it, like the days when he'd been her everything and she'd been his. He could almost feel again the intensity of her embrace when she thought he'd drowned.

"I will. And you'll be safe in the dining hall with Tate but don't go back to your tent. Right?"

"Right."

"Not for anything. If something comes up, send Kip."

She frowned. "You were too hard on him."

"I don't trust him."

"You don't trust anyone."

Anyone but you. What? Why should he trust her, this woman who had once upon a time accused him of cheating? Committed an epic lie of omission? Because he'd seen how she loved Hannah and that was the truest expression of devotion and courage that he'd ever seen. She'd learned how to love, like God wanted. Of that, he was certain.

And so the words came out.

"I trust you." It was a mumble, no more. Maybe she hadn't heard. He hoped so.

But she cocked her head in that way that made his stomach tighten and then fired off that smile, the one that zapped right to his heart. "Thank you. In view of everything that's occured, I'm surprised."

"Lot can happen in three days." Like his emotions turning him into a mush pot, for one. Hannah shot out a hand toward him and he snagged it, planting a kiss on fingers unbelievably soft and delicate. "Take care of Mommy."

They both stood shoulder to shoulder, looking at their daughter. Stella tilted her face to his.

Before he realized what he was doing, he'd kissed her lightly on the lips. The electricity sparked through him with such intensity that he jerked away. "I, uh, better get going." He didn't dare look at her as he strode outside with Bear into the cold, every nerve sizzling. He'd wondered if kissing Stella would feel the same as it had when they'd been engaged. It didn't.

It felt better.

There was a deep sensation of oneness, peace, a warmth he hadn't ever felt before, as if she were a beam of sun coaxing earth-covered seeds into life.

Things aren't different, he told himself. *You don't suddenly love someone because they tell you you're a parent.*

Parent. That was the word that explained his relationship with Stella, his new position in his own life. That was what would connect them, their twin roles as parents. He wasn't going to stay, nor did he want to, not in Cloud Top and certainly not in a relationship in which they'd both already failed. Co-parents only.

No more kisses.

As he tightened his collar against the cold, he dialed his phone and waited as patiently as he could until Legs answered.

Legs's voice was gravelly. "You are aware I've got a leveled town to deal with."

"You said you'd gotten reinforcements and I need you to check out a man who works for the Driscolls. He's their family doctor, Yanis Johnson."

"When I get a minute." He paused. "Von, what's going on in camp?"

"I'm not sure yet. We've had some incidents that don't sit right with me."

"I can't get anyone there right now."

"I wasn't asking you to. Information. Get it to me when you can."

"Roger that. Got an ID on your body in the river by the Opera House."

Von tensed.

"From out of state. Staying in town for hiking activities and got separated from his buddies by the quake. Doesn't sound like it's your guy."

Von bit back a sigh.

"Soon as this storm breaks we can land a medevac at your amphitheater."

"Tomorrow afternoon, possibly."

"Possibly? You're the weatherman. You tell me. Satellites say it's unsettled."

Satellite data was like shaking a box to guess what was inside. The whole point of his job was boots on the ground info, generating a "nowcast" rather than a half-formed forecast.

But he had none of his equipment. It was going to have to be a gut call. He peered at the sky and mentally filtered through the information he'd gotten from his basic tools that morning.

"Tomorrow afternoon," he said firmly.

"Have to be enough daylight to extract. Can't risk it at night."

"We'll have a window."

"There's the arrogant Von Sharpe I know and love. Watch your back, weatherman."

Too busy watching everyone else's. He clicked off.

After Bear had a refreshing whiff of the fabric he'd excised from Abe Lincoln's jacket, they started in. Now that he knew with certainty Abe Lincoln hadn't drowned after jumping from the roof, there was more urgency than ever to find out if he'd been in camp. It required several hours to scour the main campground itself, every tent, storage closet, the main trails in and out, the exterior of the dining hall and med tent again, to be thorough. There was an unused multiroom platform tent uphill behind the dining hall that they searched also. After Bear cleared a section, they moved on to the next. They finished up the main campground area ending with the stables.

The horses were out but they had the good sense to huddle together under the lean-to, tails swishing as they nosed the hay Archie must have put out for them. Walker stood near the paddock with his back to Von, both hands clutching his cell phone as he tapped out a text. Something about the tight way Walker was gripping the phone piqued Von's interest.

Walker glared at the screen. "Don't worry," he muttered as he stabbed out another text. "I know I owe you. You won't ever let me forget it."

Von stepped forward and Walker spun to face him. The color drained from his cheeks and he quickly shoved his phone into a pocket.

"Were you spying on me?"

"No. Bear and I are doing a security check." He decided Camy's rules about being conciliatory with the guests no longer applied. "You're upset. Who were you texting?"

"No one."

"That'd be a good trick to text no one."

"I…"

"What you mean to say is that it's none of my business, right?"

"Right."

Von kept up the unrelenting eye contact. "But if it's got something to do with keeping everybody safe here, then it is my business, see."

"It doesn't."

"Who do you owe, Walker?"

"I don't know what you mean."

He took a stab in the dark. "Does your dad know?"

Walker's face hardened, eyes glittering. "My dad doesn't know anything about me. He's never wanted to."

Archie strode over with a bucket of feed and greeted Walker and Von. "What brings you by, Mr. Sharpe?"

Von didn't see the sense in mincing words. "Checking the campground for our stalker."

He frowned. "Stalker? All I heard was that Paul fell out of bed. Did we have another incident?"

Nothing that he was going to jaw over with Archie. "Being cautious. Taking a look around for strangers."

"Haven't seen one. Only us campers." His grin faded as he regarded Walker's angry expression. "Have we got a problem?"

"No. If everyone would stay out of my business." With hunched shoulders, Walker shuffled off, the wind snatching at his long hair.

"Raincloud over his head," Von said.

"Kid's okay. He's had some family stuff is all."

"Like what?"

Archie hesitated before he answered. "You know, the usual never measuring up to your father's standards type thing. Paul's a hardnose. He shouldn't have tried to raise a kid. That's my opinion anyway. If I'd been in Paul's position, I'd have brought Walker up on a ranch, not a resort, where he'd learn how to be a proper man."

"Walker said he owes someone. What do you figure that's about?"

"I don't know. But it's probably something he doesn't want Paul to know. I don't blame him one bit. Paul can find creative ways to punish people."

"How so?"

Archie shrugged. "I probably shouldn't have started down this trail, but Paul's a piece of work. I remember when Walker

was fifteen he was really into basketball. He'd made the sophomore team, and he was on cloud nine. He got into some trouble
with his dad, I don't know what exactly, swiped some money or
a car maybe, and you know what Paul did? He made an enormous donation to the school to remodel the gym with the stip-
ulation that the construction be started right away. The school
wasn't about to say no and the gym was torn up. Basketball was
scuttled for the school year. Walker never picked it up again."

Von couldn't conceive of that cruel and covert manner of
discipline. With his dad it'd been chores and days spent cutting
everyone's lawns on the block when necessary. The time he'd
disrespected his mother he'd gotten both barrels of his father's
wrath and been grounded for a month. He'd raged about it,
but he'd never disrespected his mother again. After seeing the
disgust in his father's face he'd never wanted to.

Archie shook his head. "Amazing thing is Paul would fork
out millions just to punish Walker, and everyone thinks he's
some magnanimous benefactor instead of a world-class ma-
nipulator." Archie shook his head. "Walker got stuck with a
doozy of a dad but we don't get to pick our fathers, do we?" A
horse ambled over and Archie skimmed a palm over his flank.

A jolt rippled through him. *We don't get to pick our fathers.*

Hannah hadn't gotten to pick hers, either. What would she
think of him when she was Walker's age? That he'd been distant? Unavailable? Uninterested? Too hard on her? Expecting
her to live up to his ideas of success? His mouth went dry. He
wouldn't let that happen. He'd be there whenever he could,
however he could and he'd read books, he decided. Plenty of
books out there about how to raise well-adjusted kids, wasn't
there? But he still couldn't manage a proper swallow. "Horses
all getting along?"

"Better than the people."

He decided to press further. "Bridget doesn't seem to like
Doc much."

"I wouldn't know anything about that."

"You wouldn't? Being around the family for how many years? You must know plenty about Paul."

"Paul deserves what he gets, but even if I knew the family dirt about Bridget, I wouldn't dish it out. Not right to talk about a lady."

Von nodded. He respected a man who didn't impugn a woman's reputation.

"She's a good person. That's all you need to know."

"And Doc's the friendly family physician? Does he do anything else besides basic healthcare?"

"I don't have much to do with him, but he's in Paul's pocket for sure." Archie offered a handful from the bucket to the horse, who whisked it from his palm. "When do you think Paul's gonna make it to the hospital?"

"Tomorrow, if the weather cooperates. We'll get the road clear soon, too, unless there are more aftershocks to destabilize it." If Von had to take a shovel and do it himself, it'd get cleared.

"Good. No offense, but I'm done with this whole campground scenario."

Von left with Bear and expanded their search of the grounds. Almost six hours later they returned to the dining hall, cold to the bone and exhausted. Stella was asleep on the floor, curled around the baby. The bedraggled cat lay in the cardboard box, only its tail showing under a pile of blankets. Bear gave it a quick once-over, which didn't seem to bother the cat. Stella stirred when he entered and sat up.

"Are you okay?" she whispered.

He chuckled softly. "That's my line. Cold and hungry, but none the worse."

"Wait a minute. I saved you something."

While she went to the kitchen, he surveyed the room and tried to restore circulation to his wooden limbs. Tate sat in a camp chair next to Paul, chin on his chest, Opie curled at his feet. Zoe and Kip were on the porch where they'd gotten a respectable fire going. As he stared at the sleeping baby, the warmth began to eat through his chill, one painful twinge at a time. His knee was going to complain about their arduous day. Bear crept close to Hannah and shot a look at Von.

"Greet," he murmured. Normally, that would be a quick friendly sniff, which might be reciprocated by a pat or scratch from his new acquaintance.

But Bear immediately assumed the spot where Stella had lain, his furry side nestled next to the baby's. Von chuckled. "You know that's not your baby, right?"

Bear laid his head down and watched Hannah sleep.

Stella returned, holding a tray. Her eyes went wide at Bear. "Will he get upset if she bops him in her sleep or pulls his hair?"

"No, but if you're uncomfortable…"

She shook her head and pointed him into a chair in the corner. "We can watch them from there but I get the feeling nothing bad will happen to Hannah with Bear around."

He sat, stifling a groan. He didn't want to sound like an old man, but when she handed him a tray with a bowl of chili and two buttered cornbread muffins, he almost moaned aloud anyway.

"Bowl too hot?" she said.

"No. I'm having a chow appreciation moment. Bear will, too, when he's done with babysitting and he feels like eating. Thank you for saving me some."

"I used to save you dinner all the time when you worked late."

And that was practically every night toward the end of their engagement. The memory made him smile. "You never kept any dessert for me, though," he teased.

She waved him off. "I am not to be trusted around desserts, as you fully well know."

He laughed, watching the firelight fleck her hair with bronze.

Sitting with her, laughing with her, filled him from the inside out. Strange. All he wanted to do was stay next to her and watch their baby. The thought chimed an alarm bell somewhere deep. To keep himself from staring he spooned up some chili.

Tate roused, tiptoed over and made to grab Von's muffin.

"You will be down a finger if you try," Von said. He was instantly swamped with remorse. What if Hannah heard him say something like that? Would he have to spend the rest of his life filtering what came out of his mouth? All the brusqueness that came naturally to him? What was he worried about? She couldn't even talk yet.

Tate merely laughed, and Stella brought another muffin, which Tate leaned against the mantel and ate. Von was annoyed that Tate had interrupted. He'd wanted to savor the moment with Stella. They'd be few and far between when he returned to duty.

Tate was giving Stella a rundown on Paul's condition.

Von paused eating only to open a message on his voice mail. They were both eyeing him for a report when he finished listening. "Interesting. I checked Doc Johnson out with Legs. About thirty years ago he was in private practice and a woman accused him of botching her hernia surgery. The case was dismissed at the last moment and Doc went to work for Driscoll."

Tate arched a brow. "Think Paul paid somebody off and secured himself a doctor and a loyal lapdog?"

"Why bother? Paul could have any doctor he chose," Stella said.

Von thought it over. "Unless he wanted a personal physician he could ask to do things outside the lines."

"Like what?" Stella asked.

"Not sure. Tate?"

Tate wiped the crumbs off his shirt. "It might be useful to have someone in your pocket who could write prescriptions or supply medicines on demand. A doctor directly responsible for whatever happened on resort property."

The more Doc did that was on the shady side, the deeper Paul's hold on him would become. "Still doesn't give him any motive to harm his boss."

"I gather there was no sign of Abe Lincoln in camp," Tate said.

"None. I'm certain he hasn't been on the property." Which left Von conflicted. It hadn't been Abe Lincoln who swung a branch at Stella. An act of nature? Or another enemy not yet on his radar?

"If we could get some sort of ID, that'd go a long way," Tate said.

"I described him to Legs, but their systems are down."

His comment seemed to startle Stella.

"The photo." She disappeared for a moment and returned with the visitor bios that had been pinned to the kitchen wall. "This one, with Walker at the beach. I've been going bananas trying to figure out why Abe Lincoln seemed familiar."

Von and Tate looked at the photo where Stella pointed.

"This man in the background. It's fuzzy, but he...well, I mean I think... I could be wrong, but..."

Von touched her arm. "Trust your gut."

She blew out a breath. "I think he might be Abe Lincoln. Look at the shape of his chin, even though it's not clear."

He tapped on the porch window and crooked a finger at Zoe and Kip. They entered the dining hall. Stella showed Zoe the photo.

"You taught Walker's class, right? Do you know this person?"

Zoe shoved her glasses higher and peered. "Maybe. He's out of focus but..."

Von clamped his teeth together to keep from hurrying her.

"That could be Gus... I can't remember his last name. He

was kicked out his sophomore year for drug possession on campus, I believe."

Tate was texting Camy as they spoke.

"Were they friends? This Gus and Walker?" Von asked.

"I'm not sure, all I remember is I encountered Gus once in the parking lot after he was expelled. I told him he had to leave, and he laughed in my face. I was scared of him. Not sure what would have happened if another teacher hadn't walked by. Maybe I was overreacting, but I got this sensation in my spine that I should head for the hills."

Von was on his feet. "Walker knows this guy. Has to if they're in the photo together. I'm going to talk to him."

"Cool your jets, Von," Tate said. "It's almost eleven o'clock and accosting a guest without facts is a bad idea."

Von glared. "Now isn't the time to worry about your Yelp reviews." It was a cheap shot fueled by fatigue and frustration.

Tate went still. "I'm not suggesting we ignore it. Camy has internet access and she's going to dig us up some facts."

"That's not…"

He interrupted. "Facts, not supposition. All we have now is a blurry photo and a possible first name. When we know for sure that Gus and Walker were acquainted, or at least classmates, we can confront him."

Stella pinned the photo back on the wall after Tate and Von took pictures of it.

Von burned to march over to Walker's tent and get answers, but deep down he knew Tate was right. Walker would deny knowing the kid, say he was some random photobomber and they'd never get the truth.

That wasn't going to be the outcome.

Not if he and Bear had anything to say about it.

Bear twitched a nose in his direction before settling nearer to Hannah.

Von wished he could move closer to her.

It poked at him again that she might very well find another man someday. Someone who was there physically for every recital and soccer game, and emotionally available to raise a child with her, as a spouse, not just a parenting partner.

The thought flipped his stomach.

His child.

But not his Stella.

That was a picture he didn't want to see.

Chapter Fourteen

In spite of the tumult of the evening, Stella fell into a deep sleep until Bear's bark shot her upright. She had no idea the time, but the tent cabin was completely dark except for the lantern she'd left on the small camp table. By its light, she saw Bear standing near the rocking chair where she'd fallen asleep with her legs tucked up on the seat. There was a strange shimmering around him. The door was open, freezing air infiltrating the pocket of warmth. Bear tugged at her blanket, barking again.

How long had the door been ajar? The baby. Terror shot through her. She leaped from the chair, instantly plunged in a bone-chilling cold up to her midcalf. Her brain spun. Darkness, cold, Hannah. She fumbled for the lantern but it toppled over along with the table, disappearing with a splash. What was happening? Water, she finally understood. The tent was filling with water.

Her sudden lurch tumbled her forward and she fell on hands and knees in the ice bath until Bear yanked her upright. She splashed toward the cot where Hannah slept. The water level was rising rapidly. Had it already crept over her helpless infant? *Please, God. Please.*

"Zoe," she yelled as she slogged.

Zoe wasn't there. Stella vaguely remembered her aunt volunteering to fetch a warm bottle from the dining hall and check on the cat. "Help," she screamed.

Bear plunged ahead of Stella toward the cot. The flow was deepening, flooding in through the back corner of the tent, the weight of it pressing against her. Her foot impacted something and she went down on one knee, the intense cold clawing at her lungs.

Gasping, she struggled upright. What if she was too late? What if her baby had drowned? She floundered on.

Bear got to the cot first and blocked Stella's view.

In a blind panic she realized the water was as high as the top of Hannah's cot.

No. She couldn't be too late. *God, please don't take my baby.*

"Hannah," she screamed as she flopped forward. The cot was inundated, water inching upward to consume it.

But Bear had gotten there first, put his front paws on the mattress, clamped Hannah's pajamas in his mouth and hoisted her above the water. She wriggled and jerked but Bear held firm, teeth dug into her fleece so only one toe of her sleeper was dampened.

"Here, Bear, I'm here." Stella snagged the baby and Bear released his hold. She held Hannah as high as she could as the water swirled around her legs, sucking away her sensation until her limbs were frozen stumps. How long could she continue to keep Hannah dry when her arms were trembling? She had to get to the door but she could not fight the overwhelming numbness.

Bear shoved at her hip, trying to move her to the exit. He swam to her waist, biting at her jacket, attempting to tow her along. She forced one foot to move but her legs were failing, her grip on her daughter weakening. She was going to fall, drop Hannah into the water.

And then Von splashed inside. He tried to take the baby but she could not make her clawed fingers let go. She simply couldn't.

Instead, he hoisted them both, cradled them to his chest and shoved one boot in front of the other until they reached the door. The water continued to pour in, floating the chair she'd been sitting on until it wedged in the doorframe.

"Hold tight to me," Von said. With every bit of remaining strength she clung to his neck while he kicked at the chair. It wouldn't move. Bear barked and Von lashed out again. Once, twice… On the third try he succeeded in bashing the chair out of the way.

Outside, the path between their tents had turned into a swiftly moving current that was almost up to Von's knees. Bear surged along next to them. Hannah cried out, and she reveled in the sound.

"Where's Zoe?" Von shouted.

"She w-went to the d-dining hall."

Over Von's shoulder she deciphered that the water was coming from the river, which must have overwhelmed the sandbag wall. It had encircled Stella's tent cabin and was quickly engulfing Von's as well. Von stopped at his door, hooked a hand out and yanked it open. "Gear!"

The dog splashed inside and returned with Von's backpack. Von looped it over his shoulder and kept going. He carried them away from the river until the slope increased enough and the water shallowed out. He didn't put her down and she didn't offer. Her legs were trembling so badly she didn't think they'd support her.

The closest safe building was the office across the meadow and up a low hill. Von headed there. She could feel him straining for breath as he carried them. It was all she could do to clutch Hannah and pray that she hadn't gotten wet in the deluge. Every few steps Hannah would wriggle and voice her displeasure, barely audible as they rushed along, each sound a blessed reassurance. The way seemed endless, minutes ticking into eternities.

At the office Camy appeared, wearing sweatpants and obviously just woken when they slammed inside. "Water's breached the sandbags." Von settled Stella on a kitchen chair.

Camy's mouth dropped open. "How did that happen?"

"I don't know," he snapped.

"You said it would hold." The accusation threaded her words.

She saw the vein jump in Von's jaw. "I'll find out. But they need help."

Camy immediately texted Tate while Von knelt and took hold of Hannah. "Let go of her, honey."

She realized her fingers were knotted in Hannah's clothing. In an instant she was drowning in fear. "Von..." Her voice cracked in two. She was too afraid to look. The baby had gone quiet in the last few minutes. Or had it been longer? Time had blurred and twisted. What if...? Darkness seeped up from the past and flooded her senses. Bear shook himself in agitation, water droplets flying as he crowded close. He whined and barked until Von ordered him to sit.

With one hand on Hannah, Von put the other on Stella's face. "Look at me, Ella."

Unable to breathe, she focused on his wet hair, the exhaustion and fear, the scar next to his eyebrow from a long-ago car accident, the droplets spangling his lashes. "Hannah is moving and her eyes are open. As a matter of fact, she's yankin' on my beard."

She still could not force herself to look. What if he was wrong? Lying to protect her?

"Honey, let go. Trust me."

Trust me.

She forced her fingers to unclench, and Von removed the baby. It hurt as if he'd amputated her hand.

She hadn't seen Kip come in, but he appeared next to Von, handing over a dry blanket as Von carried Hannah to the sofa. He draped another over Stella's shoulders and squeezed her in a sideways hug.

Stella couldn't breathe, move. She wasn't even sure whether she was conscious or not until Hannah let loose with a big bellied chortle. Everything drained out of her in a huge rush except the exquisite relief.

"That's my brave girl," Von said. "You're right as rain, aren't you? Only a little damp from Mommy's clothes and a tiny bit of your sleeper got wet."

"B… Bear," she finally managed. "He held her above the water." Tears started down her frozen cheeks, but she could not feel them.

Von spared a look at his dog and it was filled with such love and loyalty that it was almost painful to witness. How she'd longed for that same look from Von. Maybe she was jealous of the easy affection he showered on his dog. She'd never be jealous again. Bear had demonstrated what unconditional love looked like. She loved him, too, now, every bit as deeply as Von did.

Von smiled at Bear. "You're the best. No question."

Bear whined, and Von allowed him to approach the baby. He bounded up, sniffing and licking her until she squealed and Von returned him to a sit.

Von turned to Kip. "Can you find Hannah something warm to wear from the dining hall? Tell everybody there to stay put until I assess." Kip nodded and jogged out. "Camy, text the guests and direct them to remain where they are until they're told otherwise."

"Already did. Fortunately, the dining hall and outer tents are high enough they're not going to flood so we can stage everybody there if necessary. Med tent is dry, too, so first aid supplies are secure." She gave Stella a once-over. "I've got something you can wear. "One sec." She was firing off more texts as she retreated.

Von moved close, repositioning Hannah so Stella could see her. He took a knee next to her chair. She longed to snatch Hannah into her arms, but her sodden situation prevented that.

"The kiddo is in mint condition, but unfortunately she's wide-awake." Von's smile faded. "How about you?"

"W-wide-awake, too." She couldn't produce a smile to reinforce the joke. "I was asleep and then all of a sudden…" She gulped and shivered. "If Bear hadn't been there…"

He squeezed her knee. "Then I would have. Either way."

She was surprised when Von let out a deep sigh and laid his forehead on her knee, the baby wrapped in a dry blanket in the crook of his arm, held away from his clothes so she wouldn't get wet. Stella reached out a hand to touch his rust-red hair, smoothing away the water droplets. With the other she stroked her daughter's. If only they could stay like that for a little while, the three of them, connected, safe, a solid trio that could withstand whatever life dished out.

But it wasn't what Von wanted.

Maybe she didn't, either. She was a different woman and part of her heart now traveled around outside her body with Hannah. Perhaps another part would always remain with Von, too. That would be enough to connect them.

Von stood and moved away before Camy returned from upstairs with Flash. The droopy dog meandered over toward Hannah and Von but Bear got between them. He wasn't aggressive, but he seemed to be saying, "No visitors for my baby at this time." Unperturbed, Flash contented himself by sniffing the puddles of water collected on the floor.

Stella slowly put her hand out to Bear and stroked his fur, hoping he could feel her gratitude. He had saved Hannah.

Lord, thank You for Bear.

And Von had made sure the dog was on duty.

And thank You for Von. On shaky legs, she hurried to the bathroom, hoping her body would not give out on her, and clumsily changed into dry clothes.

Kip returned, winded, and provided a warm bottle, a dry diaper and a pink baby sleeper. She reached for it, but Von intercepted it first, laid the baby on the tiny sofa and set about putting it on her, his movements tentative and awkward. She only had to correct him once when he was about to put the diaper on her backward. His intense concentration made her smile. He might as well be packing a parachute with all the gravity he applied to the task. He must've been freezing cold, wet up to the waist, but his hands were steady and his smile proud when he held her up for inspection. "Got her all sorted out. Ship shape, right?"

"Well-done, Sharpe," she said.

Camy tapped her phone. "Tate says Walker arrived looking for a midnight snack about forty-five minutes ago."

Von lost his smile. "Is that a firm timeline?"

"Tate can't be more specific since he was changing Paul's bandage. He's gotten texts from Bridget, the doc and Archie. Their tents are dry as expected. He reaffirmed they should hold in place until we give the all-clear. I'll go with you and we'll pray we can shore up the sandbags."

Kip held out his hands. "Sounds like you two have to go. I'll keep the fires burning here."

"No," Von started, then stopped. In her frozen state it took Stella a moment to decipher Von's hesitation. He didn't want to leave her and the baby alone with Kip, nor did he want to pull Tate from Paul's side. The waters were rising in more ways than one.

"Von," she said firmly.

With Hannah snug in dry clothes cradled in his arm, he turned to her, brow raised.

"You said you trust me."

"I do," he said.

"Then you need to believe me. I couldn't have made a good home for Hannah if it wasn't for Kip. He loves us both and he'd never hurt us. We're safe here with him."

Von started to argue, but she moved closer. "You know what—" she swallowed "—what happened at the birth. I was lost and Kip took care of me, of us. Believe me."

Would he? Put down his stubborn perception and accept her word?

His mouth worked as he considered. It was such an odd sight, Von, dwarfing the small room with his size, his scowl making him all the more formidable, holding their baby as she tugged a handful of his beard with gusto. Stella clutched the blanket Kip had given her and tried to control her shivering.

"Kip will watch over us," she insisted. "You need Camy's help. Go."

Kip sighed. "I got plenty of sins on my soul, but she's right, Von. I would never intentionally hurt her or the baby. On that, you have my word."

Von's scowl softened and he looked one more time at Stella. "All right." He gently prized Hannah's fingers from his beard before he handed her over and stepped away. "Bear's staying here, though."

Stella was too cold and wrung out to properly argue. "You need him."

"No. He's wet. He'll stay here with you and dry off. Alert if needed."

There was no arguing that point. Von towel dried Bear and ordered him to guard. The dog took up a position where he could see the doors and windows and track every move the humans made.

"Lock up," Von said to Kip.

She wanted to tell Von to change his clothes, but he'd be soaking in a matter of moments anyway. Thoughts of hypothermia left her short of breath. Kip used a tiny propane burner that Camy had brought to the office to fix her a cup of tea and took the baby while she drank it. Bear tensed a fraction when the baby changed hands, but he did not react.

She managed only a few sips before she took Hannah back, brushing her chin over the hair and breathing in the scent of her. Hannah was clearly wide-awake, as Von had said. No sense offering a bottle. Instead, she began a few choruses of Hannah's favorite songs. When her shivering slowed, she began to joggle Hannah in slow, soothing circles around the cramped room until she relaxed.

Settling on the sofa, she offered the bottle, which Hannah now accepted. Through the windows, the darkness seemed impenetrable. How would Camy and Von be able to see well enough to repair the place where the sandbags had failed? Or maybe they couldn't. What would happen then?

Kip was staring out the window, hands cupped so he could get a better look.

"What is it?"

He turned with an airy shrug. "Nothing. Nothing to worry about."

"You're a terrible liar."

The genial mask fell away and for a moment she got a glimpse of anguish underneath. "No, I'm a good liar. That's part of my problem."

She had the strangest feeling he was trying hard to conceal something. "Then why don't you tell me the truth? Even if it's something I don't want to hear? I meant what I told Von. I know that you love and care about me and Hannah and you wouldn't hurt us. Not on purpose."

"I…" He stopped, shook his head and returned to staring out the window.

"What do you see out there, Kip?"

"I may be mistaken, but it looks to me like the water's flowed down into the amphitheater."

"At least it's contained and the remaining tents are okay."

"Very positive attitude, considering you and the baby might have drowned."

She squelched a shiver. "I try very hard not to dwell in *what-ifs*." That would turn into a spiral of intrusive thoughts that would hold her hostage.

"You're right. I'm sorry. I forget how strong you are sometimes." He was weary; she read it in his drooped shoulders and the lines at the corners of his mouth.

He heaved out a breath. "This campground is rugged and hilly. Mountainous in many parts."

"Yes. That's part of the reason Ronnie loved it so much, Von said."

"Uh-huh. So the only good spot for landing a helicopter is the amphitheater."

The helicopter that was set to arrive as soon as the storm broke. She'd forgotten all about it. "And if the amphitheater is flooded…"

"There's no rescue coming, not by air anyway, and the roads are still blocked."

She felt the chill return. No rescue for Paul.

Or any of them. And she was still stranded and unable to flee if the person who shot Matt Smith was still alive and hunting. Bear shifted closer as she sat with Hannah on the couch. She sang softly and hoped to soothe them both.

When Hannah was asleep with a chair placed to keep her from rolling off, and Kip snoring, Stella was left to wander. An hour had passed without any word from Von or Camy, only a text from Tate checking in, she suspected to be sure she or Hannah weren't experiencing hypothermia. Tate wasn't the only one worried but she'd checked Hannah obsessively and found no signs of concern.

After another aimless loop around the room, she noticed Von's backpack where he'd left it in the corner. The bottom fabric was dark with moisture. A worn book protruded from the outside pocket, one she recognized instantly.

She wiggled it free. *Seeds of the World*, the guide to Von's beloved hobby that he'd consulted as long as she'd known him. At least she could lay the book open on the table and let the pages dry if it had gotten damp. As she fanned them open, she felt something heavy adhered to the back cover. She opened it.

A ring, her engagement ring, was wrapped in a bit of plastic and taped inside. For a moment she could do nothing but stare. With her fingertip, she felt the hard edge of the pink diamond solitaire and the gold band that had encircled her finger and meant the world. Memories crowded in.

They would have been married.

She would have been a bride. Her vision back then was awash in sparkling gowns, diamond rings, showers and honeymoons. They'd live that happily-ever-after life where romance colored every day and grief would never touch them. Oh, how naive she'd been, and how ignorant of the agony that lay around the corner. Love couldn't be enough without the bedrock of faith. She knew that now.

Why had Von kept the ring? Why not sell it? Shove it in a drawer somewhere?

Something else was taped on the previous page. It was a postcard from Yosemite. *Camp is gonna be awesome. Visit when you can.-R*

It was a message from Ronnie. And tucked underneath, the photo she'd given him of their son.

The three things secured there, reminders of love turned to ashes.

Her gruff ex fiancé.

So wounded.

So grieved.

The prayer came softly and silently as she returned the book to the pack.

Help him heal.

Von and Camy struggled to fill more bags to replace the ones that had been swept away. Fire burned inside him while cold blasted his outsides. He'd examined the sandbags and he knew the truth but there wasn't time to wrestle with it. They stopped to give their aching muscles a break.

"We can't continue much longer," Camy said as they trudged back for more sand. It was heavy with moisture now, like shoveling rocks.

He didn't want to agree, but he knew he had to. He could hardly grip the shovel. At least the snow had slackened, but the water was excruciatingly cold when they heaved on the sandbags and there was no way to avoid being splashed as they climbed on the submerged ones and piled new on top.

If they let the water continue to overflow, it was certain to inundate the amphitheater to the point where it would be inaccessible to the helicopter. Who was he kidding? It might already be too late, but he couldn't accept that. If there was a chance they could keep even part of the amphitheater dry... He tried to force his quivering muscles to obey, but the shovel fell from his fumbling hands. Muttering, he bent to retrieve it.

Camy gasped. "Reinforcements."

Von snapped around to find Archie and Walker, bundled in jackets and ski hats, standing at the edge of the sand pile. Surprise didn't quite capture the level of Von's astonishment. "What are you doing here?"

"Tate said you were still working. Figured if you hadn't gotten things under control yet, you probably weren't gonna unless you had some extra muscle." Archie jerked a thumb at Walker. "Young buck volunteered, too."

Walker was hunched in his jacket, not exactly brimming with

enthusiasm. In light of their suspicion about Gus and Walker being friends, Von couldn't decide on a motive for Walker that made sense. He was still trying to work out what to say when Camy handed him a shovel. "Now we have a chance."

Archie and Walker worked in tandem, faster than Camy and Von, who were clumsy with cold. They gradually closed the gap and in another hour they'd sealed off the bank. All four of them were soaked to the skin.

"We're done," Camy said. "Into dry clothes, pronto."

Archie clapped Walker on the back. "That's stepping up in man shoes, son." The comment teased a smile from the shivering Walker.

"There will be hot cocoa in the dining hall after you're changed if you want. I'll have Tate load up the fire. No hot showers yet, but at least we can provide warm beverages."

Archie and Walker hurried off into the darkness. He and Camy took the path back to the office, each step a painful effort. When they made it back, Stella's gaze searched them both. She had the heater blasting and the microwave heating something. Kip was awake and alert as he'd promised. Bear welcomed him.

"Did you fix it?" Kip said.

Stella shushed him in a mom voice. "Change of clothes first. They don't say a word until they're dry."

His hands were flabby and useless as he tried to unzip his pack. Stella took over, pulling out a sealed plastic bag of clothing. "Here."

He grabbed it with an awkward lurch. She chafed his arms with her hands. He could not actually feel anything but a slight pressure, but having her closer infused a bit of strength into him. He staggered to the bathroom and managed to pull off the pants and get the new ones on, but his arms wouldn't lift high enough to put on the dry sweatshirt. He felt like headbutting the door. There was a tap and it opened.

Kip. "Stella is helping Camy. I…thought you might need a thawed set of hands."

No, I don't. But his arrogance and stubbornness were outstripped by the truth. "C-can't get my shirt on."

Kip immediately stepped in, tugged the garment over Von's shoulders. "We'll do socks and boots at the table."

Like a helpless child, Von stumbled after Kip, landing on the chair where Kip threw a blanket around his shoulders that he'd somehow warmed, maybe on the heating vent. Von's body went into full-on shiver mode. Kip rolled dry socks onto his feet and the spare pair of boots Von always kept in his go bag.

"See there? I'm not an altogether bad guy." He sighed. "I'm trying to live better, be better."

"Th-thanks." Von couldn't say more. He glanced at Hannah, sleeping soundly, Bear attentive of his charge.

Stella and Camy returned. Camy's lips were still tinged blue, as he suspected his were. Stella piloted Camy into a chair across from him where they shivered together. Mugs of hot liquid were produced, he couldn't tell if it was coffee or tea, and his palms shook too much to grasp it. Stella held the mug for him to sip. Agonizing minutes passed as life crept back into his body, one stinging millimeter at a time.

Camy spoke first. "We'll have to wait until daybreak to see if the amphitheater is accessible."

"Bad timing," Kip said. "To have the wall fail."

"It didn't, not by itself."

They all stared at Von.

"Center bags were slit with a knife. When the sand poured out, the wall caved."

"A knife?" The muscles in Stella's throat convulsed in a swallow. "Sabotage?"

"Yes." The placement of the breach told him it was meant to cause flooding both to the amphitheater and Stella's tent. Bear hadn't alerted to Abe Lincoln's presence, which meant either the storm had hidden his actions, or one of their very own happy campers was the culprit. He knew they were all mulling over those possibilities.

For a moment there was only the sound of the wind driving against the window.

"Plan?" Camy said. "Obviously, the first is to get Stella, Hannah and Zoe somewhere dry and protected. We can pile everyone in here…"

"Too crowded. I was thinking the empty tent behind the dining hall. It's got multiple rooms. I'll run an extension from the generator to power lights and heat." It was also up higher than the office, which would afford him and Bear a better view of any approaching threats.

"Okay." Camy was trying to tap out messages to Tate. "At sunup I'll check about helicopter access. In the meantime, we'll update Legs and tell him we need police backup as soon as they can swing it. I'll do a sweep when I warm up and keep watch tonight."

He looked at Stella. "She's right. We have a confirmed threat in camp now. No one goes anywhere alone."

She nodded, face tight with fear. Kip placed a palm on her shoulder. It should have irritated Von, but he found it didn't for some reason. Kip had or hadn't changed, but something in Von must have.

"We're almost out of the woods." Von forced a lighter tone. "Matter of hours before access is restored." *Hours left for someone to try again to kill Stella.* "I'll get the generator heating the tent, and then I'll come for you."

Stella didn't answer. She'd gone to gaze out the window. Painfully, he got to his feet and approached her. His hands were still cold, so he gently rested his head on her shoulder. "Gonna be okay, Ella." She reached up and stroked his beard, her fingers toying with the fuzz like Hannah did. In spite of his earlier vow, he brushed his lips against her cheek, a kiss of encouragement for them both. And then he levered himself out the door, this time with Bear, since Camy was recovered enough to take over watch. She was already powering up her laptop. "While I'm warming up, I'm going to try the internet to dig up info on Gus and Walker."

In the dining hall he secured an extension cord to run to the tent.

"Do I get to check you for hypothermia and frostbite?" Tate asked.

"No."

"Figured. Camy?"

"She's good, far as I can tell."

"Doesn't reassure me."

He grabbed the diaper bag, extra blankets and the rocking chair, determined not to let Tate see his lingering clumsiness. "I'll move Zoe, Stella and Hannah with me. Baby's gonna need some rocking," he said by way of explanation for taking the chair. He didn't wait for Tate to reply before he hauled the items up to their new location, mulling over the possibilities. Abe Lincoln, Archie, Walker, Bridget, Doc. Who had the opportunity to slit the sandbags? Probably all of them. But which had a motive to flood Stella's tent? Ruin the chances for a helicopter rescue for Paul?

Archie and Walker had shown up to help shovel sand. Did that mean they weren't involved? Not in his book. They'd arrived an hour after the repairs were in progress. Could be a diversion to make themselves appear innocent as the proverbial driven snow. Would they work together?

Bridget and Walker were likely Paul's heirs, so he could see their motive for wanting to see that Paul died before help arrived. Maybe they'd even knocked him out in the med tent, and Stella had arrived at the wrong moment.

But what did it have to do with Matt Smith and the shooter

who'd tried twice now to kill Stella? Maybe a third if he'd been involved in the flooding?

A headache punched his temples as he hooked up the extension cord and turned on the heater in the tent cabin. The place smelled of dust and age but there was nothing to be done about that. There was a private room on either side and a central communal area. Perfect setup to monitor Stella, Zoe and Hannah all at once.

He put blankets on both beds and bottles of water in each room. There was no mattress on the space he'd occupy, but he'd make do with a couple of blankets once he told his knee to clam up with the complaining.

The fact was he was on the edge of nauseated, his body barely going along with his brain. Though he wasn't thirsty, he forced himself to drain a bottle of water, overriding his stomach's rebellion at the addition of anything cold.

Camy was her usual intense self when he returned to the office, he was happy to note. She wasted no time getting down to business.

"Finally got a text back from the principal. Gus, last name Richardson, was enrolled at Cloud Top High as a sophomore the same year Walker attended but he was expelled after four months for drug possession like you told me Zoe remembered."

He perked up. Now they had a last name. Immediately, he texted it to Legs. "Any proof that he knew Walker?"

"Nothing concrete, but I did find an online yearbook photo that shows them both in shop class. See?" She pointed to the screen. Stella moved closer with Kip and they all examined the photo. Two young guys, amid a half dozen others, holding wrenches and all smiling. Gus's arm was looped around Walker's neck.

"They look pretty chummy to me," Von said.

"Not proof. But suggestive. I'll interview him tomorrow."

"I want to be in on it."

"Agreed, but you'll let me do the talking. Retired cops outweigh weathermen in this case."

Her tone brooked no argument so he nodded and turned to Stella. "Are you okay to go to the new tent?"

She nodded but there was something tight and coiled about the way she held herself. Before he could act, she'd scooped up the baby. At least he managed to get the door and send Bear in recon mode before they made it outside. She moved quickly and he kept up in spite of the ache in every single one of his muscles. Zoe was ready at the dining hall and joined them in walking to their new shelter. He was pleased that the main area was warm when they entered. He checked the room, to be extra cautious, and used his night binocs to scan the campground. Nothing out of place.

Stella immediately put Hannah down to sleep on the bed, drawing the chair close to keep her from rolling out. Her brisk, "Good night," let him know she was done with his presence. Had he said something wrong? Been too pushy or overbearing? Maybe it was the Kip thing, the way he'd telegraphed distrust until she put her foot down.

Mostly, he didn't much ponder how he came across to people, but with Stella it was different. Zoe, too, went to her tent room and he heard the squeak of her cot. He poured water for Bear and gave him a handful of treats along with his bowl of kibble. Dog deserved a T-bone and a featherbed.

Though he should be resting, too, he knew he wasn't going to fall asleep anytime soon. Not with what he knew. Exhaustion rendered his thoughts fuzzy and unsettled. There was an energy drink in his pack. He rifled through and picked it up. But he'd told Stella he wouldn't drink them.

She wouldn't know. He stared at the can.

But he couldn't lie and someday tell his baby that lying was wrong.

Is this the way it's gonna be? Every choice, good or bad, an example for his child? Would he have to tell her someday how he'd failed his brother? That left him even more exhausted. The blankets on the floor promised to be anything but comfortable. He eased carefully into the rocking chair instead, listening to the sounds of the windblown snow. His gaze traveled to the stout beam above the door. Carved into the wood was an R and an S. Ronnie Sharpe. It hit him like a blow that this was the original tent structure Ronnie had installed on the property, the beginning of his dream.

Why didn't I come when you were dying?

He flashed on the memory of his mother lying still and white in the bedroom of their house. His father's trembling hands as he'd grabbed the phone to summon help. The light had gone out of their family then, though he hadn't realized it. That moment was pressed into his psyche, like a knife plunged into a slab of clay. But it had been imprinted on Ronnie, too.

Never want to be cracked open like that again, Ronnie had said years later as they fished together off a rotted pier.

Funny how he'd forgotten his brother's remark until that moment.

Ronnie'd lived it, also, the sudden loss of their mother.

Could Tate be right? That Ronnie would have understood?

And if so, was there a possibility that Von could let go of the punishing guilt?

A whimper caught his attention.

Bear's ears arrowed up.

He listened to a second small cry, but it wasn't Hannah. He went to Stella's door and tapped.

"Ella?" he said softly. "Everything all right?" When she didn't answer he pushed it open a crack. She was sitting on the bed, hands balled into fists against her chest, as if she'd been struck. He hesitantly entered, Bear inviting himself along.

Her breath was coming in and out in shuddering waves. With a jolt he moved closer, frantically scanning the baby, but

Hannah's eyes were closed, her respirations steady and smooth. Quickly placing his hand on her tummy confirmed what his senses told him. The baby was perfectly fine.

Stella was not. She panted, tears running down her face as she began to rock back and forth. Bear was confused, too. Von tried to touch her but she recoiled. He should get somebody. Tate maybe. Zoe.

"Stella, tell me what's wrong."

The tears fountained down, wetting her borrowed sweatshirt as she stared at Hannah. "She'll get hurt. She'll die. I won't be able to stop it."

After a few seconds, he understood. It wasn't about this moment; it was about all the moments, the terrifying ones in camp and on the mountain and those that had taken place with Daniel. She'd faced them all.

Kneeling, he tried again to make contact, grazing his finger light as a breeze on her wrist. When she didn't pull away, he stroked the back of her hand and bent to look in her eyes. "Hannah is okay. I know you're scared, but she's safe."

Stella shook her head violently, unseeing, deep in the grip of the panic attack. Her breaths were sharp and shallow. "I won't be able to protect her. She'll die, like her brother."

Vaguely, he remembered something Tate had told him about panic, how feeling something solid could be helpful. With slight but steady pressure he pulled her up and guided her to the floor, scooting her back to the banged-up dresser until he was sure she could feel the wood surface behind her. They were only feet from the bed where she could see Hannah clearly.

Her sobs strung together into a wail. Zoe poked her head in. His heart leaped. Zoe would know what to do. He opened his mouth to ask her in, then stopped. Hannah was their baby and Stella was her mother and that made both of them his to soothe. He was going to stand and face it, for her, and him and them.

With a jerky nod, he gave Zoe an "I got this" look and she slowly closed the door again. Part of him longed to go with her.

Stella was still crying, so clearly his plan wasn't working so far. "Hannah is safe," he repeated.

Stella bit her lip so hard he thought it might bleed. *Do something, Von.*

"Close watch," he ordered Bear.

The dog was moving before Von finished. He leaped onto the mattress, sitting erect and alert inches from Hannah's toes. Nothing and no one would hurt Hannah. Now, if he could only convince Stella. He lowered himself onto the floor next to her and gingerly took her hand.

"Bear and I are going to stay right here until you feel better. We'll just breathe together, slow and easy."

The minutes passed.

There might be a blizzard blowing outside, or another earthquake ready to knock the whole place down, a killer stalking outside, but his whole world at that moment was the slow breaths they took together, fighting away her panic with each exhalation.

He moved only once, in a bone-popping stretch that enabled him to reach a tissue box and extract one. She took it with a whispered, "Thank you."

Progress. She mopped her face and they kept on with the breathing. When her crying slowed and stopped, she blew her nose.

"I'm sorry." Her voice was barely audible. "I've…had some problems with fear, since…"

He nestled his shoulder to hers. "You don't need to be sorry, honey. No one on this green spinning planet could handle everything that you've endured without some trauma."

She kept staring at Hannah. "I deal with fear every day and mostly I win."

"Yes, you do."

"But sometimes I can't stop myself from going back to what happened with Daniel."

He brought her hand to his mouth and kissed her knuckles. "I'm no expert, but that sounds perfectly natural to me."

She offered a watery smile. "The worst thing isn't the fear or wondering if I'm doing everything right for her…"

He waited for her to continue but she didn't.

"It's okay. You can say it." He desperately yearned to be that safe place where she could empty herself of the burden she carried.

She gulped and a new tear fell. "It's that I have guilt about being joyful."

It wasn't what he'd expected to hear. "Guilt?"

"Hannah is perfect, the greatest blessing God ever gave me, but I sometimes can't look at her without remembering losing her twin brother. I feel joy, and then I remember I shouldn't."

He got it and the old ache flared up. "I guess I'm the perfect person to understand guilt. Everywhere I look around this camp I see Ronnie and I remember that I didn't come when I should have." And he hadn't been there for his son, either, nor Stella. "Difference is you did nothing wrong. I'm…" His voice cracked and Bear tilted an ear in his direction. "I'm sorry I wasn't with you when it happened."

"I didn't tell you."

"I gave you reasons not to." He gripped her hand. "Doesn't mean you made the right choice by keeping it from me, but I don't know if I would have handled it well anyway. I don't have a great track record." An unexpected moisture collected under his lashes. "I'm sorry."

"Me, too."

Her fingers, laced through his, felt like a perfect fit. "How…?" he stopped.

She looked at him. "What?"

"How did you…know how to be a mother?"

"I'm not sure what you're asking."

"Before, when we were engaged, you seemed so young and impulsive and now since you had Hannah, it's like you just know how to give her what she needs."

Her gaze went to Hannah. "I don't know, a lot of the time, but God gave her to me so I think He's helping me learn along the way."

Bitterness coated his tongue. "And He took another child from you. I don't get why that doesn't make you angry." He was horrified at what he'd said.

She stared at their linked hands. "Even if He'd taken them both, I'd still consider myself blessed."

Her comment landed like a boulder rolling down a mountain peak. How could she think that? Believe it? "I can't understand that. The blessing part yes, but Daniel died before you... we...got to know him."

"That doesn't mean he wasn't a blessing." She reached up to brush a tear from his cheek that he hadn't known was there. "Von, I loved both our children with every last breath, but God loves them more." She paused. "He loved Ronnie that much, too, in a more perfect way than you could."

Von shook his head. He'd been angry, hardened, scorched, by his brother's death. If God loved Ronnie, He'd have let him live. If God loved Von, He'd have made him strong enough to show up.

"I was afraid to be there." Von's voice was hoarse. "I was too scared to watch my brother die. I was in Germany at the time but I could have gotten leave if I'd asked. I knew it was coming with the info Tate provided and I was too much of a coward to face it." A truth he'd never uttered to another living soul. She didn't flinch or withdraw from him in disgust or disappointment.

"I wouldn't have faced what I did, either, if I'd had a choice," she said. "The only difference is I didn't have one."

He was so grateful that he hadn't seen his loathing reflected back at him in her eyes. How could she be like that? Love like that? Endure what she had? She was wiser and more breathtakingly gracious than he'd ever be. In that instant he longed to have her peace. "I wish I was a better man." It was as if the desire came shouting from every cell. A better man who could be a good husband and father.

"You're getting better every day, Von Sharpe. And now you have a chance to start fresh with a baby."

Another chance? To love better? To be better? Was God giving him that?

Instead of talking he pulled her close and tipped his cheek onto the top of her head. Together, sitting on the worn plank floor, they watched their baby sleep.

Chapter Fifteen

She vaguely remembered Von helping her into the bed, covering her with two blankets, Bear curled up in the corner watching Hannah. The pouring out of her panic and grief drained her to the point where she could hardly force her eyes open when Hannah cried at some point during the night.

"You sleep. I got this," Von whispered.

She hadn't known he'd stayed there, sitting on the floor, but he eased Hannah from the mattress and put her to his broad shoulder. Too early for a bottle, she thought. Probably she needed to be soothed and allowed to fall back asleep, but Stella found herself too exhausted to utter one iota of advice. All she could do was watch through slitted eyes as Von marched in precise loops over the floor, patting Hannah on the back.

When Hannah whimpered, he laid her on the foot of the mattress and changed her diaper, holding the clean one up to catch the lantern light before he applied it correctly this time.

"That was a good pee," Von whispered. "Very productive. You have champion kidneys."

Stella smiled.

Von began another series of loops and back patting, and when Hannah wouldn't settle he began to quietly chant a military marching cadence.

"Took away my faded shoes, now I'm wearing air force blues," he murmured, executing a tight-heeled reverse when he reached the tent wall. "Baby, baby, can't you see, what encampment's done for me?" After another snappy turn he continued. "Standing tall and looking good, you oughta be in Hollywood."

If she'd had the energy she would have laughed heartily, until sadness took over. This was Von, the man who could not consider himself whole without his duty. It nourished and defined him. And that was the important thing she'd learned along these unsettled eighteen months they'd been apart. He didn't like who he was, what he'd done, how he'd failed. He thought all he had was his profession.

She could not be what Von needed.

And he needed his job more than he needed them. She'd learn to accept it. No matter what the future held, Von was trying to be a father the best way he knew how. That was an offering she would always treasure. He would give what he could, with what he had.

When he laid the baby, sound asleep, next to her, she pretended to be sleeping, too. She felt the brush of his lips on her forehead before he retreated.

Mission accomplished, Von. Good night.

The next morning Kip brought a warm bottle for Hannah from the dining hall and cups of fruit juice for Zoe and Stella. Von and Camy were in deep conversation when Stella emerged in the communal area.

Von gave her a half smile and pointed.

She had not realized he'd brought the rocking chair over. Cheeks warm, she nodded gratefully and settled in with the baby and bottle. Bear was instantly at her side, observing every suck and swallow.

"I didn't see any signs of an intruder on the property at all." Camy leaned close and offered Von her phone. "Tate sent up the drone. Here's the footage I relayed to Legs and his team. The decision is the northwest corner of the amphitheater is accessible enough for a chopper to hover and they'll take Paul up in a basket. We'll have to transport him there and be ready, though, so it will be a hike. They figure we'll have a weather window in about an hour. Do you concur?"

Von nodded. "Storm should abate by then. Everyone ready?"

"Tate's good to go. I explained to Bridget that she won't be allowed on the chopper. Doc pushed to go along but that isn't permitted even if he is an MD. They're both consoling themselves with raisin toast at the moment."

Von's stomach growled. "Toast sounds good."

"Yes, it does," Zoe said. "And we've got to take care of our feline camper who needs breakfast, too."

He turned to Stella. "I'd like you and Hannah to stay here while I'm gone." She knew why. He didn't trust the other campers. "Is that okay? Bear will be with you," he hurried to add.

"And me and Kip, too," Zoe said.

He was treating her as if she was made of porcelain again. Recollecting her massive panic attack the night before made her squirm. "Yes. Of course."

He nodded and turned to Camy. "Can you…?"

"Yes," she said. "I'll climb to the roof of the dining hall and watch your progress with binoculars. You and Tate can handle the transport with help?"

"We'll need to recruit," Von said.

They moved en masse to the dining hall where they found Bridget sitting next to Paul. Camy opened her laptop at the wooden table while Zoe offered the cat some milk in the dish. Bear, Opie and Flash watched the cat lap it up.

"That feline's got some nerve," Tate said, "with all these dogs watching."

Zoe chuckled. "That's probably why he survived the quake and the cold."

"We should name him Hercules or something heroic like that." Kip helped himself to a slice of toast.

Von looked around. "Where's Walker?"

"Sleeping," Archie said. "He'll be along when his stomach wakes up."

Von didn't reply but Stella knew he wasn't going to be put off much longer from interrogating the young man about his connection to Abe Lincoln no matter what Camy said. She fetched the plate she'd fixed for Hannah the previous day.

The baby grabbed a handful of rice puffs and crammed them into her mouth at once.

Von grinned. "I feel hungry as a bear, too." He took a huge bite of his toast. Stella wanted to relax and enjoy the warmth and the relief that Paul would soon be delivered to the hospital where he belonged, but thoughts tumbled through her mind, the tent flooding with water, Abe Lincoln jumping off the roof of the old theater, the fractured earth all around them. It would all be over soon, in a matter of hours maybe.

And Von would be gone.

And she'd be alone again.

Not alone. Quit all this emotional stewing. She took a slice of raisin toast and forced it down. She was reaching for a glass of water when the liquid sloshed and the windows rattled.

Her stomach knotted. Another quake. She clung to the table. Von made it to her side. With one arm, he bundled Hannah to his shoulder, the other urging Stella to her feet.

"Get under the table," Camy shouted. The guests complied. Tate ran to Paul. Opie followed. Glasses shook themselves off the table and smashed onto the floor. There was no room left underneath so Von guided Stella to the edge of the room, pressed against the wall where the roof would be less likely to fail. Bear followed. Von caged her and Hannah with his body, prepared to deflect any debris. Zoe and Kip held on to each other from their spot in the doorway.

Stella clung to his arm.

Von tightened his grip on her. "We'll be okay."

Hannah cried.

"Daddy's got you," he murmured.

Another sharp jolt would have thrown Stella to her knees if Von hadn't anchored her against his strong side.

Abruptly, the shaking stopped.

It left her breathless. He kept up steady pressure on her fingers. "It's gone."

Hannah fussed. Von handed her over. "Stay here for a minute, just to be sure." He hastened to the table to help the guests crawl out.

"Aftershock," Tate said. "A doozy."

Stella felt as if the floor was swaying. In spite of his reassurance, Von, too, was alert, waiting to see what would follow. Was there more coming? The room remained still except for the lazy swish of the plaid curtains. Camy swept up the glass. Gradually, the group resumed their seats. Stella tried, but her nerves felt like hot coals that could burst into flame at any moment.

"While I have your attention," Camy said wryly, "I'm going to ask that everyone stick close to the main structures."

Doc's dark eyes narrowed. "Why?"

"Due to the flood, there's a wide area of ground that's been saturated, and the quakes only unbalance things more. We need to be cautious of liquefaction."

"What might that be, exactly?" Archie stopped with a slice of bread halfway to his mouth.

"Short story is the ground turns to liquid," Von explained.

Archie grimaced. "Liquid ground? Sounds nasty."

"It is," Von said. "Aftershocks make things worse."

Camy returned her attention to her laptop. A minute later she pumped a fist in the air. "Score. The national guard is going to begin clearing the roads starting this morning."

Bridget looked up. "We'll be able to get out of here?"

"Soon as they can get past the slide, unless that bonus quake changed any of their plans." Camy blew out a breath. "Finally."

Archie applauded. Stella watched Bridget. Her brows crimped, lips thin. "Back to life as we knew it," she said softly, staring at Paul. Her gaze wandered to her son.

"We'll arrange transport for you and Walker to the hospital," Camy said.

Bridget didn't answer. What was her expression communicating? Sadness? Fear? Resentment? Archie looked as though he was trying to decipher it, too.

Doc stared at Bridget.

"We'll need your help." Von aimed the words at Archie and Doc.

Doc started. "Help? Oh, you mean moving Paul?"

"Yes. We're gonna have to do it on foot with the stretcher. Skirt the amphitheater and take the long way around."

Doc's eyes rolled in thought. "I've got a back problem. Bulging disc."

"You can carry the IV and gear, then," Tate said.

Doc nodded.

Archie hesitated. "I guess I'm in no position to decline. Will you be okay here by yourself, Bridget?"

"Walker can join her." Von smirked. "When he wakes up."

Stella noted that Doc did not offer to keep Bridget company. He merely picked up his toast and a cup of coffee.

Archie slugged some of the strong brew. "All right. I'll go roust Walker and meet you back here in ten."

Von helped Tate load Paul onto the stretcher. When Archie returned, they took it up and headed for the door.

"Probably take us about an hour to make the round trip. Stay inside, okay?" His eyes shimmered with intensity; she'd never forgotten how they reminded her of the Yosemite sky before a storm.

Again, she fought the urge to tell him to be careful.

You've got no claim on him.

But Hannah does, doesn't she? Didn't Stella have the right to worry on behalf of her daughter?

When they'd gone, she took the radio Camy offered, scooped Hannah up and returned to her tent with Kip and Zoe. Bear was practically welded to her hip.

At the thirty-minute mark, she heard the *thwop* of rotor blades in the distance, and they all crowded to the window openings to see. A helicopter hovered, backed by iron-gray clouds, until a man in a jumpsuit was lowered down, standing on a litter. Stella realized she was holding her breath.

After an interminable wait, the litter was raised up again with the medic steadying the rig until both were loaded again into the helicopter.

"What a relief..." Kip said. His words were lost in a series of deafening pops.

Simultaneously, her radio crackled. "Shooter!" came Camy's desperate cry.

Bear barked and yanked her to the floor so abruptly she almost dropped the baby. "Get down," she called to Zoe and Kip as a row of bullet holes punched through the canvas walls.

Shooter. As soon as Von heard Camy's radio traffic he took off at a sprint, leaving Tate, Archie and Doc staring after him.

How? He'd scoured the camp with Bear. How had Gus known the moment they'd be farthest away? Walker had to be feeding him information. He ran as fast as the sodden ground would allow, sticking to the spots that wouldn't suck his boots into the mire. His body flooded with jolts of electricity as more shots pierced the air.

Bear's with them.

They'll be okay.

But the dog couldn't protect them from a shooter taking aim from the woods.

"What've you got, Camy?" he shouted as he floundered through a deep pocket of snow.

"Flash and I are making our way to their tent, but we need cover. Saw the gun for a moment. It's an old Remington twenty-four rifle. He's got from eleven to fourteen rounds before he's gonna have to reload."

Camy was right about the weapon; he had no doubt. She and Ronnie were gun history enthusiasts. He cleared the edge of the amphitheater, which opened him up to fire. Since he was a big target, moving quickly, the shooter changed trajectories. A bullet whizzed past his temple and he crouched and zigzagged as best he could. "How many?"

"By my count that's eleven."

Anywhere from one to three shots to go before the reload. "Tell them to let Bear out," he puffed as he sheltered behind the woodpile.

If they weren't hurt… If someone was left alive…

Bear would be an impossible target with his speed. The door banged open and he whistled. Bear rocketed to his side. He wished the dog could tell him what he craved to hear, that Stella, the baby, Zoe and Kip were unharmed. The pause in the shooting made him think the ammo had been depleted.

"Get to them," he told Camy. "I'm going for the shooter."

Another bullet screamed by his temple, carving a chunk from the log above his head. So much for the eleven-bullet count. Unwilling to delay any longer he'd have to risk it. After a breath, he gave Bear the command and they burst from their hiding place and beelined for the trees. He pulled his own weapon and fired high into the brush as insurance to give Camy some protection.

Camy burst out of the dining hall and sprinted at full speed with Flash jouncing next to her, a weapon in her hand. He heard the tent door slam open as she entered. He didn't pause. There was only a short window before the reload would be complete. They ran to the thickest bunch of shrubs bordering the dining hall. From his shelter of branches, he tried to calm his thundering heart enough to hear any indications of the shooter's location.

Bear's nose quivered, and he went stiff in that way that meant he'd gotten a bead.

He gave the silent command, and Bear guided him along. The snow covered the layer of needles, and leaves muffled their approach. Bear's steps shortened as they got closer until he came to a full stop behind a twisted pine. Von peered through the screen of foliage. Gus was down on one knee, attempting to reload.

Von gripped his weapon and stepped out.

"Drop the rifle."

Gus jerked to his feet, the weapon tumbling to the snow. He was wearing different clothes since they'd encountered him on the roof, nose running and eyes puffed and bloodshot. He looked at Von and Bear and the starch went out of him. Slowly, he raised both palms.

"No river to jump into here," Von said.

Gus exhaled. "Guess you got me. Didn't think you could make it back so fast from the helicopter. My fingers are stiff so I missed."

Von got a degree warmer at that remark. His shot to kill Stella had been offline. "Your name's Gus Richardson, right?"

"Yeah."

"Friend of Walker's."

"Never heard of him."

"You can cut out the lying and save us some time. You went to school together, and he'd been feeding you information. Did he hire you to kill Stella? Matt Smith?"

Gus shook his head. "Walker's not behind this."

"I'm supposed to believe that?"

He coughed and lowered his hands until Bear's intense bark made him hastily raise them again. "If you're gonna shoot me, go for it. I'm cold. This assassin stuff isn't for me."

"You're going to jail and whoever hired you is, too. If you won't talk to me, you'll tell the cops. Walker's gonna be in the cell across the hall if he was an accomplice. Lie on the ground, face down."

With a groan, Gus flattened himself in the snow. Von moved closer and pushed the rifle farther out of his reach.

Bear stiffened and looked at his paws.

The snow where they were standing quivered as if there was some massive animal burrowing underneath them.

Gus tilted his head to look at Von. "What was that?"

Von didn't have time to react before the ground turned liquid, caving in and churning the soil and trees into a bubbling stew.

He reached out to grab Gus's arm and pull him back toward solid ground. He caught hold, for one brief tick, before Gus slipped into the rippling sludge. Bear crouched next to Von as he struggled to get to his feet but his boots found no purchase as the earth disintegrated. The dog's sharp bark hovered in the air as they were sucked under.

Chapter Sixteen

From her position crouched on the floor, Stella felt the rumbling before she heard it.

Camy poked her head up to look out.

Horror infused her words. "Oh no."

"What?" she asked.

Camy yelled into her radio. "Tate, ropes! The ground west of the dining hall liquefied. Von's there." Camy dropped the binoculars and ran outside with Flash, sprinting out the door without a backward glance.

Stella's hand shook. *Von's there.* She grabbed the binoculars and peered out the side window. Gus? Von? Bear?

"I can't see them. Any of them." She scrambled for the radio Camy had given her. "Von, can you hear me?"

"There," Kip said.

She followed the direction of his outstretched finger. Now she could make out Tate and Opie tying a rope to a tree. Below, the ground shimmered with movement. Tate took a tentative step forward before quickly retreating. He signaled Camy to stop when she and Flash raced toward them.

Stella understood. "They can't get close." She stared until her eyes burned. "They're too heavy. The ground is collapsing under them. I have to help."

"No," Zoe said. "Von wouldn't want…"

"I can save them. I'm smaller and lighter. They can rope me."

"No."

"I have to try."

She kissed Hannah. The baby, their baby…and they were so close to losing him. She ran out of the tent. There was nothing on her mind but getting there as quickly as she could. Her feet punched through the crusted snow.

Tate yelled as soon as he saw her. He was trying to steady the rescue rope and prepare a harness. Camy and Flash poked a stick along the edge of what looked like a wide pool of wet cement.

"No, Stella. Get back," Tate shouted.

She shook her head. "Can you see them?" *Please, God, let the answer be yes.*

Camy pointed to a spot a few yards from where she was prodding. "I can't get closer without sinking."

Alive or dead? A rescue or a recovery? She could hardly force a swallow. "You can tie me. I'm lighter and smaller than both of you."

She didn't wait for a reply. She grabbed the harness out of Tate's hands. Reluctantly, he fastened another around her.

He gripped her wrist. "If they're too heavy, you can't let yourself go under to save them."

Without a reply, she hooked the harness to the rope and walked gingerly toward the spot Camy pointed. The ground was a swirl of mud, snow and rocks shoved in every direction. Keeping as best she could to the solid parts, she walked until the surface under her felt like sponge. She sank ankle-deep into the sludge, then up to her knees. The only way to progress was to pull herself forward in a kind of swimming motion. Submerged rocks cut into her shins as she approached the spot

Camy had pointed out. At first, she could only see a kaleido-scope of grays, tumbled rocks, branches that floated and some that protruded from the surface.

"Von," she yelled. "Bear. Where are you?" No answer. Panic began to pull at her along with the sucking muck, which roiled around her waist. Her second call was practically a shriek. "Von!"

"Here," came a faint reply. Joy fueled her forward as she hauled herself through the liquefied earth. The top of a tree jut-ted from the mess and there, at long last, she found them. Von's arm was crooked around a branch and his other clutched Bear. Both were so covered by ooze that they could have been made of wet cement.

When Von saw her, the whites of his eyes widened, bits of light in the dark palette. "No, Ella," he said, after a coughing jag. His voice was weak as if it required all his strength to keep them there. "Get out."

"Bossy." She hoped he didn't detect the tremble in her voice. "I'm bringing you a harness."

"No." Now his voice was louder. "Throw it and get back."

"I have to come closer."

She shut out his rebuttal and inched forward. Her feet had no purchase as she clung to the rope. "I'm gonna throw it now."

She did, only her aim was off and it tumbled far short of him. She reeled it in, dripping and covered in debris, heavier now. "One more time."

He mumbled something but she ignored him. Her second effort made it close enough that he snagged it.

His limbs were shivering violently.

"If you can't attach it, I'll…"

"Negative," he snapped. "I'll do it. Tell them to pull you in."

Good, she thought. He's strong enough to be rude.

She peered across the lake of mud. "Where's…?"

Von didn't look at her. "I lost him."

Her heart squeezed. What a way to die, swallowed up by liquid ground. Gus had escaped death when he'd plunged into the river behind the theater. This time, she was certain he hadn't. After a hard swallow she yelled to Tate,

"We're harnessed."

When she saw his thumbs-up, she gave one of her own to Von.

Her limbs were cold, stiff, but she clung to the rope as they extracted her from the goo. They helped her away from the sucking muck.

Von and Bear were next, sliding forward together. It must have been a supreme effort. Inch by inch, Tate and Camy pulled them free and carried them to where Stella waited. Von lay on his back, Bear curled up next to him. Stella crawled over. Tate knelt at Von's side.

"Don't need help. Stella and Bear…" Von croaked.

"I'm fine, you stubborn, stubborn man." Stella choked back tears. "And so are Hannah, Kip and Zoe."

But Bear was covered in muck, his tongue coated in sludge as he panted.

Tate poured water from a bottle in Bear's mouth, rinsing some of the debris, and scooped the sludge out of his ears. The dog turned his head and vomited.

Von's expression was agonized. "He needs help."

Tate nodded. "Gotta get this stuff off right now and restore some warmth." He turned to his sister. "Dining hall okay structurally?"

"Yes," Camy said. "It's on bedrock. Ronnie saw to that. And there's no liquefaction within a hundred yards."

She radioed to Kip and Zoe. "Von, Bear and Stella are safe but they need dry clothes. Meet us at the dining hall in ten."

Tate helped Von to sit up.

Camy stripped off her jacket and wrapped it around Stella.

"Can you make it by yourself? I need to stay here with Flash for a while, in case…"

In case there was a chance of finding Gus. Stella swallowed. "Yes. Tate, if you can help Von, I'll carry Bear."

Von's filth-covered brow creased and he opened his mouth, but only a cough came out.

Stella fired off her most forceful glare. "I'm carrying him, so you'd better tell him it's okay because we don't have time for an argument."

To her surprise, Von did. Stella bent to Bear. "Okay, big boy. Consider me your temporary partner." With Tate's help, she hefted the dog, carrying him upright as if he was a baby on her shoulder. He was a heavy bundle, but she steeled her muscles.

Tate supported one of Von's shoulders and they stumbled along. With achingly slow progress, they made it to the dining hall.

Kip was there holding Hannah. "Zoe's got the showers going. Hot, because Camy and I fixed the water heater last night while everyone was sleeping."

"If I wasn't filthy with an armful of dog, I'd kiss you," Stella said.

There were two bathrooms with small showers. Tate lowered Von into a chair. "Let's get you cleaned up." He untied Von's boots.

"Bear first," he rasped.

"Von," Tate started, then exchanged a look with Stella. There was no way they would get Von tended to until Bear was taken care of.

"Relegated to dog washer." Tate took the dog from Stella. Zoe handed him a towel and he disappeared into one of the shower rooms.

Zoe gave another to Stella. "Water's hot and ready for you. In you go."

She passed Von and he reached out a filthy hand. She took it, their palms gritty and cold.

"You shouldn't have risked yourself," he said.

"You can take it out of my pay for disobeying an order."

He blinked and his filth-covered face split into a grin. "Yes, ma'am." But his mirth dimmed quickly as he heard a low whine from Bear. She squeezed one more time. "He'll be okay."

She thought his grip became a little desperate before he let go and Zoe escorted her to the shower. The hot water was absolute bliss. Stella tried to sort out her tumbling thoughts while she scrubbed away the filth.

She offered up a prayer of gratitude that Von and Bear were alive and an entreaty that Gus would be found. Von's weary smile replayed in her thoughts.

What was happening between her and Von? Did they have a chance at love? They were now a ready-made family, and he was slowly accepting his role in Hannah's life, but that new mission did not seem to involve them becoming a couple. A family, but not together. She washed hard until the gray sludge ran down the drain.

Dressed in yet another borrowed outfit and socks, she padded to the dining room where Kip was poking at a fire. Tate deposited Bear on a blanket in front of the fireplace, bookended by Opie and Flash. The rescued cat watched unconcernedly from the mantel. Stella accepted a quick hug from Kip.

"How about you don't ever do a thing like that again?" Kip said.

"I'll try not to."

He stoked the fire until the flames danced.

Camy entered, her face grim. "Found him."

Stella's stomach dropped at her expression. There would be no second chance at life for Gus this time.

Von emerged a few moments later. He was clearly pained and holding his shoulder stiffly, but he walked right to his dog. He dropped to his knees with a groan and Bear shoved his head in Von's stomach.

"You okay, boy?" Von whispered and only Stella heard the catch in his voice. The dog was not his usual high energy, but he perked up at Von's gentle stroking. Tate brought a bowl of liquid and put it in front of Bear.

"Water and a couple of teaspoons of beef broth."

Stella held her breath as Bear sniffed, then lapped up the contents with two envious dogs looking on. Von exhaled, murmuring and cooing to his canine friend.

She settled in the farthest corner to give them some privacy. Camy joined her. "He sure loves that dog," Stella said.

Camy sighed. "At first, when I got to know Ronnie, I didn't understand that dog-person bond. I'd only owned a goldfish, so to be honest I was jealous. I researched, as I do for everything in life that puzzles me. Turns out the pet attachment is akin to a parent-child bond. When I inherited Flash, I guess I became a mom to an overgrown, slobbery hound."

A parent-child bond? The thought startled Stella. Von was clearly becoming more comfortable with the human parent-child bond. It made her feel such a rush of affection for him, she was taken aback. That affection felt like something very close to love.

"Hey," Camy whispered, tapping her shoulder. "He loves you and Hannah, you know."

Stella meant to wave off the remark, but instead she slumped. "He doesn't love me the same way…"

"That you love him?"

A wave of tears crawled up her throat, leaving her unable to answer.

"I get it. Sometimes love's not enough but you're blessed to be able to have a chance." Camy's mouth wobbled. Stella reached for her hand, but she moved slightly away. Ronnie, the love of

Camy's life, was gone forever. It was a private grief and Camy wasn't going to accept comfort.

Walker, Doc and Bridget entered, with Archie following.

"We stayed together like you ordered," Archie said. "But man, that was a lot of gunfire. What happened to the shooter?"

Von got to his feet. "He's dead. I tried to extract him, but he was sucked under by the liquefaction."

Tate cleared his throat. "I've notified the police."

Walker's eyes were wild. "Is there a chance he crawled out? Got away?"

"No. There's not. Camy located his body." Von's eyes were hard stones. "And you're gonna answer my questions now. We know you were classmates with Gus."

Walker's expression shifted from shock to defiance. "Doesn't mean I knew him."

"You were in shop class together. Stop lying."

"I…"

Bridget put her arm around Walker. "You can't browbeat my son."

"I'm not browbeating anyone. Look around. It's amazing there weren't more people killed in this last escapade. Because of Gus and whoever was helping him, we were all put at risk. He knew exactly when we were taking Paul out of here so someone had to have told him." Von blazed at Walker. "It was you, wasn't it?"

"No, I…" He trailed off.

"Look, kid," Von said harshly, "I get he was your friend, but he was a murderer and he almost added to his body count today."

Bridget's fingers dug into Walker's shoulder. "Stop talking to him like that."

Archie stepped closer. "She's right. This isn't…"

Walker startled them all. "Yes. I helped him."

There was a moment of shocked silence. Bridget's mouth twitched. "You don't know what you're saying. You couldn't…"

"I fed him the information, Mom."

"But…why would you do that?"

"Because I owed him. I'm sorry." Walker started to cry. "It was me back in high school that had the drugs, not Gus. I bought them to hand out at school, some lame attempt to be a big shot with the other kids. When we realized there were narcs at the school coming to arrest us, Gus took the blame. He jokingly told the cops his name was Abe Lincoln. I've been paying him ever since he got out of jail. He texted me."

Camy's voice was calm. "When?"

"A couple of times right when we hit camp."

"You told him you were here?" she said.

"He already knew that, somehow. I figured he saw us roll in. Driscolls never do anything without attracting attention. The last time he texted me was a couple hours ago, right after breakfast. He said he messed up his phone so he stole one. Lost all his contacts. Mine was the only number he'd got memorized. He wanted to know when Dad was getting out."

Von glowered. "So you told him all about your father's evacuation and where exactly Stella would be? Why does he want to kill her? Who hired him?"

"I don't know. I told him the time the helicopter was coming and who would be there with Dad. He warned me to stay away from Stella's tent. That's all. I didn't know he was gonna shoot at her. He's…he was…my friend."

"More like he didn't want the cash cow to stop giving milk," Doc said.

Bridget drilled him with a glare. "Shut your mouth."

Doc shrugged, but Stella thought she saw a gleam of satisfaction in his eyes.

Walker hung his head. "I never knew which friends were

with me because Dad is loaded and who liked me for me, but I figured Gus didn't have to go to jail in my place."

"That's enough." Bridget hustled him to the door. "You're not saying another word without a lawyer."

Stella felt suddenly sorry for Walker. It was all too much to think about who and why and how the murderous plans had come to pass. She took Hannah from Kip.

She rocked the baby, feeling Von's gaze on her.

Bear perked up and wagged his tail at the sight of his little friend, and Stella's stomach unclenched a notch. Whatever had taken place, they were still here. Gus was not a threat anymore, and Walker would answer to the police for whatever he had or hadn't done.

Camy pocketed her phone. "The police anticipate arriving by sundown."

Doc perked up. "So we're getting out of here?"

"Yes."

"Excellent." He beamed.

"Thanks for being so concerned," Bridget spat. "About Walker."

Doc shrugged. "He needs to answer for his choices for a change."

"Oh, it's time for a change, all right." Bridget's eyes slitted.

Doc shot her a defiant look. "What are you mad about? We're about to be rescued. Aren't you eager for your husband to reach the hospital?"

"Yes, because the moment he wakes up, I'm going to tell him I fired you."

Doc's mouth fell open. "You won't do that."

"Bridget," Archie said, a warning in his tone. "Maybe now's not the right…"

"I've done some reading up. If Paul is mentally incapacitated, I act on his behalf."

"Do you really want to cross me?" Doc said. "Considering…"

Stella wondered. Considering what?

"Like you said, it's important to answer for your choices." Bridget gathered Walker and guided him to the door. "We'll be packing."

Doc blinked as if he'd been slapped, then strode outside to the porch. Stella caught the bitter scent of a cigarette.

"What was that about?" Camy asked Archie.

"I dunno, but if Paul comes out of this, he's going to need a playbook to figure out the score." Archie frowned at Von. "You got any proof that Walker was conspiring with Gus?"

"Police will check his phone."

"If they can find it," Archie said. "Could be it gets lost between then and now, like Gus's."

Camy arched her brow. "There are phone records the cops can tap."

"If they have enough cause. Seems to me like we got a troubled youth six feet under the muck and everybody else is fine."

Stella shook her head. "Matt Smith isn't."

"That's on Gus, not Walker." Archie shrugged. "He's just a kid."

"His mother's shielding him from the consequences," Von said.

Archie shot him a look. "You just found out you're a dad. Give it a while. You'd do anything for your kid." He shrugged. "I'll get the horses taken care of and then I guess their care is turned over to you all after we leave tonight."

Tate nodded. "Thank you for your help."

"Text me when the road is clear." Archie left.

Stella's mind whirled. She got up and walked the baby in aimless circles. "Whatever Walker did or didn't do, I can't figure out how that connects to what happened with Matt Smith." The others exchanged glances. The sudden shift in the room prickled her nerves. "What?"

"About that," Camy said. "Legs and Von and I have been

discussing something. He called and caught me just before we transported Paul. I shared with Von via a text, but you probably need to hear it now."

Camy looked grim. Stella nestled the baby closer. She didn't know how much more she could take.

"I'll dial Legs and see if he can talk." Camy clicked the phone and set it on the table. "You're on speaker with me, Stella, Tate, Zoe, Von, Kip, a baby, three dogs and a cat."

"Sounds like a three-ring circus." There was a sound of Legs shuffling papers. "All right. Let's get right down to it. Like I told you earlier, we have an ID on Matt Smith. He was a private investigator."

"What?" Stella could hardly take it in. "Why did he want to meet with me?"

Legs continued. "Still working on that. You told me when we met that you didn't go to school here in Cloud Top."

The line of conversation surprised her. "That's correct. I grew up in Fresno."

"Something about the photo that Smith gave you bothered me and I finally figured out what it was. The background. It's a whitewashed brick wall. I know that because my dad was a custodian here in Cloud Top for years and that's where the school always staged photos before the gym was built."

Stella gaped. "Wait a minute. Are you saying…?"

"It's not a photo of you," he finished.

The truth clicked into place. "It's my mother."

Zoe sighed. "I always said you two were carbon copies."

"Why would a private investigator have my mother's photo?"

Camy cleared her throat. "Maybe it's a good time for me to chime in. Von told me the facts about your father's death, that he was killed on a TexAm oil rig and the year."

She stared blankly. "Yes, that's right."

"I did some research." Camy looked at Von.

He put his hand on her shoulder. "This whole mess keeps

going back to the meeting with Matt Smith and the photo. I figured it had to be connected to your past in some way."

"What did you find out?" Her heart whacked against her ribs.

Camy cocked her chin. "There was no one killed on a TexAm oil rig the year you mentioned."

She must have misheard. "That's not possible."

"I'm telling you that there is no TexAm employee by that name at all that I can find," Camy said. "And I'm pretty good at finding things."

"I don't understand."

Von took a breath. "The letters you got. Perhaps they weren't actually written by your father."

Zoe groaned. "Oh no. I knew this would happen." Stella gaped at her. "What?"

Kip folded his arms and looked at the floor.

Zoe twisted her hands together. "Um, well… Your mother moved to Fresno when she was nineteen and pregnant. Alone."

The word circled slowly in her brain. "Alone?"

Zoe nodded. "She wouldn't speak about your father to anyone, not even me. Only that he was a horrible, manipulative man and you were better off not knowing him. She was scared he'd find you someday, which is why she didn't want to visit Cloud Top often. He'd told her she'd never be able to leave him, that she belonged to him."

"But the letters…"

Kip cleared his throat. "Your father didn't write them." He sucked in a deep breath. "I did."

Stella's mouth dropped open and she clutched Hannah close. "You…pretended to be my father in those letters?"

He nodded miserably.

"Why?" she whispered. "Why would you do that?"

Kip groaned. "I didn't think it through. Even Zoe didn't know until I blurted it all out to her before Hannah was born. She's been pushing me to tell you since the day she found out."

Stella fell mute with shock.

"I got to know your mother when she moved to Fresno as a young woman and then you came along and you were the sweetest, cutest baby. I watched you grow. Greatest privilege of my life." He wiped his eyes. "I... I felt bad seeing the other kids with their dads and you always asking where your daddy was, and Frannie told you he was away on an oil rig because she didn't know what else to say. There was a kindergarten project where kids were supposed to share something about their dads and I found Frannie crying one day over it. I came up with this nutty idea to write a letter so you'd have something to share, too, and you got so excited. I... I sort of continued it. Frannie was uncomfortable with the whole thing, but she saw how happy it made you, so she let me continue for a while until she decided to tell you he'd been killed."

Stella paced the room. Lies. Her mother, Kip, Zoe. They'd fed her a steady diet of lies.

"Are you angry?" Kip said.

"Yes," she blurted. "And hurt and confused." She didn't make eye contact with Von. He'd been right about Kip all along. Her stomach knotted.

"I'm sorry, Stella. I never should have written you those letters. Another one of Kip's colossal mess-ups. I wanted to tell you so many times." He looked at Von. "I know what you're thinking and you're right. I lied and I deserve whatever is coming."

Stella's stomach churned along with her thoughts. "So who's my father, then?" Silence descended on the room. "Are you all thinking it's Paul Driscoll?"

"Everything fits," Von said. "He could have hired the PI to find you. Maybe he arranged to come here for camp so he could get you to the area under the ruse of an arborist consult."

Camy nodded. "He owns a small property near where you met with Smith."

"Why lure me? For what purpose?"

"That's a good question," Camy said.

"Gus almost killed me along with the PI. Do you think Paul arranged to have me shot and got Matt Smith instead? Why would he?"

"Archie said Paul believed in punishing people."

Her mind spun. "My mother's dead. There's no way to punish her anymore. None of this makes sense."

"You can have a DNA test," Camy suggested.

Stella squeezed her eyes shut and opened them. "This is all too much." She hurried to the door.

"Where are you going?"

"To the tent. I need to be alone."

"I'll walk you," Von said.

She didn't wait, almost running along the path, the baby heavy in her arms.

"Stella."

She couldn't hear any more. Not after she'd almost lost Von, been shot at and terrorized. Now to find out the man who was more like a father than anyone had systematically lied to her? The father that she'd only known in letters was a complete fiction.

He caught up to her as she shoved inside. "We have to figure out what Paul was after."

"I don't care anymore."

"You should. You and the baby might still be targets."

"How? Matt Smith and Gus are dead. Paul is in the hospital, and Walker has to face the police."

He reached for her arm but she jerked a step back, confused.

"I know you're hurting…"

Her vision blurred with tears. "What do you know, Von? Your life didn't turn upside down again."

"I'd say finding out I'm a father was pretty revolutionary."

Her blood turned molten with too many emotions, too much loss. The fire tumbled out of her mouth before she could stop it. "You've played Daddy for a few days and it was fun, right? You're going to leave and return to your old job. Nothing has changed for you."

"Yes, it has."

"So you'll dabble on and off in the fatherhood thing. You know what? My life just did a one-eighty and the circle of people I can trust got even smaller." She swallowed a sob. "I'll take care of Hannah by myself." Without the man who'd been her rock since the baby was born. And Zoe had lied to her, too. It would take a while to forgive that as well.

His mouth firmed. "It doesn't have to be that way."

"Really? What are you prepared to do? Stay with us? No. That's what you do with a woman you love, not just someone who's raising your child." What was she saying? *Stop, just stop.*

He shook his head in confusion. "Ella, I…"

"Never mind. I'm sorry. I'm tired and upset. I want to be alone now. Please."

He limped out the door. Through the window pierced with bullet holes she saw him hesitate, turn back, but she stepped out of view.

Von would return to his duty and when he couldn't continue, he'd find something else to occupy his energy. Pain knifed through her at the thought and she could deny it no longer. The inescapable fact was that for the second time in her life she'd found herself in love with Von Sharpe.

But this love was deeper, richer, wider, a connection that could take them into the future and beyond. She knew who she was now, who God had made her to be. And she loved Von Sharpe with her reborn heart.

Except that he did not feel the same.

She was alone again, and even though she had Hannah, the loss felt so much greater.

Her tears of hurt and pain and disappointment fell on Hannah's soft blankets as she held her daughter close. Outside, the clouds formed an angry gray wall that mirrored what she felt inside. The squeak of the rocking chair marked off the passing moments.

What seemed like only a moment later, Zoe tiptoed in with lunch.

"Thank you." Stella stiffly rejected Zoe's offer to feed the baby. Her aunt laid the food on the table next to the rocking chair, and Stella hoped she would leave.

Instead, she sank onto the cot. "For what it's worth, Kip feels terrible. So do I. I should have insisted he tell you the moment I learned about it, but you'd lost Daniel and…" She shook her head. "No excuse. I'm very sorry."

Her cinched heart loosened and she heaved out a breath. "I know. You wanted Kip to tell me. This quake situation and shooter wasn't exactly the opportune moment to reveal it. I don't blame you. I've certainly been guilty of keeping secrets." Relief coursed through her as she realized it was true. She didn't blame Zoe. It would take a lot of soul searching and prayer to say the same about Kip.

"Thank you, honey." She got up and kissed Stella, both of them wiping tears away. "Von's leaving to escort Bridget, Doc and Walker to the trailhead where the national guard will meet them."

"What about Archie?"

"He's already left. He volunteered to ride with the two rescued horses along the trail to Cloud Top where they've got a relocation point for lost animals."

"Should we put up a flier about Hercules the cat?"

"Yes. That's a good idea, but if he doesn't find a home, I'll take him. He'll love my little sunporch once I get the debris cleaned away."

Zoe's little sunporch. It seemed like a lifetime ago she'd been eager to visit her aunt's cabin and have a relaxing vacation. That was before the earth had imploded along with everything else.

Zoe left to help Camy pack up supplies and tend to the cat. When Hannah went to sleep on the mattress for her late-afternoon nap, Stella consolidated their belongings into a meager pile. Not much and no van to carry it in. Von would no doubt insist on driving her. Kip would, too. She didn't want to be around either one of them. Maybe Tate or Camy would give her a lift.

She heard the door open. "Did you find a way to transport the cat, Zoe?"

As she zipped the diaper bag closed, something smashed into the back of her head and she blacked out.

Von helped the national guard soldiers shovel debris until it became clear he was in their way. His body was shouting at him to stop anyway. Why did all the men and women around him look so young?

Old man.

He felt as if he was aging by the minute as he whistled to Bear, who was supervising from a spot of sunlight he'd found. Von couldn't blame him, after what he'd been through. The dog was sluggish but alert as ever. Von's chest ached, and he didn't think it was simply from almost being liquefied. Stella was hurting and he couldn't do anything about it. As a matter of fact, he was part of her pain.

That's what you do with a woman you love, not just someone who's raising your child.

A woman you love…

He had loved Stella once, passionately, recklessly, selfishly, and they'd blown each other up. What was he feeling now, that deep ache, the heart-clenching sensation rolling through him? Maybe it was simply the impact of sudden fatherhood.

You'd do anything for your kids.

But the paternal issue was only part of the weight pulling at him.

He leaned against the tree to share Bear's sunbeam and forced his brain to sort through the mishmash of information. The events refused to align themselves in any orderly fashion. If Paul was Stella's father, and he'd hired a private investigator to track her down, what was his purpose?

Posthumous revenge against Francine, the woman who'd taken his child away? No. Perhaps the opposite. A lawyer had been on his way to camp before the earthquake disrupted Paul's plans. To change a will? To award Stella some of his wealth? But Paul wasn't a magnanimous man. Likely, he'd change his will not simply to benefit Stella but to punish someone else.

Bridget? Walker?

Maybe there was some provision in the inheritance for Doc? Archie?

Stella's situation barged back in. A father who wasn't her father...

You'd do anything for your kids.

He went hot. Then cold. Bear stared up at him. Without a word he grabbed his phone and ran.

Chapter Seventeen

Stella blinked awake; her first sensation was a cleaver chop of pain in her skull. Flashes of white snow and dark rock interwoven with the sound of rushing water finally penetrated as cold seeped into her clothing. She was lying belly down on the ground, staring at a pair of booted feet. In a rush, she sat up.

Archie looked down at her. "Sorry. I really am. Nothing about this is your fault, and I just wanna say that up front."

"What?" He'd hit her with something. Dragged her from the tent cabin. Had he taken Hannah, too? She stared wildly.

"She's here." He pointed under an oak. Her heart lurched as she took in the wriggling bundle. "She can't be on the ground," Stella blurted. "It's too cold."

"Unless you do exactly as I say, she's going to be dead soon anyway." He sounded almost apologetic.

Dead? She struggled to understand through the pounding in her head and chest.

"Like I said, not your fault, or hers, but I know you're not going to cooperate unless I give you a good reason."

"Cooperate with what?"

"Stand up."

She tried, legs shaky, head splitting, until finally he grabbed her forearm and hauled her up. They were a few feet from the ruined bridge, the yellow caution tape fluttering in the wind.

"Why, Archie? Why did you bring me here?"

He shrugged. "A father's got to do what he's got to do, right?"

A father?

He pointed to the bridge.

Her lungs constricted and her vision blurred. He could not mean it.

But his pointed finger told her he did.

"Is she in her tent?" Von panted into the radio as he and Bear hurtled over a deep, snow-filled gully.

"Give me a minute to check," Tate said. "But the guests have left, Von. Who would…?"

"Archie. I can't explain now. Check."

Tate didn't argue. Von could hear the sound of him running, calling to his sister as he did so.

Von kept going, heart in his throat. He was wrong. Had to be wrong. His imagination was running amok. Maybe he was inventing ways to care for Stella and Hannah by protecting them. Fine. If that was the case, he'd eat crow with Tate as soon as he reported that Stella was fine. He was forced to stop running when his knee threatened to give out. Bent over, he watched his radio, willing Tate to reply that all was well and he was a dope.

"Von…" The tone said it all. "Stella's gone, and so is Hannah."

His heart came to a full stop.

"He came on horseback," Camy said. "Tracks show he's heading toward the bridge."

The ruined bridge over the swollen river.

"En route." He started to run again. Why had Archie done it? He had a feeling he knew. Archie's constant support of Walker and Bridget, his defense and refusal to speak badly of her. Paul might be Stella's father...but maybe he wasn't Walker's.

You'd do anything for your kid.

Including killing the person who would be given an inheritance if Paul recovered and Stella was proven to be his daughter.

Would Archie kill Stella and Hannah to keep Walker's future safe?

Anything...

All he could do was run.

And pray.

Hannah cried, her wails piercing the winter air. The sound arrowed right to Stella's core. Her baby was cold, the moisture no doubt soaking her pajamas. Black, tarry fear coated Stella's insides. She had to talk him out of whatever he was planning, get Hannah somewhere warm and safe. "Why are you doing this? If you're going to kill me, don't you owe me an explanation at least?"

He shrugged. "Same old sad story. Boy meets girl and loses girl. Bridget was my girl before Paul hit town. Did you know that? Paul took my family land and her. Not that she wasn't pleased as punch to go with him, I'll say. All that money? Her head was turned. I don't blame her, but she should have told me the truth."

She took a stab in the dark. "That Walker is your son, not Paul's?" She knew from his balled fists that she'd hit the target. "How did you find out?"

"Paul was making sounds like he was doubting Walker was his. Even had Doc run a DNA test, but Bridget paid Doc off not to reveal the real results, she told me. Paul's a hard one to redirect, though. Walker's always been a disappointment to him. He read your mama's obit and began to wonder if you were his kin. The timing was right. Frannie ran from Paul, I take it, and never wanted him to know about you, which was the smartest thing she ever did. But sure enough, the private eye uncovered the truth. You're a Driscoll, Stella. Congratulations."

Driscoll. She remembered the double l's on the faded mailbox near where she'd met Matt Smith. "I don't want any of his money. I'm no threat. Walker can have it all."

He prodded her shoulder, moving her toward the lip of the bridge.

"Not if Paul wakes up. Doc will tell him the truth now that Bridget's lost her temper and fired him. She's been paying Doc to lie about the DNA results. Paul will punish her and Walker. That's what he does." When she dug her feet in, Archie shoved her forward. "You're gonna walk out there and jump."

Stella felt as if she was lost in a nightmare. Nothing was real, except the sound of Hannah's sobbing. "So that's it? You and Bridget decided to kill me so I don't get Paul's money?"

"Not her. She's the catalyst only. You have to know that. Bridget is a solid person, deep down. She got scared that Paul was going to change his will so she reached out to me, told me about my son." Archie sighed. "How do you like that? Turns out the man I cannot stand raised my kid for twenty-three years."

If Bridget wasn't involved in Paul's accident then… She tried another guess. "Is that why you pushed him off the horse? You wanted to speed up the inheritance?" She scanned the dirt for a stick or rock she could use to defend herself, but it was all cloaked by a fine layer of snow.

He laughed. "You figured that out, huh? Easy to do. I hired Walker's friend Gus to kill you, but he got Matt Smith instead. I figured the next best plan was to kill Paul. The inheritance would go to Bridget and then to Walker when Paul went to his fiery reward. Plan worked pretty well until Gus lost his phone. Dummy couldn't remember my number. He contacted Walker for details so he could follow through on his job to kill you. Kids these days. Too used to pushing buttons instead of remembering using the little gray cells." He sighed. "Imagine my surprise when you showed up in camp. I mean…if Paul woke up for even a few minutes and recognized you, all my work would have gone up in smoke."

She moved as slowly as she could, looking for a branch she could grab, a rock. "Paul managed to survive in spite of you, didn't he?"

"Tough old dog. It was easy to spook the horse so he'd get thrown but he pulled through. I heard Tate say he was starting to come around. I tried again at the med tent but you surprised me."

"You were behind the flood, too."

"Yeah. Figured the safest way to make sure you two never met was to kill one or both of you. I even told Gus before he lost his cell that you were sneaking off to your aunt's. I'm a thorough man. I believe in covering my bases. The will hasn't been officially changed yet. The earthquake stranded us all here together so it should have been easier than shooting fish in a barrel. It's more complicated now that Doc is an enemy, but he won't be able to make trouble after you die in an accident. Eventually Paul will, too."

He moved closer and bullied her forward until her toes touched the bridge planks. "Go."

With a gulp, she inched onto the nearest board. The wood creaked under her shoe. "What's Walker going to think? Having a murderer for a father?"

"He's not going to know what I did, and neither will Bridget. When I find a way to kill Paul, Bridget and I are going to reunite and she'll tell Walker the truth. He'll be ecstatic to know that Paul wasn't his father. I'll have my land back and Walker can tend it with me. Your death is an insurance policy in case he lives long enough to try and change his will."

"You're living in a fantasy."

He shrugged. "Whatever. Walk out onto the bridge. Maybe it will collapse and you won't have to jump."

Tears gathered in her eyes. "Are you trying to make it look like suicide?"

"I don't care what it looks like. No one will be able to tie it to me or Walker or Bridget. Move it."

"No." She clung to the wooden railing.

"Don't make this hard." He looked at Hannah. "If you don't cooperate, I'll throw the baby in first. If you do what I say, I'll leave her here and she'll be found. She dies or you do. What's it gonna be?"

The blurred white bundle…her daughter, her everything.

Would Archie keep his word?

There was no choice.

She dies or you do.

On unsteady legs, she stepped farther onto the bridge.

Von pulled up abruptly, lungs shouting at him. He didn't need binoculars to figure it out. Stella was on the bridge almost halfway out. Archie was watching intently, his back to Von.

His stomach plummeted until he picked out the bundle lying on the ground. Still, his heart refused to beat until he saw a kick of her leg as she tried to roll herself over. Bear was practically vibrating, but he remained silent per his training.

Archie was probably armed, but it didn't matter. Nor did the fact that Camy and Tate were a few minutes behind. No chance of taking a shot that might injure his daughter or Stella. There was only one way. He'd get Stella and Hannah to safety. No matter what.

He looked at Bear and held up three fingers. "Wait and watch close."

Bear's ear twitched, his gaze hyper-focused on Von's fingers as he silently counted down.

Three…two…one…

Bear raced for his charge, moving so fast his paws were a brown blur. Archie did not hear until Bear had skidded to a stop, straddling Hannah, teeth bared and barking viciously. Archie jumped back, reaching for something in his pocket, only looking up in time to see the freight train that was Von Sharpe running straight at him.

Von's head plowed deep into Archie's stomach. He heard the man's exhalation as he drove him backward. Archie landed in a heap, gasping for air. Again, he went for his pocket, but Von pinned his hand and wrestled a revolver free, tossing it away.

"Give me a reason to throw you into that river," Von grunted.

Archie twisted under Von's grasp. "I had no choice." His mouth bled. "That's why your baby's mother is about to fall in. We all do what we have to, right?"

Bile filled his throat as he scrambled upright. Camy, Tate and their two dogs roared up in the ATV.

"Secure him," Von yelled, calling off Bear so Tate could get to Hannah and Camy could handle Archie.

He ran to the edge of the bridge. Stella was almost halfway out, at a place where the boards had broken away. She jerked a look at him, face pallid with fear.

"Stella," he shouted, but as he took a step forward, the wood fell away and the structure swayed. Hastily, he jumped off.

She clung to the wobbly railing with both hands. It would not hold much longer. He was too heavy to risk going after her and bringing the whole thing down.

"Here." With Hannah bundled against him with one arm, Tate tossed him a rope and harness.

Von looped it securely around the nearest tree before he called to Bear. The dog immediately took hold of the rope end. Before he set him into action, he held the dog's chin and looked into his eyes. It occurred to Von that all the major blessings in his life were here in this one spot on the globe. Stella, Hannah and Bear, the three he loved most dearly, who loved him, in spite of every single failure. A second chance...

After one more moment he released the dog, and Bear crept

to the bridge, trailing the rope and harness rig. He watched with his muscles turned to stone as Bear edged past the ruined sections, staying close to the more solid beams until he reached Stella. Would she be able to secure herself?

"Can you tie it on?" he called.

After a moment of fumbling, he watched as she knotted the rope around her waist.

"That's good. Real good," he called. "Now, walk back toward me, okay? Slow and easy. You're secure. I've got you if you fall."

Expressionless, Stella took a step, clutching the rope around her waist. A crack echoed like a gunshot. The planks broke and she crashed through, plummeting toward the river.

Bear was able to grab her sleeve, scoot onto the remaining beam, balanced there, his teeth buried in the fabric. No choice now. Von ran.

All around him the wood creaked and buckled as he charged on. Stella's face was locked in a grimace, her torso protruding above the bridge and her legs dangling below, angled toward the river.

Von grabbed both her wrists and yelled at Bear to release and return to safety. Reluctantly, the dog obeyed. Von pulled the extra rope toward him and looped it around them both. She was crying.

"I've got you, Ella. We're gonna ride this rope outta here."

"H... H..."

"Hannah is okay," he said, before she could even get the word past her chattering teeth. She sagged, weak as a rag doll. She pressed her cheek to his chest.

"Enough with this bridge stuff, right?" He kissed her ear. "We're secure, Tate," he directed and the rope was pulled taut. Wood fragments pressed into her back as they moved. Von wriggled and turned his body to shield her as best he could, but the broken wood stabbed at her anyway. They slid slowly off the bridge. He lifted her and carried her to the ATV.

"It's over, honey." Every pore and sinew filled with the deepest relief he'd ever experienced. Tate supplied a blanket and Von wrapped it around her. Camy cradled Hannah.

"Stay awake, Stella," Von said as her eyes closed.

"Hannah," she whispered.

"I'll take care of her and we'll get you to the hospital." He kissed her tenderly. "We need you, Ella. We love you."

Love. The word sounded foreign on his lips, strange and alien...

And he felt as if he'd been waiting to say it his whole life.

Stella woke in a haze. Exhaustion kept her eyes closed but she listened to the rumble of a masculine voice. Von's.

"The Pribby plant is part of the coffee family. It's a critically endangered species. It lives on an island called Montserrat. Do you know what, Hannah? There's a volcano there that spits out all kinds of stuff on those poor little plants. And goats eat 'em, too, but they keep on growing. Yes, they do." She heard the munching sound of Von pretending to gum Hannah, and her baby's giggle. "So what do you say? Should we go there and get some seeds and plant them? We'll have to ask Mommy first if it's okay."

She listened to him read from his beloved book, chatting with their daughter, planting seeds with her as she drifted off to sleep again.

Stella felt every bump and bruise when she fully awakened in the hospital. Zoe sat at her bedside with Hannah.

"Well, hello, Stella. Pookie Pie has been waiting for her mama to wake up. You've been in and out a while."

Stella touched her daughter's hand. "She's..."

"In tip-top shape. Tate administered first aid until she could be checked out here, but she doesn't have so much as a scratch." Zoe helped Hannah to stand on her lap, joggling her from foot to foot. "And you're going to be tip-top, too. Some sutures and a broken rib, slight concussion, but you got a good report."

Stella rubbed her eyes. "Where's Von?"

She hesitated. "He was right by your bed every minute for the past twenty-four hours. He interviewed, well, let me say interrogated, the doctors, first about Hannah and then about your condition until they threatened to toss him out on his ear." She clapped Hannah's hands together and the baby grinned. "And he brought you those roses." She pointed to a vase brimming with white blooms. "He said something about getting more."

The door opened and someone came in behind a bouquet of pink roses. Von poked his head around the arrangement. His face lit when he saw her awake. "There she is." He picked up the water pitcher to make room for the flowers.

She felt herself blushing. "Didn't you already bring the white ones?"

"I figured I'd keep getting different colors so you'd have a nice selection when you woke up."

Zoe laughed. "Hope you appreciate them, Stella. I haven't received flowers since I was in high school. I'm going to find good old Uncle Kip to handle Hannah's diaper change."

Von sat in the vacated chair. "How are you feeling?"

"Alive. Ready to be a mommy again."

"Now that the doctor is speaking to me once more, he tells me you're going to be fine. I was banished for a while, but I made good use of the time."

"How?"

"Bought a new car seat and set up a checking account for you in case you or Hannah need anything while I'm overseas."

"Oh." Stella blinked and then sank back on the pillows. "When will you go?"

"I refused to report until you had some recovery time. I

wanted to be sure you were okay and you and Hannah were settled. See if you need anything. They agreed to let me start my training online stateside for another month if necessary, so I'm staying right here until you're fully recovered." His mouth twisted. "After I complete the initial phase in Germany, I'll be able to get leave and come visit."

"That'd be great."

"I'll call often. Maybe we can do some video things, too. Babies change so fast." He was talking fast, up and pacing now.

"Yes, they do." Stella kept her tone even and calm. Why did it hit her so hard that he was leaving? He'd never said anything different. She knew he loved her on some level, and he definitely adored Hannah, but he'd said nothing about them becoming a couple; never mentioned any more permanent plans. That was really the source of her sadness, she realized. It wasn't that he was leaving, but the fact that he didn't want to try again with her. He didn't love her, not in the way she loved him.

"I…feel bad about leaving."

"Don't," she said. "You'll do what you can, when you can. That's enough."

"Is it?" He looked confused.

She felt the same. Would it be enough? Could she coparent with Von and not long for something deeper? She'd have to. No choice. She smiled with extra brightness. "Yes. We can be great parents in any circumstance, right?"

He looked at her, tall and strong and tender. "Is there anything you need right now? You or Hannah?"

"Not a thing," she said, trying to make herself believe it.

Stella pulled a batch of Christmas cookies from the oven, which scented the whole Fresno apartment. She'd cheated, bought premade dough and added red and green sprinkles. Von probably ate way better at the chow hall where he was stationed, but at least she'd tried. Since he'd been gone, that's all she could manage—trying. Doing her best, getting through the days with the strange sense that there was something out of place in her life, a stumbling in her stride that she could not correct. While she placed the cookies onto a cooling tray, she snuck a glance at Von through the sliding glass door.

He was inspecting the greenhouse he'd built on her tiny balcony, brooding over the plants. He'd already spent a half hour trimming, deadheading and fertilizing during Hannah's afternoon nap. Restless, she thought, distracted by thoughts he wasn't willing to share. Bear sat on a patio chair, watching Von.

She sighed. He finished his perusal and let himself back inside, Bear following. "Honey, not to be judgmental, but the lilies needed repotting. Root-bound."

Sometimes she felt that way too. She picked a handful of tiny socks from the basket of laundry and began to pair them. "That's not high on my list."

"I understand, but it's critical." He wandered the cramped space, skirting the baby swing.

"Nope. Not really critical at all."

He blinked. "Right, well, just pointing it out."

Weariness circled through her, fraying her patience. "I'm doing the best I can, Von, but there's a baby to look after and I'm adding clients. I'm too busy or too exhausted to fuss with the plants."

"I get it. I…"

"Von," she snapped, louder than she'd meant. "The gardening is *your* passion and you want it to be Hannah's someday. That's lovely, but the work falls to me and that's not fair. Trees are my business and passion. Backyard gardening isn't."

His mouth opened and closed. "Oh. Right. Of course. I'm sorry. I wasn't thinking."

Guilt and irritation and many nights of interrupted sleep piled up on her along with the knowledge that he was leaving again, and she desperately wanted him to stay. The baby monitor crackled with Hannah's chortling. She threw down the socks. "Nap time's over."

"I'll get her," Von said.

While she fixed a bottle, he paced with Hannah in his arms. Normally he'd be chanting a marching song or one of the many odd tunes he'd picked up. Now he was quiet. Strange.

"What is it?" she said as she shook up the formula.

"What's what?"

"The frown on your face. What's wrong?"

"I'm not frowning."

"Do you want me to take a marker and trace the furrows on your forehead so you can see them?"

He lifted a broad shoulder, settling onto the sofa. "It's nothing."

"No, it's not." She handed him the bottle and he nested Hannah in his lap. Bear lay as his feet, staring at his beloved baby. The dog's steadfast devotion to Hannah had not diminished one iota in the time they'd spent apart. She sat down next to Von. "We've been through enough for you to trust me, haven't we?"

He stared at Hannah, the baby reaching out to try to snag his beard. "I... I've been thinking about the greenhouse and my job and all kinds of things."

She readied herself for the blow. He was unhappy with his training position, unsatisfied—she'd sensed that in him. He must have somehow found a way to return to deployments. This life divided between his post in Germany and visits to Fresno was causing him to wither like the plants in the greenhouse.

Unfair, she thought. *He can thrive without you, but the reverse isn't true.*

"When I'm there at work, it's great and all," he said. "The people are incredible, their drive, focus. The mission's clear, achievable. But..."

She waited in silence, stomach tense.

"But it's like not all of me is there. The plant, but not the roots. I thought I could give my all in both places. Turns out I was wrong."

Not what she'd expected. "What do you mean?"

The seconds ticked by. "I've been listening to the chaplain…"

Her eyes flew wide. "You have?"

He shrugged and wiped a dribble of milk from Hannah's chin. "He does services and I infiltrate, sort of sneak in the back, under the radar."

She hid a smile at this bearded giant of a man thinking he could sneak in anywhere unnoticed.

"Most of it's Greek to me, but…" He trailed off.

"But what?"

"Chaplain says God gives second chances." His gaze caught hers. "Do you believe that?"

"Yes, I do. Seconds and thirds and fourths…as many as it takes." Her heart beat hard in her chest. "What do *you* think about that?"

"I'm not completely sure, but I've been chewing on what Tate told me, that the point here on this planet is to learn how to love. It'd be hard to learn that big lesson all in one shot." He brushed a kiss on Hannah's head. "I never thought I could feel like I do when I'm around her." He added softly, "And you."

Her? Loving Hannah was one thing, but her? She blinked back tears. She would not tell him that she missed him with a terrible aching need. She would not, could not, add that weight. Whatever choices Von made, they would not be the by-product of any guilt she added. It had to be born of love, pure and simple.

His alarm beeped and he sighed. "My flight leaves in an hour."

The moment evaporated and her hopes with it. Whatever God had started up in Von's heart, he'd work through on his own. She nodded, steeling herself for the pain that would begin again soon.

"I'm going to figure this out, Ella. For myself, but also for you and Hannah. I love you both." He took her hand and kissed the knuckles.

She gulped. "We love you too." There was safety in the *we* she knew. Not nearly the same as telling him she loved him as a woman loves a man. Merely as a mommy loves a daddy.

That was safe, wasn't it?

"I'll be back in a month."

"Sure," she said. And then after a few days he'd be gone again. At least he was opening his heart to healing, and for that, she thanked God.

In the meantime, she watched him cradle their daughter, the unbreakable bridge between them.

On a chilly February afternoon three months after the disastrous quake, Tate met Von outside Kip's tidy one-story bungalow. A Happy First Birthday Hannah sign, hand lettered in pink marker, was taped to the door.

"You look nervous," Tate said.

Von clutched the two bouquets of pink carnations. "Doesn't everyone attending a toddler birthday party get the jitters?"

"Umm, no. They usually aren't sweating and dressed in BDUs and a grey beret."

He shifted, feeling a flush of worry that he should have changed out of his battle dress uniform. Would the camo print scare Hannah? Too late. "I wanted it to be a surprise. I came right from the airport. I washed Bear last night, though."

Tate laughed and eyed the dog. "Well, that makes all the difference. And you even got a pink handkerchief around his neck. Very sporty."

"He destroyed the bow tie."

"Smart dog." Tate handed him the box. "Per your request."

He shoved it into his cavernous pocket along with the small gift he'd painstakingly wrapped. He hesitated a moment on the porch step. "Tate, I didn't say it before but you were right. About everything. I apologize for the things I said and the way I behaved." He stuck out a hand but Tate grabbed him in a tight hug.

"I'm going to write that down and show it to you the next time you mistakenly think I'm wrong."

Von gripped his shoulders. "And thanks for being there for Ronnie," he murmured.

"It was my honor." Tate released him. "All right. Go get 'em, champ."

His hands felt suddenly cold. He knew all the party details, since he called Stella on a weekly basis, trying hard to keep up with the ins and outs of their lives. He could recite Hannah's nap routine, Stella's scheduled therapy appointments, the wake-up times and go-to-sleep times, even a list of Hannah's current most liked snacks. They'd discussed anything and everything, like they had when they'd first dated, and each call added to his certainty. He'd told her all that was on his mind save one. That message had to be delivered in person.

He felt like a nervous high schooler showing up for the prom. "Anything I should know first?"

"Stay low when Hannah gets her hands on that cake. And quit stalling."

They strode into the house. Camy leaned against the wall at the entrance to the living room, sipping from a can of soda, Flash lolling at her feet. Opie watched the proceedings from the top of a stuffed ottoman. The tiny front room decorated in dark woods and fishing photos was embellished with pink-and-white streamers. A garland of tissue paper pompoms hung from the overhead fan, and a pink-papered table housed a round cake and one smaller cupcake. Both were decorated with swirls of frosting, and the larger one read Happy Birthday Pookie Pie. The cupcake, decorated in blue, sat neatly on a plate. For Daniel. A lump formed in his throat.

Hannah was sitting on Stella's lap, batting at a wrapped package Zoe handed her. Kip danced around snapping photos, using an enormous telephoto lens. Camy crooked her neck at Von. Bear's tail whirled as he caught sight of Hannah, but Stella had not yet noticed their entrance.

Camy grinned. "You made it. 'Bout time. Quit hiding and get in there, why don't you?"

"I…"

But he didn't move fast enough for Camy's taste, so she hastened the process by stepping aside and announcing, "Late arrival to the party."

Stella looked up and his heart whammed as her eyes widened to luminous pools.

"Von?" She spoke as if she couldn't believe it. "I thought you couldn't make the birthday party."

He took a breath and stepped fully into the room. "Surprise." Bear whined in excitement and he stared at Von, begging permission.

Von quietly gave it and Bear bounded forward until he drew close enough that Hannah grabbed his ears. Bear slopped her with his tongue. She'd grown in the weeks he'd been away. A proper toddler now. He wondered how many small changes he'd missed. If all went according to plan, he wasn't going to miss any more.

Stella's mouth was a round "o" of surprise as he handed her one of the bouquets. Dressed in jeans and a soft pink top she looked like a gift more lovely than anything on the table.

She found her voice before he did. "You didn't say anything when we talked on the phone last week."

"I hope…you're happy to see me."

"Yes."

Every day since he'd visited at Christmas had further convinced him of what he'd already known deep down. Now he had to convince her, too.

He offered the second bouquet to Zoe.

"Why?" she said, cheeks flushed. "It's not my birthday."

"You said you hadn't received flowers since you were in high school. That was a wrong that needed to be set right."

"Aww, you," she said, kissing him on the cheek. "I'll find some vases."

While Stella settled Hannah in the highchair and turned to scoop him a cup of punch, he knelt next to his daughter. "Hey there, baby girl. You're looking fine as frog feathers."

She grabbed his beard. "Dog," she said.

He laughed loud and long. "It's not quite Daddy, but I'll take it."

Stella offered the punch. He got to his feet and handed her his gift. "I brought her a present."

"That's so nice. Let's have her open it now."

He took a breath. "How about you do it for her? Outside, okay?"

She frowned but nodded.

When Zoe returned, he put the punch down, left Bear in a sit where he could stare devotedly at the baby, and the two of them walked outside. It was difficult to remember that the area had been turned upside down by a quake only three months prior. The damage would take a long time to clean up. He hoped his own personal restoration plans would be quicker.

She opened the present and revealed the small child's Bible inside.

"Oh, Von. How sweet." She turned the colorful pages. "This is perfect for Hannah."

"I, um…" He found there was a brick in his throat and he tried to clear it. "It's, uh, for both of us, me and Hannah."

She cocked her head, brow furrowed. "I don't understand."

He squared his shoulders. "I have a lot to learn. The chaplain said to start at the beginning, so that's what I'm gonna do." He blew out a breath. "I've been mad at God for so long, mad at myself. I need some spiritual remediation. I figured I could learn with her, remember the basics, and we could tackle it together, me and my girl."

She pressed her lips together and held the book to her heart as if she was soothing a pain there. "That would be lovely. How perfect. I'm so glad."

Her smile rendered him speechless for a moment. He'd stared at her photo every day he'd been gone, but no photographed smile could capture her real-life grin, the way it burrowed down into his soul and lit a fire there.

"How long will you be here this time?"

"Here?" He'd been so focused on his plan, he'd checked out for a moment.

"In town. On leave."

"I'm not on leave. I resigned my position and my commander agreed. I had to complete the three months to onboard the next guy, but it's just a matter of the paperwork being processed at this point."

Her mouth dropped open. "What? You worked so hard to get back as a trainer."

"I know. I've worked all my life to try and prove I matter. I thought the only times I succeeded were when I served. My civilian life is a train wreck. I messed up with Ronnie. I messed up with you. Then...everything changed."

"What changed?"

He forced himself on. There would be no turning back from this moment. "God gave me another chance, and I fell in love with you again, Stella."

A pink flush crept up her cheeks, but she didn't say a word. He plunged on, desperate to get it all out.

"I fell in love with the new you, the incredible woman you've become, and it forced me to examine myself." He struggled to find the words he'd practiced. "You are the most breathtaking example of strength I've ever witnessed."

She shook her head. "I did what I had to do. That's all."

"It's the way you've done it, honey. With grace and courage and love."

A tear leaked down her cheek, and her gaze dropped to her feet.

"I want you to look at me while I say this." He tipped her chin up until her eyes were fixed squarely on him. "I love you. I want to learn from you, grow with you, protect you and plant gardens with you. I love Hannah. I didn't think I could love someone so much that it would make me want to face my mess and try to clean it up instead of hide from it, but here I am." He took her hand, the fingers slender in his calloused grip. "I want to be in your life and Hannah's forever, and I don't want to miss one moment."

He dropped to a knee, still grasping her fingers, pulling out the box Tate had given him. "Let's build a life in Cloud Top. I'm staying on at MDWG. You, me, Hannah, Bear, Kip and Zoe, Tate and Camy, we'll all be close. I want to plant new seeds. I don't understand much about God, except for one thing. He made us to be together and He loves me enough to give me a second chance with you. I want to give one hundred percent to you both." He gulped. "You asked me when I was going to grow up, Stella. I think I finally did." He snapped open the lid.

Her engagement ring caught the light, so familiar, but now the pink diamond was sandwiched between two smaller white ones. He pointed to the center stone. "This is you, honey. The strong diamond, the anchor, and these two…" He could not stop the tears that blurred his vision. "These are for our children, Hannah and Daniel." His voice broke on the name of his son. "We can add on as necessary and I hope we will. Guess I'm the band, because I'm going to try my best to love and support us, keep us together as long as God will allow."

She was so quiet his heart rattled his ribs. "Do you love me too, Ella? Enough to marry me?"

And then she was collapsing onto her knees next to him, wrapping her arms around him, whispering words that glued his world back together and set his heart beating in perfect rhythm.

"I love you, Von. So, so much."

He clung to her, face buried in her shoulder until he could gather himself. Then he kissed her, all the love and loss and heartache and hope twined between them. With hands that only shook a little, he removed the ring from the box and slid it on her finger.

She cried quietly as she looked at it, and he kissed her again before he helped her to stand. "There's something else in there."

She pulled out the bottom of the box and inside was a minuscule packet of seeds of all kinds, the biggest the fragile propeller seed.

"I was saving them, to plant at the right moment. Do you think you and Hannah would like to start a garden with me? Don't worry. I'll do all the work this time." He could not contain his glee. "It's going to be amazing. Tomatoes the size of your head."

She laughed and tipped her face to his. "We would be delighted, Mr. Sharpe."

He thought his buoyant heart would float out of his body.

Zoe appeared at the door, shoving her hair back. "Kip's tripped over Flash and dropped his camera into the cake, which splattered Hannah with frosting so she's crying and Bear is about to lose his doggy mind. Are you two coming back in to help?"

Von and Stella looked at each other and broke into guffaws. They laughed so long that Zoe shook them off and retreated inside. When their mirth subsided, he wiped his eyes and embraced her again.

She squeezed him close. Hannah's wails carried on the winter wind, strengthening in volume as they approached. "You sure you're ready to take on this duty, weatherman?"

"Yes, ma'am," he said. "There's nothing in this world I'd like better."

★ ★ ★ ★ ★

Get 3 FREE REWARDS!

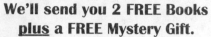

We'll send you 2 FREE Books plus a FREE Mystery Gift.

Essential inspirational novels reflect traditional Christian values. Enjoy a mix of contemporary, Amish, historical, and suspenseful romantic stories.

FREE Value Over **$40**